SAINTLY REMAINS

A NICK BERTETTO MYSTERY

SAINTLY REMAINS

TONY PERONA

FIVE STAR
A part of Gale, Cengage Learning

GALE
CENGAGE Learning⁻

Detroit • New York • San Francisco • New Haven, Conn • Waterville, Maine • London

GALE
CENGAGE Learning·

Set in 11 pt. Plantin.
Printed on permanent paper.

LIBRARY OF CONGRESS CATALOGING-IN-PUBLICATION DATA

Perona, Tony.
    Saintly remains : a Nick Bertetto mystery / Tony Perona. — 1st ed.
      p. cm.
    ISBN-13: 978-1-59414-856-9 (alk. paper)
    ISBN-10: 1-59414-856-2 (alk. paper)
    1. Bertetto, Nick (Fictitious character)—Fiction. 2. Investigative reporting—Fiction. 3. Youth and violence—Fiction. 4. Good and evil—Fiction. 5. Indiana—Fiction. I. Title.
    PS3616.E75S25 2010
    813'.6—dc22   2009046967

First Edition. First Printing: March 2010.
Published in 2010 in conjunction with Tekno Books and Ed Gorman.

Printed in the United States of America
1 2 3 4 5 6 7 14 13 12 11 10

For my dad, John Anthony Perona, 1924–2007

ACKNOWLEDGMENTS

First of all, I want to thank God, who continues to bless me far beyond what I deserve. Right behind God I thank my wife Debbie, who makes it possible for me to do this, and my daughters, Liz and Katy, for their support.

Second, I want to recognize many people who provided their expertise during the writing of this book. Any mistakes or misinterpretations must be attributed to me and not to these people, who know what they're doing. They are, in no particular order:

Father Joseph Moriarty of the Indianapolis Archdiocese, for information about the priesthood and exorcism, and Bob Smith for making the introduction; Father John Schipp of the Old Cathedral, Basilica of St. Francis Xavier, Vincennes, Indiana, for showing me the reliquary collection that belongs to the Old Cathedral and answering my questions about saintly relics; Dr. R. Blake Deckard, for information about how veterinarians would handle certain issues and for not turning me in to the police for asking such questions; Larry Brinker, former police chief of the Plainfield Police, for answering my theoretical questions; also Sgt. Michael A. Black of the Matteson, Illinois, Police Department and Sgt. Dave Case of the Chicago Police Department, for information about how SWAT teams would handle certain incidents; Mike Ellis, an editor with the *Indianapolis Star*, for his thoughts on certain situations and how they would be handled; Rita Milandri, an associate professor at IUPUI, for help with the Italian; Michael Wolfe, EMS Captain with the Plainfield Fire Department, for advice; Dale Hanke of Hanke Studio, for the photos and for photographic advice; Brent David of Mission Control, for information about LAN gaming locations; and Lance Burris of the Indiana State Police Academy, for answering police procedural questions.

Thanks also to my agent, Lucienne Diver, John Helfers of Tekno Books, and Tiffany Schofield of Five Star for their help in getting this book in print. And my son-in-law Tim Dombrosky, my friend Elizabeth Gilbert, and proofer Toby Bradford for reading the book cover-to-cover one last time and catching way too many mistakes that I'd made.

Last, but certainly not least, I want to thank the members of the Indiana Writers Workshop who read this manuscript several times and provided much needed advice. They are Teri Barnett, Pete Cava, Bob Chenoweth, John Clair, June McCarty Clair, Nancy Frenzel, Pat Watson Grande, Joyce Jensen, Kathy Nappier, Lucy Schilling, Kitty Smock, and Steve Wynalda. There is no finer group of writers and critiquers anywhere!

PREFACE

Because of the dark nature of this book, I've veered a bit from the pattern I set in the earlier two Nick Bertetto mysteries, of using real locations. The town of Jasper exists, but West Jasper High School, along with St. Barnabas, New Vienna, St. Aelred's (thank you, Terence Faherty) and most of the other places I mention are fictional. Though I genuinely prefer to set my books in places people can visit, I couldn't imagine using a real high school to stage such a horrific massacre, nor attribute some of the atrocities to places that existed. So those of you who know the area, I hope you understand and can appreciate why you'll only find a few landmarks you recognize.

But southern Indiana is just as beautiful as I've described it, and Jasper is a friendly town with an authentic, celebrated German heritage. If you've not been there, I encourage you to visit.

PROLOGUE

The answer was not in the pattern. The answer was in the exception.

Keri Schoening, age sixteen, dead in a Columbine-style massacre, was that exception. The non-jock, the non-bully, the sweet, loving young woman who answered "yes" when asked if she believed in Jesus, was the only one of the five dead students who didn't fit the pattern.

So no one asked, what if she was the reason for the massacre?

I'm Nick Bertetto. I'm a freelance investigative reporter, and I didn't ask the question, either. Not that I was looking for the answer. It wasn't my story, not until five months later. And even then, I was asking a different question when I stumbled upon the answer.

The shootings occurred one gray Indiana afternoon on January 23 at West Jasper High School, the alma mater of my wife, Joan. Two students returned to school after lunch, shot five students, then shot themselves. None of the victims survived.

It was heartbreaking. The school closed for the rest of the semester. Students were transferred to Jasper High, the other community high school in town. Though there had been rumors the killings were the work of a Satanic cult, the police found no evidence of it, other than a cryptic verse of no known origin left on the wall of the library:

> *"When night is at its lowest ebb,*
> *And Vict'ry's sung from heav'nly tower,*

11

Then evil spins its strongest web,
And Satan has his finest hour."

The authorities believed that the two students who did the shootings sought revenge on athletes who had bullied them. It was said that, for years, the slain had inflicted misery on the shooters and their friends—and that, as in Columbine, the school had ignored what the popular jocks had been doing.

That's what the police and the media concluded. Keri Schoening, huddled under a table in the library with other students, had been an afterthought. The wrong person at the wrong place at the wrong time.

We took the news of the massacre hard, especially Joan. Keri had been the daughter of one of her good friends from high school. Susan Schoening and Joan were close enough that when we were in Jasper, our families always got together. Keri had treated our daughter, Stephanie, like a little sister and even babysat her on occasion. Steph, like all kids Keri came in contact with, really liked her. We'd had eggnog at the Schoening's house after Midnight Mass on Christmas morning. A month later, Joan and I went to Jasper for the funeral.

Not one of us asked, what if Keri's death was not the exception?

Because we saw the pattern instead, the evil that had been in the boys lived on unnoticed. It lay low for a short while, but that time was very short. Just five months later, it resurfaced.

CHAPTER ONE

Mr. Jangles was missing and Stephanie was not happy about it.

"Daddy, where's Mr. Jangles? I want to pet him," she said. Her eyes, a deep coffee brown that reminded me of my mother's, held such innocence that I smiled at her bewilderment. She couldn't figure out why the tomcat wouldn't want to be with her this morning.

I wasn't surprised. The black-and-white shorthair, ten years old and cagey as a reformed gambler secretly playing the ponies again, had been wary of us since we'd arrived for our annual summer visit to Jasper. Stephanie loved the softness of his Oreo-colored fur and wanted to pet him in the way that smaller children do, hands stiff, without grace. Most times he either hid under a bed or lurked among the high shelves of the Strassheims' basement storage, well out of reach. When he could persuade my mother-in-law, Janine, to let him out, he would scoot past the screen door and disappear into the bushes of a neighbor's front lawn. He'd be gone for hours after that.

"Honey, I'm sure Mr. Jangles will get hungry and come home for breakfast," I said. Janine had told me that while it was unusual for the cat to still be out after a night of prowling, it had happened before.

She may not have been worried, but I was. I worried that Stephanie had pushed Mr. Jangles to his limit last night, chasing him around the kitchen trying to pet him when all he wanted to do was get to his food bowl. I restrained her when I heard

13

the bells on his collar making the sound that earned him his name, but the cat was agitated. When my father-in-law took out the trash, Mr. Jangles rushed to the open door, escaping into the dimming sunlight. He would be happy when we were gone, no doubt about it.

"Doesn't Fluffy spend a lot of time outdoors, away from Melissa's house?" I asked. Melissa the Motormouth was one of Steph's best friends back in Franklin.

"I guess. But Fluffy doesn't hiss at me."

"Maybe you should give Mr. Jangles some room when he comes home, let him get used to you."

Steph looked around like she wanted a second opinion. "Where's Grandpa Hugo?"

"Grandpa is getting ready to go on a fishing trip with his buddies. He's out in the garage." She left to find him.

I poured myself a third cup of coffee and relaxed in one of the twin recliners in Hugo and Janine's living room. I looked forward to this week of vacation every year. Joan's parents were wonderful hosts, and although their relationship with me, of late, hadn't been as warm, I always felt their enjoyment at having us here. Plus, Jasper is a beautiful little city in southern Indiana. Founded in 1830 and populated largely by Germans during its early years, the town still today celebrates its German heritage. In that way, I likened it to my own hometown of Clinton with its Italian roots. The first time Joan brought me home to meet her parents, I was enchanted by the way traces of German ancestry permeate everyday life. It was an easy town to feel at home in, no matter what your ethnicity.

Daylight poured through the windows. I checked the time; it was nine A.M. The forecast was for a sunny day, warming into the mid-80's by late afternoon, and we planned to visit a local water park around eleven. Our goal was to be there while it was still a little cool and the bigger kids hadn't yet arrived. We would take our lunch with us and vacate the place by two. Joan didn't really like the heat, especially out in the sun. If we left on schedule, we could be back in the air conditioning before it got really hot.

Today's *Jasper Times* sat on the kitchen bar across the room from me. I sipped the coffee and struggled with indecision as to which was worse: sitting there with nothing to read or making the effort to get out of the comfy chair to retrieve it. I got up to get the paper. Janine and Joan entered the front door, returning from their morning walk, just as I sat back down.

"Where's Stephanie?" Joan asked.

"Out in the garage helping your dad get ready to go fishing," I said.

"With all those lures around? One of us should go out there."

"I'm sure Hugo's watching her. Besides, she went out no more than five minutes ago."

Joan paused, facing toward the garage. She made an unconvincing move in that direction, then decided in favor of sitting in the matching burgundy leather recliner next to me. "All right. I'm sure it's okay."

I was pleased to hear that. Joan had a history of post-traumatic stress syndrome, the result of her being abducted during one of my investigations. At first, she'd rejected therapy, and then when she finally agreed to it, we ended up with someone who hindered us more than helped. Now we were seeing a new therapist, Dr. Patricia Grande. Under her guidance, our relationship had strengthened and Joan was making a lot of progress.

Joan looked at the headline on the newspaper's front page. "I wonder how long the West Jasper shooting will continue to make headlines. It's been nearly five months."

"It's got to be hard on Susan and Aaron," Janine said from the kitchen. "Tough enough to be faced with Keri's empty room, let alone have the whole thing pop up again and again."

"Can I see that part, Nick?" Joan asked.

I handed over the front section and moved on to sports. The Yankees won again. Big surprise. Money talks.

"The parents of the students killed are considering filing a lawsuit against the Goebels and the Fleischmans," Joan said. "Susan didn't mention anything about that when we talked yesterday."

"Probably some kind of legal issue," I said. "The parties involved can't say anything to anybody."

"Or maybe Susan and Aaron aren't involved in the lawsuit. Susan told me she understands the Goebels and the Fleischmans are grieving, too. They lost kids."

"I agree," Janine added. "It's not like the Goebels weren't good parents. And no one's going to get anything out of the Fleischmans. Everyone knows they've got money problems."

Joan continued to skim the article. "The police are still trying to figure out how the kids got the guns. The serial numbers were filed off, and the guns were assembled from a mix of parts. Experts say they may never know who passed them to the kids."

I'd read the article before I'd given it to Joan. "I'm still not sure the motive is right. There was never any evidence to back up the police's claim that the boys had been harassed by the athletes they killed. It seemed circumstantial to me, like the police didn't know what to make of it and decided to go with the pattern established at Columbine and Virginia Tech. I wonder if there wasn't something more at work."

Stephanie burst through the door, Hugo behind her. "Daddy, Grandpa Hugo wants to teach me to fish. Can I go with him? Can I, please?"

"Honey, I don't think that's a good idea," I said. "Grandpa is going to be gone overnight at a cabin with friends. But when he gets back, I'm sure if he wants to take you to the lake for a few hours, it'll be okay."

Behind her, Hugo smiled with relief. He was in his fishing clothes, a lightweight, stone-colored long sleeve shirt that kept the sun off his arms and olive green chinos with a drawstring waist. Topping his head was a fisherman's cap with hooks stuck in it. "That's what I meant, Stephanie," he told her, bending down to pat her on the head. "I'll give you a lesson or two on Wednesday."

Stephanie stared up at him. Dressed in pink shorts and a pink flowered top, she looked adorable with her chestnut hair pulled back in a ponytail. "But I want to go with you now."

"If you do that, you'll miss going to the pool," Joan said. "You'll miss going down the slides and getting to eat a hot dog and barbeque potato chips for lunch."

Stephanie considered that. "I'll wait," she told Hugo.

He laughed. "I'll make it worth your while on Wednesday," he promised. "Well, I better get going."

This was Hugo's annual summer trip to a cabin one of his friends owned on Christmas Lake, just south of Jasper. Usually it wasn't the week we came down to visit, but his friend had shifted the date to accommodate a family celebration at the cabin. Joan's father lived for fishing, and while he had talked of skipping the trip because we were coming down, we insisted he go for at least part of the time.

"Why don't you take my cell phone?" Joan asked. "That way we can get hold of you if we need to."

"Thanks, but you know I hate these electronic gadgets. And what if it rings while I'm out on the boat and scares the fish away?"

"You can turn it off while you're on the boat." Joan got up, retrieved hers from her purse, and showed him how to operate it.

Hugo fumbled with the phone. "I don't know if I can

remember this."

Joan assured him it was easy, but I was convinced he would never turn it on. The cabin didn't have a phone, so if Hugo didn't want to be reached, he wouldn't be. But he put the phone in his pocket.

After kissing Joan, Janine, and Stephanie goodbye, he nodded at me, got in his black Buick Rendezvous, and left.

Hugo, Janine, and I have a strained relationship. It didn't used to be that way. But with the abduction, and then my investigation into a state congressman's disappearance that ended badly for Hugo's sister and their niece, they've been wary around me ever since. I don't think they doubt my love for Joan and Stephanie, but they behave as if I'm a bad luck charm.

Janine went back to her bedroom. I returned to the recliner. Joan walked over and nudged me.

"I'm going to get ready for the water park. Aren't you going to get ready, Nick?"

"I will after I finish the paper. It's only 9:30. The park doesn't open until 11:00."

Joan huffed and clomped up the stairs, just a little more loudly than usual. I joined her shortly. The *Times* is not a large paper.

We arrived at the water park precisely at 11:03, found a spot, spread out all our stuff, put on sunscreen, and prepared for a few hours of hanging out by the kiddy water playland. Joan humors me by allowing my inner child to spend some time at the big slides in another area of the park, especially the "Freakin' Nightmare Plunge," a 40-foot-high, nearly free-fall slide that takes my breath away every time. She thinks I'm crazy. I do it anyhow.

But I never got to the slides.

Janine called my cell phone at 11:45. Joan and Stephanie were in the pool, Stephanie shooting water through a pistol at people crossing the children's area on a rope bridge. Neither heard the phone.

"Nick, can you come back to the house? Please?" Her voice was strained.

"Is something wrong, Janine?" I asked. It was very unlike her, especially of late, to ask me for a favor.

"Yes, and I can't get hold of Hugo."

That Hugo hadn't turned on Joan's cell phone was not a surprise. "We can be back in fifteen minutes. Is it bad?"

"Not the girls," she said. "Just you. Please hurry." And she hung up.

It was bad, I thought.

I got out of the deck chair and went over to Joan, sitting in the kiddy pool with the cool water swishing over the tops of her toes. "Your mom just called. She needs me to come back to the house for something. Why don't you just stay here? I'll be back soon."

Joan's head snapped around. "What's happened?"

"I don't know that anything's happened. She just said she needed me to come home. Could be anything. She said she couldn't get hold of Hugo. Maybe it's the car or something."

"That's not like Mom."

"I'll get my hand stamped on the way out and be back as soon as I can."

Joan frowned but didn't argue. I put on my white T-shirt. Joan said something to Stephanie, who came over and gave me a hug before I left. I watched her go splashing back into the pool, most of the water falling on Joan. The two of them laughed.

It was a quick trip back to Janine's house. I pulled the screen door open and went in. I could hear a cat meowing, but the sound was muffled.

"Janine?" I called.

"In here, Nick." I followed her voice into the living room.

Janine sat stiff and upright in her recliner. On her lap was a light blue bath towel with something wrapped up inside. When she saw me, Janine started to cry.

"It's Mr. Jangles," she said, and she dropped one side of the towel.

Mr. Jangles was on his feet, shaking. His eyes were glassy, and his meow sounded distant, pained.

And he had been skinned.

CHAPTER TWO

I turned my eyes away for a moment, trying to grasp what I had seen. Then I looked back.

Tears welled in my eyes. The fur was still on his head, paws, and tail. Clinging to the rest of the shivering body was raw muscle and fat and a little blood, like a plucked chicken with the skin removed. Mr. Jangles continued to cry a fading, high-pitched howl. Something clutched at my heart.

"Oh, my God," I said. I could feel the bile rising in the back of my throat. I turned away and gagged but managed not to vomit. "Oh, my God."

Janine cried harder. She covered Mr. Jangles. "I . . . need you . . . to take us . . . to the vet," she said, in between sobs.

"The vet," I repeated.

Momentarily I couldn't remember where her vet was. My mind couldn't comprehend what had happened to the cat. I tried to force myself to think of streets and roads. All I could think of was U.S. 231, the main drive through Jasper. Newton Street. Most everything was along there.

"Dr. Thom," she said, in between sobs.

Thomas Haase, DVM. The spot came to mind now. Like Hugo and Janine's house, it was located out on the western edge of the city, along S.R. 56. We passed it every time we came to see them.

"Sure," I said. My cheeks were now wet, tears sliding down

them uncontrollably. I stood and offered to take Mr. Jangles from her.

She shook her head. "I'll carry him."

Bundled up, he continued to meow, but he held still in her arms as she stood. In shock, I thought. Both of them.

Janine followed me to the van. "What . . . do you think . . . he'll do?"

The vet, she meant. "I don't know," I said, but that wasn't true. Mr. Jangles would have to be put to sleep. He must be in tremendous pain; there would be no way he could survive. I helped the two of them get settled on the passenger seat. "I'll drive carefully," I said.

Sitting in Janine's lap, Mr. Jangles was probably as safe as he was going to be, but I backed slowly down the driveway anyway. I couldn't bear the thought of inflicting any more pain on him.

The drive was mercifully short, only a couple of miles. Mr. Jangles's meows grew more desperate but weaker. I had to grab several tissues from the box between my seat and Janine's to mop up the tears streaming down my face.

"I swear I will find out who did this." I wasn't sure if I was talking to Mr. Jangles or Janine, but I meant it.

I pulled up to the red brick building, slowing gently to a stop. I got out of the van and ran around to the passenger side, gently lifting Mr. Jangles from Janine until she could get out. I held him close to my chest, still wrapped in his blanket, cradling him in my arms.

When Janine was steady, I carefully transferred the cat to her and kicked the door shut with my foot. I walked ahead to open the door, but a soccer mom leaving with a golden retriever took care of it for me. I scooted in behind Janine and followed her to the counter. The receptionist said something, but Janine stood there with a blank look on her face.

"This cat," I whispered to the receptionist, "he's . . . he's been skinned." I reached over to where Janine held Mr. Jangles and pulled the blanket back just a little so the receptionist could see.

She stared at the cat. Her jaw clenched. I could read the horror in her eyes, mixed with pity. "I'll take him," she said. She reached across the counter but Janine wouldn't let go. Tears formed in her eyes.

"Follow me," the receptionist told Janine. She opened a gate into the office area and led her into the back. I debated whether or not to go back with Janine. On the one hand, she had asked me to come back to the house and drive her here, which indicated some kind of trust. On the other hand, this was the anomaly in our current arms-length relationship, and I didn't feel comfortable intruding on what would no doubt be her last moments with the cat. I decided to sit in the waiting area and wait for her to ask me to come back, if that's what she wanted. I watched the two women disappear into the back, Mr. Jangles's blue blanket a blip of color in the sterile environment. "Dr. Haase!" I heard the receptionist call as the door shut.

I sank into a chair in the waiting room and tried to deal with my emotions. I didn't care what the others in the room thought. Mr. Jangles wasn't my cat, of course, but I had known him ever since Janine and Hugo had acquired him from the animal shelter. I couldn't believe that anyone would treat a helpless animal so horribly.

After a few minutes, I managed to collect myself. I looked up and saw a box of tissue on the counter. Taking a few of them, I wiped my face and eyes. A man with a Yorkshire Terrier and a woman with a white cat in a carrier glanced at me with sympathy. Then they turned away, not wanting to stare. I appreciated their kindness.

The veterinary clinic had ample seating room for people and pets. I took in the white walls and ceiling, and the grayish white linoleum floor. The effect was antiseptic, clean, softened only by photos of pets on the walls.

A rotund man in a Harley Hawg T-shirt came out of an examination room with his bulldog on a leash. He took a seat two away from me. The bulldog patrolled in front of him. The man looked at the vacant counter and then at me. "Where is everyone?" he asked.

"In the back," I replied.

The counter swept elliptically around the office, creating a division between the waiting area and the clinic. On either side of the counter were doorways to examination rooms, one of which the bulldog had occupied. The receptionist appeared again. She indicated that I should come to the counter.

"Please come with me," she said, swinging open the gated section Janine had used. "Dr. Thom would like you to come back." Seeing the other pet owners, she said, "There's been an emergency. We'll be with you very soon. Please be patient."

She led me inside to a room in the back, a small examination room, barely eight foot by eight foot. It had a stainless steel examination table to one side. Janine sat in a chair, a vacant look in her eyes. I put my hand on her shoulder and gave it a gentle squeeze. A couple of tears ran down her checks. I took a seat and the receptionist left.

Dr. Thom came in no more than a minute later. He had a rugged, outdoor look, with a ruddy face and a full, neatly trimmed beard. He wore stone white chinos with a burgundy knit shirt, the shirt and pants mostly covered by a knee-length white lab coat. His eyes were blue, and he sat on a stool with rollers on the bottom. He rolled up to Janine and hugged her in sympathy. To me, he simply nodded.

"Mr. Jangles is in extreme pain and is dehydrated," he said. His voice was soft and calming, the kind of voice physicians who have great bedside manner use. "We've given him butophanol, which is a narcotic, to alleviate the pain for the moment. Can you tell me how this happened?"

"I . . . he . . ." Janine stammered, then went quiet. Dr. Thom looked at me for help.

"I don't know how it happened. Janine called me. I was at the water park with my wife and daughter. Janine found him outside the door when she went to call him. He was . . . well, you saw him." I could feel the nausea returning as I pictured the cat. I closed my eyes and tried to forget it. Breathe, I reminded myself. My stomach held.

He looked to Janine again. "I need your permission to put the cat to sleep. He can't survive like this. I'd be surprised if he lasts the day. He's in shock, which is how his body has managed to survive so far. When was the last time you saw him?"

Hearing that Mr. Jangles needed to be put down seemed to snap something in Janine back into place. She answered, "He went out last night. In the evening. He didn't come back."

"It's amazing that he had the will and the ability to make it back today, after what was done to him." Dr. Thom put his hand on Janine's and tried to get her to look him in the eyes. "I need your permission. It's the right thing to do."

Janine openly cried. Dr. Thom gently held her hand. I put my arm around Janine's shoulder. "I'm sorry," I said, having no idea what else to do.

"I know it hurts you to think of this, but Mr. Jangles is in a lot of pain," the vet said. "If you want, you can stay right here and be with him when he goes to sleep."

She nodded. Dr. Thom left the room and returned with an assistant who was carrying Mr. Jangles. The cat was wrapped in the blanket, but there was no movement. If I hadn't known better, I might have thought he was already dead. The assistant handed the blanket to Janine, who pulled back a corner to reveal Mr. Jangles's white and black head. She petted it. "Mommy loves you," she choked out. Then she closed her eyes and turned her head to the side. "Please do it now," she said.

I couldn't look either. My eyes were staring at the opposite wall. The next thing I knew, the vet was giving Janine another hug and the assistant had removed Mr. Jangles from the room.

"Would you like us to have Mr. Jangles cremated so you can scatter his ashes?" Dr. Thom asked Janine.

She blinked. "How long would that take?"

"He'll be picked up tomorrow, and his ashes returned a week later."

"No . . . I can't . . . bear to have this stretch out. I need to put him to rest today."

"Are you certain? It might be easier on you if you didn't have to look at him again. You'll want to remember him as he was, not like this."

She somehow pulled herself together. "I want to bury him today," she said again, wiping her nose with another tissue. "If I need to, I can ask Hugo or Nick to handle him."

The assistant returned and handed Janine the blanket containing Mr. Jangles. Dr. Thom walked us out to the van. I opened the door for Janine and helped her in. When the door was closed, I asked the vet, "Why would anyone do this to a poor, defenseless animal?"

He shook his head. "Don't know. It's so cruel. I wish I could say this was the first case I've seen, but it isn't. I've been around too long for that. Just last week I had a beagle mix in here from Janine's subdivision that had its ears and tail cut off."

"That's awful," I said. "Could the same person have done this?"

"I wanted to bring that up with you. I'm required to report this to the police. You can better judge when Janine is able to handle a talk with them, but I'd urge you to go sooner rather than later. Perhaps even before I file my report. First, because the details are freshest in her mind now, which will help the police. Second, it will help deflect any suspicion that either of you did this."

I gagged at the thought. "Janine would have walked through fire for Mr. Jangles, and I could never do that to anything."

"Not unless you're a good actor," he said.

We stared at each other for a moment.

"You're not a hunter, are you?" he asked.

"No, why?"

"Unless the person who did this has been getting a lot of practice, I think it might have been done by a hunter. I shot squirrels as a kid, and we used to skin them to get the meat. Of course, they weren't alive, but the technique is the same."

"Wouldn't the cat have fought back? Surely it would have taken more than one person to subdue him. Should we be looking for people who have been clawed and bitten? Or was Mr. Jangles drugged?"

"I examined the head, and I think the cat was clubbed and knocked out. His paws were probably duct-taped together at that point."

I started to taste the Rice Chex I'd eaten for breakfast in the back of my throat.

"I'll give the police the details," Dr. Thom said. "It could have been done by one person, or two." He paused and looked at Janine in the car. She'd been sitting there a long time holding Mr. Jangles, but she hadn't moved. "I wouldn't let Janine look at him again. I would put him in a box and bury him as soon as possible."

"Thanks."

He shook my hand. "I'm sorry that we had to meet under these circumstances. Don't forget to go to the police station— today, if possible. Don't put it off."

I got in the other side of the van, made sure Janine would be fine, and drove away. I realized that no one had given us a bill or asked for payment, but I imagined that was how it was done in these cases. They would probably send a bill later.

Janine's breathing was still a little ragged when we got back to their house.

I thought about calling Joan. I had been gone for almost two hours, and I knew she'd be worried. Then I remembered she'd given her cell phone to Hugo. It was probably better that it worked out this way, though. As long as I could keep Stephanie from hearing, telling Joan in person would be preferable because I could assess her frame of mind. Though she was doing much better, I still worried about a relapse. I wondered if I always would.

Janine shuffled into the house. I followed. The Strassheims' house was a modified Cape Cod, with a living room on the right off the entryway. To the far left was a dining room, and to the near left was the stairway leading upstairs. We went past the living room and into the kitchen.

Janine sat down at the table, still cradling the blanket with Mr. Jangles's body. She sat like that for a minute. "He was a good cat," she said finally. She swallowed hard. "How could anyone do that to him?"

"I wish I had an answer."

"Please hold him for me a minute."

I took the blanket from her. She went back to her bedroom and returned with a medicine bottle. I knew she had Valium, but I had never seen her take one before. She did now.

"Janine, I know you don't want to think about this, but Dr. Thom said we need to report this to the police, and the sooner the better." I handed the cat back to her. "He said he would report it also."

"Do we have to go down to the station?"

"I think that would be best. But I'd like to go get Joan and

Stephanie first. They've been at the water park a long time. They're probably worried."

"Go on. I think I'd like to have some time alone with him. Just to tell him how much he meant to me and how I'll miss him."

"Perhaps we can bury him here on the property, after we finish talking to the police."

Her eyes were rimmed in red. "He'd like that."

"I'm going to go now. You'll be okay?"

"I will."

My heart went out to Janine. I remembered losing two cats to car accidents when I was a teenager. One of them was a black-and-white like Mr. Jangles. Those accidents had been bad, but nothing compared with the horror of what Mr. Jangles had suffered. I drove in silence to the water park.

Joan saw me right away when I walked in. She waved as she sat in a shallow pool, keeping one eye on the gate while she watched Stephanie. Steph was about ten feet away, laughing and playing with other kids in a fountain spray that came up from the concrete. A mist washed over Joan from the spray, beads of water sticking to her blonde hair. It was a hot day, and I could understand why she sat in that particular spot, with the cool mist on her face and water around her slender legs diffusing the sun's heat. As I got closer, she turned toward me. Her eyes were large.

"What happened? I tried calling Mom's house but didn't get an answer. You've been gone a long time."

I looked over at Stephanie, who was splashing water at a little dark-haired boy. The boy, in turn, splashed back at her. They giggled and were having so much fun Stephanie hadn't noticed I was back.

I knelt in close to her. "It was Mr. Jangles. He . . ." All of a sudden I choked up. I thought I'd been through it enough that

I'd be able to talk about it. But as the image of the skinned cat came back in my memory, the tears began forming again. "The vet had to put him to sleep. He'd been . . ."

"Nick, he'd been what?"

"Skinned alive." I looked away. I didn't want her to read the look in my eye and know how bad it had been. It would be bad enough in her imagination.

"Please tell me I didn't hear that right," she said, stunned.

"I wish I could."

Joan looked over at where Stephanie was happily playing. I guess she knew we couldn't say too much. She lowered her voice. "That's so horrible. Poor Mom." She had tears in her eyes, too.

"I need to take your mom to the police to report it. The vet said this is the second incident of animal mutilation that he knows of in your parents' subdivision."

The corner of her mouth twitched. "Oh, God. Someone living in my parents' community is that twisted? It's scary."

"It may not be someone living close. It could be someone driving in and snatching the animals. The police need to be aware of it."

She shuddered. "We'd better get going. Stephanie!" she called.

Stephanie looked over and saw us. Her face lit up. She came splashing through the ankle deep water, and when she got to me, reached down and swooped up some water, aiming for my shorts. She didn't get me very wet, but enough that the trunks I was still wearing would need to dry. It was then I realized I'd spent the last two hours in a swimsuit. Fortunately I'd worn one that looked enough like regular shorts no one would have thought a thing about it, but I still thought I should change before going to the police station.

I picked Steph up. "I suppose you think that's funny, don't you?"

"Are you mad?" she asked.

"Of course not." I paused. "But you're gonna pay for it!" I turned her upside down, and holding her by the legs, I walked over to the spray fountain where I dangled her in the shooting water. She shrieked with laughter.

Immediately all the other kids in the fountain wanted the same thing. "Mister, can you pick me up and do that, too?" asked the little boy Stephanie had splashed when I arrived.

"I'm sorry," I said, "but you need to have one of your parents do this. They might not like it if I did it to you."

"Pick me up!" said a little girl in braids, who looked to be a year or two younger than Stephanie.

"Well, you've done it now," said Joan, standing behind me.

I turned Stephanie over and put her down, getting myself even wetter in the process. "I guess I did." I turned to all the little kids who were now looking at me expectantly. "Listen, I would like to stay and play with you, but Stephanie and her mom and I have to go."

They looked disappointed, but not for long. By the time we'd gathered up all our stuff, they were running around splashing each other again.

On the way out, Joan pulled me in close to her and asked, "Can you help find this guy?"

I was shocked. This was the first time in several years she actually wanted me to investigate something. Maybe we were truly getting back to the way we were before.

"I might be able to," I said, "but I want to see what the police do, first."

CHAPTER THREE

Janine and I arrived at the police station around 2:30. The receptionist behind the glass partition asked us what we needed. Janine seemed unable to respond right away, so I told the woman we wanted to report an instance of animal cruelty, that Janine's cat had been the victim. The woman, wide-faced with small black glasses that exaggerated her heaviness, nodded at Janine sympathetically and told us to have a seat. We found a couple of uncomfortable waiting room chairs next to each other. Ten minutes later, a uniformed officer came out.

"Can I help you folks?" he asked, then stopped as he looked at Janine. "Mrs. Strassheim, they didn't tell me it was you." He put out his hand. She shook it without emotion. "Do you want to come in?" he asked.

Janine nodded.

"That would be great, thanks," I said.

"Who are you?" he asked.

"I'm her son-in-law, Nick Bertetto."

He gave me a once-over. "You're the guy that married Joan?"

"I am."

"Huh." He turned away from me and unlocked the door to the secure area of the station. Janine went in first. The officer cut in front of me, forcing me to grab the door before it shut. I followed behind him.

Who was this guy? He recognized Janine and knew Joan was her daughter. Of course, Jasper is not large. I guessed that he was about my age, so perhaps he had gone to school with Joan. A quick check of the patch on his sleeve indicated that he was a patrol officer, no special rank.

"First room on your right," he said to Janine, who had reached a row of offices.

The table in the small conference room was rectangular, and Janine took a seat on the far side. I sat next to her. The officer took a seat near the door, opposite us.

"I'm Officer Day," he said to me as we shook hands.

"Nice to meet you."

For the first time, Janine smiled. "I'm glad you're going to be helping us, Johnny."

"It's good to see you again, Mrs. Strassheim." He had a form in front of him and was playing with a Bic pen. "How can I help? The receptionist said something happened to your cat?"

Janine looked at me and nodded. I guessed that meant I would be doing the talking.

"This morning my mother-in-law found her cat, Mr. Jangles," I said. I put my hand on her arm to provide some comfort. "He had been skinned. She called me—we were at the water park—and I came back, and we took him to the vet and had him put to sleep. The vet said it was the humane thing to do. Mr. Jangles couldn't survive in that condition."

Johnny's brow furrowed. He turned to Janine. "That's awful. When was the last time you saw the cat before this morning?"

"Last night. He wanted to go out."

"Does he often stay out at night?"

"A lot when he was younger. Now, not so much."

"Where did you find him this morning?"

"By the back door." She paused. "When I saw him, I almost fainted. Most of his beautiful fur had been . . . he had some blood . . ." Janine gave a small sob and closed her eyes. "I went and got a towel to pick him up."

33

"Then what did you do?"

"I tried to call Hugo. He's away fishing for a couple of days. He had Joan's cell phone with him, but I didn't get an answer. I don't think he turned it on."

"And after that?"

"I called Nick." She indicated me with her hand. "He and Joan and Stephanie are staying with us this week. They were at the water park, like he said."

"At the time you picked up the cat, did you see any evidence in the backyard, like footprints or a weapon that might have been used?"

"No, but I don't remember it clearly. I was more concerned about Mr. Jangles." Tears ran down her face.

"Has anyone been in the backyard since?"

"No, unless Stephanie goes out to play back there while we're gone."

"Before we left I told Joan not to let her go out back," I said to Johnny. "I thought the police might want to search there."

Day looked at me. "Are you a policeman?"

"No, a reporter."

"I see. What paper are you with?"

"I'm a stay-at-home dad and freelance writer. Sometimes the *Indianapolis Standard* hires me."

He stared at me for a few seconds. Then, as though something clicked inside his head, he said, "Oh. Okay."

He turned back to Janine. "Do you still live on Wayside Drive?"

"586," she said.

"I remember. Your yard backs up against the Tinsley field, right?"

"Uh-huh."

"We'll need to search your yard. If possible, we'd like to do that yet today. Will you be home?"

Again she nodded.

"I'm going to ask you not to say anything about this until we've had a chance to investigate. We'll talk more about it later today, okay?"

We both agreed.

"Have there been any other incidents like this?" I asked.

"Later," he said.

While the interview had been going on, I had noticed one or two officers sporadically dash past the window of the room we were in. Now I saw lots of officers in groups of two or three go by. They were definitely in a hurry. It looked like the building was facing mass evacuation. A sergeant opened the door and stuck his head in.

"Sorry to interrupt, folks. Johnny, can I see you for a moment?"

Johnny looked in our direction. "Excuse me." As he was just shutting the door, I heard him say, "We're just about done here."

Call it reporter's instinct, but I crossed to the other side of the room and listened through the crack in the door. Even though I was far from my home territory and unlikely to benefit from what I might hear, I couldn't help myself. Something big was going on.

"Should you be doing that?" Janine asked.

I don't think she had ever seen me in reporter mode before. I put a finger to my lips to indicate she shouldn't talk.

"When you finish the interview, I need you out at the . . . cemetery," the sergeant was saying. I didn't catch the cemetery's name. He'd mumbled it. "A grave's been dug up, and the body's missing."

"Someone important?" Day asked.

The sergeant whispered a name, but I didn't catch it.

"Dispatch will give you the details. How soon can you wrap this up?"

"I was getting ready to show Mrs. Strassheim and her son-in-law out. I can be ready in a minute."

I took that as a cue to get back to my seat, and sure enough, I was just easing in the chair when the door re-opened and Day appeared. I pretended to have just shifted in my seat. The sergeant passed by the window, heading toward the exit.

Day spoke to Janine. "Sorry about that. Is there anything else either of you think I need to know?"

We both shook our heads.

Day stood up. "If I can, I'll get out to your place later this afternoon to look around. I'll call first. In the meantime, if you'll stay out of the backyard, that would be helpful."

Janine and I stood. Day opened the door, his hand motioning for us to exit first. We walked down the hall to where he'd let us in, shook hands with him again, and left.

Janine was quiet on the way home. I was, too, but for reasons other than hers, I was fairly sure. Part of me wondered just who this Officer Day was and how he knew so much about the Strassheim family. The other part wanted to know why a grave had been robbed.

Janine broke the silence. "He was Joan's boyfriend for about a year in high school. They went to the prom together her junior year."

"Did she break up with him or was it the other way around?" I asked.

"She broke up with him."

"Is he married now?"

"Has been. I don't think so now."

I wished I'd looked at his ring finger, although it might not have meant anything if there was no ring. Some policemen I knew chose not to wear jewelry on the job.

Janine went quiet again. I did the guy thing. I compared myself to the former boyfriend. He was maybe an inch or two taller, about six feet. He outweighed me by probably twenty-five pounds, but he had a bit of a paunch. His face was young-looking, like mine. He had brown hair, also like mine, but his was cut short, military style. Mine had at least a little length. Well, except for the bald spot in the back.

Why was I even thinking like this? It had been at least fifteen years since Joan had dated him. And it wasn't like Joan left him for me. I figured there were five years, college, and a couple of boyfriends between dumping him and dating me.

Still, I thought she'd made a wise choice in marrying me.

"How do you feel about our police visit?" I asked.

"I feel okay about it. I don't know what I expected them to do, really."

"Well, for what it's worth, I think they're taking the right approach. I just hope they find the person who did this."

I decided to be low key in what I said to Janine. Eventually I wanted the police to answer my question about other reports of animal cruelty in the area. The vet had mentioned a dog that'd been mutilated. I didn't know if it was in Janine's immediate neighborhood or elsewhere in the subdivision. There might have been other cases, too, and I wanted to see if there were any links. Day had indicated he would talk to me about this later, and I intended to take him up on that offer.

We pulled up to the house. Stephanie ran out the front door before we were out of the van.

"Daddy, we can't find Mr. Jangles. He's gone."

"Has Mommy talked to you about this?"

"She said you would tell me where he went."

"Let's wait until Grandma Janine and I get inside and then we'll talk about it." I knew how to stall for time as well as Joan did.

37

Stephanie went over to the other side of the van and took her grandma's hand. I wasn't sure if she sensed Janine needed the support or it was something natural she would have done anyway, but it was the right thing to do. Janine gave Stephanie a hug and then she straightened, held her head high, and the two of them walked into the house. I followed.

Janine took Stephanie into the kitchen where Steph gladly accepted a brownie. She took one for herself and offered one to Joan and to me. Joan declined, as she had been watching her weight recently. I thought she looked pretty good, but she said she still wanted to lose about five pounds. I think it's a woman thing.

I declined the brownie also. I wasn't on a bodybuilding diet anymore, having decided it just wasn't what I wanted to do, but I still tried to watch the fat calories. Mark Zoringer, my bodybuilder friend who owned the gym where I worked out, had smirked when I told him I was dropping the mass-building diet and exercise program. He knew my heart hadn't been in it for some time. When Joan had been abducted a second time in a copycat effort to stop a recent investigation, I'd risked my life to save hers. The first time, I'd failed to do that, relying instead on Mark's strength and fortitude. In rescuing her the second time around, I'd proven to myself that I could conquer what I regarded as inadequacies. That smacks of machismo, but it was important to my psyche that I reacted as I did. Mark, ever the friend, was less disappointed in my dropping bodybuilding than he was pleased by my new-found confidence.

Stephanie had not forgotten about Mr. Jangles. After finishing the brownie, she approached Joan and me in the living room. "Daddy, where has Mr. Jangles gone?"

I pulled her onto my lap. Joan and I exchanged a look. I was sitting in one of the twin recliners, Joan in the other. Janine, in the kitchen, busied herself with the dirty dishes.

"Honey, do you remember the story about Freddie the Leaf? We read it when your great Aunt Hildy died last year."

She nodded her head slowly.

"Well, Mr. Jangles has gone to Heaven where Aunt Hildy is," Joan said.

"Was Mr. Jangles sick? He didn't look sick."

"Well, Mr. Jangles was . . . in a fight of some kind last night, and it left him badly hurt. Your grandma found him this morning. We took him to the vet, and then he went to sleep."

"And he woke up in Heaven?"

I'm a believer in what Billy Graham says on the subject, that in heaven we will experience great happiness, beyond what we know on earth. If pets are essential for that kind of joy, then our pets will be there also. "Yes, honey, he went to sleep here and woke up in Heaven."

Janine suddenly dropped a plate. It shattered and startled us all. She bent down to pick it up and started crying. Joan rushed into the kitchen. Steph and I followed.

"Let me get that, Mom," Joan said, squatting next to her. She picked up a few of the larger pieces. Janine tried to do the same, but she kept stopping to wipe her face with the back of her hand. Joan took the pieces from her mom, placed them in a pile, and helped her stand up. She put her arm around Janine.

"Why don't you get some rest, Mom? You've been through a lot today. I'll take care of this."

Janine hugged her daughter tightly. Joan watched as she picked her way through the kitchen to the hall and over to the master bedroom. She closed the door behind her. Stephanie eased her hand out of mine and went to the bedroom. She knocked on the door, and hearing no response, said "Grandma?" There was still no response that I could hear, but Stephanie went in.

Together Joan and I cleaned up the shattered dish.

"She'll be okay," Joan told me.

I knew Joan was right, or would be in time, but so far this visit hadn't brought Janine the joy our visits usually did, though it was not our fault. I just hoped we could turn it around.

CHAPTER FOUR

Joan and I agreed that for everyone's sake we should bury Mr. Jangles as soon as possible. An hour or so later, when her mother was a little more composed, Joan made the suggestion. After a measured sigh, Janine agreed but said she would like to have Father Dan Klein from St. Barnabas Church say a few prayers. I didn't know that there was any kind of ceremony for burying pets, but I called the rectory.

The secretary told me Father Dan was just finishing up hospital visits and put me through to his cell phone. He said he would stop by on his way back to the church and that we could expect him in about twenty minutes.

When Father Dan stopped outside the house, he was in a fairly new red Toyota Tacoma, which seemed sporty for a priest wearing the traditional black shirt and white collar of a clergyman. I judged him to be in his early 50s, with a receding hairline made less noticeable by keeping his hair short. When I introduced myself, he looked at me with kind blue eyes.

"How are Janine and Hugo taking the death?" he asked. His voice was gravelly.

"Hugo is at the lake fishing and doesn't know about it," I said. "Janine is doing as well as can be expected. There's something else you should know, though." I paused. I still found it difficult to accept what had happened. "The cat had been skinned alive. Janine found him that way this morning. I took him to the vet, and the vet had to put him down."

Father Dan shook his head in disbelief. "Skinned? How horrible! Poor Janine must be devastated. I can't imagine what she must have gone through seeing him like that. I'm glad I was able to come over."

I ushered him inside. Janine met him in the family room, and he hugged her in sympathy. He was only slightly taller than she, about five feet six. She introduced Joan.

"Thanks for coming," Joan said. "We didn't know what to do, but Mom said you did a 'blessing of the pets' ceremony last year. Is there a ceremony for burial, too?"

"There isn't, but I get requests for this kind of thing from time to time. Pets can provide an essential friendship in a person's life. The church has a history of recognizing the importance of animals in our world. It goes back to St. Francis of Assisi."

Father Dan took Janine's hand. "I'm so sorry, Janine, for your loss."

"He was a good cat."

Father Dan nodded. "I think pets mirror the unconditional love of God in their devotion to us, and that makes them special. We become attached to them, and naturally their deaths affect us."

"How do you want to conduct this?" I asked. "We've picked out a place to bury him. Do you want to see it?"

"Sure," he said. "We can have the ceremony there."

We walked out to the side yard to the maple tree Janine had suggested for the burial spot. Father Dan looked around. "I'll make it just like a funeral. Burying a pet is similar. We need time to look back on its life and celebrate it. Accept that it's gone. We complete the circle of life, say goodbye to those animals we love, and grieve."

After a brief discussion with Janine about Mr. Jangles and what he meant to her, Father Dan started. I'd dug the shallow grave before he got there. It had been easy to do in the shady spot, still soft from recent rains.

We stood under the tree. Joan had her arm around Janine. Stephanie and I stood next to them, holding hands. The box with Mr. Jangles rested in the grave. Father Dan thanked God for creating Mr. Jangles among all his creatures, to be a source of friendship and love for Janine and Hugo. He gave a brief summary of how the cat had brought joy to the household, using Janine's earlier words. Then he pulled out a jar of holy water and blessed the box, asking that God bless Mr. Jangles in death as he had been a blessing in life. After that he said the prayer of St. Francis, turned and hugged Janine, and then shook our hands and blessed us. We made the sign of the cross as he did, and the ceremony was over. Janine cried. Joan comforted her mom. Then Stephanie started crying, and I picked her up. We all went into the house. Later I would go out and cover the box.

By now it was suppertime. Janine invited Father Dan to stay for dinner, but he politely declined, saying that he needed to get back to the rectory. Janine and I walked him to the front door. Joan persuaded Stephanie to go watch a video and followed behind us.

"I remember Mr. Jangles from the blessing of the pets last October," he told Janine. "A black and white shorthair, wasn't he?"

"He was," Janine said. "I brought him in his cage because he just won't behave on a leash."

"Thanks for the burial ceremony," I said. "It was very touching. I guess you've conducted more than a few?"

"Too many recently," he said, "several in this vicinity. Some smaller dogs and cats have disappeared, and we've had to do those in absence of having the pet's body. Happens sometimes when a subdivision like this is located so near a rural area. The coyotes will come up close to the houses if they think they can pick off some easy prey. I have to say, though, this is the first time I've heard of a cat being skinned. Scary. I hope the police catch the person who did it."

"Me, too," I said.

"Sometimes I wonder what's going on around here. One of my parishioners at the hospital told me that Keri Schoening's body has been stolen out of her grave. That it happened last night. Awful."

"It was Keri Schoening?" I asked. "I heard something about that at the police station, but no one mentioned names."

"Sad, really. I called their house to see if there was any help I could provide, but I didn't get an answer. They're probably tied up with the police investigation right now. I thought I'd try again tomorrow. I haven't heard from them in a couple of weeks."

Joan stood with us, blinking without saying anything. I began to get a little nervous that maybe there had been too much going on for her to absorb in one day when she said, "Keep trying, Father. I'm sure they could use your help right now. I'm going to try to get hold of them, too. Susan Schoening is a close friend of mine."

I breathed a sigh of relief at the normalness of Joan's response.

She was more expressive after Father Dan left.

"Can you believe the Schoenings have to go through this whole thing again? Bad enough they had to suffer when their daughter was killed and then be in that media spotlight. Now it's all going to be resurrected."

"Why would anyone want to steal the body?" I said.

Neither Joan nor Janine had an answer for that. I wondered if I could get some information from the police when they came to examine the back yard.

No one really felt like eating supper, but I offered to make something light and they took me up on it. I scrambled eggs and served them with whole-wheat toast, cantaloupe, and skim milk. Joan picked at the eggs—I guess I hadn't scrambled them dry enough—and decided on a piece of toast alone. Stephanie took small bites of everything except the cantaloupe, which she ate with gusto. Janine retired to her room without anything.

The police showed up at seven o'clock. It was still daylight, typical for June. I had somehow managed to abide by Officer Day's request not to snoop around the backyard. While Mr. Jangles's burial in the side yard had kept me busy most of the afternoon, I'd still had to use restraint after supper, deciding to surf the internet instead. I had looked for information about skinned cats, not a pleasant subject. All the time I was doing it, I hoped I couldn't be traced. Wouldn't want anyone to think I was a wacko. Most of the references I found were on Satanism.

In charge of the investigation was a policewoman, Detective Kim Whitmeyer. Johnny Day came along, though. He let us know that he was off-duty but had volunteered to help out the detective. Johnny's presence was understandable after the first five minutes. He was supposed to be interviewing us, but he seemed more focused on impressing Joan. Having already decided Joan had clearly made a good choice by dumping him so many years ago, I asked if I could shadow Detective Whitmeyer. She didn't say no, so I followed her as she prowled around the backyard, carrying a camera and an evidence bag.

She methodically paced from one side of the yard to the other. "Have you or anyone else been back here?" she asked.

"No, we've been careful to stay up near the house."

"Your mother-in-law says the cat came to the back porch. Did she say what direction he'd come from?"

"Not that I recall. I had the impression he was near the porch when she saw him. You'd need to ask her."

Janine and Hugo's back yard, which is long and narrow, is mostly septic field. Since nothing but grass can be planted there,

Janine had focused her landscaping fervor on the perimeter of the yard, now well-stocked with bushes, trees, plants and mulch. It took us awhile to examine everything for clues. Nothing. When we reached the back, we walked through a narrow, grassy, utility easement and into the cornfield behind the property. The county road that ran by the field was about fifty yards to our right. Neat rows of waist high green cornstalks stretched as far as the eye could see. Whitmeyer turned toward the road and began walking along the easement.

She stopped suddenly. "Wait a minute."

I halted before I blundered into her. "What is it?"

She had bent down and examined the grass. "Does that look like blood to you?"

It wasn't much, but there was a small red patch of something that looked like blood. "Could be," I said, staining to see. "There's not much there."

"The vet said that a skilled hunter would've been able to get the skin off without much loss of blood," she said, "but that vessels near the outside of the muscles could have leaked. That would leave a small trace, which this might be. I'll take a sample. The lab'll be able to determine what kind of blood it is."

She took a photograph and then scraped up a sample, placing it in an evidence bag. After that we followed the path to where it intersected with the road. "My guess is that the cat was dropped off here," she said. "We haven't found much, but I don't think we'll find anything more."

"Could he have made it back to the house from here?"

"The cat was in shock and dehydrated. It needed water, and it needed help. The vet said in that condition, it could've man-
. _ake its way to the house."

_oked around. Other than the usual trash along the ay—plastic McDonald's cups, burger boxes from White _le, assorted beer cans—there wasn't much to see.

"There's so little evidence," I told Whitmeyer.

"It's quite probable that whoever did this must've seen the cat in the field, coaxed it here, then captured it. Afterwards, they returned it to the same spot. Why, we don't know. Did the cat prowl the field regularly?"

I thought back to other vacations we'd spent here. "I think so. The cat has brought us 'presents' before—half-dead field mice he's played with. Janine won't let him in until he drops them on the porch."

Whitmeyer shook her head. "There's not much to go on. No footprints, no weapons, no clues. Whoever did this was careful to stay by the road where he would leave little evidence. We'll have to canvass the neighborhood to see if anyone saw a car sitting on the county road last night."

"You said 'he,' " I noted. "Why do you think it's a 'he?' "

"In cases like this, the crime is usually committed by a male."

We walked back to the house.

"Dr. Haase mentioned that a dog in this area showed up with evidence of torture, and then earlier this afternoon Father Dan from St. Barnabas mentioned several dogs and cats had gone missing. Do you think they're related?"

"At first we thought the missing animals, especially since they were small, were taken by coyotes. But now that a dog has turned up missing its ears and tail and Mr. Jangles has shown up in his condition, we're more inclined to think they're part of the same case."

"Why would they return some of the animals but not others?"

"Probably to spread fear. Seeing what happened to the pets has introduced a grisly psychological element that wouldn't have been there if they all just disappeared."

I opened the back door for Whitmeyer. "Do you have any suspects?"

"Just the usual ones. There's an old guy east of town we know is a former child molester. The sheriff's department keeps an eye on him, and we've let them know the kind of activity we've seen." She was careful not to mention names, and as an outsider in the community, I hadn't a clue as to his identity.

"Are those crimes related?"

"Sometimes. Animals, like children, are weak and defenseless, so the same types of people prey on both. In my experience, though, it usually goes the other way, from animals to children and then to adults, if they're not stopped."

She didn't look old enough to have that much experience, but I didn't say so.

Officer Day sat on the navy plaid couch along the wall adjacent to where Janine and Hugo's recliners were located. Day appeared to have made himself at home. He was sitting close to Joan, who rigidly hugged the far edge of the couch.

"Those were good times, weren't they, Joan?" Day was saying. "Ever wish you were back in high school again?"

Joan strained to be polite. "High school was a phase, Johnny. Everyone passes through it; but no one can remain in it." She got up and put her hand in mine. "I like to look forward in my life, not backward. It's okay to look back, but we can't spend all our time staring in the rear view mirror."

Dr. Grande would be proud, I thought.

Whitmeyer didn't seem given to reminiscing, either. Or maybe she sensed that Johnny was making Joan uncomfortable. "Please take this out to the car," she said, handing him the empty evidence bag.

He glared, but her stare was unyielding. "Excuse me," he said to Joan. "Got to help out the detective." He left.

Whitmeyer glanced around and then asked about Janine.

"She's in the kitchen," Joan told her.

With a nod, the detective left to find her.

"So, how have you been getting along with your friend?" I asked.

"Can you believe him?" Joan whispered. "He acts like I'm not even married."

"I think he'd make a pass at you if I weren't here."

"Let's not give him the chance."

Day re-entered the house. Joan and I both looked at him. I think he read our looks correctly because he didn't say anything for a few moments.

Then he began to speak sincerely. "It's terrible what happened at our high school, wasn't it, Joan? All those families who suffered. Who would have thought it could happen here? It used to be a great place to grow up."

Joan softened. "It still is, Johnny. But no place is immune to tragedy. Even here. You're a policeman, you know that."

"Did I tell you I was one of the first ones there after the shooting ended?"

Joan shook her head.

"It was horrible—the blood, the kids crying, the bodies. Do you remember Mary Beth Eastbeck from our class? I checked her son Evan for a pulse. Broke my heart when his skin was cold. My mind couldn't even conjure up a heartbeat."

We were all silent in the moment. I was glad Stephanie was in the other room watching the television.

Day started to say something else, but Whitmeyer entered, talking with Janine.

"It'll be a week before we get the results of the blood sample," Whitmeyer said. "That's just how long it takes for the lab to turn things around. In the meantime, we may not be able to put much effort on this. I don't want you to think that we're not taking this incident seriously because we are. But for the next few days we have to focus everything we've got on something else. I'm afraid it's going to put Jasper in the headlines of the national media. Again."

We all knew what she was talking about, but someone needed to say it. Naturally it was me who couldn't keep his mouth shut.

"Is it true that Keri Schoening's grave was dug up and that her body is missing?" I asked.

Whitmeyer was quiet for a moment. "It's not much of a secret, I guess. Word's been getting around the last few hours, and all the media that covered the West Jasper shooting have called about it. It's not a media circus like it was before, at least not yet, but we're getting lots of inquiries."

"Why would anyone take her body?" I asked. "What would they do with it? And how did they manage to dig it up without anyone seeing?"

"I don't know," Whitmeyer said, "but the rest of my division is over there right now. Hopefully they'll have some answers soon."

Joan spoke up. "Susan Schoening is a friend of mine. I've tried calling her, but I always get voice mail."

"They're not answering the phone. I've been over to their house, and it took them a long time to open the door. They've been through this before. They're afraid of what's coming."

Whitmeyer looked at Day. "Ready to go?"

He nodded.

"We're going door-to-door in the subdivision to alert people to what's happened to your pet and ask if they've seen any suspicious activity we should know about," Whitmeyer said. "We're encouraging them to keep a close eye on their pets. It would be a help if you'd also spread the word."

We all agreed to do that, and they left.

"I think Susan would answer the phone if she knew it was from me," Joan said. "I wonder if they've got caller ID."

"Do you think it's wise to keep calling? Maybe she's seen you on the caller ID but doesn't want to talk right now."

"Maybe. I know it's a tough time for the family, and I know she has friends that are closer than me. But I still want her to know that I'm here for her if she needs anything."

Later that evening, Joan was able to reach the Schoenings. They didn't talk long, but Joan said Susan was sincerely glad she had called.

Little did I know that I would push the limits of their friendship the next day.

CHAPTER FIVE

Tuesday began early and ominously for me. Someone walked past the bedroom door just before midnight. I knew because I checked the giant green numerals on the clock on Joan's side of the bed and saw it was 11:58. Joan was still here, sleeping beside me. I closed my eyes and concentrated on listening.

The feet moved to the back staircase, the one that went down to the kitchen. The footfall was light—either a deliberate attempt to be quiet or someone who didn't weigh very much. It was probably Janine, I thought, still upset over what had happened to Mr. Jangles and tired of tossing and turning in bed. But I decided to make sure it wasn't Stephanie, who had also gone to bed anxious. She wasn't given to frequent sleepwalking, but it had happened before when she was stressed. If she became disoriented in the dark, she could fall down the stairs and get hurt.

Rising quietly, I opened the door and stepped out in the hall. The bedroom was carpeted but the hallway floor was wood, and I felt the coolness on my feet. I saw a faint light down in the kitchen as I approached the top of the stairs. I quietly padded down the staircase.

Stephanie stood at the back door. There was just enough light from an electronic security device near the jamb that I could see her. She had pushed the curtain to one side and was staring into the darkness of the backyard through the window.

The bells of a carillon began to chime midnight, Westminster-style. Their peal was faint, but unmistakable.

"Stephanie," I said, approaching her softly.

She didn't answer.

I stood behind her and gently put my hands on her shoulders. "Stephanie," I said again.

"Who makes the bells play?"

"I don't know. It's probably automatic, like our grandfather clock at home."

"Mr. Jangles is dead."

"Yes, he is."

We were quiet again.

"Something bad is out there," she said.

I turned her around and looked in her eyes. They had a vacantness to them. She was sleepwalking.

"There are lots of good things out there, too," I answered. "But you're in here, and you're safe. Now, you need to get back to bed." I picked her up and carried her up the stairs. She didn't resist, and I knew she would fall asleep once I put her under the covers.

Closing her bedroom door after I tucked her in, I stood in the hall and felt the stillness of the night. The carillon still played, this time a melody that haunted me even after the ringing ceased. It might have been my lack of musicality, or maybe the bells were simply too faint, but I wasn't able to determine the song. I wondered where the carillon was located. Maybe St. Barnabas. The distance would explain why I had only heard it at night.

I contemplated Stephanie's words. "Something bad is out there." Involuntarily I reached for the religious medal I wear around my neck. Touching it, I found some reassurance, but maybe not as much as I had hoped for.

I returned to bed and slept fitfully until morning.

★ ★ ★ ★ ★

The first phone call of the morning was for me, and it was early, at least for vacation—7:30 A.M. Janine had to knock on the door to tell me to get the phone since I'd turned the ringer off before we'd gone to sleep. I looked to the other side of the bed and noticed that Joan was already up. Groggily I picked up the receiver.

"Well, aren't we sleeping in today?"

"Ryan?" I sat up. Ryan Lockridge was my best friend and former college roommate. He still worked at the *Indianapolis Standard,* and we occasionally shared assignments, him on staff and me as a freelancer. He had been my partner last year when we investigated the Calvin Cahill disappearance.

"The very one," he said. "The legend."

"I am on vacation, you know."

"And I'm not due into work for another half-hour, but I'm calling you anyway, so don't complain to me. Besides, as a stay-at-home dad, you're always on vacation."

"As a stay-at-home dad, I'm always working."

"So you'd like me to believe. Nonetheless, I have an assignment for you."

"What part of 'I'm on vacation' didn't you hear?"

"Clarisse called me and said we needed to get someone down to Jasper, and I told her I knew someone who was already there."

"Ryan, I'm on vacation."

"What is that, some kind of mantra?"

Since he wasn't giving up, I gave in to my curiosity. "What kind of assignment?"

"If you weren't lying around in bed all day, you'd have been up by now, read the paper, and discovered that the body of Keri Schoening, one of the victims of the West Jasper shooting, is missing from her grave. We want you on that story."

"Even if I were willing to do a little work on my vacation,

which I'm not saying I am, why wouldn't you send Jackie Corbis down here? She covered the original shootings, and it's not like Jasper is so far from Indy. She could be here in a few hours."

"She could be, if she hadn't just given birth to twins. Mother and boys are doing well, but I think they need her more than we do right now."

I'd forgotten she was due. "What about Zimmerman? Didn't he help her on the assignment?"

"He did, but he's on vacation, too, and not conveniently located in Jasper, like you are. He's in Yellowstone with his family."

I was just getting ready to make another retort when I heard the sound of a smoke alarm going off at the other end of the connection. "Ryan?"

"Damn. I forgot I was toasting a bagel. Just a minute."

I heard all kinds of cursing going on at Ryan's end, along with the "ow, ow, ow," of someone juggling something hot. Then the sound of a sliding glass door opening. More cursing. The alarm made a sound like it had been strangled. Finally there was silence.

"I had to disconnect it," Ryan said. "Too much smoke in the house." He took a bite of something.

"You're not eating it, are you?" I asked.

"It's not too bad with enough cream cheese," he said with his mouth full. "I can hardly taste the burned parts. Did you know cream cheese will melt on a hot bagel?"

"Of course, when your bagel is hot enough for nuclear fission."

Ryan swallowed. "I don't have a lot of choice. The only other thing in the house is cat food. I would try it except we're down to 'shrimp feast,' and that doesn't sound like a breakfast food. Now if it were time for cocktails . . ."

"That's disgusting."

"So, there's a reporter down there we want you to watch out for. Sally Kaiser at the *Jasper Times*. She was Jackie's arch nemesis in the days after the shooting. Nearly every time, Kaiser got the story before we did. Since Kaiser's a native, she snagged interviews with people we didn't even know were important. Ended up having to lift her stories off the AP wire more than once. You've got contacts down there, too, so exploit them and try to stay ahead of her."

"*If* I take the assignment. I need to think about it. Let me call you back."

"Got to check with Joan, don't you?" Ryan said, baiting me. He feels I defer to my wife too much, and I probably do, but I still worry about the post-traumatic stress syndrome that has dominated our lives the last two years. This was especially touchy since we knew the Schoening family, although I didn't tell Ryan that. He'd only push harder if he knew.

I started to answer, but Ryan had a coughing fit.

"Are you okay?" I asked.

"The smoke doesn't seem to be going away."

"Open more windows. You need to get a cross ventilation going. As for Joan, of course I'm going to check with her. We're on vacation. For me to give up that free time and start filing stories when we had planned to do other things is not a solitary decision. I'll get back to you."

"Well, don't make it too long, Sherlock. If you're not going to take it we need to get another reporter down there immediately." He coughed again.

"I'll be in touch within the hour. Maybe by then the smoke will have cleared." I hung up and flopped back onto the bed.

I didn't need this—an assignment on top of trying to find the culprit who hurt Mr. Jangles. Not classic vacation material. Unfortunately I hadn't had an assignment from the *Standard* in a month or so, so we could use the money. And I liked to stay on friendly terms with the paper.

The comforting smell of pancakes drifted into the room. Janine makes a special kind of thick Dutch pancake with apples baked inside it that Stephanie loves, and I knew we'd have it at least once while we were here. They're huge; one is enough for all but the biggest appetite. I put on a robe and headed downstairs.

Joan was in the kitchen warming slices of ham while her mother stood at a counter making pancakes in an electric skillet. The fact that Janine was cooking was a good sign—it meant that she was coping with Mr. Jangles's death as best she could.

Stephanie had received the first pancake of the morning and was already working on it. I walked over and gave Joan a hug.

"Who was that on the phone?" Joan asked me.

"Ryan."

"Uncle Ryan?" Stephanie asked. Her eyes lit up. She was very fond of him and called him "Uncle," even though he was no relation. He loved playing children's games with her like *Candyland* and *Chutes and Ladders.* In many ways, Ryan's never grown up.

"Yes, it was Uncle Ryan," I told her. I turned to Joan. "The paper wants me to start filing stories on the disappearance of Keri Schoening's body."

"Why you?"

"Mainly because Ryan knew I was already down here. The reporter they'd normally send just had twins."

"Are you going to take it?" Joan sounded slightly annoyed, which I could understand. I was slightly annoyed myself. I wanted to be on vacation, not working.

"Normally I wouldn't, but I'm not sure I should turn it down. May was kind of dry for me, and I haven't had an assignment from the *Standard* in a while. It would be good from a relationship standpoint to do this."

Joan thought for a moment. "I suppose you're right. I know it's important to you." That was something Dr. Grande had helped Joan recognize, and I was glad to hear her verbalize it. "If you decide to take it, it'll be fine."

I looked over at Stephanie, who was busy with her breakfast. She seemed to have tuned us out.

"I promised I'd let them know in an hour."

"I've got another pancake done, Nick," Janine said, pulling the plate-sized treat from the skillet and sliding it on a dish, which she handed to me. It hung over the edge on all sides. "Why don't you take this one so you can get started on the day? Just in case you need to."

I thanked her and got a smaller dish for the meat Joan was cooking. With a plate in each hand, I chose a seat next to Stephanie and then got coffee, black, since Janine's coffee was on the weak side. I dusted the pancake with powdered sugar and cut it with a knife and fork. The apples inside oozed with a cinnamon and sugar coating.

"How does yours taste?" I asked Stephanie.

"Good," she said, between bites.

I cut a piece and placed it in my mouth with anticipation. The warm, doughy goodness of the pancake, the sweetness of the cinnamon sugar, and the tartness of the apple made my taste buds soar. While the Italian in me wasn't overly fond of German cooking, Janine's pancakes were superb. Soon Joan and Janine were seated at the table eating with us, all of us in a contented, sugar stupor.

"Janine, last night I heard a carillon playing music after it chimed midnight," I said. "Is that the carillon in St. Barnabas's tower?"

"Probably. The parish just recently re-started it chiming every hour. A song plays at noon and midnight. We went for a long time without it working. Personally, I find it comforting at night when I hear it."

I nodded. There was something old and beautiful about steeple bells ringing. In retrospect, it was probably Stephanie's sleepwalking that had made the incident feel ominous.

I thought again about Ryan's call, and especially my relationship with the *Standard*. Although I knew they already liked me there, I decided the newspaper was too important to my income and professional life to turn down the job. True to her word, Joan seemed fine with the decision. Stephanie was more interested in finishing her pancake. I left to call Ryan and plan my next move.

Ryan didn't answer his cell. Probably still coping with the burnt bagel incident. I left a message and then retrieved the morning paper from the front door to check what the *Jasper Times* had published about the incident. Sure enough, the byline was from the great Sally Kaiser.

According to the paper, Keri's grave was located in a family cemetery in a secluded meadow bounded by woods on the western edge of Jasper. The acreage was part of the old farmstead where the original Schoening family had settled when they emigrated from Germany in the late 1800s. At one time the family members were major landowners; now they were no longer farmers but businessmen. The family still owned the homestead and the 500 acres surrounding it, which included the cemetery, but the land was tilled by someone else. A gravel road led back to the graveyard. About a half mile long, it went past the farmhouse, which had been turned into a retreat center used primarily by the St. Barnabas parish. Since no one lived there, there was no one to notice any activity at the cemetery. The fresh digging at the grave site was first noticed by a young woman who had gone there to pray.

I called into the dining room. "Joan, do you know where the Schoening's family cemetery is?"

"Sure, it's no secret. Everyone around here knows."

"Can we go out there?"

"I can take you out there later. You'd probably never find it if I gave you directions. There're a lot of country roads you have to take."

"Would it be treading on your relationship with Susan for you to get me an interview with her?"

"Maybe."

"Would you do it anyway?"

Pause. "Let me see if I can find a way to do it more naturally than just calling her up and asking her to give you the interview."

I'd had enough with the long-distance shouting so I walked into the dining room. "I won't have a lot of time. They'll want a story for tomorrow's paper."

"I understand that, but I don't want to infringe on my friendship. I'll figure something out."

"Okay." I heard the "back off" in her tone. And I trusted her to get it done.

After a quick shower and shave, I put on jean shorts, a faded, plum-colored T-shirt and shoes and was ready for the day. Returning to the living room, I started through the paper again, this time for pleasure, when Stephanie came in and asked me to read her the comics. It had become something of a ritual with us. She didn't ask for it everyday, but when she did I enjoyed our time together. Joan and I had been reading to her for many years, but since she would be starting kindergarten in the fall, lately we'd made more of an effort to show her the words when we read. The comics were perfect for that. I also liked that it helped her develop a sense of humor.

This morning I didn't have to explain any of the strips, which is a good sign. "Garfield," which appeals to the kid in all of us, is almost never a problem. But "Baby Blues" sometimes is, since it's often aimed at adults. But today she got it. Stephanie retrieved a Dr. Seuss book afterwards to "read" to herself. I know this is the father in me, but I think she's a very bright child. She's getting the hang of the words and the rhythm of Dr. Seuss. I don't know if she's really reading, but I think she will be soon.

With Stephanie occupied and Joan upstairs in the shower, I pulled out my cell phone and called the police station. I asked for Detective Whitmeyer and got put on hold. When she came on, I told her who I was and asked if she and Day had been able to contact the neighbors in the subdivision last night about their animals.

"We visited everyone who was home," Whitmeyer said. "I think they were alarmed at the idea that a person was behind the missing animals. If you hear any talk around the neighborhood, be sure to let us know."

"I was wondering if you could tell me the names of the people who had missing pets, and also the name of the family whose dog had had his ears and tail cut."

"Why do you want them?"

"My goal is like yours. I want to see whoever is doing this gets caught, and quickly. I believe I can be a help to you."

Whitmeyer didn't respond right away, but I knew what she was thinking. She knew I was a reporter, and she was wondering how much she could trust me, especially since she'd only just met me. In the end, the police know they need us as much as we need them, but they like to get to know a reporter before they start sharing information. I hoped she'd give me the benefit of the doubt since I didn't have a lot of time to prove myself.

"Okay, especially since I'll be tied up with that body disappearing from the Schoening cemetery. But I want your promise that it's a two-way street, and you'll give me any information you come across."

I assured her that I would. After all, I wasn't doing this as a reporter, this was a personal grudge match. The secrecy I might normally reserve for an investigation wasn't necessary.

She gave me the names and addresses, and I wrote them down. After we hung up, I stared at the list. The pattern that I saw was one I was sure the police hadn't missed either. Every house with a missing pet was on the outside ring of the subdivision. The beagle mix the vet had told me about belonged to the house a few doors down. I wondered which of the remaining houses had pets, and if vigilance by their owners would cause the felon to go elsewhere. Or, if he might simply become more desperate.

CHAPTER SIX

"How well do you know the Muellers?" I asked Janine. It was about 9:30 A.M. She'd just come into the living room looking for Stephanie. She smelled of a citrus hairspray that held her short silver-gray hair in place.

"The woman four doors down? Why do you ask?"

I stood and walked closer to her so Stephanie wouldn't overhear. "Their dog has been a victim, too."

Janine winced. "The Muellers? That's awful. They have such a sweet-natured dog. I haven't seen it in a while. Tell me they didn't have to . . ."

"No, I don't think so. The police told me the dog lost its ears and its tail. I'm sure they're frightened, though. That's probably why they're keeping it inside."

"Who's frightened?"

Janine and I turned to see Joan descending the staircase near where we were whispering. She was dressed in jeans and a light blue T-shirt that fit her just snugly enough to emphasize her trim figure but not enough to make it look like she was trying to attract attention.

I took her hand in mine and pulled her into the hushed conversation Janine and I were having. "A neighbor's dog. The police say it was abducted also. It lost the outer part of its ears and its tail. Your mom said she hasn't seen it in a while, and we figure it's probably frightened to go outside."

Joan kept an eye on Stephanie. "They may not want to let it

out," she said in a quiet voice. "I know I wouldn't under those circumstances."

"Someone needs to find the person who did this," Janine said, and I think the point was directed at me.

"After we get back from the cemetery, I'll talk to the Muellers," I said. "But first we need to get over to see where the body was dug up."

"I'm ready if you are," Joan said.

We said goodbye to Stephanie, who seemed uncharacteristically subdued. I wondered if she was missing Mr. Jangles or if she sensed something was going on. Janine and Steph went out to the porch swing. They waved to us as we backed down the driveway.

Stephanie wasn't the only one subdued. Joan and I were lost in our thoughts as we drove. We passed field after field of soybeans and corn, mesmerizing me with waves of green. Periodically Joan broke the hypnotic effect with her directions. She was right—I would have gotten lost without her. We went down no fewer than eight different small county roads. By the time we neared the old farmhouse, I had no real idea where we were relative to our starting point.

"Slow down here," Joan said as we rounded a particularly sharp turn. There was a long, straight stretch ahead. "That's the house," she said, pointing to a large old farmhouse about a quarter mile off the road on the left.

It was a big two-story Colonial Revival with a red brick exterior. It sat on a hill overlooking the surrounding fields. From that elevation in the 1880s, a landowner would have been able to keep watch over the farmhands, the cattle, and the rest of the property. Strategic.

"Turn in at the next driveway," Joan said.

I would have done so, but the police department had blocked the driveway with sawhorses. Since there were no cars behind me, I stopped on the road.

"I'm surprised the police have jurisdiction out here," I told Joan. "Wouldn't the sheriff's department be in charge?"

"Mom said the town annexed a lot of farmland out here in an effort to control growth. But we're really not all that far out. It's just there's no straight way to get here."

There was no one around—no one to see what I was about to do. Joan made a token protest when I got out of the van and she realized I was going to move the sawhorses, but I moved them anyway, returning them to their blocking positions after I pulled into the drive.

The drive back to the cemetery was a little more than a half-mile. We passed the farmhouse, now used as a Catholic retreat center, on the left, and a wooded section on the right. Past the woods, the gravel road took a sharp turn to the right and went back into a meadow. The cemetery was there, marked by a black wrought iron fence with spikes on each post.

We stopped at the edge of the cemetery. The woods had grown up to it on two sides. I parked near the smaller of the two gated entrances, which was down by the wooded area.

"For a private cemetery, this is bigger than I thought it would be," I told Joan as we got out of the van. There was nearly one full acre of land within the fence. I reached into the back seat to get a notebook and camera before I shut the door.

Yellow police tape marked off the two entrances. The closest one was narrow and clearly for pedestrians. The larger one I took to be for vehicles, like the backhoe they probably needed to dig graves.

It was easy to tell which grave belonged to Keri Schoening. It was the one that was now a big hole with a mound of dirt piled up beside it. To the other side was a small lean-to shelter that protected an array of candles, crosses, and flowers. A large terra cotta jar with a lid was in the center. I'd seen kids put crosses and candles and memorabilia at sites along roads where their friends had died, and I figured this was Keri's friends' way of paying tribute.

"Hey!" we heard someone call. Joan and I turned around to see Father Dan hustling up to us. He looked much like he had the previous day, priestly collar and black, short-sleeve shirt with jeans. His tennis shoes looked rather white for an old pair, and I thought he'd probably cleaned them recently.

"This area is closed," he called. "The police don't want anyone trespassing."

"Father Dan, I'm Nick Bertetto, Janine Strassheim's son-in-law. This is my wife, Joan. We met you yesterday."

"Oh, that's right. Nick. And Joan," he said, nodding to my wife. As he got closer, I noticed a faint smell of incense. "Sorry, I didn't recognize you from a distance."

"Where did you come from?" I asked. "We didn't see anyone when we pulled in."

"I'm staying in the retreat center." He pointed back toward the road. "I've been there since I learned Keri's body disappeared. Thought it would be a good idea to keep an eye on the cemetery."

"For the police?" I asked.

"Well, not officially. But I know they don't have the manpower to patrol out here all the time. So I can't really let you hang around. The area's a crime scene."

I told him I was a freelance writer for the *Indianapolis Standard*. "The paper is interested in the body's disappearance, so I thought I'd swing by and take a look at the cemetery. We're not going to be here long, and I won't disturb anything."

"I suppose if you want to take pictures from here, that's okay," he said, noticing the camera. "But you can't go inside the fence. The police have it blocked off."

I shifted my attention back to the graveyard. "Father, what's the little lean-to all about, the one next to Keri Schoening's grave?"

"It's so people can leave things for Keri's blessing or petitions for her to take to God."

"Really?" I said. I opened my notebook. "I thought people only did that at shrines for the saints or places where the Blessed Mother had appeared."

Joan turned to me. "Haven't you heard the talk about Keri being a saint?"

"Yeah, but she's not a saint yet, I mean, officially . . ."

"Technically, no," Father Dan said. "But she died for her faith. She was shot after she made the affirmation that she believed in Jesus. That makes her a martyr, and according to Catholic doctrine, martyrs are believed to automatically go to heaven, where they would be saints."

I made notes. "But aren't there steps the Church has to go through in order to declare someone a saint? Isn't there some kind of inquisition? Mother Teresa hasn't even made it yet."

"Let me differentiate between being a saint and being *declared* a saint by the Church. A person like Keri Schoening can die for her faith and go to heaven and be a saint. Just because the Church doesn't declare her a saint, doesn't mean she isn't one. We place that in God's hands. But people who demonstrate extraordinary faith on earth, such as Mother Teresa, are examples for the Church. We want to recognize them as saints. So a process was set up to determine whether or not they're saints. You're right. Mother Teresa's been declared 'blessed,' which is one step away. That means someone prayed to Mother Teresa for a miracle, it occurred, the Church investigated it and not only validated it but attributed it to her intercession with God. For canonization—sainthood—a second such miracle has to have occurred."

"But all that takes years."

"True, and the investigation process doesn't even begin until five years after the presumed saint's death, although the Pope waived that in the case of Mother Teresa. But the five-year time frame won't stop people from asking saints to help them obtain miracles, especially if they believe the candidate has a special 'in' with God. And therein lies the appeal of Keri Schoening. She likely *is* a saint."

We stood there in the humid June air. Though we were in the shade, it was still hot. Father Dan wiped perspiration from his forehead.

I wanted to get in the cemetery and head over to Keri's grave, examine the little shrine, and just see what I could. But with Father Dan there, I was reluctant to flagrantly ignore the rules. Plus, it wasn't a good idea to disturb the area since the police investigation was still open. With the ground loose from all the digging, I was sure to leave footprints that could be tracked.

"I'd like to include the information about people leaving petitions and why in my story," I said. "Is it okay if I quote you?"

He tried to look appropriately humble about the whole thing, but his eyes held a little bit of sparkle, making me think he was flattered to get some attention from the press. I couldn't recall if he had been quoted or not when the West Jasper shootings had been covered.

"If you really think it's necessary to use my name, I guess that's okay," Father Dan said, "but I'm not an expert on church procedure regarding saints. You should probably contact someone in the Evansville diocese office."

I noticed that he said Evansville and not Indianapolis. Jasper must be in the southern Indiana diocese rather than the larger Indianapolis archdiocese.

"Do the police know how they got the body out? Wouldn't they have had to bring in a lot of equipment? I would think that could be tracked."

"You should really ask the police," he said, looking at my notebook. "I mean, since you'll need something official. But I thought I heard them say the body must've been dug up by hand."

"What about the concrete vault the casket is buried in?" Joan asked. "Those things are heavy. There's no way they could have gotten that thing up without some equipment."

"There was no vault."

I was surprised. "How could there not be a vault? I thought those things were required by law."

"I don't think so," the priest said, "at least not in a private cemetery. I've done a lot of funerals. Most cemeteries require them, but I don't think it's a law."

A cell phone rang. Father Dan pulled up a phone hooked to his belt and flipped it open. He looked at the number and closed the phone. "I need to return that call in a moment," he said.

"Wouldn't it take a while to dig a casket up by hand?" I asked, getting back to my notes.

"You're questioning the wrong person," he said, "but if you didn't have to worry about the vault, I would think a couple of strong people working on it could have it dug up in six or eight hours. The thieves reburied the empty casket, too, but I think that would take less time."

I looked around. The cemetery was a long way from the road and the view was blocked by the woods. If no one was at the retreat house, which we could see from where we stood, a person would be able to dig without interruption for as long as necessary.

"How often do people come out here to leave petitions?" Joan asked.

"I don't know, but I'm guessing someone comes out here every day. That's how the police knew someone had dug the

69

casket up. A visitor noticed the loose soil."

"Then they probably had to do most of the digging at night," I said. "Otherwise, they wouldn't have the time needed to get it done. But if they did, wouldn't the lights they'd have to use attract attention?"

Joan shook her head. "The nearest neighbor is the Barber property, and they wouldn't see a light from here unless it was a searchlight."

I nodded and tried to imagine the scene. People digging up a grave late at night, out here partially surrounded by woods. Faint light put out by some kind of lantern. Shadowy figures moving around gravestones. It felt very creepy.

"I'd better take some photos," I said, mostly to push the images from my mind.

I ran the zoom lens as far as it would go. The cemetery was large enough, and Keri's grave was far enough away that the zoom still couldn't get me very close. I took a couple of photos anyway, hoping that the definition of the camera was good enough we could enlarge the picture with a software program and extract a decent close-up. If not, I'd hire a photographer and charge the *Standard*. We'd have to deal with Father Dan and then maybe the police, but I could handle that later.

"Do you know whether the police have any suspects?" I asked Father Dan.

"I haven't heard of any."

Joan asked, "Have you talked to the Schoenings today?"

"Yes. They're upset by the whole thing, but they're taking it better than I thought. I was afraid this would open up the wounds of Keri's death again. It has to some degree, but they seem to be more angry than devastated."

To my mind, this meant the Schoenings would be more likely to talk to the press, especially if it meant they had a better chance to recover the body. Since Joan had asked if he'd contacted them, I was fairly sure she hadn't talked to them yet. I didn't want to push her into getting me an interview, but the time was getting close to try that avenue again.

"I need to get back to the retreat house and return that call," Father Dan said. He looked at us as though he expected us to leave now, too.

"I've probably got enough to get started," I said. "Thanks for your help. Will you be staying here the rest of the day?"

"I'll be here on and off. I have appointments, but whenever I can, I drive back."

Father walked us back to the van and waved as we drove away.

"Don't you think he's exceeding his authority a little?" I asked Joan.

"What do you mean?"

"I mean, telling us we couldn't go into the cemetery. Like he's the one who makes the decision."

"C'mon, Nick. *You* know you shouldn't go back there. Father Dan didn't tell you not to do anything common sense wouldn't. The police had it blocked off for a reason."

"Maybe. Do you think you could call the Schoenings now? I really need to get the interview done and start on the article because if I need more information, I want to have the time to get it."

Joan thought about it. "Okay." She pulled my cell phone out of the pocket between our two seats and dialed the number.

"Hi, Aaron, it's Joan Bertetto. Is Susan there?" Joan paused. "Oh, she is? Do you think it will go on much longer? No, that's okay. I'll try back." She hung up.

"Susan is doing an interview with the *Jasper Times* right now," Joan told me.

"Did Aaron mention the reporter's name?"

"He did, but I don't remember."

71

"Maybe Sally Kaiser?"

"That sounds right."

"Figures," I said.

I was being scooped even as we drove home from the cemetery.

CHAPTER SEVEN

I felt confident that if Susan Schoening was giving an interview to the *Jasper Times,* she would give one to me, too. After all, I was married to one of her best friends. All that was left was for Joan to make the connection that would get us over there.

When we got back to the house, Hugo had returned from his fishing trip. I knew he'd heard about Mr. Jangles because, right after he said hello, he pulled me out onto the front porch and shut the door behind us.

"Thank you for taking care of the situation while I was gone," he said. Hugo's jaw clenched and unclenched, making the bristles of his gray mustache stick out. "I have to ask. Who did this? Do you think you can find him? Because I want to make sure this bastard gets what's coming to him."

"I think I can find him, but it's not going to be easy. Now that Keri Schoening's body has disappeared, the police aren't going to be digging into this case as hard as they might. That's going to limit the information available to us. Honestly, I'm as distracted as they are, Hugo. My paper wants me to report on the body's disappearance, too."

"I thought you were on vacation."

"I was. Still am, to some degree. But when a front-page story drops in your lap, you just have to move on it. Especially if you're a freelancer. They don't come around very often."

"But will you find out who did this to Mr. Jangles?"

"I promise I'll try, Hugo. I want to see justice done as much as you do."

Joan opened the door and came out onto the porch. "I just got a call from Susan. She doesn't want to do another interview."

"What?"

"She says you should get the information from Sally Kaiser."

The blood must've rushed to my face in anger pretty fast because Hugo backed his way through the front door.

"Does she understand that reporters don't share interviews?" I said. "That we're competitors, not good buddies? That we have to do our own research?"

"I tried to explain that to her, but she didn't want to listen. You can imagine how distraught she is."

"Of course she's distraught. I know that, and I know this sounds selfish, but I've got an article to write. You're one of her best friends; I've known her for years."

Joan shrugged.

"Let's go over there right now. Maybe she'll be willing to talk in person."

"I am going to go, Nick, but not until 1:30. That's when she said she'll be able to see me." Joan frowned at me. "I'm not sure she'll be any more willing to talk to you then than she is now."

"I've got to take that chance," I said. "I'm going with you."

Joan put her hand on my shoulder. "We need to be gentle, Nick. She's going through a lot."

"True. But she's already done one interview."

"And one may be all that's in her right now. I'm going to get some lunch. You want any?"

After several deep breaths, I followed Joan into the kitchen. Stephanie was there with Janine, eating macaroni and cheese, occasionally with a fork, mostly with her fingers. Steph goes through phases where she wants to eat the same thing over and over again; right now it was a macaroni and cheese phase. Janine was indulging her, but the last thing I was going to do was tell Steph's grandmother not to spoil her. That was her job.

However, Stephanie knew better than to think macaroni was a finger food. "Steph," I said. "How do we eat macaroni?"

She licked her fingers and then hid them. She smiled at me. "With a fork?"

I nodded. "With a fork."

She picked it up.

Joan and I made sandwiches from deli meat Janine had purchased for our visit. While Joan opened a bag of barbeque potato chips and had those with her lunch, I tried to be virtuous, opting for carrot sticks instead.

I sat next to Janine. "Do you think the Muellers would be home now?" I asked her.

"Kevin might. He's their son, just turned sixteen. Brenda's a nurse and works odd hours. She might be home. Her husband travels a lot, and we don't see him much."

If the kid was there, he'd probably be a good source of information, but I didn't want to talk to him unless his mother was home too. Parents don't like strangers talking to their kids, even when they're sixteen. It was worth a walk down the street, though, just to see who was home.

After lunch, I took to the sidewalk and went four doors down to their house. The Muellers' home, like almost all of the houses in this relatively new subdivision, was a two-story with an attached garage over which sat part of the second story. The home was part brick, part siding. I walked up to the porch. Both the screen door and the front door were closed. I rang the doorbell.

Immediately a dog began yapping. A few seconds later I heard someone say, "Be quiet, Buddy." A high school kid answered the door. Kevin, I assumed. He was about my height, with brown eyes and curly brown hair. Like many boys that age, he was working on his growth spurt but hadn't filled out his frame. His thinness was emphasized by his one-size-too-big Outkast T-shirt. There was an air of resignation about him, as though the world was throwing too much his way. Through the screen door I could just make out the shape of the dog, cowering behind Kevin. It growled, but it hadn't barked since the door opened. Kevin looked at me. "Yes?" he said.

"I'm Nick Bertetto. I'm here visiting the Strassheims down the street," I said, pointing in the direction of Hugo and Janine's house. "I'm their son-in-law. Is your mom or dad in?"

"My mom is," he said. "Just a minute." He turned and yelled, "Mom!"

When Brenda Mueller came to the door, I could see which side of the family Kevin had inherited from. She was trim, with short, wavy brown hair. I repeated my introduction and told her why I was there.

She nodded. "The police stopped by yesterday and told us about the cat. I'm sorry to hear it. C'mon in." She held the door open. "We'd like to get hold of the person who did this, too."

The Mueller home was very nearly the same floor plan as Hugo and Janine's, with the living room off to the right of the hall. I followed Brenda into the room, where she sat on an antique rocking chair and I took a seat on the leather couch. Kevin chose a matching leather chair near his mother. The dog, which looked sturdy like a beagle but had longer hair like a collie advanced toward me, growling suspiciously. I could see where the vet had cauterized the wounds left when the ears had been cut. They were healing but still looked ugly. What little was left of his tail had been wrapped in bandages. The missing ears and tail gave the dog a pitiful look, and my heart ached again thinking what torture Buddy and Mr. Jangles had endured.

"How long ago did this happen?" I asked.

"It was a week ago yesterday," Brenda said.

"Do you have an idea how Buddy was captured?"

"We think he had to have been taken from the backyard Monday morning. No one was here then. Kevin is getting his Health requirement out of the way this summer. His classes are in the morning."

"The dog wanted out before I left," Kevin said, interrupting, "and I didn't have time to wait for him to finish doing his job. I feel really bad about what happened, but sometimes he likes to stay outside all day. We've never had a problem before."

"No one's blaming Kevin," Brenda said. "He just hates that it happened."

I could understand why Kevin seemed depressed. If he had waited to let the dog back in, Buddy would be fine.

"There's no way you could have known, Kevin," I said. "And if it hadn't been that day, it might have been the next day or the one after that. Let's just hope that now the neighborhood's aware of what's going on, it won't happen to another animal. When did your dog come back?"

"Not until that night," Kevin said. "He was gone when I got home at lunchtime. I rode my bike all over the neighborhood looking for him. I was going to put up posters the next day if we couldn't find him."

"About one in the morning, I heard him yelping outside," Brenda said. "Since my husband isn't home, I got Kevin up. We didn't know what to do. Buddy was bleeding pretty badly. Since we know Thom Haase, the vet, we called him at home. He told us to bring Buddy to the clinic, and he fixed him up."

We all looked at Buddy. He had progressed from growling at me to sniffing my shoes. I bent down to pet him and he snarled, baring his teeth but backing away from me. I snatched my hand away.

"He didn't use to act this way around strangers," Kevin said.

77

"It's okay. I understand. Did the vet speculate on whether they drugged the dog before they did this to him?"

"We had a hard time believing that someone had done this deliberately, even though the vet said it was possible. We thought it was coyotes, that Buddy had broken through the electric fence and wandered too far. The vet wasn't absolutely sure. The ears and tail had been ripped so badly there was an outside chance they might have been bites. We told everyone to watch out for the coyotes. Several other dogs and cats have gone missing, and we assumed coyotes had gotten them. We didn't know the truth until we heard about Mr. Jangles."

"It's so sick," Kevin said, picking up the dog and holding him. The dog didn't object.

"Have you or the police looked for footprints or other clues on the property?"

"I did," Kevin said. "But I didn't see anything."

"I probably won't find anything either," I said, "but would you mind if I looked?"

"Not at all." Brenda turned to Kevin. "Would you show Mr. Bertetto the back yard?"

"Sure."

"Please call me Nick," I said.

Kevin led me through the hallway to the kitchen. We went out a sliding glass door onto a deck. From there, I surveyed the sizeable yard. It was long and narrow like the Strassheims' but without the landscaping Janine had put in. The only obstructions were at the end of the yard, a line of pine trees that weren't very old. "I'll bet you can play a good game of football out here," I said.

"Yeah." Kevin smiled for the first time. "Or soccer. I like to play soccer."

"Great," I said. "Are you on the team at the high school?"

The smile was short lived. "I tried out but didn't make it.

The coach already knew who he was going to play."

"I'm sorry," I said.

"Nothing you did."

I stepped off the deck into the yard. Kevin followed. I pointed toward Janine and Hugo's place several yards away. "Over at the Strassheims', the police said they believe whoever did this lured the cat to the back, nabbed him, and then after they . . . well, when they were done they dropped him off at the county road, back by the cornfield. The police think they didn't actually come into the yard. What do you think happened here?"

"Probably something like that," he said. "If they came up through the cornfield, Buddy would have been going nuts with his barking and been right up against the electric fence line. They could have grabbed him and pulled him through it. It would have shocked him at first, but then he would have been all right."

"Would he have bitten whoever grabbed him?"

"Absolutely."

"Then they may have sprayed him with something to temporarily knock him out. Did the vet say anything about that?"

He shook his head.

"I may ask him," I said.

We walked to the back of the property. "When did the police learn about this?"

"Not until they stopped by yesterday to tell us about Mr. Jangles."

"The vet didn't report it?"

He shook his head again. "We thought it was the coyotes."

"Yeah, but he wasn't so sure. He described it to me as an act of cruelty. I would have thought he'd have reported it."

Kevin shrugged. He stopped walking at the tree line. "This is as far as Buddy can go."

I continued past the trees and walked to the edge of the cornfield. Between the trees and the cornfield was the utility easement, a narrow, grassy strip of land that also ran behind the Strassheims' property. It led to the county road. I walked the grassy part all the way to the edge of my in-laws' property, looking from right to left and back again for anything that seemed out of place.

Kevin followed me. "What are you looking for?"

"Some kind of clue. A footprint, a matchbox, a scrap of clothing that might have gotten caught on a bush, anything."

"I don't see anything, do you?"

"No, unfortunately."

"You've done this before, haven't you?"

"What do you mean?"

"I mean, you've looked for clues before. Are you a detective?"

I smiled. "I'm an investigative reporter."

"I want to be a reporter," he said, brightening. "I'm on the newspaper staff at school. What paper do you work for?"

"I'm a freelancer now, but I used to work for the *Indianapolis Standard* full time. I still do some work for them."

"Sweet," he said. "I'd like to work for them some day."

"Keep writing while you're in high school. If you can get into a good journalism program in college, there's no reason you couldn't get a job with a good newspaper."

Kevin paused. "Have you ever seen a dead body?"

I looked at Kevin with concern. "Yes, and you wouldn't want to see one."

"I already have. Several," he said bluntly. "I've written articles about it. I was in the high school when the shooting started."

I took in a sharp breath. The West Jasper shootings. It had infected this community with a kind of malaise, not obvious to outsiders like me but very much still there. It suddenly hit me that this kid had seen too much in his short life. "I'm sorry, Kevin. That must have been terrible."

"Yeah, it was. I had to go to counseling and stuff for awhile. I'm okay with it. None of us talk about it much anymore."

"None of whom?"

He stuck his hands in his pants pockets and pushed them down, making the waistband of his baggy jeans tighten as it rode low on his hips. He looked at the ground, not at me. "You know, the other kids who were there."

"Where were you when it happened?"

"I was in one of the main hallways. It was my study hall time, but I had written a pass to go to the media center to work on the paper. If I hadn't stopped at the bathroom on the way down, I would have been in there, too."

"Were any of your friends among the . . . I mean, were any of them involved?"

"Two of them were injured."

"Are they okay now?"

"Yeah. Physically, anyhow."

"I'm so sorry."

"It happened."

"And now this with Buddy. It must be hard on you and your mom."

"I wish my dad were home more often."

We stood there for a short time reacting as guys do, shuffling our feet and not looking at each other. I wondered about the absentee father. Kevin's words sounded like an SOS. Perhaps Janine would know what the story was.

In the end, a quick glance at my watch made me remember the trip to the Schoenings at 1:30, and I decided to get back to the reason I was there. "Kevin," I asked, "do you or your mom have any enemies, anyone who would want to threaten you by hurting your dog?"

"I've thought about that, but I can't come up with anyone."

"All of the known disappearances and cruelty acts have come from this neighborhood. You're probably in touch with kids around here. Have you or anyone you know spotted people who don't belong here, or seen someone acting suspicious, or anything like that?"

He hesitated. Then he said, "No, not really."

"You're sure?" I said. "You paused before you answered."

"I was just thinking. But no, I don't know of anyone around here."

I searched his eyes for a few seconds before I let him go. The way he had added "around here" made me think he knew something. "You're really sure?"

"Yeah."

We started walking back toward his house. I may have overstepped my bounds a bit, but I put my hand on his back as a father might. "Promise me you'll let me know if you hear anything or if something suddenly comes to mind."

"I will," he said, but he didn't make eye contact when he said it.

I hoped that whatever he knew, he would decide to tell me soon. He seemed to be carrying around a lot of baggage, and deep down in there, I believed, was something important he knew but was afraid to talk about.

CHAPTER EIGHT

When I got back to the house, I found Janine and Joan in the kitchen. Joan drizzled icing on a coffeecake she had made earlier to take to Susan and Aaron.

"Kevin Mueller's a nice kid," I said to Janine.

I got a spoon from a drawer to sample the icing and headed toward the bowl. "Not too much," Joan said.

"Just a little." I don't know what it is about icing, but it just begs to be tasted.

"Kevin *is* nice," Janine said. "It's a shame about his father, though."

"That he travels a lot?"

"Hugo and I don't think he's traveling anymore. We think he's settled down in California."

I licked a bit of icing off the spoon. "Does Brenda not want to move out there?"

"He doesn't want her to go. From what we've heard, he's got a second family out there."

"He's married to two women? That's illegal!"

Janine shook her head. "He's married to Brenda, the other woman he lives with. I guess he's had to go to San Diego for so long and so often he worked out this scheme. But the last few years he's basically chosen the California family. So Kevin rarely sees his dad—and when he does, his father ignores him. It's affected him."

I finished licking the spoon and set it in the sink. "Why

doesn't Brenda divorce him?"

"We're not sure. We think there must be some kind of financial reason. Anyway, Brenda works as a nurse at the hospital, doing the evening shift three or four nights a week. Kevin gets left alone a lot. It's sad."

Joan and I nodded.

Joan looked at her watch. "We need to be leave in about fifteen minutes, Nick."

"I'll be ready," I said.

Leaving the kitchen, I decided to make good use of the time by hooking the camera to my laptop and downloading the photos from the cemetery. Just as I'd thought, the zoom hadn't gotten me close enough to Keri's grave. I dropped the first photo into Photoshop and enlarged it to see what I could do.

It was of the lean-to that contained the flowers, crucifixes, petition jar, and other items left by Keri's friends. I used the cutting tool and deleted everything but the lean-to, then enlarged it. The photo was still pretty clear. I saved the changes and went on to the next one.

The second photo was of the gravesite. I thought I had done a particularly good job positioning that one, given that I wasn't a real photographer. On the left side of the photo you could see slightly into the hole of Keri's dug up grave, and beyond it, in the background, were other graves and gravestones. On the right side was the dramatic, out-of-place mound of dirt from the grave. Keri's rectangular gravestone could be seen sitting at an odd angle on the far right of the photo, half on the dirt and half on a flat, adjacent grave site. It practically screamed that something was very wrong. I framed the part I wanted and then enlarged it.

Something stopped me. There was a shadow back behind one of the graves that couldn't be caused by anything in the vicinity. I did a double take. And a triple take. I enlarged the photo even more, to the point where it became very fuzzy. I stared at the screen.

It wasn't a shadow; it was a person. He or she, I couldn't tell which, was leaning out from behind a memorial in the background. I tried to judge how tall the person was. The memorial was half a foot or so above his/her height, so if I knew how tall the memorial was, I could figure out the size of the person. I tried to imagine why someone would be back there.

Whoever it was had been in the graveyard before we got there. They'd hid once Joan, Father Dan, and I showed up. Being so far away, they would have had to check from time to time to see if we'd left. I'd just happened to take the photo at one of those times.

I walked to the top of the back staircase and called down into the kitchen. "Joan, could you come up here, please?"

Two minutes later she was upstairs standing next to me at the computer. "What is it?"

"Look at this," I said, pointing.

"From the Schoening cemetery?"

"Uh-huh."

She studied the screen of the laptop intently for a moment. "It looks like a person."

"My thought exactly."

"What does it look like in the big picture?"

I backed out of the close-up. Joan leaned in toward my face trying to see the photo straight on.

"Where is the section you just showed me?"

I used the mouse to point out the shadow.

"Can I see the enlargement again?"

I switched views.

"Can you make it any clearer?"

"That's as clear as I can get. You remember we were so far back that I wasn't sure the resolution would be good enough for a close-up? Well, it was good enough for Keri's grave, but not for a close up of whoever was hiding in the background."

"It's too pixelated to make out any details," she said. "Could be a man or a woman. In fact, it might not even be a person, really."

"What else would it be?" I asked, not wanting to speculate myself. My imagination gets me in trouble too often as it is.

She looked at her watch. "I don't know. Print it out, and we'll take it with us. We need to leave."

I hit the print button and made copies. We said goodbye to Janine, and then to Hugo and Stephanie, who were having an animated discussion.

"Grandpa's taking me fishing!" Stephanie said, excited. "Grandma tied my hair in a pony tail so I wouldn't get too hot." She swished the brown mane behind her head to demonstrate. Then she held up a plastic bag. "We're taking animal crackers with us for a snack."

"I know you'll have a good time," Joan said, giving her a hug. "Now be sure to mind Grandpa and wear your float vest, especially around the water."

"And bring home lots of fish," I told her when I gave her a hug of my own. "I'm really hungry for fish tonight."

"I will," she promised.

We chuckled at the idea of Stephanie fishing as we left for the Schoenings'. She was somewhat squeamish when it came to handling things that crawled, so neither of us could imagine her baiting her own hook. We also felt she would be very kind-hearted when they actually reeled in their first fish. If they caught a lot, by late afternoon she might be willing to bring home a few fish to eat, but the first ones would most certainly be thrown back.

Both of us were relieved, though, that the fishing trip distracted her from asking where we were going. Stephanie had thought the world of Keri Schoening, who had treated her like a little sister whenever we visited her parents. She hadn't been to Keri's house since the death, and we didn't think this was a good time for that to happen.

"What did you tell the Schoenings about our visit?" I asked when we were about halfway there. Nothing is very far from anything else in Jasper, so getting to the Schoenings took about ten minutes.

"Only that I wanted to help in any way I could and that you hoped to interview them for the *Standard*."

"Which she promptly refused."

"This isn't easy for them, Nick. Remember that, and you might get an interview yet."

"I'm sorry. That came out harsher than I meant. I do feel for them. If the pressure wasn't there to get something for tomorrow's paper, I'd be a lot less pushy. It's just that right now everything is background. Without their comments on the body being dug up, it's just a rehash of whatever the *Standard* pulled off the wire yesterday."

"Also remember that I'm on your side. Give me some time to work."

We pulled into the Schoenings' driveway, and Susan ran out to meet us. She threw her arms around Joan and held her longer than would be normal. I could see that her eyes were red. Except for Susan's reddish hair, the two of them could pass for relatives. They're both about the same height, weight, and shape. Susan's face is a little broader, and Joan's lips are a little thinner, but with similar hairstyles, eye color, and orthodontically-corrected smiles, they have a definite likeness that seems to have held up despite the years and miles between them. They pulled away, still holding onto each other's hands.

"I'm so sorry, Susan," Joan said. "I know we planned to get

together this week, but not under these circumstances. Are you doing okay?"

"I could be better," she said. "Hi, Nick."

"Hi, Susan." I gave her a hug. "I can't imagine how difficult this must be for you."

"I keep going over and over this in my head. I can't seem to get my hands around it. I still can't fathom that anyone would have wanted to hurt Keri, but they did, and now I have a hard time believing that anyone would want to desecrate her grave, and yet they have."

Joan put an arm around Susan's shoulder. "We want you to know that if there's anything we can do, you just need to let us know."

"I appreciate that. Thank God for friends."

Joan offered her the coffeecake. Susan smiled.

"You always did know what would help," Susan said. She led us inside.

The Schoenings' house was decorated in what can only be described as country chic. The kitchen was wallpapered in a rustic blue pattern with a border of red barns around the top. A decorative wrought-iron egg basket hung from the ceiling in one corner, and a cow-over-the-moon cookie jar was prominently displayed on a counter. She placed the coffeecake on the counter near the cookie jar, took a knife from a drawer, and cut pieces for us. "I haven't been hungry enough to eat anything today," she said, "but this looks good." She put the plates in front of us. She offered to make coffee, but Joan told her to relax, that she would take care of it. I opted for milk.

"What have the police done so far? Do they have any suspects?" I asked as we sat down at the solid oak kitchen table.

"They've questioned us about who might have had grudges against Keri or our family, and they've interviewed a number of Keri's friends who've left things at the cemetery." Susan forked a small bite of cake and nibbled at it before continuing. "I know they examined the site before they dug up the casket. If they found any clues, they haven't told us about them."

"Do you think this has anything to do with the original shootings at West Jasper?"

"Nothing that's apparent. What happened to Keri at the high school . . ." she had to stop for a moment while she closed her eyes and composed herself, ". . . that was over and done with. When the boys killed themselves, it was finished."

I understood what she meant, but her response sounded rehearsed, liked she'd told it to herself a lot. Probably helped her believe it.

"Do you have any idea why someone would want the body?" Joan asked.

Susan carefully put her fork on her plate. "No, not really."

This was a replay of my talk with Kevin. She said "no," but she didn't mean it.

"Are you sure?" I asked. "Even if you've got a guess that seems farfetched, it could be worth mentioning."

She leaned her head conspiratorially toward us. "Aaron and I talked about something this morning. We hesitate to bring it up. If I tell you, you can't tell anyone else."

Susan looked at Joan. Joan looked at me. I gave my head a subtle shake and widened my eyes as a sign not to agree.

"We won't tell anyone," Joan said.

"Unless you change your mind later," I added quickly. I could see my article shrinking rapidly.

Susan took a deep breath. "Relics," she answered.

"What?" Joan asked.

"This is either going to sound crazy or make you think I'm trying to turn my daughter's death into something more significant than I should."

Joan put her hand on Susan's. "We won't think that at all. Please tell us."

"There are people out there who collect the relics of saints," she said. "Now I'm not saying that Keri was a saint. She was a wonderful child, and we couldn't have loved her more, but she wasn't perfect. We're not saying she led a saintly life. We believe she's in heaven with God, and that's as far as we want to take it. But people who have been talking about her dying for her faith see her as a modern-day saint. It's possible someone who collects relics may have taken her body."

"You mean relics as in body parts? Saints' bones?" Joan asked.

Susan nodded. "Yes. Personal belongings count, too."

Joan grimaced. "That's horrible!"

"Do you have any evidence that someone would want her body for that reason?" I asked.

Susan wiped away tears that were forming at the corners of her eyes. "We can't put our trash out at night anymore," she said. "Someone goes through it. Aaron tried to catch him one night a month or so ago, but he got away. After that we stopped putting anything out until daylight."

"Why would they be searching through your trash for relics?"

"I mentioned personal belongings. Apparently anything Keri owned or touched would be regarded as a relic. That's what Father Dan thinks."

"So Father Dan knows."

"He was here one morning seeing if we were okay. This was after the third or fourth week our trash had been searched. The police had come out yet again, but they had stopped taking it seriously. Eventually we stopped calling them."

Susan fell silent. It seemed so bizarre, and yet I knew that, at least during the Middle Ages, the collecting of relics had been of particular importance.

"How much would something Keri touched be worth?" I asked. I decided not to ask the same question about her body parts.

"Probably not much now. But it might become valuable in the future if the Catholic Church declared her a saint."

Speculation in saintly relics, I thought. It was like trading stocks. Buy those stocks now that you think will be worth more tomorrow. Buy and hold. Or, in this case, steal and hold.

"I mentioned to you that Nick is working on this story for the *Indianapolis Standard*," Joan said. "He might be able to help you, or at least get the word out. The more people that know, the more clues the police might be able to get."

"I don't want this relic thing to get out to the public. I don't want people to think we're trying to make Keri out to be a saint." She started to cry.

"We don't have to speculate about the relics situation right now," I said, hoping to salvage at least part of an interview. "In fact, I won't ask you any questions about it. We'll just talk about what's happened so far." I thought that if I could get Father Dan to talk about his relics theory, it would take the pressure off the Schoenings. They wouldn't be the ones trying to make Keri out to be a saint, it would be someone else.

"I can't do the interview, Nick." Susan reached for a tissue out of a box that had been sitting at the table. It was three-quarters empty.

"It's just a conversation, Susan, like we're having here. Only I'd be taking notes." I started to pull out my notebook.

"No, Nick, I mean I can't do it anyway. I promised Sally this morning my interview would be an exclusive."

A few strong words popped into my head. What I said, though, was, "I see. The great Sally Kaiser?"

Admittedly, the remark was a little snide. I certainly shouldn't have said it in that tone.

Susan let me have it.

"Do you know how many conversations I've had with reporters since Keri died?" she demanded. "More than I can possibly count. The only person who's been nice to me through the whole process is Sally Kaiser. She's the only one I've come to trust."

"I'm sorry, Susan. I shouldn't have said that. I'm just disappointed. I don't know what the other reporters were like, but you know you can trust me. We've known each other a long time."

She was quiet for a time. We all were. Susan had stopped crying and got up to blow her nose. Then she sat down again. I took a couple of bites of the coffeecake Joan had made. It had chocolate chips in it. Chocolate usually made me feel better. But not now.

"I won't agree to give Sally an exclusive anymore," Susan said. "But I can't do anything about what I told her today. How long does an exclusive last?"

"Until she publishes it. The *Jasper Times* is an afternoon paper, so if she interviewed you this morning, it'll probably be out this afternoon. If it is, I can still use anything you give me in tomorrow's paper."

"Okay," she said, "but nothing about relics."

"I promise I won't quote you about the relics."

I could tell by the hard stare she gave me that she'd caught my non-committal response, that I hadn't fully promised not to mention them, only not to quote her. But she let it go.

Retrieving my notebook, I went over some background information to get quotes about what had happened so far, and then I covered the same ground we'd already covered, only this time I took notes. Joan sat quietly throughout, interrupting just once to offer us both additional cake. She also unobtrusively slipped the copied photos from our cemetery visit away from my other materials and leafed through them. When the conversation led toward the visit, Father Dan's arrival, and his discussion of the petitions people were leaving, Joan slid the photos across the table to Susan.

"While we were out at the cemetery, Nick took some photos," Joan said. "We'd appreciate it if you could look at them, especially the one Nick enlarged. We'd like to get your opinion on something he spotted."

Susan cocked her head toward Joan. "What is it?"

"This one," I said, moving the close-up of the shadowy figure in front of her. She lifted it up to get a better look, and then gasped.

"It's him," she said.

"Who?" I asked.

"The guy who's been going through our trash. I'm sure of it."

"Really? You've had that good a look at him?" Joan asked.

"The photograph is fuzzy, but you see that extra darkness around his jaw? That could be a beard, and he has a beard," she said pointing. "And he's kind of short, too. This memorial is much taller than I am, about six feet. That would make this guy five foot five or so. I really think it's him."

"We need to find this guy," I said. "Do you think he still hangs around here? Is he still interested in your trash?"

Susan shrugged. "I don't know. It's been so long since we put our trash out overnight, I didn't even think he was still in the area."

"When is your next trash day?"

She thought a moment. "Wednesday. That's tomorrow."

"Yes it is," I said. "Maybe Aaron and I could set up a trap for this guy tonight. Try and catch him in the act."

"Aaron already tried it once."

"Did he have help, or did he do it on his own?"

"On his own."

"Maybe with two of us, we'll have a better chance. Can you call Aaron at work and see if he's willing?"

"It might be dangerous," Joan said. "Shouldn't you call the police?"

Susan spoke up. "They weren't much help before."

"But that was before this happened. Now they might be more responsive."

I had to think about that. The police probably would be more receptive now, but they would also be against Aaron and me doing *anything*. On the other hand, would they set up a trap at all, especially one based just on our hunches? I thought it unlikely. All we had was a blurry photograph of someone hiding among the graves at the Schoenings' private cemetery today, someone Susan thought was a man who had gone through their trash months earlier. There was no reason to believe he would go through their garbage again tonight. The police were more likely to station someone at the graveyard to prevent anyone from getting in. Which would also include me. If they did anything in the neighborhood, it would be to increase nightly patrols, which would only scare the guy away, not catch him. As for any danger, he hadn't turned on Aaron in their earlier confrontation, just run away. If all he was after was relics, I didn't think he'd be armed or dangerous.

I explained this to Joan and Susan. Both of them seemed to be worried now about the danger to Aaron and me, but I persuaded them to have Susan call Aaron at work anyway, just to see what he thought of the idea. Since he was something of an adventurous guy and had already made one attempt to catch the relic hunter, I was counting on Aaron to agree. He did. I heard the anger in his voice, mixed with some excitement. Too many bad things had happened to them in the last six months. Their only child dead, now the body missing. I'd be excited about catching the guy who took the body, too, even if the chance was remote.

"He was an older guy," Aaron said after Susan handed me

the phone. "Maybe faster than I was ready for, but we'll get him this time. Come over about 8:00. Since Indiana went on Daylight Savings Time, it doesn't even start to get dark until around 8:30. We'll have time to figure out how to set this up."

"You realize he might not show?"

"It's worth a try. Better than just sitting around, especially since we know he's in the area."

Joan and I visited with Susan for a few more minutes before leaving. When I said I would see her again around 8:00, Susan tensed up.

"It's probably your reputation," Joan said, needling me a little when I mentioned it to her in the van. "She knows the kind of trouble you can get into."

"But it's their daughter's body, for heaven's sake."

"But now Aaron's in potential danger."

"Am I doing the wrong thing?"

She paused.

"Probably not. I think you're right in guessing that the police won't help you set a trap. There's no real reason for them to believe the trash would be searched. It's been a while since they even put the trash out at night."

"I'm glad to hear you say it. I know police pretty well. They would view this as a waste of manpower."

"It might be a waste of your time, too."

"It may."

"And you have to admit it might be more dangerous than either you or Aaron thinks."

"I know. Are you going to worry?"

She turned in her seat and put her hand on my shoulder. "Always, Nick. But there are things you do better than other people. I'm starting to understand and accept that."

"Thank you."

"But don't push too hard, okay? I still think the police should know."

"They will," I said.

I just hoped I could control the circumstances under which they found out.

CHAPTER NINE

Back at Hugo and Janine's house, I used my notes to write the story for the *Standard*. Much as I would have liked to discuss the body being taken for relics, I couldn't get hold of Father Dan for a quote. I did call the police station and ask for an update, which netted me the tidbit that the police were keeping an eye on the graves of the other West Jasper victims.

I hadn't thought of them until that point. Frankly, that was embarrassing. Perhaps the Keri Schoening raid had not been an isolated incident, although I couldn't see how anyone could dig up the other graves, which were in much more public cemeteries. Nonetheless, I wrote myself a note to contact the parents of the other victims.

As the deadline crept up on me, I called Father Dan again. Still no answer. Why had he not called me? Was he avoiding me, or simply too busy with his own work? I left a more urgent message. Then I read the article over one last time and e-mailed it to Ryan.

Pushing back the chair from the computer desk, I contemplated what to do next. It was four o'clock. Stephanie was still fishing with her grandpa, and Joan and Janine had gone to the grocery store. I decided to go for a run.

Since the day was hot and muggy with only a few hazy clouds in the sky, I dressed for the heat—a gray tank top and black nylon shorts. I left a note on the kitchen table and went outside. After warming up and stretching, I started running at an easy pace to get my heart rate up. I passed the Muellers' house on my way down the street.

A few minutes later, just as I hit my regular running pace, Kevin Mueller rode up on his bicycle. I didn't really want to stop and talk, but neither did I want to ignore him. I glanced at my watch so I'd know what time I started the run, then looked at him and said, "Hi."

"Hi," he replied. He didn't say much else for maybe a minute. He seemed content to ride beside me while I focused on running. Then he said, "I thought you might be a runner. You looked like you were in good shape for a person your age."

I laughed inwardly. I was only in my mid-thirties, hardly old, but I supposed it was more than twice as many years as he'd seen at sixteen.

"Thanks," I said.

"Do you do triathlons?"

Now I laughed outwardly. "No, those are for real ironmen. I'm not that tough."

"Oh. I thought maybe you lifted weights, too. You look like it."

"Thank you. I do lift weights, a little."

"More than a little," he said.

Again I glanced over at him. He was looking at my biceps. Now, no one would mistake me for Arnold Schwarzenegger, but Mark Zoringer at the gym did say that my arms responded well to training. I guess Kevin thought so, too, but it embarrassed me. "I don't have that much size," I said, trying to pace my responses so they didn't interrupt my running. "I try to make the best of what I have, though."

"I lift, too," he said.

"That's good."

"You probably can't tell."

"I can tell you're athletic."

"How did you bulk up?"

"I'm really not all that muscular, Kevin. You should see the guy who helps me with my programs. He's a Mr. Indiana. He's huge."

"Really? That's cool."

We continued on for another minute or two, me running, him riding. We reached the end of the street, turned right, and went into another part of the subdivision. I was settling in on a good pace when Kevin said, "I can't seem to gain any muscle."

"Have you tried talking to someone at your school? A P.E. teacher or a strength and conditioning coach?"

"The strength coach is a jerk. He only wants to deal with top athletes, like the star football or basketball players."

"That's too bad."

"Tell me about it," Kevin said.

I was beginning to wonder why he didn't talk to his dad about it when it hit me that his father was never around. That might explain this whole situation. I slowed down to a walk. Kevin slowed with me.

"Let's talk," I said.

I glanced at my watch. I hadn't done more than five minutes at running pace, but this seemed more important.

"Do you think you can help me?" Kevin asked.

"Probably. Have you ever kept a food diary?"

"A what?" Kevin jumped off his bike and started walking beside me, the bike between us.

"A list of everything you eat. It'll help you figure out how many calories a day you consume. Then we can determine how much you'll need to help you put on some muscle. We may need to revamp your weightlifting program as well."

"How long do I need to keep the diary? I can start doing that right away."

"Probably just for a few days, so we can get a good idea of

your eating habits. I won't be going back home until Sunday, so if you start now I can look it over and make suggestions before I leave. Record everything you put in your mouth—quantity, too—and what time of day you do it."

He nodded enthusiastically. "What about the lifting routine?"

"If you'd write down what you're doing now, that would help. I want to talk to my friend Mark Zoringer, the guy who writes my programs, before I suggest anything. I won't leave without making sure you know what you're doing."

His expression brightened and he grinned from ear to ear. "Sweet," he said.

I trusted Mark would help me deliver on that promise.

We continued walking. Kevin said, in a soft voice, "Before school ended, there were rumors about a cult."

I stopped and turned to him. Matching his near-whisper, I said, "What kind of cult?"

He looked around nervously. "Devil worshipers."

"You think they may have something to do with what's happening to the pets?"

"Yeah. Part of the rituals."

My first thought was skepticism. Rural kids are always talking up Satanic cults. But I liked Kevin, and I didn't see him as the gossipy sort. "I knew one of the theories the police floated about the two kids who shot up the school was that they were members of a cult, but they couldn't find any evidence. Didn't they conclude the two acted alone?"

"I'm not saying the two events are connected. I'm just saying this cult may be involved in what happened to Buddy and Mr. Jangles."

I was silent for a moment, pondering this. I could see possible connections all over the place.

Kevin spoke up. "Just because the police concluded they weren't members of a cult, doesn't mean they weren't."

"The police said the two took revenge against kids who bullied them."

Kevin leaned over the bike toward me, so I stepped in to meet him part way. "You're right," he said. "That's what the police said. Did you ever see a photo of Drew Fleischman with his family?"

Drew Fleischman was one of the shooters. "Not that I can recall."

"His brother Eddie, who's only a year younger than he was, was heavily recruited to play offensive tackle on the football team. Drew wasn't as big as Eddie, but he wasn't a pushover, either. And no way would Eddie have put up with anyone bullying Drew."

"Are you saying the police lied?"

"They had a conclusion. They didn't look too hard at evidence that didn't support it."

I searched his eyes and tried to remember what it was like to be sixteen, the adolescent struggling to become a man. Did he really know something about what happened at West Jasper, or did he just want to feel important? Were those rumors of a cult still relevant, even though the police had discarded them? I reminded myself that Kevin was a reporter for the school paper. He might have good instincts in that direction.

"Let's just focus on the possibility that there's a cult and that it has something to do with what . . ." my throat suddenly got a lump in it again, ". . . what happened to Buddy and Mr. Jangles. Where would you look for evidence supporting that theory?"

He glanced away from me and down at the bicycle. He pushed his left foot at the pedal closest to him, making the bicycle chain go around backwards. "If I wanted to, I could find out."

"When the police originally suspected there was a cult, did they not talk to the right people?"

"I don't know, but if they did, the people they talked to had reasons not to be helpful."

"Do you know who these people are?"

"One or two of them. I can ask around."

"I don't want you to. That's something I should do."

"They didn't talk to the police, why would they talk to you?"

"I'm not a policeman, I'm a reporter."

Kevin held out his hands palms up. "Like it matters. You're an adult."

I considered that. When I was sixteen and thought I was far smarter than all the adults around me, would I have said anything to a reporter? About this, probably not.

"I won't do anything dangerous," he said.

Where had I heard that before? Out of my own mouth. I didn't know if Kevin was any more trustworthy on the danger aspect than I was when it came to following up a lead.

"What if I asked you not to do this?"

"What if?" he replied. It was a challenge, not a question.

"Let's go back to my in-law's house so I can give you one of my business cards. It has my cell phone number on it. I really *don't* want you to do this. I'm giving you the card because I want you to call me with the names of the guys I should talk to. But on the other hand, if you make up your mind to do this, promise that you'll call me before you do anything or go anywhere."

He shrugged. "Okay," he said, but the excitement in his voice betrayed feigned nonchalance.

It didn't take long to get back—I ran and Kevin biked. No one else was home, and I was glad of that. This was a major dilemma. Kevin wasn't going to give me those names. I could see that in his eyes. What I had to do was try to get him to call me before he did anything. To be honest, there wasn't a lot I could do to stop him. If he'd already made up his mind to find out what he could, all I could do was keep tabs and try to keep him safe.

I handed him my business card. "Please keep this with you at all times. Don't hesitate to call me in any situation, at any time. You understand?"

He crossed his arms over his chest. "So we have a deal."

"Do we?"

"You'll help me with my workouts, and I'll get you the information we both want."

I sighed. "As long as the information is just the names. You're not to put yourself in any danger. And I'd help you with the weight-lifting stuff anyway."

He grinned and hopped on the bike. It was just then I noticed the brand name, Cannondale.

"Hey, that's a serious bike," I said.

"Yeah."

"You do much cycling?"

"Now that I'm not in soccer." He started to pedal and moved away from me.

"Remember, I just want the names," I said.

He didn't answer. I watched him pedal away. It was no mystery why he couldn't put on size, if that's what he was after. Soccer and cycling were highly aerobic. He was burning through calories like a wildfire through California.

I went back inside to lock the house up so I could go running again. My cell phone rang. I hoped it was Father Dan returning my urgent call, but the voice on the other end was definitely not the priest.

"I just read your story. That's all you've got?"

"Hello, Ryan."

"Sally Kaiser's article in the *Jasper Times,* which was published two hours ago, said pretty much the same thing. What are we paying you for, anyway?"

"Because I'm a darn good-looking reporter?"

"Save it for your dwindling fan club. Don't you have anything new?"

"I haven't read Sally's stuff yet. Did she mention anything about a relics hunter?"

"A what?"

"Ah. Tomorrow I may have something for you that even Sally Kaiser doesn't have." I told him about the figure in the photograph of the cemetery and the trap Aaron and I were setting for that evening.

"Can't you put any of that background stuff in this article? It would really help."

"I need to cite a source. I promised Susan Schoening I wouldn't quote her because she doesn't want it to look like she and her husband are trying to claim their daughter is a saint. I've tried getting a hold of the local priest, but he hasn't returned my phone call. And you're the one who set the deadline."

"Did you try the archdiocese of Indianapolis?"

"They're in the Evansville diocese down here."

"So, did you try them?"

Actually, I hadn't thought of that, mainly because I'd expected the priest to call me back. But I certainly wasn't going to admit it to Ryan. "No time," I answered. "Plus, I don't know anyone there who could expedite comments. You know how cautious our archbishop is. It's probably worse down here."

"You don't know that. I want you to give them a call. In the meantime, I'll see what I can do about getting a quote from the archdiocese up here. I'll tell them it's purely speculative, based on rumors you heard that relics might be the reason for the body disappearing."

"Okay, I'll call the Evansville diocese. If you don't hear from me, it means I didn't get a satisfactory answer or I'm waiting for a call back."

"I expect results, Bertetto."

"Ryan, how did this story get the attention of the national media? I mean, someone digging up a body is not that important in the scheme of things, even if was someone from the West Jasper massacre."

"Don't know. Must've been a slow news day. You know how some stories get a life of their own? Can you say 'JonBenet Ramsey?' Anyway, all I know is, people are following this one and I'm under pressure to get more out of you." He belched. "See? It's upset my stomach. Now get busy."

He hung up.

I really should have tried the diocese office earlier. I didn't need Ryan to point that out. I looked up the phone number and dialed, reaching a live person. Naturally, she wasn't the person I needed, but I gave her my name and what I was looking for. She promised to get back to me. I slipped the cell in the pocket of my running shorts and took off.

Within ten minutes I was drenched in sweat. By thirty minutes I was pretty much wiped out. This time of the year the heat and humidity take a real toll. Since I had already doubled back, when I slowed my pace I wasn't that far from Hugo and Janine's house. Walking past the Mueller's house, I again had a few pangs about what Kevin might be doing, but I kept thinking that there couldn't possibly be anything that sinister going on a second time in Jasper. Or, if there was, that Kevin could manage to find it. Those in charge would surely be working hard to keep themselves hidden.

Stephanie bounded out of the house as I started up the walk toward Hugo and Janine's. I picked her up and hugged her.

"Ewww, Daddy, you're all sweaty," she said.

I laughed. "I was out for a run. Sorry." I put her down.

She straightened her pink top.

"How was fishing with Grandpa?" I asked.

She looked back at the door to make sure he wasn't there. "Boring," she said.

I chuckled. "I was afraid you might think that. Did you catch any fish?"

"Grandpa did."

"Are we having fish tonight for dinner?"

"Uh-huh. It's fish Grandma took out of the freezer."

"Didn't you and Grandpa bring home any fish?"

She wrinkled up her nose. "Uh-huh."

I decided not to ask about the fate of those fish.

I went in to wash up and change for dinner. The diocese of Evansville didn't call me back, and neither did Ryan nor Father Dan. I guessed the article would have to stand as I'd written it.

Dinner was wonderful—pan-fried bluegill with Janine's homemade tartar sauce, coleslaw, and fresh fruit. I ignored the fat calories. Not long after Joan and I had finished the dishes, I received a phone call from Aaron Schoening.

"You know you can't drive the van tonight," he said. "Do you want us to come pick you up?"

"Why can't I use the van?"

"Because," he said, sounding exasperated, "if it is the same guy, he might recognize it from the cemetery."

"Good thinking. Let me see if I can borrow Janine's car. That way you won't have to bring me home."

"Bring a flashlight, too. I've got a plan."

"What is it?"

"I'll explain when you get here."

After I'd agreed, Susan got on the phone and asked for Joan. From this end of the discussion I could tell she wanted Joan to come over, too. Probably to make her feel more secure about the whole thing. At any rate, Joan agreed and said we'd see them later.

106

When we told Hugo and Janine what was going on, they seemed less than enthusiastic. Part of it, I'm sure, had to do with the possibility of danger, which they've come to believe I attract just by breathing. The only thing they seemed pleased about was that at least we were helping the Schoenings. They did agree to let us take Janine's car.

As we left, I could tell Joan was struggling with emotions that were welling up in her, but I was also proud of the way she controlled them. I think she felt she had some measure of power over the situation since she was going to be there.

I wondered at it all: our life together appeared to be returning to normal, and my needs were becoming important to her again, as hers had always been important to me. I closed my hand on the Miraculous Medal I wore around my neck. In order to get that return to normalcy, I'd been coaxed into asking for it by Elijah Smith, a guardian angel of sorts. He believed that making the wish on this medal would make it come true. The medal had been given to me by a person who claimed Mary, the Blessed Mother, wanted me to have it and had endowed me with a special gift. I still wasn't sure how much of it I believed. But I prayed now that whatever I encountered down the road wouldn't change the new direction of our lives.

CHAPTER TEN

Aaron was waiting outside when we arrived. His trash was by the curb—two big, rigid, black plastic trash containers with wheels and lids, and three small boxes of odds and ends next to them. I started to pull Janine's Honda Civic alongside the curb next to the trash, but Aaron shook his head. As he started toward the car, I rolled down my window. The sticky heat invaded our air-conditioned space. "What's going on?" I asked.

While Joan and Aaron's wife Susan have a lot in common physically, Aaron and I do not. My features are dark and Italian; he's more Germanic—taller by nearly half a foot with sandy hair, a mustache, and a stocky build. His blue eyes blazed with a mixture of anger and excitement. Hunting the relics hunter was something I guessed he really wanted to do.

"Park the car down the street." Aaron said. "I want to keep the front of the house clear. I'll explain in a minute."

I nodded, parked two houses away, and Joan and I walked back. Soon the four of us sat in the Schoening's country kitchen. Dinner smells were in the air, although the dishes had been cleared away. From the spicy scent of cumin, I guessed Mexican.

"So you've got the trash out already. Tell me about your plan," I said.

Aaron didn't need much encouragement. "The trash has been out since supper. I wanted to make sure it was there in case this guy drove by to check us out. That way he'd make plans to come back at night."

"Sounds like a good idea."

"I've really thought about this. The last time I saw him going through the trash, he parked his car across the street and waited to see if anyone was around. That was about 2:00 in the morning. Then he got out of the car and ran over to the garbage cans. He pulled off both lids and looked inside with a flashlight. He had some kind of large stick that he used to poke around the trash. I thought I'd be able to go out and grab him, but the second I stepped outside, he dashed back to his car and got in."

Susan, who was seated next to Joan, leaned up against her. Joan put her arm around Susan's shoulders. I could tell the whole thing was upsetting Susan. Nonetheless, Aaron and I had to get our plan together.

"Why do you think he went back to the car?" I asked.

"Maybe he was just being careful. I don't know. Since I wanted to catch him in the act, I waited, figuring he'd go back. The light had come on in his car when he opened the door, and I saw him talking on a cell phone. Then the light faded out. He started the car and drove off. I ran out when he was leaving, but I couldn't get the license plate number. He pulled away pretty fast."

"Describe him to me."

"He's short, has a beard. The beard's bushy. His hair is thick, but it's receding. I'm not sure about his age, but I'm guessing he's somewhat older than we are. Maybe late forties."

Susan pulled a tissue out of her pants pocket and wiped her nose. She wasn't crying, but she was emotional.

Joan focused on Susan. "We don't have to be a part of this conversation," she said. "Do you want to go in the other room?"

Susan shook her head.

"Can I get you anything?"

"Tea would be nice. I know it's summer, but it would make me feel better," Susan said.

"I'll make it," Joan offered. She rose and filled the teakettle.

"I'm going to have a beer," Aaron said. He looked at me. "Want one?"

"No. I'm fine."

"Come on, have a beer with me."

"Are you sure this is a good idea? We don't want to get too relaxed."

"One beer won't do that. Besides, it might be good to take the edge off."

We were all nervous. Anyone could see that. "Well, okay. Maybe one."

Aaron brought us each an imported German beer from the fridge.

"Do you know if this guy saw you that night?" I asked Aaron.

He popped the caps off our beers. "Unless he was looking in the rear view mirror, probably not. Anyway, my plan for tonight is to put you in the car down the way. If he drives off before I can get to him, you can follow him. Susan's going to be parked down the street in the other direction with the binoculars. That way she can get a license plate number and a description of the perp."

"Perp?"

He shrugged it off. "I watch *CSI*, you know."

I took a drink. "What if the 'perp' drives in from the other direction?" I asked. Unlike some states, Indiana only has rear plates. "Then no one is facing the right direction, and I don't have the binoculars to get the license plate number."

"No problem," said Aaron. "We have an extra pair for you."

Joan spoke up. "I don't think Susan should do this. I can sit in the car instead of her." She turned to Susan. "Is that okay with you?"

Susan nodded. "I want him caught, but I don't know if I have it in me to be a part of it."

Aaron put his beer down and kissed his wife on the cheek. "We'll catch him, honey, and don't worry, you've already done enough." He massaged her right shoulder while he talked to Joan and me. "It was Susan's idea to put out the boxes with odds and ends. We're hoping he'll think they're things from Keri's room."

"How do you plan to get hold of him?" I asked Aaron.

"I'm going to tackle him and wrestle him to the ground. Then you'll help me get him into the house where we can question him."

"When are you planning to do that?"

"As soon as he's got the lids off and is poking around. He'll be too preoccupied."

"Aaron, I'm not trying to be negative, but I see a few flaws in this plan."

"What?"

"Well, the trash, for example. Out by the curb, it's not really your property anymore. You can't nail a guy just for going through your trash."

"I can't?"

"No. What you need is to get him to trespass on your property."

"We could move the trash up by the garage so it looks like I just moved it around from the back and plan to take it out to the curb in the morning."

"That's a start. Although, if he's seen it by the curb before this, he might recognize it's a trap."

"Oh."

"But at this point we'll just take the chance. Now, about your tackling him. How are you going to get that close? You can't just come charging out of the house. He'll head for his car the instant he sees you."

"No, I'm going to sneak up on him. When I see him pull up,

I'll go out the back door and around the back side of the garage, behind his line of vision. I'll be able to get close without him knowing it. That's why I'm wearing black."

Indeed, Aaron was wearing a black T-shirt, black jeans, and black canvas tennis shoes. If he had told me he was going to wear black make-up on his face, I would have believed him.

"What if he has someone with him?"

"We may have to change the plan at the last minute." He held up a Target sack. "That's why Susan also bought these walkie-talkies, so we could talk to each other and figure it out."

The teakettle whistled, and Joan poured the boiling water into two mugs containing tea bags.

"Well, it might work," I said. "But about this dragging him into the house. That's confinement, and it's illegal. But we could hold him for as long as it takes the police to get here, and we can try to question him during that time."

"Oh, man. We have to call the police?"

"That's the only way this is even quasi-legal. And let me ask you this, what if he has a gun?"

"That's the part that really has me worried," Susan said. "Aaron plans to have a gun, too."

I looked at Aaron. "How long have you had a gun?"

"Maybe six or seven years. And before you ask, I have a permit for it."

That wasn't much of a relief. "Do you practice with it?"

"Oh, yeah. I go down to the shooting range at least once a month."

I could understand why Susan was worried. My sudden vision of a shootout in front of the Schoenings' house included someone getting hurt. Probably Aaron. Or a neighbor. Or Joan or me—if stray bullets were flying everywhere, anyone could get hit. Cars were not necessarily a protection. We didn't know how good the relics hunter was.

And Aaron was drinking a beer.

"I'm not comfortable with you carrying a gun. Why don't we wait to see if the guy has one before you make any moves?" I asked. "It's so hot tonight that we'll see if he's wearing one. I doubt he'll have a jacket on. And he'll be moving around a lot with the trash cans. I would think it'd be obvious."

Aaron clenched his teeth, and I could see his mouth working. Finally he spoke. "It's not your decision whether or not I wear a gun."

Joan jumped to my defense. "No, it's not, Aaron. But Nick has more experience with criminals than you. I think you should listen to him. And much as I love you and Susan, I won't be a part of this if a gun is involved."

Aaron looked to Susan. "I've never liked the idea of having a gun in the house," she said, "let alone you using it."

Aaron set his jaw again.

I shrugged. "It's unlikely the relics hunter will have a gun. We don't know a lot about him, but it doesn't seem like the kind of thing he would need. And if he has one, we don't want to sneak up on him. We'd be safer just to get the license plate and go from there."

"Well, I guess I'm outvoted." Aaron picked up his beer and took a long pull on it.

It's going to be a long night, I thought.

After we moved the trash so it was near the front of the garage—and obvious from the street—Aaron and I went to the basement to shoot some pool and pass the time. Joan and Susan gabbed in the living room and drank their tea. By 11:30 when we moved upstairs to begin the vigil, Aaron had had three beers. This was against my better judgment, but after insisting the gun would stay in its hiding spot, I was treading lightly with Aaron. Granted, the beers had been consumed over a period of two hours, but Aaron was nevertheless showing some effects. His manner had become more brusque, almost bellicose. I'm not much of a drinker beyond the occasional glass of wine with dinner, and my single beer was making me a little braver than I should have been, especially coupled with Aaron's manner.

"It's time for us to go to our stations," Aaron announced. Easy for him to say. He could stay in the air-conditioned house. Not only would Joan and I not have air-conditioning, we had to stay inside the cars with the windows mostly rolled up so they wouldn't look suspicious.

We all got into our positions. Joan backed Susan's car down the driveway and parked in front of a neighbor's house, two doors down. I got into Janine's car, which I had parked two doors away in the other direction. Aaron watched us from the front window until we were settled. Then he moved to the kitchen, on the far side of the house from the garage, and called us on the walkie-talkies.

"Can you hear me?" Aaron whispered.

"I can hear you just fine," I said.

"Me, too," Joan squeaked.

"Aaron, whose house is Joan parked in front of?" I asked.

"Ida Mae Kaiser. She's an older, widowed lady whose husband passed away a year or so ago. He was a retired policeman who did private detective work."

I heard the last name and made an instant connection. "Any relation to Sally Kaiser?"

"She's her granddaughter."

The ease with which Sally had gotten the interview with the Schoenings now made even more sense. "Oh," I said.

Susan, who was listening in on Aaron's walkie-talkie, bristled, even though I hadn't really said anything. "It had nothing to do with my giving Sally an exclusive interview. She's earned the right to that exclusive, as kind as she's been to those of us who've lived through what we did. We didn't know Sally was

Ida Mae's granddaughter before she started reporting on the shootings."

"I didn't mean it that way," I said. At least not intentionally.

"Sally never brought it up to us. Ida Mae was the one who told us. She's proud of her granddaughter."

"I didn't mean to imply Sally doesn't deserve the reputation she has," I said. "Does Ida Mae know it's one of your cars parked outside her house? Does she know what we're doing?"

"Of course not," Aaron chimed in. "You want to scare the poor lady to death? Anyway, she goes to bed early. She won't even notice we're here."

I hoped not because it was too late to notify her. I didn't want to be the one ringing her doorbell after midnight to advise her not to worry about strange people parked in front of her house. "What about the house I'm parked in front of?"

"They're gone. Left Saturday on vacation."

"Good," I said.

We settled back in. People with regular jobs think investigative reporting is glamorous or exciting, but in reality it can be very boring. Private investigators say the same thing. A lot of what we do is research, which is often done in a library or over the Internet. Occasionally, but not often, we do some surveillance, and that means a lot of waiting around. Sometimes you can stake out a place for days with nothing happening. Every now and then you get a short burst of activity. Beyond that, staying awake is the hardest part, especially at night.

"Can I listen to the radio?" Joan asked over the walkie-talkie. She must've been struggling with the same boredom.

"If you keep it really, really low," said Aaron. "We don't want this guy to come down the street and hear someone rockin' two doors down."

"I wasn't going to be loud," she said, a little testy.

I wished I could turn on a reading light and settle in with a good book, although this late it might have put me to sleep. I thought momentarily about authors who could keep me awake—Harlan Coben, Robert Crais, Janet Evanovich, among others. Didn't matter anyway, since turning on a light might attract unwanted attention.

"Everyone awake?" Aaron asked about every ten minutes.

"Must be nice to be in the house where you can do whatever you want."

"Hey, I'm keeping the vigil just like you are. The TV is not on, if that's what you're asking."

I thought some more about Aaron's plan. The biggest risk I could see, aside from the perp having a gun, was him having a partner. If he had both, that would be really bad. If not, though, I thought it had a chance to succeed. Aaron had had some experience with the guy before, and he didn't sound particularly dangerous by himself.

At about one-thirty, something finally happened. Unfortunately it was the wrong thing. Red and blue rotating lights split the darkness as a police cruiser rolled up behind Susan's car. I sat up quickly and got on the walkie-talkie.

"Sit still, Joan," I said. "We don't know what it is, but let the policeman come to you. They get nervous if you get out of your car."

Aaron's comment was less informative and more graphic. "Shit," he said.

The police car door opened. The officer had a large flashlight which he turned on. I watched out the back window of Janine's car as he strolled over to the window of Susan's. He flashed his light on the driver's side window, and I saw it being lowered half way. The beam of the flashlight reflected a bit back on the officer's face and I recognized him—Johnny Day. I shook my head.

I knew Joan could hold her own with him, but still I got out of the car. This was taking my dislike of the guy to a whole new level. I started toward him, remembering to hold my hands up so he would be able to see I did not have a weapon. I had no sooner reached the beginning of the Schoenings' driveway when another car appeared out of the darkness. It passed Susan's car and then the police cruiser. When it was under the streetlight across from the Schoenings' house, the inside of the car was lit up just enough that I had a profile view of the driver. He had a bushy beard and a good head of hair. From the way the man sat low in the seat, I also guessed he was short. The evidence was circumstantial, but I was fairly confident who I'd just seen.

The relics hunter. He was alone. And we had just blown a great chance to get him. Helplessly I watched as the car accelerated and he sped off into the darkness.

CHAPTER ELEVEN

"Nick Bertetto," I said to remind Officer Day who I was, although I was pretty sure he would remember me as the guy who had married his ex-girlfriend. He shined a light on my face, but I was the one who asked, "What are you doing here?"

"I could ask you the same," he said. "Mrs. Kaiser called us. Said there was a strange car outside her house with someone in it. We came to check it out."

By this time Aaron had made it out of his house and came up next to Day and me. We all looked up at the picture window in the front room of the Kaiser home. The light in the room was on, the curtains held back by a small hand. I could see the face of an elderly woman staring out.

Aaron waved at her. "Hello, Mrs. Kaiser," he called, almost disgustedly.

Day turned to Aaron and me. "So before I arrest you, what are you doing out here? And why did you," he added, looking pointedly at me, "get out of a car four houses away?"

"You're not going to arrest us," I said confidently, "so don't start in with that stuff. As for why I was parked in that car, it's kind of a long story. You know Aaron Schoening, don't you?"

"Of course." He nodded at Aaron. Joan got out of the car.

I was going to continue, but Aaron interrupted me. "Well, there's no sense in standing out here making a spectacle of ourselves," he said, pausing to wave unhappily again at Mrs. Kaiser, who was still staring at us. "Let's go in the house, and we'll talk about it."

"I think we need to reassure Mrs. Kaiser first," Day said, "and I need to call in, let Dispatch know everything's okay."

"I'll go talk to Mrs. Kaiser," Aaron said. "Go ahead and make your call."

Aaron trooped up to the house while Day returned to his police car and stopped the lights. I turned to Joan.

"Did you see the car that went by? It was him."

"What car? Who?"

"What do you mean, 'what car'? That mid-size Chevy that went by after Day pulled up behind you."

"I was a little preoccupied at that point."

"It was the relics hunter."

"Can you describe the car? Did you get the license plate?"

I thought back to the scene. It had all happened so quickly. "I'm not real familiar with Chevy models. I'd have to go online to look at them. It was definitely a four-door Chevy sedan, though. As for color," I hesitated a moment, scraping around for bits of memory. "There just wasn't a lot of natural light. I think it was some kind of red. Maybe darker, like cranberry."

"The license plate?"

I shook my head. "It caught me by surprise. I know I should have thought to look, but I didn't. It all happened so fast."

Aaron came back from Mrs. Kaiser's. "She's okay. I told the truth, that we were trying to catch someone who had been getting into our trash. I apologized. We should have told her what was going on so she wouldn't worry."

"Do you think it was wise to tell her that much?" I asked.

Aaron frowned at me. "Why not? We're going to have to tell the police the truth. It won't hurt to have the neighbors alerted to what's happening. They may know something we don't."

I hadn't meant to tick Aaron off. "You're right," I said. It didn't matter what I thought since Aaron had already spilled it.

Besides, given that Mrs. Kaiser was Sally Kaiser's grandmother, the whole thing wouldn't be a secret for much longer. I wondered what Ryan would say, now that we'd blown our one hope for an exclusive story. I wasn't looking forward to telling him in the morning.

Day came back from the cruiser, and the four of us went into the house. The smell of coffee hit me the minute we were in the door. Susan had brewed a pot while watching us outside. She immediately offered us all a cup. No one turned it down. Aaron started a second pot. Servings of the coffeecake Joan had made sat on a platter on the kitchen table. We explained the situation to Day.

"I can't believe the kind of things you civilians try to do on your own. You should have called us. That's all I can say," Day scolded. "If you'd done that, and if this guy is for real, we'd be questioning him now."

"Of course he's real. And if you hadn't blazed in with lights flashing, Aaron and I might have caught him," I retorted.

"Using lights is standard procedure," Day said defensively. "It's not like I had the siren blaring."

"You might as well have. Police lights put everyone on edge, especially at night. I'm sure you scared him. I know I saw him in that Chevy that passed us."

"If you'd been really alert, you would have gotten us some kind of identifying features of the car, like a license plate number."

"I told you I couldn't *see* a plate . . ."

Aaron interrupted me. "Nick's not the one who needs to be questioned," he told Day. "How are we going to find this guy now that you've wrecked . . . I mean, now that our first plan is wrecked?"

Day thought about Aaron's question. "What's to stop us from trying the same setup next week?"

"Oh, come on, Johnny, do you think for one minute he won't see a trap here?" I said. "The first time Aaron and Susan put their trash out in two months, a police car shows up."

"*If* this guys exists, he doesn't know why I was here. He might wonder if the two are related, but he doesn't know for a fact. There's no reason to believe he won't come back. We just need to be discreet, which we can do, now that we know what's going on."

I shook my head. "He had to have seen me standing out by the road. I watched him go by. Granted, I only had a profile view, but he's bound to think there's a connection."

"The connection is that you're a nosy reporter. And if you only had a profile view, how can you be sure it's the same guy?"

"I'm working off Aaron's description."

"You know, if you'd let us professionals do our job, we wouldn't be in this jam."

"If we'd come to you ahead of time, no way would you have agreed to set up a trap. You're not even sure you believe us now. You would have discounted the whole thing."

Joan nudged me. She made an ever-so-slight movement with her fingers over her lips. *Zip it.*

Aaron said, "We all believe there's a relics hunter looking for things that belonged to Keri. Whether you think so or not doesn't matter. We do, and we think it's related to—" He stopped, and banged his fist on the table.

Aaron put his hand over his forehead and hid his eyes. I knew he wasn't an emotional guy, but it was late and he was talking about his daughter who'd died only five months ago. Susan went over and hugged him. She had tears in her eyes.

After a moment, Aaron continued. He seemed drained. "We think it's related to what happened at Keri's grave. But it's late. Not the best time to figure out a new strategy. Let's all just get some sleep, let Johnny go back to his patrol, and we'll come up with something in the morning."

He was right, of course, but Day and I grumbled anyway.

Day left, but Susan wanted us to stick around for a little while. I think she was still wound up from the excitement.

When Susan finally started yawning, Joan and I made our excuses to leave. Aaron and Susan saw us out to our cars. It was then we got the news that added insult to injury.

The trash was gone. Aside from a few items that had fallen out of Susan's decoy boxes, the two plastic trash containers and the other boxes had vanished.

As we stood there gaping at the empty spot by the garage, Mrs. Kaiser made a sprightly run toward us from her house. She was waving several pieces of paper.

"I got him," she cackled as she got closer. She stopped to catch her breath. "He took your trash but I videoed the whole thing. Here are some pictures."

"You got him on tape?" I snatched the photos she held out.

"Why didn't you call us?" Aaron asked.

She gave Aaron what my grandmother used the call the evil eye. "I know you, Aaron Schoening. You would have just gotten yourself in trouble. And this way, we have proof."

"How was there even enough light?" I asked.

"I used a night vision video camera, then downloaded the file and took some images off it. My husband used to do that all the time when he would trap cheating spouses. Sometimes I would help him."

Aaron, Susan, and Joan gathered around me as I looked through the photos. They had an eerie green caste to them, which I attributed to the night vision equipment. It was almost as if the night was a dark liquid in which the objects swam. But the photos themselves showed the sequence of events—him getting out of the car, him looking through the trash, him loading it into his car, and him driving away.

"This is great," I said. "It's not crisp like it would be in daylight, but you can tell what the relics hunter looks like."

"Did he see you shoot the video?" Aaron asked, concerned.

"Not unless he could see in the dark. I was standing in the shadows by my house."

"We need to get Day back here," I said. "This proves what we were trying to tell him."

I made the call to Dispatch, and Day was back in no time. We showed him the photos, and while he was impressed with Ida Mae Kaiser's detective work, he still found things to grumble about.

"Yeah, well, we still don't have a license plate number," he complained.

Mrs. Kaiser smiled. "I got that, too."

I couldn't hide my amazement. "How?"

"He parked under the streetlight, and he was there long enough for me to use my binoculars." She read off the license plate number, which Day wrote down.

I was still looking through the photographs. "Can we keep these?"

"I believe they're my responsibility," Day said, snatching them out of my hands. "I need to take them down to the police station and see what information we can get from them. Could we get a copy of your video file, too?" he asked Mrs. Kaiser.

Aaron turned to her. "Would you make that two copies?"

She gave him a big smile. "Sure."

We waited in Mrs. Kaiser's living room while she download the file and made two DVDs, which she gave to Day and to Aaron. Day was satisfied and left. Then she printed out duplicate photos for Aaron and me. Before we said our goodbyes, Mrs. Kaiser made us promise to keep her informed on our progress in catching the guy. I could see the information going straight to her granddaughter, but what could we do? She had been a big help.

It was four o'clock in the morning before Joan and I trudged into Hugo and Janine's house. Neither of us expected that anyone would be out of bed, so we both registered surprise when Joan used her mom's spare key and the door opened to Janine sitting in her leather recliner. Her eyes were closed and her head was tilted to the side. Tony Hillerman's latest novel lay open on her lap, a handmade bookmark dangling out of pages that had slumped across her hand. Joan went over and gently rubbed her shoulder. "Mom?" she said.

Janine stirred but didn't sit up, so she must have been in a deep sleep. "Mom?" she said again, gently shaking her.

"Joan?" Her eyes opened to a slit. "You're home. What time is it?" She groggily moved her right hand, realized it was in a book, and started to put everything together. She used the bookmark to hold her spot and slid the book onto the end table. She opened her eyes fully and focused on us.

"It's four o'clock. You didn't need to wait up for us," Joan said.

"Stephanie got me up an hour ago," Janine said, now alert. "She'd been sleepwalking. She hasn't done that here in a long time."

I felt guilty now. I hadn't told anyone about Stephanie's episode the night before. It wasn't an intentional slip, but with all the activity of the day I just hadn't found the right time.

"She did it last night, too," I said. "It got me up. I'm sorry I forgot to mention it."

"I wasn't even sure she was sleepwalking at first," Janine said. "She was downstairs in the kitchen looking out the back window."

The same place she'd gone last night. "Did she say anything?"

"The carillon at St. Barnabas was chiming. Stephanie asked

me who made the bells ring. It was a good question, so I didn't think much of it. I told her I didn't know, but that it was time for her to go to bed. When she didn't answer, I gently turned her around. It was then that I saw her eyes had that unfocused look. She said, 'Something bad is out there.' I told her there were lots of good things out there, too, but that no matter what, she was safe inside with us. I took her upstairs and put her to bed."

I felt something press against my chest, a sensation I hadn't felt in a long time. I put my hand to where I felt the heaviness and realized it was the Miraculous Medal I wore around my neck. It hadn't weighed on me like that since I'd been shot back in my hometown of Clinton while looking into Gregorio Iavello's death. I wondered what connection there could possibly be.

"Did she say anything else?" I asked.

"On the way up the stairs she mumbled something about seeing a girl playing with Mr. Jangles."

Joan interrupted. "Nick, do you think it means anything?"

"I don't know. Maybe we need to watch her more closely. Mr. Jangles's death had to affect her. And then we've been talking about Keri Schoening, too. You know how she adored Keri. Maybe we're seeing her anxiety come out at night."

"Well, it scares me," Joan said.

I took her hand and squeezed it. "It scares me, too."

Janine asked, "Did your trap work? Did you catch the guy?"

"No. Thanks to Joan's old flame, Johnny Day, our relics hunter got away, not only with the trash, but also with some decoy boxes Susan had set out." Joan and I told her the story, ending with the big surprise we all got when Mrs. Kaiser showed up with pictures. I handed her my set of photographs.

"At least you have something to go on now." Janine looked them over.

I yawned. "That we do. But it needs to wait until morning.

125

Very late in the morning."

Joan nodded.

Janine said she would turn off the lights. Joan and I plodded up the front staircase. I fell asleep as soon as my head hit the pillow. But I didn't sleep in the next day. An important phone call took care of that.

CHAPTER TWELVE

Joan woke me at nine A.M. "Father Dan is on the phone," she said.

I sat up, disoriented. I had been sleeping so heavily I had a difficult time figuring out where I was at first.

"Father Dan?"

"You called him yesterday, asking about relics, remember?" She held out the portable phone.

"Oh, right." I took the phone and tried to focus. "Hello?" I said. Joan left the room.

"This is Father Dan, Nick." His voice sounded thick, like he'd spent the night outdoors in humid weather. "Sorry I wasn't able to get back to you last night. I had a couple of difficult visits at the hospital. What is it you need?"

"I was calling about the disappearance of Keri Schoening's body. Someone speculated that it was related to her growing cult status as a saint, that the person who confiscated the body wanted it for relics. I'd like to get some comments from you."

"I'm not sure what I can say, Nick. It's all speculation. However, the relics idea seems far-fetched. Keri is not an official saint of the church." He cleared his throat.

I was scrambling around the room looking for my reporter's notebook. It wasn't under the mystery novels Joan had brought with her, nor was it with the newspaper articles tucked under the old photo of Mr. Jangles. I finally located it in the midst of Stephanie's coloring books. "But so many people left petitions for her at the cemetery," I said, jotting down a few notes while talking. "They think she's a saint. Does it matter to them that the Church hasn't officially declared it? Isn't the value in the eye of the beholder?"

He was silent for a moment. "So you think it's possible the person who took her body intends to use it like they used the saints of old, dividing up the bones and venerating them?"

"Or worse, turning a profit on them."

There was quiet at the other end again until I broke the silence. "I know this sounds crass, but aren't relics worth something?"

"I suppose there's value if the relic can be authenticated. And if there's a demand."

"Can someone buy relics on eBay?"

"The modern Church frowns on that kind of thing, Nick. We don't encourage the buying and selling of relics."

"But people do, don't they?"

Father Dan paused. "Even the church will buy relics on occasion, to keep them from being treated like souvenirs or from passing into the hands of profiteers."

I was busy making notes, so I let a moment or two more of silence pass before I started to ask another question. Then Father Dan said, "I suppose there might be a black market for this kind of thing. There are instances where people have tried to steal relics. I don't know if it was to sell them, but I guess it could have been."

"How far back would I have to go to find an instance of someone stealing relics? And where did it happen?"

"You wouldn't have to go far. A year or so ago, an attempt was made here in Indiana."

"I didn't know we had relics in Indiana."

"Sure we do. Most of the older churches have a relic or two in their altar stones. It's not required, the way it used to be centuries ago, but when they opened the big new church in Fishers, St. Maria Goretti, there were relics from several saints and a vial of Mother Teresa's blood."

"That's gruesome," I said, scribbling it all down. It would be great background for the story.

Father Dan pushed on. "The largest collection of saintly relics in the state used to be at the Old Cathedral in Vincennes, at least until there was an attempt to steal them. Now they're in a special vault at St. Aelred's Archabbey. Supposedly it's more secure."

St. Aelred's wasn't all that far from Jasper, about a half-hour southeast. Although I'd never been there, I'd heard of it. It was very influential, one of only a handful of archabbeys in the world. In Indiana, Catholic congregations from all over the state held retreats there, and most were conducted by priests who received their degrees from its school of theology.

I imagined the Gothic buildings I'd seen in photos of St. Aelred's. "I'm sure it's a formidable place. Have there been any attempts to steal them since?"

"Not that I've heard."

I made a note at the top of the pad to see if I could get into St. Aelred's to view the relics. I had no real idea what they might look like. "Well, thanks for the information. Are you still monitoring things at the cemetery?"

"I'm at the retreat house now and looking out the window at the cemetery. Before I called you I visited Keri's grave. It looks like nothing has changed since yesterday."

"They removed the police tape for you?"

"Not at all. The police have just been good about letting me get close to the grave to say some prayers."

Must be nice to have friends on the police force, I thought.

We said our goodbyes and hung up. I made my notes a little more legible and added a few thoughts after the conversation.

Father Dan's presence at the retreat house hardly provided protection. It was so far from the cemetery that he would only know someone was there if they drove by the house on their way to the gravesite. Unless he had binoculars and happened to be looking at the right time, anyone who approached the cemetery on foot from the opposite direction, through the woods, could sneak in unnoticed. The relics hunter whose shadowy image I'd captured yesterday had escaped his surveillance. I thought I could probably do the same if I needed to, if I knew where to park and how far I would have to go to enter the woods. Joan might know as well, having lived around here.

Now fully awake but yawning, I dressed and went downstairs to see what might be around for breakfast.

The delicious aroma of fresh bread filled the kitchen. Janine had used her breadmaker to bake some kind of multi-grain loaf. Slices had already been cut from it, so I cut a couple for myself and then looked in the refrigerator for eggs. Janine had two dozen, so I figured it would be okay to use a few. I decided to whip up a mostly egg-white, for extra protein, omelet. While I was doing that, Stephanie came in.

"Haven't you eaten yet, Daddy?"

I gave her a kiss on her forehead. "No, sweetheart, I haven't. But I bet you have."

She nodded. "Grandma made me bread." Stephanie loves homemade bread, and not just the plain white variety. She'll eat almost any whole grain bread if there's nothing crunchy or chewy in it, like seeds or dried fruit. And as long as she can spread it with her favorite topping.

"Did you put honey on it?"

She nodded and then watched as I whipped the omelet mixture and poured it into a hot pan. When it was ready to be flipped, I did it with a little flourish because she finds it funny. I threw some cheese on top, then slid it onto a plate, folding it over. I buttered the bread slices and moved to the table.

"What are we going to do today, Daddy?"

"I don't know. Did you ask Mommy?"

"She said she didn't know either. She said she was tired."

I wasn't surprised. I was, too, and she must have gotten even less sleep since she was the one who woke me up.

"This may be a really laid-back day for Mommy."

"I think Grandma wants to take Mommy shopping," Steph said.

"Oh." That would mean Stephanie would be largely my responsibility—or Hugo's—but since he had taken her fishing yesterday, I suspected he would be doing something with his cronies today. Not that I didn't want to have Stephanie with me, but since I was dogging not one, but two investigations, it would be difficult. Still, I'd done it before.

I looked at the clock on the stove. It was after 10:00. The local shops were open. If the two women were going shopping, they'd be leaving soon.

"Would you go find Mommy and see when they're leaving?"

She scampered off.

Joan came back with Stephanie a few minutes later. "Mom needs a new dress and wants me to go with her to pick it out," she said. "I think we'll leave in a little bit, and we shouldn't be gone that long. You don't have to run out, do you?"

I said I didn't, especially since I hadn't had a shower and looked pretty disheveled. I rinsed my dishes and was placing them in the dishwasher when the doorbell rang. I went upstairs quickly, into hiding, while Janine answered the door.

I was no sooner in the bedroom when Janine came upstairs and knocked on the door. "It's for you."

"The phone? I didn't hear it ring."

"No, the person at the door is for you."

"Who is it?"

"Someone I think you should meet."

"Do they have a name?"

"Just come down, Nick."

I wondered why Janine was being so mysterious. I combed my hair and tried to look as presentable as possible, then began to trudge down the front staircase, but stopped halfway.

A woman in her mid-to-late twenties was in the entryway, her back against the doorframe and her arms crossed over her chest. She was dressed in high-end jeans that hugged her lean, long legs and flared out at the floor around black boots. Her hair was blonde and short, with a part slightly off center, revealing an ear that was double-pierced. Despite the summer warmth, she wore a black, stylish sportcoat over a turquoise top that said business without sacrificing youth. She had red, pouty lips and a neutral eye shadow with a slight shimmer to it. From her stance alone, I could tell this lady was trouble.

"Hello?" I said. Janine and Joan stood off to the side in the living room, amused looks on their faces.

"I hear you used my grandmother's photographic skills last night," the woman replied. She bent down, opened a tan leather messenger's bag at her feet, and pulled out copies of the photos Ida Mae Kaiser had given us. "You want to tell me who this guy is and why he's stealing trash from the Schoenings?"

"You must be Sally Kaiser," I said, coming the rest of the way down the stairs. "I'm Nick Bertetto." I held out my hand. She shook it with a firm, no-nonsense grasp.

"Now that we have the formalities out of the way, let's get down to business." She waved the photos around. "Who is this guy?"

"I'm not going to tell you any more than you'd tell me about your investigation," I said. "I'm a reporter, too, you know."

"Oh, yes. I know. The legendary Nick Bertetto from the *Indianapolis Standard.* You've come to Jasper to break the story and show us local reporters how it's done. You're the reason the Schoenings have suddenly clammed up and won't give me exclusives."

"I happened to be here on vacation when the press picked up your story about the body disappearing. The editors of my paper knew I was here and asked me to file some reports. I may be your competition, but that's no reason to barge in here with that kind of attitude. If you weren't expecting me to cooperate, why did you come? Do you really think I'm going to tell you who the guy in the photos is just because you demand it?"

She picked up her bag and flung the strap over her shoulder. "I don't need you to tell me who he is, if you're going to be that way about it. I can find out myself. I just think you should know this is my town. I know it inside out, and no one is going to get the story before I do. Even you."

"Are you sure you want to start out this way? Because I don't see any reason not to be friendly competitors. There may be some instances where we could trade information."

"Ah, so you concede that you need my help in getting this story?"

"I concede nothing, only that it's stupid for us to make this personal."

"So now you're saying I'm stupid?"

I bit the insides of my cheek to suppress a smile. "Only your attitude."

"Well, then I don't see any reason to talk to you any longer. I'll just get going and plan on filing better stories than you every day, this one included." She stuck her head into the living room where she could make eye contact with Janine. "Thank you, Mrs. Strassheim, I won't bother you again."

Kaiser opened the screen door and let herself out. She stomped down the porch stairs, heels clacking, and walked out to her bright blue Ford Focus, driving off with a roar.

Joan laughed. "That went well, didn't it?"

I joined her and Janine in the living room. "I wouldn't want to be on *Survivor* with her," I said. "I think she'd eliminate the other contestants by eating them alive."

"I agree, she could have been nicer," said Janine, "but you have to consider her experiences five months ago when the national press descended on Jasper. She was used over and over again, and when the TV cameras and the big name reporters left, she was still here. She's got ambition but hasn't been successful at getting a job in a larger city. I think she sees your involvement here to be the same kind of thing. You're not the national press, but you still represent a bigger paper. She doesn't want to get walked over again."

I hadn't known that, but it still didn't justify her attitude. She didn't know me. All she had managed to do was get me riled. I was all about filing a major story for tomorrow's paper just to show her up.

I excused myself and went back upstairs to shower. Standing beneath the hot spray, I tried to summarize what I knew so far and figure out what I needed to do next. There was nothing quite like a hot shower to get my creative juices going.

Here's what I knew: Keri Schoening's body was missing from the cemetery where she'd been buried. Why, we didn't know. It might be related to the fact that she was popularly regarded as a martyr for her faith, making her an unofficial saint, and that the relics of her body had some worth. That worth might well be monetary since the remains of saints were valued by the Church and others. Of course, it might be something else. Ryan had noted that the volcanic Sally Kaiser was investigating the possibility that it was related to the original massacre, checking to see if anything had happened to the bodies of the other victims. I needed to check out that angle as well, although until something happened I couldn't see putting much effort there.

My instincts told me that wasn't the right direction, that there was another reason for the grave robbery, even if it wasn't the track I was on.

Kevin Mueller had mentioned rumors of a Satanic cult in connection with what was happening to missing pets in the community. That was my first indication that the two events might be connected since one of the original theories about the massacre was that it was related to some kind of cult. But no evidence had shown up to point the police in that direction. In fact, with the two killers dead, the police's evidence had indicated it was something they'd done on their own, related to bullying by most of their victims. But Kevin seemed to think there was something else there, and for the moment I put enough faith in him to keep that possibility in play. What if there had been a cult that went deep underground after the massacre and had resurfaced now? It was scary, but possible. I had no idea where to look for leads, though. Unless Kevin found something. That had its drawbacks, too, with him being so young.

So, what could I do? Well, as far as finding the person or persons who had been hurting pets, I could call my favorite officer, Johnny Day, and ask him if there had been any more attacks reported. Lots of promise there. A better bet would be keeping in contact with the neighbors in the hopes of hearing any buzz if something happened.

As far as my work for the paper, Father Dan had mentioned that the relics from the Old Cathedral at Vincennes had been transferred to St. Aelred's because someone had tried to steal them. I wondered if that near-crime was related to what was happening here. Probably not, but since St. Aelred's was only a half-hour away, it wouldn't hurt to see what they had and learn more about relics in general. Someone was interested in Keri's relics. Maybe he'd been interested in others, as well. The police knew as much as I did about the guy who had taken the Schoenings' trash last night, especially with Ida Mae's night vision photos, and they'd be looking for him. I needed to move in a different direction.

Joan came in while I was drying off and said that she and Janine were leaving and that Stephanie was watching a video. I asked if Hugo was still around, but he had gone golfing.

After shaving and getting dressed, I checked on Stephanie, who was absorbed in a SpongeBob Squarepants cartoon, and then got on the Internet to look up St. Aelred's. On their well-designed, easy to follow website, I located the Contacts page and scanned the list of names and phone numbers until one of them stopped me. Father Vincent Kennedy. It was possible he wasn't the priest I knew, but it seemed unusual that two priests from Indiana would have that same name. The Father Vince I knew had been investigating apparitions of Mary, the mother of Jesus, for the Church while serving as a professor at St. Mary-of-the-Woods College in Terre Haute. We'd come in contact when I'd been in Clinton poking into the death of Gregorio Iavello, a case which involved a former lover of mine, Anna Veloche, who claimed to see visions of the Virgin Mary.

Although it had been almost two and a half years ago, Father Vince could easily have been transferred to St. Aelred's. I wrote down the phone number and signed off.

Guessing the phone number would be long distance, I pulled out my cell phone and dialed. When the voice answered, I knew immediately it was the same Father Vince by the flat tone and clipped delivery. "Retreats. Vince Kennedy."

"Father, I don't know if you'll remember me, but we met a couple of years ago. My name is Nick Bertetto. You were looking into an apparition . . ."

His low-pitched, rumbling chuckle overtook my explanation. "Of course, Nick, I remember you. Are you well?"

"Very well, thank you." We exchanged pleasantries, but before I could get down to business, he jumped to it.

"So what may I help you with, Nick? I doubt this is a social call."

"No, Father, it isn't. I'm in Jasper looking into the disappearance of Keri Schoening's body from her grave—she was one of the West Jasper High School shooting victims—and there's speculation that whoever did it who wanted her body for relics. She was the one who died after saying she believed in God. I understand St. Aelred's has quite a collection of relics, and I wondered if I could talk to someone there about them."

"May I ask how it is that you know about our relics?"

"Father Dan, the priest at St. Barnabas here in Jasper, told me."

"Interesting. I'm surprised he was so free with that information. Well, since you know we have them, I probably don't need to tell you they're here because someone tried to steal them."

"That's what Father Dan said. Is it possible I could see them?"

"I think that would be all right. However, Brother Richard, who oversees our collection of historical artifacts, is away in Europe for study and won't be back for another two weeks. Is this something you need right away?"

"I'm afraid it is. I'm trying to put together a story for tomorrow's edition of the *Indianapolis Standard.*"

"Did you say you were in Jasper?"

"Yes, I'm staying with my in-laws."

"Why don't you go ahead and come down? Brother Richard's duties are being handled by another monk, but I'm fairly certain I can talk him into letting you see the collection. I'll arrange for it while you're driving here."

"Thank you. I appreciate it. There is one problem, though. I'm taking care of my daughter, Stephanie, and I'll need to bring her with me."

"Ever the doting father, eh, Nick? I remember her. Such a sweet child. Of course, bring her along."

"Thank you. Where do I find you when I reach St. Aelred's?"

He gave me directions, and I went to tell Stephanie about our trip. After I turned off SpongeBob and let her go through a short tantrum, I told her where we were going. She didn't remember Father Vince, which didn't surprise me given that she was only three years old when we saw him last, but she said she'd be good.

I gathered up some necessities, buckled Steph in her car seat, left a note for Joan and Janine, and took off.

CHAPTER THIRTEEN

"Isn't this pretty, Stephanie?" I asked, trying to keep her occupied as we drove to St. Aelred's. "It's so different from where we live. There are lots and lots of trees here."

Southern Indiana is a beautiful drive during the summer. We were going through the lush, green woods of the Hoosier National Forest. They roll through hilly terrain, making the countryside seem like a completely different state from the farmland of the north, which was crushed flat by glaciers during the Ice Age. Here, the plethora of leafy oaks and maples encroach on everything, even the highways, which are cut out of the forest like ski runs on a mountainside.

Stephanie didn't respond, so I continued. "Look how blue the sky is? Doesn't it look like it could go on forever?"

I hoped she was looking out the window, although I suspected she was too young to appreciate what was out there, like the many shades of green that stretched upward until they met the bright blue of the sky. It pulled a driver's eyes toward the heavens. I wondered if that led to many wrecks around here. Probably one becomes immune to it over time.

Stephanie, who I knew was nervous about going somewhere that a) wasn't fun, and b) she'd never been before, interrupted my travelogue.

"Daddy, why couldn't I go with Mommy and Grandma?"

"You know you hate to go shopping with them, Stephanie, and besides, they'd already left before I found out I needed to go to this meeting. Now, I know you're a little nervous because you don't remember Father Vince, but he's very nice. You'll be fine."

It wasn't like I hadn't prepared for this trip, short as it was. I'd packed a travel bag with several Dr. Seuss books, a snack bag of Cheerios, and a juice box. I had also reluctantly added the handheld video game Hugo and Janine had purchased for Stephanie. I don't really approve of video games, which I view as time wasters, but I try not to censor what her grandparents get her. Joan's brother, Ron, has two boys, both older than Stephanie, who play the games nonstop. I guess Hugo and Janine thought she was missing out.

"Do we have to stay a long time?"

"We won't stay longer than necessary, I promise. And we're almost there, so relax and try to think about what you might want to do this afternoon." I had hopes, probably not valid ones, that we could do something fun in the afternoon, all three of us.

I turned at a sign that pointed the way to St. Aelred's, and twenty feet further passed a sign indicating the archabbey was two miles away. Soon I was directed to take a right onto St. Aelred's Pass, a narrow, one-way road that looped around the archabbey's campus. We left the state road, passed through an open wrought-iron gate, and plunged into a dense forest. It was beautiful but made me somewhat claustrophobic—the overhang of the trees completely covered the road and blocked nearly all the direct sunlight, except for a few rays that dodged in and around the branches.

We went through a few intersections with signs pointing to other areas of the campus, but we turned at the fifth intersection, which led to the retreat house. I followed the road until we reached a venerable, two-story stone farmhouse, circa 1900. The rustic exterior contrasted with the freshly paved asphalt driveway leading to the house on one side and back to the street on the other. Father Vince had said to park on the driveway in front of the house. I guessed he wasn't expecting anyone else.

But he was expecting us. By the time I had opened the sliding side door and let Stephanie jump down, he was outside to greet us.

"Nick, nice to see you again," he said, warmly shaking my hand. He looked very much the same as I remembered, tall and thin, with a young face that had enough lines to make me guess he was in his early thirties. Since then, though, he had acquired rectangular, black frame glasses that gave him a trendy but nerdy appearance. He knelt to Stephanie's level. "How are you, Stephanie?" he asked. "You've grown quite a bit since I saw you last. I bet this much," he said, indicating about six inches between two outstretched hands.

Shyly she said, "Hi," and then looked to me for some kind of clue as to what to do. Before I could give any, Father Vince asked her, "Would you like a Rice Krispies Treat?" She immediately nodded. "Well, let's go inside then," he said. "I have one for you that I just bought this morning."

We followed him into the retreat house. The building may have looked old on the outside, but the inside had been remodeled into a comfortable, modern meeting place. Father Vince led us through the living room, which had a wide-screen plasma TV mounted over the fireplace, and into the adjacent dining room, which was dominated by a dark, cherry-wood dining table that could easily seat ten. It was covered with a white lace tablecloth, on which sat three golden crosses, each about a foot and a half tall with a wide base so they stood upright like a statue. Each had a large circular centerpiece covered with red felt and studded with tiny mountings, similar to what you would find on an engagement ring, only much, much smaller. A circle of glass protected the red felt and mountings. I couldn't see much detail without getting closer, and I thought I should wait until invited to do so. There was another golden object next to the crosses, shaped more like a tiered castle, with four golden turrets on each side of a center spire. Like its cross-shaped counterparts, it had a red felt center with things mounted in it.

"I took the liberty of getting these reliquaries out of storage to show you," Father Vince said. "Have a seat."

I sat at a chair near the fanciest of the reliquaries, the one with turrets. Since it was more ornate, I figured it must have some fairly precious relics. Father Vince took a chair next to me. Stephanie stood looking at the two of us.

Father Vince smiled at her. "I did promise you a Rice Krispies Treat, didn't I?" He rose and went into the adjacent kitchen, bringing back a box of them. Pulling one out, he handed it to her along with a napkin.

"You may have half of it," I said. I didn't want it to spoil her lunch, but it was also the best way to get through this visit in peace. Father Vince helped her climb onto one of the dining room chairs where she knelt and could reach the table. He scooted the tablecloth back a little so she wouldn't get marshmallow goo on it. I helped her unwrap the treat, divided it in half, and placed one piece on the napkin. I handed her the other one.

After cleaning up my sticky hands, I sat next to the turreted reliquary again. "May I touch this?"

He nodded. I picked it up. It was heavy at the base end. I used both hands to tilt it back and squinted to see what was under the glass.

"You probably can't read those, can you?" he asked.

"Are they in Latin?"

He nodded.

There were mountings spread out all over the red felt, each accompanied by its own identification strip of white paper. The center relic was a little larger and seemed to have some significance.

"All of these little mountings are relics?"

"The center one contains a fragment of the cross which is reputed to be the one upon which our Lord Jesus hung. I have a paper of authenticity, signed by the Vatican. Of course, you've no doubt heard the same stories I have, that if all those fragments were gathered up and put together, they'd make up six or seven crosses. We don't know anything for certain, but it does at least have some kind of certification."

"Do all of these have certifications?"

"No. We really don't know that much about them, other than they were brought here from France back in the early 1800s when a parish was being established at Vincennes. However, they were revered in France as being authentic."

Father Vince handed me a magnifying glass. The relics were still so small it was hard to identify what they could be.

I could see the "St." mark ahead of the names on the identifying strips of paper. "Are they bone fragments?"

"Mostly. That's consistent with what we know of the early church. It sounds grisly, but the saints of the early church were so revered that everyone wanted a piece of them, something to remember them by. It didn't help that the living couldn't leave the bodies in graves, for fear of pagan raiders ransacking their resting place. So the practice of dividing them up began. Legends grew up about their healing powers, and the practice was perpetuated."

"They still do this?" I asked, keeping an eye on Stephanie while still trying to concentrate on the conversation. Her hot little hands were now covered with marshmallow, and I could see us headed for a crisis if she tried to wipe them on the tablecloth.

"Not really. The Vatican has clamped down on that sort of

thing. Although they still take bodily remains from a sainthood candidate's grave when the body is exhumed to prepare for beatification."

"Who gets those?"

"They're presented to the pope, then turned over to the Apostolic Sacristy. The diocese or religious order presenting the candidate's cause for sainthood will likely hold some, too."

Stephanie was almost through her piece of the Rice Krispies Treat and slowing down. Soon she'd wipe her hands on something. I decided to pre-empt that. I took her hands and guided her down from the chair.

Fishing around in my bag, I came up with a wet-wipe. I cleaned Stephanie's hands and put her back in the chair. With the tablecloth out of immediate danger, I reviewed the names on the reliquary through the magnifying glass. "Do you know whose remains these are?"

"There's a reference key that was created with the reliquary. I made copies for you." He handed me papers that had been sitting near his elbow. "I went ahead and marked the abbreviations so you'd know what they stood for."

I looked them over. I was glad he'd written them out because it wasn't obvious to me that V.M. meant Virgin and Martyr, which were used after St. Ursula and St. Lucy.

I did a quick count. "There're around eighty relics here," I said.

"In the four of them put together. Of course, those are first class relics. There are others in the collection I didn't get out. Second and third class."

"What?"

"I'm sorry. I thought you understood the class system when it came to relics."

"No, I don't. Not all relics are created equal?"

"There are three types. First class relics are parts of the actual

144

saints themselves—bone chips, hair, nails, blood, etc. Second class are things that belonged to the saint, like an article of clothing or a well-used Bible. Third class relics are things like pieces of cloth that have touched first or second class relics."

"First class relics are the most valuable, I imagine."

"Yes, if it can be proven they came from the saint. Second class may be valuable if they're well-connected to the saint, like a Bible that has the saint's writing in it or something like that. Third class relics are less valuable, but that's in the eye of the beholder."

Stephanie couldn't seem to sit still any longer. "Daddy, I want a drink of water."

I lifted her off the chair and onto the floor. Father Vince went into the kitchen. I heard him filling a cup with ice then a faucet running. Stephanie followed the noise to get her water. Father Vince returned, leaving her behind.

"Such a well-behaved child," he said.

"You helped a lot with the snack. Thanks."

"It's no problem. I have two nieces and a nephew about her age. They need distractions, too. You said Father Dan Klein at St. Barnabas told you the relics were here?"

I nodded.

The priest scratched his chin. "I guess there's no denying the grapevine among the priesthood is an active one. The press knew about the break-in at the Old Cathedral, but we didn't publicize it when we moved the relics here. We didn't want to give whoever had tried to get them another chance. Since then we've been pretty discreet about who knows. It's not a secret, but still I'm surprised Father Dan told you."

I shrugged.

"I guess you're easy to talk to," Father Vince said.

"Father Dan has been very helpful. He seems very conscientious."

"He is, and a good fit for this area since his parents came from Germany and Dan speaks it fluently. The Evansville diocese thinks so highly of him they've assigned him extra duties. He's kept quite busy. And the Jasper Police love him. He's their chaplain."

"Is he being trained for a higher position, like bishop?"

"The pope appoints bishops, not the diocese, so it's difficult to be certain that could happen. But I could see Father Dan as an administrator, if not a bishop. Did you know he's also the exorcist for the diocese?"

I raised an eyebrow and looked at the priest, wondering for a moment if he was putting me on. "Seriously? You have priests assigned to do exorcisms? I thought the Church didn't do that anymore."

Father Vince smiled. "Every diocese has an assigned exorcist, but there's not much call for one anymore. We have a better understanding about mental illnesses now. Generally we only do it if the person thinks they are possessed and requests an exorcism. Father Dan handled one awhile back. Sad case."

"When was that?"

"It was a couple of years ago." He walked down the hall and disappeared into a room. I looked into the kitchen and saw Stephanie walking around, still drinking her water. The cup Father Vince had given her was plastic, so I didn't worry too much.

The priest returned with a folder. "I thought I'd saved something on that, only because it was so unusual. Of course, I can't give you specific information that would enable you to identify her. But I can tell you in general what happened, if you want to know."

We both sat down at the table. I leaned toward him. "I am curious."

He set the folder on the table and opened it. "She was in her early forties, divorced, depressed, and convinced she was possessed. When I read the report, I figured it to be multiple personality disorder. Her psychiatrist believed the woman wouldn't get better until we did something, so the bishop sent Father Dan in. A few weeks later she committed suicide. She'd been threatening to do it for some time, the psychiatrist told us."

Father Vince scanned the notes. Since I could read upside down, a trait I'd developed from years of sitting across the desk from police officers when interviewing them, I could read her name. It was April Kensington.

"I bet Father Dan felt terrible," I said.

"He did. He asked to be relieved of those duties, but the bishop told him it was not his fault. Father Dan was reluctant, but he's still the exorcist. No cases have come up since then."

I didn't know what to say. Fortunately Father Vince changed the subject.

"So tell me, what's been happening with you since I saw you last? Have you had anymore close encounters of the spiritual kind?"

I told him about how I'd come across Elijah Smith last year, how he'd given me clues to the disappearance of state representative Calvin Cahill, and how I suspected he'd been an angel. Father Vince listened and nodded when I reached the end.

"I don't find it surprising that this has happened to you," he said. "In pagan days, people would have said 'the gods favor you.' I think you have a knack for stumbling onto things that Heaven cares about, and that your participation makes a difference in how it gets resolved."

"I think maybe it's just a big coincidence."

"And that's the other thing. I believe your humility and skepticism are delighting God. He knows you won't take Him for granted."

There was an uncomfortable silence. I didn't know what to believe, but the notion that I had some kind of 'in' with God wasn't it. Father Vince must've sensed that, as he changed the subject.

"So you mentioned this interest in relics relates to Keri Schoening's body disappearing. Can you tell me more about that?"

I filled him in on how I'd come to be in Jasper before it happened, how the paper had assigned me the story, and about the person going through the Schoenings' trash. I also told him about the possibility that it might tie into some acts of cruelty against animals, that there might be some kind of Satanic cult involved.

"I took a course about Satanism once," he mused. "Fascinating and scary." He cocked his head at me. "I bet it's no accident that you've become involved in this investigation. You still wear the Miraculous Medal, don't you?"

I nodded, flipping the chain with its medallion out from under my shirt.

"Don't stop wearing it," he advised.

About this time I noticed Stephanie hadn't come back from the kitchen. I shifted my chair to get up and find her. "What about you?" I asked. "How did you come to be here instead of St. Mary's?"

"I graduated from St. Aelred's. Some of the best years of my life were spent here. I was delighted when an opening appeared and I had the opportunity to return. Right now I lead retreats, which I enjoy, but I'm hoping a teaching position will open next year. I'd like to be a part of the faculty."

I nodded at his comment. "Stephanie?" I called.

There was no answer. I walked into the kitchen, Father Vince behind me. Stephanie stood on a rug in front of the back door, staring out into the yard, as she had the night I found her sleepwalking. I knelt next to her. "Stephanie?" I asked, this time more quietly.

"She's out there," Stephanie said without turning toward me.

"Who is?"

"The girl I told Grandma about last night, the one playing with Mr. Jangles."

I looked out but didn't see anyone. "Honey, there's no one out there."

"Yes, there is. She's the one who told me there's something bad out there."

"She said that?"

"Last night."

"Has she said anything today?"

"She's crying."

"Oh."

"Now she's looking at you. She says you have to help her."

"I do?"

"She says not to let the prophecy come true." Stephanie strung out the word "prophecy" as though someone were telling her how to say it.

"I don't know of any prophecy, Stephanie." I waved my hand in front of her face. She didn't blink or turn her head. Gently I turned her around to face me. Her eyes had that vacant stare of sleepwalking, but it was the middle of the day, and she hadn't been asleep.

A shiver ran through me.

CHAPTER FOURTEEN

Father Vince knelt down beside us. "Stephanie," he asked, "does the little girl have a name?"

"She's not little."

"How old is she?"

Stephanie turned her head to look at Father Vince. Her consciousness seemed to return, and her eyes began to focus. "How old is who?"

I pulled her close. "Don't you remember what you said?"

"I was drinking my water," she said. "Where is it?"

Father Vince took her glass from the counter and handed it to her. "You don't remember putting it down or going to the back door?" he asked.

She shook her head. She took a drink of water and went back to the dining room.

I glared at the linoleum floor like it had some explanation for what just happened. After a moment I looked up to see Father Vince watching me, his face full of concern.

"What do you make of that?" I asked him.

"I don't know. I heard her say she's seen this girl before."

"She's had two sleepwalking episodes since we got here. Last night Joan's mom found her in the kitchen. She mentioned a girl in the back yard playing with Mr. Jangles, my mother-in-law's dead cat, but that's it. The other time, I found her. She said there was something bad out there, but she didn't mention seeing anyone."

"If Stephanie is seeing something, there's a reason," he said. "What is this prophecy she's talking about?"

"First I've heard of it. Do you know of any local prophets, past or present? I mean, this is a fairly religious area."

He shook his head. "The Church would frown on those kinds of things. Since Jesus is regarded as the fulfillment of all Old Testament prophecies, the Church's position is that there is no need for additional prophets."

"Yeah, well, I might check at the Jasper library to see if they have any insights. This whole thing is really creepy. And I'm worried about the effect it could have on Stephanie if it continues."

"She seems to be okay now."

We moved back into the dining room where the reliquaries were, and Stephanie did seem back to normal. She was looking at a Dr. Seuss book I'd brought along, *Horton Hears a Who,* trying to read it.

"This could be a vision Stephanie is having. You know other people who have visions," Father Vince said pointedly.

Of course, I did—Anna Veloche, the visionary from Clinton, where I'd met Father Vince. I asked him about Anna, and he said she still receives messages from the Blessed Mother. "As far as I know, though, there are no other developments," he added.

I didn't want Stephanie to have any kind of visions, Anna's kind or otherwise. I wanted her to have a normal life.

We prepared to leave. Father Vince made sure I had the list of relics. He asked me not to make a big deal about their location if I used any of this as background. "Some parishioners of the Old Cathedral are still unhappy they no longer have the relics," he said. "It's not that we won't let them have them back on a temporary basis because we will. On All Saints' Day they always have a nice ceremony and display the reliquaries, and that won't change. But for security reasons, they're here for the foreseeable future."

I promised to do what I could and left. Stephanie smiled at Father Vince and waved at him through the van window as we began our drive back to Jasper.

My mind was a jumble. Keri Schoening, Stephanie, a ghostly girl who played with a ghostly cat. Relics of long dead saints. I kept trying to create a lead for my next story in the paper, but my own fears for Stephanie kept breaking in and sabotaging it.

But at least now I knew more about relics. I should be able to flesh out a story that Keri Schoening's body was possibly taken for that reason. Without a lead on the man we thought was a relics hunter, though, the story wasn't a strong one.

My cell phone rang. I pulled over to the shoulder and answered it. Aaron Schoening was on the other end, and he sounded elated.

"The police got the relics hunter," he told me. "Caught him outside a Hampton Inn on the other side of Jasper. They've asked me if I want to identify him as the person who raided my trash several months ago. I said I did, and we're headed downtown. They're going to question him about Keri's disappearance. We asked if you could be there, and the police said it's okay."

This could be a break. "I'd like to. Problem is, I'm still a good twenty minutes from Jasper."

"Well, when you get here, come to the downtown police station. We'll be waiting for you there."

I looked back at Stephanie. No way was I exposing her to that. I phoned Hugo and Janine's house, hoping someone would be there. Hugo answered. I explained the situation to him, and he agreed to meet me at police headquarters.

Perhaps now I could focus on getting a story for tomorrow's paper. I just hoped it was a big one, big enough to offset anything the annoying Sally Kaiser could come up with.

Police headquarters in Jasper is located at the corner of Sixth and Mill in a two-story, speckled brick and white vinyl-sided building with a shingled awning out front that that bears the word POLICE in big silver letters. I've always wanted to go in and ask them if this is a police station, just to see if I could get a reaction of any kind, even an eye roll. I suspect, however, that they've gotten that question before—and from people who didn't recognize it as a less-than-intelligent query.

I'd been there recently, of course, to be with Janine when she reported what happened to Mr. Jangles, so I knew the ropes. Go in, talk to a receptionist who communicates with you through a small speaker within a huge sheet of bulletproof glass, then sit and wait for a policeman to come out and admit you into the locked inner sanctum. But I wasn't ready to go in yet, not with Stephanie in my care. I stood out front waiting for Hugo to pull up. I wondered if I looked like the type who was hanging around to make trouble.

I wasn't there all that early. I had guessed it would take me twenty minutes; it took me fifteen. I expected Hugo to pull up any minute. Stephanie sensed my impatience.

"Daddy, will Grandpa get here soon?"

"I hope so, honey."

"Why do you have to go to the police station?"

"Mommy's friend Susan and her husband are talking to someone in there who might have done a bad thing, and they would like for me to meet the person and maybe ask a few questions." That was probably more than she needed to know about something she'd never really cared about in the first place, but I occasionally articulate things just to hear how they sound.

"Will you come back to the house when you're done here?"

"That's my plan. But things might change, depending on

what the person says."

"I thought you didn't have to work."

I took a deep breath before answering. "We've been over this, Stephanie. Daddy didn't intend to do any work while we were down here visiting Grandma, but then something came up and Uncle Ryan really needed me to do this. It wasn't something we could plan for. Besides, you don't get to visit at Grandma and Grandpa's house very often. This is a chance for you to do something fun with them."

Mercifully, Hugo pulled up. Joan and Janine were with him. Joan got out and gave me a quick kiss.

"I got a phone call from Aaron asking if I could come down here to help Susan, if she needed it," she said. "We got home at the same time you called Dad, so we came with him."

Janine had already gotten Stephanie out of the van, so I pulled the car seat out and wrestled it into the back of Hugo's car. Joan helped me secure it, and then Stephanie climbed in. Soon the grandparents drove off, and Joan and I headed inside.

A policeman who introduced himself as Sergeant Kentman walked us back to the observation room. He warned us that the questioning was just about over as he led us through a maze of hallways.

"The man's name is Richard O'Brien," Sergeant Kentman said. "At this point he's not a suspect, but we do want to know where he was the night Keri Schoening's body disappeared. We found him through the license plate number we got from Mrs. Kaiser. He was checked in at a hotel on U.S. 231. So far he's been upfront with his answers to our questions. He said he hasn't done anything wrong, and we don't have any evidence to the contrary."

"Has he admitted that he deals in relics?"

The policeman nodded. "He points out that's not illegal. We asked if he was searching for items related to Keri Schoening, and he said 'yes.' He said that's because she's being treated like a saint, even if she's not officially one, and that she may be one yet."

"So there's nothing you can hold him on."

"We could charge him with trespassing, thanks to Mrs. Kaiser's photos, but they're not high quality. A good lawyer could likely get him off. His alibi checks out. He works for a funeral home in Columbus, Ohio, and they say he was there. We're left with this: if all he was after was relics and he had the body, he'd have been out of town by now and not openly registered in a local hotel with trash taken from the Schoenings' house."

I nodded. "With Keri's body, he'd have the mother lode of first class relics," I said. "Every hair, every tooth would have value. He wouldn't have wasted his time trying to get other stuff from the trash."

Joan frowned at me. "That's disgusting."

"But true," I responded.

We were ushered into a small conference room. The interrogation was on the television. Aaron and Susan were seated in front of it, watching. Joan went up behind Susan and put her hand on her friend's back. Susan saw it was Joan and squeezed her hand. Then she went back to watching the proceedings.

Detective Whitmeyer, who'd investigated Mr. Jangles's skinning, was handling the interrogation. Richard O'Brien looked understandably nervous. At this point he probably was unsure what they would do about the trespassing charge. I could see beads of sweat accumulating on his brow. He wiped his forehead with a handkerchief and scooted forward on the hard wooden chair to return it to his pocket. His high-pitched voice sounded confident, though. "I've told you everything I know," he told Whitmeyer, who sat across from him. "I was shocked to learn the grave had been disturbed. Ask at the hotel. As I said earlier,

I didn't check in until after it happened. When I heard about it, I came over from Ohio to get some of the dirt that had been around the casket. That's why I was at the cemetery. As for taking the Schoenings' trash, I was hoping to find something that belonged to Keri. It's not illegal to do that."

"We've explained before, it is if the trash's not yet at the curb."

"They would have put it there in the morning."

"But it wasn't there yet." Whitmeyer paused. "You've taken their trash before."

O'Brien nodded. "We've been over this already. Yeah, I did. Until they stopped putting their trash out at night. Then I didn't do it anymore. But I was back in town, so I decided to see if they were putting it out at night again. And it looked to me like they were. So I took it. And now you've got it. There wasn't anything in there, anyway."

Susan talked back triumphantly to the television. "Of course there wasn't. I wouldn't let go of any of Keri's things, especially to the likes of you."

"Tell us one more time about relics," Whitmeyer said.

O'Brien folded his arms over his chest and cocked one eyebrow. I guess he knew this was a police tactic to see if he made changes to his story. "Dirt from around the casket is a relic because it came from her burial plot. It touched the casket she was buried in. Relics are important because they help us connect to the saints."

"Were you hoping for some miracle from this dirt?"

"Not me. But I would have given it to someone who was."

"Given or sold?" asked a tall policeman who also sat at the table.

He shrugged. "I don't know. It hadn't happened yet."

Whitmeyer looked at the policeman. The two of them looked at O'Brien. Everyone was quiet for a few moments. In the remote room from where we were watching, there was silence as well. O'Brien set his mouth defiantly and folded his arms across his chest.

After what seemed like forever, Whitmeyer walked over to the door and leaned against it. "Well, we don't have any more questions for you at this time. You're free to go. Will you be staying in Jasper?"

"No," O'Brien said. He stood up, and I could see that he was relatively short, maybe five feet four. "I have to go back home today. I have a job to get to tonight."

Whitmeyer looked at her notes. "At a funeral home."

"You have something against funeral homes?"

She gave him a hard look, but O'Brien's demeanor didn't change. "We have your contact information if we have further questions."

O'Brien waved his hand dismissively. "Sure. Whatever."

Whitmeyer opened the door, and O'Brien walked out. The tall policeman followed him. Shortly after, the television went dark.

"We have to let him go," Kentman said to Susan and Aaron. "The trespassing charge isn't worth it, given he has an alibi for the night in question. But he probably won't bother your trash again."

Susan teared up a bit. "I don't like him at all, but I don't think he has Keri. He's just scum trying to make a fast buck off the situation."

"That's our assessment, too," Kentman said.

Aaron, who'd stood up and moved back to where I was standing, banged his fist against the wall. "Then who did it? Where is Keri?"

"We have to keep looking," said Kentman, "but we'll find her."

Aaron supported Susan on the way out. I could tell Joan's

instincts were to be by her friend's side, but she wisely let Aaron do it. The two of them would need time together to process what they'd just learned and how to deal with it. I couldn't imagine what it must be like for them to have lost their only child and five months later have the whole incident resurrected in this way.

Joan and I bid goodbye to the two of them outside the police station. We held hands and watched them drive off. Joan leaned her head against my shoulder. "I feel so sorry for them," she said.

I nodded. We made our way back to the van. Joan asked, "If this guy didn't do it, who did?"

"I don't know," I said. I started the van and put it in drive. "But there are a lot of things going on here that may or may not be clues. The problem is, I don't know which ones fit together."

"Like?"

"Like this—over a year ago, the largest collection of saintly relics in Indiana was almost stolen. To prevent anyone from trying it again, the collection was transferred to a more secure spot, St. Aelred's Archabbey. People talk about Keri Schoening as though she's a saint. Is that related? Or how about this—Kevin Mueller thinks that what happened to Mr. Jangles and his dog may be the work of a Satanic cult. He's heard rumors about it at school. That was something the police considered when they investigated the West Jasper massacre, but they didn't find any evidence of one. Did it possibly go underground and has just now come back to life? Who knows?"

I knew at this point I had to tell Joan what had happened at St. Aelred's. It concerned me, how she would react. I reached across the seat, searching for her hand. "Here's something that really worries me. Stephanie had another sleepwalking incident this afternoon. Only she wasn't asleep. It was like she was in a trance. And she saw some girl, who told Steph I needed to help

158

her, not to let the prophecy come true."

Joan reached for me. "Oh, my God! What's happening here, Nick? We've got to protect Stephanie."

"We will, Joanie, we will." Of course, I didn't know any way right then to protect her from these episodes, but I hoped I would think of something. "I would attribute the visions to the stress of Mr. Jangles's death and Keri's disappearance, except for the mention of a prophecy. I'm not even sure Stephanie knows the word."

We drove in silence for a while, until Joan broke it. "I can't believe things like this are happening right here, right where I grew up. It's still such a small town. How could there be such evil?"

I didn't have an answer for that.

We reached the house and walked up the sidewalk, clinging to each other. Her warmth was reassuring.

Stephanie, the object of our worry, was excited to see us when we came through the door. She'd already had lunch with Grandma and Grandpa and was ready to have more fun. She hugged us and asked if we could go see a movie.

My day already was a movie, an adaptation of a Stephen King novel. My cell phone rang. Kevin Mueller was on the other end.

"Nick," he said, his voice shaky. "I need you to come out here right away."

I looked up and saw that Janine, Hugo, Joan and Stephanie were all watching me intently. I covered the mouthpiece. "It's Kevin Mueller. I need to take this outside."

I stepped out of the house and out of earshot. "Where are you, Kevin?"

"In New Vienna on 56. Do you know where that is?"

I did. New Vienna was a tiny town that didn't really exist anymore, maybe twenty miles west of Jasper. "Are you on 56 or somewhere in New Vienna?"

"I'll give you directions."

"What's there, Kevin? Are you all right?"

His voice cracked. "An abandoned church. I'm all right. I want to go in there, but not by myself."

"Are you in danger?"

"I don't think so. I don't think there's anyone around."

"What do you think is there?"

"A clue as to who hurt Buddy."

"How did you find this place?"

"I can't reveal my source." He sounded like the reporter in him was starting to take over.

"You're sure you're not in any danger?"

"No. I mean yes, I'm not. I mean . . . I'm okay, all right? Just get out here before I lose my nerve, okay?"

I gritted my teeth. Kevin was doing things he shouldn't be doing, but he seemed to be effective doing them. I had to trust he was being truthful about not being in danger. "Get in your car and lock it. Keep the motor running and your cell phone on. If *anything* happens call 911 and get the hell out of there."

"I will."

"I'm leaving now. I'll be there as soon as I can."

An abandoned church in a deserted area. I didn't like the pictures my mind was conjuring up. I went back inside. Everyone stared at me. I held up my hand to indicate not to ask questions. Then I ran upstairs, grabbed a notebook and my digital camera, and dashed back downstairs.

"Kevin Mueller may have found something out in New Vienna, and I need to make sure he's not in trouble," I said, throwing open the front door. "Go to the movie without me. I hope to be back before you are."

CHAPTER FIFTEEN

New Vienna is one of those small farming communities that sprang up when transportation wasn't good, when local stores and services were needed because a trip into a larger town, like Jasper, was too far to make often. But as roads developed and everyone bought cars, the towns lost their reason for existing. Small, family-owned businesses like corner grocery stores went out of business, and buildings were abandoned. Tiny country churches became victims as well. I'd seen it happen where I grew up, around Clinton. Towns like Centenary that didn't have post offices—only the older folks spoke of being from those places. Everyone else just said they were from Clinton.

New Vienna rolled up quickly without warning. The speed limit didn't even change, as it would have for a town that still had some vibrancy. I slowed down when I saw a couple of old, two-story brick buildings on one side of a road and a deserted, ramshackle house on the other side. A cross street that at one time might have been the business address of choice now had nothing to show but vacant lots with thick accumulations of trash along fences. I saw boarded-up windows and "No Trespassing" signs. Not a "For Sale" anywhere. That hope had been abandoned, too.

I turned left at the only other cross street, drove two blocks down, and turned right onto Elm Street. From there I saw the church up ahead on the right side. Kevin's car was parked in the lot beside it. His Taurus, facing me, was running, and the windows were up as I had recommended. I drove down Elm Street and stopped in front of his car. I got out and went over. He shut off the engine and got out next to me.

"This is it," he said. His voice had a false bravado; I could hear a tremble in it.

We stood just shy of the church grounds. It was a good-sized church for a small, rural community and had probably been very nice in its heyday. The building's brick was deep red, and a cross still stood atop the steeple, but its arched windows were covered with plywood, darkened with age. The brick and the plywood were spotted with spray-painted graffiti, including a few Satanic symbols like 666, pentagrams, and broken crosses. Between us and the church was a garden, probably once well-tended. For some reason I imagined it with statues, now missing. Whatever beauty it had once had was choked by thick, overgrown weeds.

"You haven't gone inside, have you?" I asked.

"No."

We stepped through the weeds to try the side door to the church, but it was locked tight. "Let's check the front."

The front entrance faced Elm and therefore had its back to the county road that led in from Jasper. I was glad no one could see what we were doing.

At one time the church had double doors at the front; now a single sheet of graffiti-covered plywood covered the entrance. A door had been cut out of the plywood and hinges attached so it could swing. A latch had also been installed, but no lock. The door was held shut by a crucifix inserted upside down into the latch. I felt a tingle at my neck and realized it was from the Miraculous Medal I was wearing.

"Kevin, I'm not sure you should go in there with me."

"I got you this far," he said. "You're not leaving me out now." The words sounded braver than his voice.

"This is not a test of machismo, Kevin. You're only sixteen . . ."

I knew the minute it came out of my mouth it was the wrong thing to say. He jutted his chin forward, and his blue eyes looked defiant.

"How are you going to stop me? You might be stronger than I am, but you'll have to wrestle me down and keep me pinned, and then how are you going to get in yourself?"

Damn him for being so much like I was at his age.

Kevin reached past me for the crucifix in the latch. I grabbed his wrist and yanked his hand back. He got in my face. A tense moment passed between us.

"We shouldn't leave fingerprints," I said. "Let me get us some gloves."

I left him smiling as I ran back to the van and pulled out the emergency kit. I found two pairs of latex gloves, then got the flashlight from the glove compartment. I carried everything to the front of the church.

"Here, put these on," I said.

When he had managed to pull on the gloves, I said, "Ready?" He nodded. I pulled the crucifix out of the latch and swung the door open.

The smell of rotting flesh poured out of the church. I whirled around, took a few steps and gagged.

Grimacing, Kevin took the flashlight from my hand. "What's that smell?" he asked, shining the light into the darkened church.

"I'm guessing there are several dead things in there," I said. I spit into the overgrown lawn.

Kevin, apparently unaffected, started into the church.

Stomach roiling or not, I couldn't let him do that. I locked my arms around his chest and pulled him back.

"Let me go, Nick." His voice sputtered with anger.

I spun him around and took hold of his shoulders. "We have

to call the sheriff's department. And I don't want you here when I do that. Your name shouldn't be connected in any way with whatever we find here. For your own protection."

Kevin broke away from my hold. "I'm not going home until I find out what's inside."

"Whatever it is, you don't need to see it."

"I've been through the shootings at my high school. How much worse can this be? I can take it." He put his hands on his hips.

"With the massacre, you didn't have a choice. It just happened and you were there. This is different. You *have* a choice."

"And I choose to see it."

I glared at him.

He glared back. "You're not my father, you know."

"No, I'm not. But I can call your mother. Want me to do that?"

That stopped him for a moment.

Something gleamed at me from the ground. I bent down and found the crucifix from the latch. I must have dropped it when I was gagging. I put it in my back pocket for safekeeping.

Kevin switched to a different tactic. "So once I leave, you're going to call the sheriff's department?"

"I am."

"And are you planning to call them before or after you explore that church?"

He had me there. I hesitated before I said, grudgingly, "You know what I'm going to do."

"Then I'm going in, too. The price for my silence. I promise I won't be here when the sheriff arrives."

I didn't like it. Didn't like it at all. As the adult, I knew he shouldn't be going in there. But he'd found the place and led me here. He could easily have gone in without me.

"Do you have any plastic bags?" I asked.

Kevin scrunched up his face. "What?"

"Plastic bags like you get at the grocery, to tie around our feet. We don't want to leave any evidence that we've been trespassing."

Kevin raised an eyebrow. "I think so. Let's go back to my car."

The back seat of Kevin's car met my expectation of what any teenager's car would look like. There were empty fast food bags, crumpled up trash, whatever he'd needed to toss while driving. There were also several plastic grocery sacks. While Kevin climbed into the back seat to get them, I went to the van and retrieved a small bottle of scented hand lotion I keep in the glove compartment.

Kevin held up the sacks. "What do we do?"

"We're going to tie them around our shoes. Double bag them. That way we won't leave shoe prints if there's something sticky on the floor."

"What would be on the . . ." His voice faded as he realized what "something sticky" might be.

We walked back to the front of the church. When we got there, I lifted my foot, put it in a bag, and demonstrated how to use the bag's handles to tie it. After finishing, we stepped up to the church's plywood door, which had swung shut.

"I'm going to open it and shine a flashlight inside," I said. "Then we'll make a decision as to whether we go in." I pulled the scented lotion from my pants pocket and smeared a little below my nose. "First we need to prepare for the smell. It's an old coroner's trick." I gave him the bottle to do likewise. "And take an extra sack, just in case you need to throw up."

He refused the sack but put lotion under his nose. I decided not to push the sack issue. After all, I'd initially reacted to the smell, not him. When we were ready, I swung the door out. The smell was just as bad, but my stomach held. Kevin didn't flinch.

The flashlight shone into the darkness.

The door opened directly into the sanctuary; there was no entry hall. There were also no pews, just a wood floor. In fact, so many of the fixtures had been removed that it was hard to tell what denomination the church had been. Light seeped in from around plywood covering what appeared to be stained glass windows on either side of the church. In the center of the floor was a pentagram that looked to be about eight feet in diameter, with a black candle at each point. An altar, probably original to the church, had been moved into the middle of the pentagram. There were black lumps scattered on the floor beside the altar, surely the sources of the smell.

I stepped inside. Kevin followed. I swung the flashlight from side to side as I stepped, avoiding the blackened lumps. The plastic sacks on our feet made rustling noises. In a couple of places I had to pull a little harder to get my feet up—the sacks stuck to the floor. Although I was confident the sticky substance was coagulated blood, I bent down to check. The smell started to get to me again.

Kevin moved past me to the altar in the center of the pentagram. I shined the light on him. He poked tentatively at a lump on the altar. I saw a look of realization flash across his face, then horror. He made a gagging noise and ran past me back outside.

I caught up as he bent over and dry heaved. I put my hand on his back. "It'll be okay."

He regained his composure and wiped his mouth with the back of his forearm. "That was, that was . . . part of a dog."

I nodded. "You shouldn't have gone in. I was wrong to let you."

"It was my choice."

It may have been his choice in the beginning, but now it would be mine. Torn as I was between going back in, especially since I needed some photos, and taking him home, I really only had one choice. Kevin was sixteen. If Stephanie were sixteen, would I let her go back in? The fact that Kevin was male was irrelevant.

"Kevin, you don't have to be a man yet. Give yourself a little breathing room."

He started to say something, but I cut him off. "You're not going back in there. We're going back to your house. I'm calling the police, and I don't want you involved in any of this. The cops don't need to know you were here."

I don't know what I said that made a difference this time, but he didn't fight me. Maybe it was because I was leaving with him. I knew I had to do that because as defiant as he'd been, I didn't think he'd go on his own.

For just a moment I thought again about making Kevin stay outside while I took the camera in for photos. But if I changed my mind now, he'd fight me, and I didn't want to go through that. Plus, was it even necessary? I wouldn't be gone that long, and even if I was, it would be daylight for another six hours or more. What could happen?

To be sure I had some record, I snapped a couple of photos from the doorway. Then I closed the plywood door and held it in place while I patted my back pockets. Finding the crucifix, I inserted it into the latch right-side up, not upside down as it had been originally. I couldn't do that.

Kevin had removed the gloves and was in the process of removing the plastic sacks from his feet. I started removing my stuff, but in reverse. I wanted to keep the gloves on for a while.

"What do I do with these?" he asked, gingerly holding up the gloves and the sacks.

"Give them to me. We're going to dispose of them in a way that should protect us."

We returned to Kevin's car and I nabbed another plastic

sack. I shoved the gloves and our blood-stained foot protectors in it. "Follow me into Jasper," I said, "and stay close."

We made our way back to Jasper, fanning out in circles from the direct route, disposing of the gloves and trash bags. I wrapped them separately in innocuous-looking fast food bags and deposited one at each trash can I could find. At the last trash bin, in the parking lot of a Burger King, I left the car to check on Kevin. He rolled his window down.

"You okay?" I asked, searching his face.

"Yeah, I'm okay." He tilted his head inquisitively. "Why did you scatter the trash like that?"

"I don't want to make it too easy for someone to track down any evidence we were there. If the police suspect anything after I call them, it'll be difficult to find proof."

His eyes widened. "Do you really think they'll suspect us?"

I chuckled. Because I was a reporter and had come across evidence, I'd been a suspect in any number of investigations, even though the police knew there was no real reason I'd be involved in the crime. But Kevin didn't need to know that. "Probably not, but there's no sense in taking chances."

When we got back to Kevin's home, his mother's car was parked in the garage. I insisted on going with him to talk to her, and it was a good thing I did. Brenda Mueller was not happy.

"Where have you been?" she demanded, grabbing Kevin by the shoulders, then wrapping her arms around him in a fierce hug. "I've been worried sick! You've been gone a long time, and you didn't leave a note or call. Why didn't you answer your cell?" She stepped back so she could look him in the eye.

Kevin kept his head down as he fumbled in his pockets for the cell. He didn't find it. "I'm sorry, Mom. I must've left it in the car."

"He's been with me, Mrs. Mueller," I said. "If I had known he hadn't called, I would have insisted." I gave Kevin a cold stare, hoping to look as though I were reprimanding him. "But let's sit down. Kevin's found something that may be a clue to what happened to the missing pets. We need to call the police to tell them what he's found, but I think we should keep his name out of it."

Brenda's eyebrows shot up in alarm. She suggested we go into the living room. Kevin sat on the flowered couch, his mom next to him. I eased into a worn recliner. Everyone looked uncomfortable. I told the story, at least from where I'd come in. I emphasized that although it had been risky, Kevin had done a good thing by locating the site of the rituals. I stopped at the point where we opened the door to the church and smelled the atrocities inside.

"We decided to come back to Jasper before calling the sheriff's department," I said. "I thought Kevin should be safely out of the way so the police don't know he was involved. Otherwise, it could be difficult for him, especially if the people who did this find out who tipped off the police."

"Ohmigod, Kevin," she said. "I can't believe you went there. What were you thinking?"

"I'm trying to find out who hurt Buddy, Mom. And we need to stop it before more animals get hurt."

She seemed to take that well. In fact, I think it raised Kevin's stature in her eyes.

"In a church," she said, grimacing. "My God!"

"It's an abandoned church, and it looked like it's been vacant a long time," I said. "We don't know for sure what's inside now."

Kevin said, "Whatever it is, it smelled pretty gross."

Brenda turned to face me. "Thank you for bringing him home. And for keeping him out of this." She put her hand over Kevin's and looked at him. "You're brave, but don't ever do that again."

Kevin pulled away.

I interrupted. "I need to get back out there and call the Sheriff's Department. Kevin, you're going to be tempted to talk about this, but you really need to keep quiet. You can't even mention it to a friend who swears he won't tell a soul. At least until it's over."

Brenda Mueller's voice was shaky. "Please, Kevin, do what he says."

We said our goodbyes. I got back in the van and drove to New Vienna, working on what I was going to say to the police. I decided on the semi-honest route—telling enough true, traceable things that my story sounded absolutely plausible and letting them draw conclusions about the rest of it.

I would admit to being an investigative reporter, following leads trying to get to the bottom of what happened to Mr. Jangles and that I'd received a tip that something was happening at this abandoned church. I would tell them I came out here to check it out and that once I'd opened the door and had a whiff of what was inside, I'd decided to call the police.

The fact that there'd been a time gap between when I opened the door and when I called, could stay unspoken for now. Ditto the fact that I'd gone inside, although I decided if the police asked that question directly, I would tell them the truth. I'd keep Kevin out of it, whatever it took. And if anyone asked who'd given me the tip, I'd say that I needed to protect my sources, which was true.

When I pulled up at the church, I decided to take one more look inside. For one thing, I really needed better photos. I still had an article to deliver to the *Standard,* and there was no chance the police would let me get photos later. I stepped to the latch wearing another pair of latex gloves and started to pull the crucifix out when it hit me. The crucifix was upside-down again. Someone had been here since I'd left.

CHAPTER SIXTEEN

If they'd been here, they'd probably been inside, too. I wanted to check that out before I called the sheriff's department. I put the crucifix in my pocket again and opened the door.

The stench was still there, but not as bad. I shone the flashlight inside. The black lumps were gone from the floor and the altar. I checked my watch. I had been gone maybe an hour. Whoever had done this had to have been close by when Kevin and I entered the church, a thought which gave me goosebumps.

I closed the door and looked around outside. The cleanup crew might still be lurking in the neighborhood, watching. While the few business buildings in the area were abandoned and the six or seven homes nearest me either boarded up or falling down, there were still a couple of houses farther away that looked lived in. But I wasn't going to go knocking on doors. Not now. At this moment, I wanted the police involved.

The question was, what would I tell them, now that the disgusting lumps were gone? I switched the camera to display mode and checked the two photographs I'd taken before shuttling Kevin home. Though it was difficult to see from the tiny screen, I was certain I could show the police what had been there just an hour before.

But to what end? My camera would probably be immediately confiscated by the police. That, I could not afford. Not only did I need the two photos I'd taken for the *Standard*, but there were other photos on my camera, from the cemetery and from my visit to St. Aelred's, that I didn't want the police to have. So, I would, for the moment, need to pretend I had no such photos.

I opened the door again and slipped just inside, propping the door slightly ajar. The pentagram was still there with its candles, and I could see streaks on the floor that I was sure were blood. Good enough, I thought. The blood would confirm what I had seen. But I'd have to admit that I'd been in there, and that I'd been gone for an hour before I called the police. Anything else would involve a lot of lying, and while I didn't mind omitting a fact here and there, outright lies were never a good thing. I decided to be as forthright as I could, that I had taken home the person who had tipped me off, but I would leave Kevin's name out of it.

For now. He needed protection since it was possible he'd been recognized by the person who had cleaned up. But I couldn't give up his name to the police until I talked to him about it. And that needed to be handled in person.

But I had to get the police here, too. I was torn. I called Kevin at home and told him to lock the doors as a precaution and not to go out unless he had to, no explanation. He said he would. I told him I'd be by as soon as I could.

Careful not to stray too far from the door, I took photos of the altar, the pentagram with the candles, and close-ups of the bloodstained floor. What the flash didn't illuminate well could be lightened later with computer software. These I'd be able to use right away since they would be exactly what the police would see when they got here. Once I had a chance to download everything to my computer, I'd see about making a copy for the police so I could use the two photos I'd taken before the church was cleaned. Of course, if I did that, I'd have to admit withholding the photos from them initially. So maybe not. I'd have to see how this played out.

I closed the door, put the crucifix right side up in the latch, stored the camera in my van, and dialed 911 on my cell phone.

Despite my dislike of Johnny Day, I almost would have preferred dealing with the Jasper Police on this. But with New Vienna outside Jasper's city limits, the jurisdiction fell to the Dubois County Sheriff's Department. The dispatcher alerted a nearby sheriff, and in about fifteen minutes a squad car was sitting next to mine. The deputy's name was Karen Prechtel. She looked young and inexperienced, but she knew to call for backup once she had heard my story and had been inside the church. I tried to go in with her, but she made me stay out as a precaution. When she came out to make the call, I slipped back in. I used my flashlight on the walls of the church. There was graffiti all over, but the flashlight beam came to rest on one particular saying. Deputy Prechtel came in and started to scold me, but I cut her off.

"Look," I said. "Do you recognize that?"

She frowned but shifted the flashlight beam to where I was pointing. Our two flashlights illuminated the whole verse. " 'When night is at its lowest ebb/And Vict'ry's sung from heav'nly tower/Then evil casts its strongest web/And Satan has his finest hour,' " she read. "My God, it's the same verse that was splattered across the wall in the West Jasper High School library where they found the bodies of the shooters." She turned to me and flashed the beam on my face. "But why would it be here?"

I squinted at the sudden light. "Good question."

I wished I'd noticed the verse earlier and gotten a picture of it, but it was too late now.

Soon more deputies and investigators arrived. They swept me away from the church and questioned me about why I was there and what had caused me to be suspicious. I told them as much of the truth as I was prepared to reveal. They were gearing up to give me a hard time when I dropped the fact that I was working for the *Indianapolis Standard*. Thankfully they were a little wary of the press, although it didn't keep a thick-necked sheriff from going over the same questions with me time after time.

"Tell us again why you were gone an hour." He had a big potbelly, and he used it as a prop for his notebook.

"I had to get my source home before I called you."

"And that person's name?"

"I've told you. I can't reveal it."

"This person could be a part of the gang that was working in there."

"They weren't," I said, using the plural "they" so I wouldn't give away that Kevin was a guy.

"How do you know that?"

"This person's reactions to what was inside couldn't have been faked. They were just as repulsed as I was."

He drummed his fingers on his belly. "That's something we should determine, not you. Plus, this person needs to give us the names of his contacts. One of them could lead us to who did this."

I shook my head.

He insisted. "Someone who knew had to have started the rumor."

"I have to protect my sources."

They moved away and huddled again. I looked at my watch. It was nearing 3:30. At times like these when I'm really absorbed in a story, I forget to eat. At first I don't notice, but then it catches up with me. It had now officially caught up. I'd missed a mid-morning snack and then lunch. I needed to get out of here. Not to mention that I had an article to write. Ryan would be looking for one, and this would knock him off his chair.

My cell phone rang. Ryan, I thought. But it wasn't.

"Nicolo!" exclaimed my dad. "I've been reading your reports from Jasper about the missing girl's body. They are very good, but I am worried that you are there by yourself. Do you need my help?"

I needed help, but I wasn't sure I wanted my father to provide it. Too often his help meant more work for me, just keeping him out of trouble.

"Papá," I said. The deputy who was questioning me looked over. I smiled at him and gave him a small wave of my hand. Then I turned my back to him and talked to my father in a softer voice. "I'm in the middle of something. Can I call you back in a little bit?"

Dad charged right on. "I can come to Jasper anytime you want."

"No, Dad, that's not necessary. Really, I do want your help, but maybe we could talk about this later."

"You sound like you are in trouble. Maybe I should leave Clinton right away."

"No, don't do that." I had to think quickly, otherwise Dad would be on his way here within the hour. I was already worried about Stephanie and her sleepwalking; I didn't need Dad putting himself in a dangerous situation.

Someone tapped me on the shoulder. I turned to find Deputy Prechtel looking at me. "We need you to come back inside the church," she said.

"I'll be right there." I showed her my phone to indicate I was wrapping things up. I uncovered the speaker.

"Who was that you were talking to?" Dad said suspiciously. "It sounded like a woman. Is Joan there?" As bad as Dad's hearing is, sometimes he catches the most amazing things.

"That's a policewoman," I said. "I'm helping with a crime scene investigation right now."

"You don't usually have such good relations with the police," he said.

"Yeah, kinda funny, isn't it?" Deputy Prechtel had her arms

crossed. "Could you hang on just a second, Dad?"

Without waiting for him to answer, I covered the speaker again. "Really, just give me a moment," I told her. "What do you need?"

"The graffiti on the walls. You recognized the West Jasper verse. Maybe you know something about the others."

So there were more Satanic verses up there. It'd probably be better for them to contact Father Vince or Father Dan. The fact that Father Dan was the exorcist for the diocese popped into my head. That also led me to think about the burglary attempt on the relics he'd told me about. I tried to wave Prechtel off, but she wouldn't go away.

I switched to Italian. "Dad, this might be a good time to visit Aunt Augustina in Vincennes," I said.

"What?" he said, replying in Italian as well. I could hear the puzzlement in his voice as he tried to figure out what Aunt Augustina had to do with anything. "Why?"

"About a year ago there was an attempt made to steal some saintly relics that used to be kept in the Old Cathedral at Vincennes. I need to know more about it. It might be related to the story I'm working on."

"Really? You want me to go research it?"

"Absolutely. And I might have something else for you to look into." Prechtel tugged at my arm. "But I'll tell you about it later. When do you think you can get to Vincennes?"

"I will call Augustina right away," he said. Augustina was my mother's older sister. "I'm sure she would be up for a visit. I have not seen her in a year or so."

"Great. I'll call you later with the details."

"No, no. Let me call you. I've got your cell phone number, so I can get you anytime. You don't know where I will be." Dad was somewhat technology averse. He had learned how to use a computer, but he didn't want to carry a cell phone.

"Okay, but call me this evening, all right?"

He said he would. I hung up and slipped the cell phone in my pocket. Prechtel started toward the church. I followed her in. The police had put up lights and had opened the side door Kevin and I had found locked. I now saw the inside of the church clearly.

The heavy detective who'd questioned me earlier stood near the pentagram with a couple of plainclothesmen. The taller of the two was gesturing at the altar. He had a booming voice, and it carried easily in the nearly-empty building.

". . . definitely a Satanic sacrificial altar," he was saying. "Notice how it's oriented in this reverse pentagram. The top two points of the star represent a goat's horns, and the two on either side are his ears. The altar stretches across the center where the eyes would be located. The remaining point is the goat's beard."

As we passed by, I stopped to see what he was talking about.

"Why a goat?" asked the detective.

"It's a symbol for the Greek god Pan, often used to represent Satan."

Now that it was well lit, I wished I could take a picture of the pentagram and altar with the camera safely hidden in the van. I patted my keys self-consciously. "Have you had other experiences in the county with Satanic symbols?" I asked.

Everyone looked at me as though I were dirt. The tall, knowledgeable guy took a step forward. "None we're willing to talk to the press about."

"Hey, I found this place for you."

"No, your unnamed source found it." The fat detective crossed his arms and rested them on his stomach. "Maybe we could trade. You give us his name; we answer your questions."

I shook my head.

The tall guy walked around the back of the altar, placing it between me and him. He examined the now clear surface. "None of the things you claimed you saw are here. You sure you're not sensationalizing this for your paper?"

I was not going to take the bait. "The animal blood on the floor speaks for itself."

"How do you know it's animal blood?"

"I don't. But I'm sure your lab will confirm it."

The knowledgeable guy looked under and around the altar. "Did you see anything besides the flesh? Say, an *athame?*"

He stared expectantly for a moment. Maybe that was a test word I was supposed to know something about. I didn't. My blank look was genuine.

"What's that?"

"It's a ceremonial knife."

"What does it look like?"

"It's a short, double edged knife with a small handle, usually either black or red."

"I don't remember seeing anything like that."

The tall guy turned to Prechtel. "He's not likely to be of much help, but try him on the graffiti. See if he can come up with anything."

Having been rudely dismissed, I walked the perimeter of the sanctuary, Prechtel beside me. Most of the graffiti was the same—reverse pentagrams, 666's, broken crosses, and lots of profanity, but there were foreign words Prechtel said they didn't recognize. I did recognize one or two of them.

"This is Italian slang for the sex act." I pointed to the phrase. "I don't recognize the others, but this word here looks French, and this one might be Latin. These with the symbols could be Japanese or some Asian language. I'm guessing they're all variations of profanity."

"That would make sense," Prechtel said. "We've seen the German word used liberally."

I glanced around the room. "Someone must have done a lot of research to find out how to spell all of these."

Prechtel shook her head. "Probably a single website run by a twisted personality lists them all."

The deputy whose collar barely contained his neck walked up to us. "You can go now, but don't leave the Jasper area. We're not through with our questions yet."

"You know where I'm staying," I said.

Without waiting for either to reply, I walked quickly back to the van. The cell phone rang immediately. I flipped it open and looked at the number. Ryan.

"The story's coming," I said, without giving him a courtesy hello. "We've uncovered a church that's been used for Satanic worship. I've got photos and everything. I'm just leaving now."

Ryan paused. "That's great," he said, "but how does it apply to the missing body?"

"Well, we've got something of a link. The verse that was on the library wall in West Jasper has been written on the wall here. That's not conclusive, but it has to be related somehow. I mean, there were rumors that a Satanic cult was involved in the West Jasper massacre, but the police couldn't find evidence it existed. And now we've found evidence of a cult, just after Keri's body disappears."

"It'll make a good story, even if you can't link it directly. But you're behind the curve again. The *Times* has posted stories from your pal Sally Kaiser. It seems she's snagged a couple of interviews with the families of the West Jasper killers. They're considering a lawsuit against the Jasper Police for harassment. The police are trying to link them to the missing body. No one's saying what the evidence might be, but Kaiser says the harassment is real."

Damn.

CHAPTER SEVENTEEN

Ryan made it clear that I was playing catch-up and didn't have a whole lot of time. He told me to write up the story I had, then go after the information Sally Kaiser had already posted to see if I could do anything new with it.

But nothing was going to happen until I talked to Kevin. He and his mom had to know he might be in danger. I called him on the cell and was relieved to hear his voice. I told him I was on my way. I asked for his mom, and he told me she'd gone to work. Not much I could do about that, so I told him to sit tight. If he needed anything, he was to call me. I debated sending him to Janine and Hugo's house, but I wasn't that far away.

Kevin must've seen the van pull up outside his house because he opened the door while I was still coming up the walk. Hurrying inside, I pulled the door shut behind me and locked it.

Kevin's eyes were wide. "What is it?"

"When I got back to the church, things had been cleaned up. Someone went in right after we were there. They were watching us. I have to assume they saw your face. You might be in danger."

"They saw you, too."

"Okay, me, too. It's just that you're the one who lives in this area. They're more likely to know who you are. And you're only sixteen."

"You make it sound like I'm in fifth grade. I'm not. I'm a junior." Kevin stuck his hands in his pockets of his cargo shorts and paced.

"When you're older, you'll understand how really young sixteen is."

He stopped, like he had suddenly grasped the reality of his situation. "Do you really think they'd do something to me?"

"Hopefully not. At this point, the police are a much bigger threat to them. Other than revenge, they don't gain anything by hurting you. But we have to be careful."

"What should we do?"

"The first thing is, we're going to tell your mom. She needs to know the potential danger. She may want to contact the police. When does she get home?"

"She's working the three to midnight shift."

I sighed. "That's a long time."

"I don't want the police involved."

"Why not? They can provide you with protection. Plus, they can question your contacts and find out who's doing this."

He frowned. "I don't have what you'd call a real contact."

"Of course you do. Who led you to the church?"

"I just heard a bunch of talk." Kevin gave me a hard stare. "I'm not gonna give the police names of anyone who fed me the rumors they heard. Especially since I asked them. They're gonna know who told the police."

"You knew where to go to ask. That's a starting point."

He hesitated. "No."

I imagined the worst. "Where was it, Kevin?"

"What will you do if I tell you?"

"I won't know until I hear it."

Kevin's dog Buddy, who had been watching me with suspicion from around the corner, walked in and nudged Kevin with his nose. Kevin knelt on the hardwood floor and began to pet him. "I don't want the police to know. Can't you protect me?"

I rubbed my temples. "Not for any length of time. I'm really not trained to do that, and I've got reporting work to do, besides."

The truth was, on the way back from New Vienna I had mulled over the possibility that the police wouldn't have the manpower to provide much protection for Kevin. I had thought about getting a bodyguard; it was the only real alternative to the police. "I suppose we could get a bodyguard for you."

Kevin had never seemed more like a kid than when he looked up from petting Buddy and said, "A bodyguard? Cool!"

"Your mom may not think that's so cool. She'll probably prefer the police."

"No police," Kevin said. He was emphatic. Buddy growled at me. Like it was my fault Kevin was being unreasonable.

"Where did you hear the rumors, Kevin?"

"If I tell you, will you help me convince Mom to get the bodyguard?"

"That's between you and your mom. My vote still goes for the police."

Kevin stood up. "My friends and I hang out at a place called Game Central. It's where I heard about the rumors. I don't want the police to start coming there. It would wreck every-thing."

"Why?"

"We're into gaming. We play mostly sports games, like FIFA soccer. But there are other kids who play . . . games their parents don't like. We don't want the place to get shut down."

I didn't like the sound of that, but it wasn't my main concern. "We'll worry about that later. Your mom needs to know about the potential danger you're in. Now. It's too long before she gets off work."

"Mom's an emergency care nurse. She calls around 8:00 to check on me. She doesn't like me to call unless it's a real emergency."

We were arguing momentarily about whether this was a real emergency when my cell phone rang. It was Joan. "Where are you?" she asked.

"I'm at Kevin Mueller's house. It's been a difficult afternoon." I eyed Kevin. "His mother works until midnight, but I don't think it's a good idea for him to be here alone."

"What did you run out of the house for, earlier?"

"Kevin found an abandoned church in New Vienna where Satanic rituals have been held. We contacted the police, and now they're on the scene looking for clues."

There was silence for a moment. "This is for real?"

"It gets worse. It's quite possible Kevin was seen by someone in the cult. He may be in danger."

"Just a minute." I heard Joan talking with Janine. "Mom says to bring him over. She won't hear of him being there alone, not when we have four adults here."

"We'll be there in a few minutes."

I put the cell back in my pocket. Buddy must have decided I wasn't going to harm him, because he was now sniffing my shoes.

"Will you call your mom and leave a message?"

"I can't leave her a message telling her all this! She'll freak."

"All right. Tell her the Strassheims have invited you for dinner, and you're going to be over there. But tell her you really need to talk to her at eight o'clock."

"Okay."

Kevin pulled the cell phone out of a side pocket in his cargo shorts. He disappeared into another room to make the call.

In the meantime, I phoned the Franklin Iron Works gym to see if I could get hold of Mark Zoringer. He would know of a good bodyguard I could hire. Kevin and his mom needed to be watched over, whether or not the police were involved. If Brenda didn't want a bodyguard, I'd have him do it by stealth. I figured

I'd have to pay for the bodyguard initially, but one way or another I'd wrangle the *Standard* into paying for it. The story we were getting from this was just too good.

Mark couldn't do it himself, which I expected. "I've got a business to run here," he said, his low growl rolling over the background noise of clanging weights. "But I'll see if Miguel can do it. He's between jobs right now."

I vaguely knew Miguel, one of Mark's bodybuilding friends. He was strong, but that only goes so far. "Has he got any experience?"

"Miguel was a special forces guy in the Army. He also has a black belt in tae kwon do. He'll do a good job."

Mark said he would call Miguel and have him phone me. After we hung up, I briefly debated whether this was the right decision. Police or Miguel? If I remembered correctly, Miguel was short, wide, and multi-tattooed. He would not fade into the background in Jasper. But I didn't have a lot of choice.

Kevin made sure Buddy had food and water, and then locked up the house. I drove us over in the van, even though it was only four houses down. Safer that way, plus I wanted the van at the Strassheims'.

Janine and Joan were working on dinner, and Hugo and Stephanie were watching TV. After some explanations as to what had gone on that afternoon, I moved upstairs to hammer out a story for Ryan.

By 6:00 I'd finished the story, downloaded the photos, and sent the package electronically to the *Standard*. For the moment, I stuck to using the photos I'd taken *after* the church had been cleaned up. They still graphically demonstrated the story I'd written. The other photos, taken from the door, weren't as clear, but more to the point, if I used those I'd have to explain to the police why I had misled them. I wasn't ready to alienate them that much yet.

Before I joined the others for dinner, I logged onto the *Times* website to read Sally's articles. She'd been busy since we'd met this morning.

She'd managed to snag long interviews with the Fleischmans and the Goebels, whose teenaged sons had been responsible for the killings at West Jasper High School. Both families had been questioned twice since Keri's body had disappeared. They believed they were being unfairly harassed, and the Goebels were considering a lawsuit. While it was certainly no blockbuster article, it did shed light on what the police were doing and whom they suspected.

Sally's sympathies were with the families, I thought. She quoted liberally about the troubles they'd had since the massacre occurred. Much as I wanted to dismiss them, Sally had done a nice job with the articles. The Goebels and Fleischmans came across as families who had accepted the guilt and the hurt that came with knowing their sons' actions had torn other lives apart, yet were justified in asking why they had to be the suspects in this latest development. Hadn't they suffered enough?

She'd even managed to work in a quote from Father Dan. How was she managing to get to him when I had to wait forever for him to call me back? Favoritism to the local paper? I was getting tired of that.

The real coup, of course, was that she'd gotten the families to talk at all. Since the massacre, they'd refused time and again to be interviewed. Sally didn't mention anyone's current address, of course, but she noted that the Fleischmans had moved out of the area.

The Goebels still lived in Jasper but also had recently moved. Sally reported that the Goebel's younger daughter had been having problems at West Jasper High School and had transferred to the local Catholic high school. I wondered if Joan or Janine knew them or knew where either family lived. I needed to go back over some of the same ground Sally had covered if I was going to have something even remotely original for the *Standard*.

I logged off the Internet and made one more call, this one to the Jasper library. I asked the librarian in their archives area if she knew about any local prophets or prophecies. She told me she was a lifelong resident of the county and had never heard of such a thing, but that she would do a little searching. I thanked her and gave her my number before we hung up. Then I went down to supper.

I had told the group not to wait for me since I didn't know when I'd have the article done. Joan, Janine, Hugo, Stephanie, and Kevin were seated around the dining room table having ham, green beans, and cornbread. I joined them in mid-course, and it wasn't long before I could sense everyone was stiff and uncomfortable. Not because of me, I thought, or because of Kevin, who was doing his best to be personable. What we had seen in the abandoned church was the elephant in the room no one wanted to talk about. Especially with Stephanie there.

"So, did you get everything written and sent off?" Janine asked, passing me the plate of ham.

I nodded. "My story doesn't directly tie to Keri Schoening yet, but I think it's going to make people sit up and take notice about what's going on here."

Sally Kaiser's interviews were still on my mind. "Do any of you know much about the Fleischman or Goebel families? What happened to them after the shootings?"

"I used to be friends with Jaime Goebel until she transferred to Bishop Koenig High School," Kevin said. "She got tired of everyone treating her like dirt, like she was personally responsible because of her brother. She asked her parents to let her go to Koenig."

"She used to be active in the youth group at St. Barnabas,"

Janine added. "They moved to the other side of Jasper in the spring. I think they go to St. Joseph's now."

Hugo looked up from where he was spearing the remaining green beans on his plate. "What happened afterward was really hard on the family. The community blamed the parents, like they should have seen what was coming and taken steps to prevent it. Yeah, they should have done something, but we probably blamed them for not seeing stuff that any of us would have missed. No one thinks their son could be capable of what those kids did. Although with the Fleischman boy, there were some apparent signs."

"Kevin said something about him yesterday." I cut my cornbread in half and spread apple butter on it. "What was he like?"

"He was the creepy one," Janine said. "You'd see him around town dressed all in black with tattoos on his arms. He made me nervous."

I looked over at Kevin. "What kind of tattoos were they?"

"He had one that looked like a bunch of thorns going around his right bicep. And he had several snakes tattooed on his right forearm."

"Always had an angry scowl on his face, too," Hugo added, "like he was mad at the world and ready to take it on."

I bit into a piece of cornbread and savored the combination of crumbly sweetness with the slightly tart taste of the apple butter. I swallowed and said, "Sally Kaiser has written two articles for tomorrow's *Times* based on interviews with the Goebels and Fleischmans. She implies that the Fleischmans had to move, too."

"They moved out of town," Hugo said.

Kevin took a drink of milk and set the glass on the table. "I still see Eddie Fleischman around from time to time."

"Where did they move?" I asked.

"Vincennes," Janine replied. "Tim Fleischman had just gotten a job at the Toyota plant over in Princeton when the shootings occurred. They'd planned to move at the end of the school year but hurried it after all that happened."

"But why Vincennes?" I asked. Vincennes was a half hour away from Princeton. While that wasn't an extraordinarily long drive, why not move to Princeton?

"It was probably the first thing they saw on the market that fit their needs," Hugo said. "The housing market's been a little tight in Princeton since the Toyota factory opened."

That may have been the case, but I was willing to bet there were other reasons. Vincennes. Was it a coincidence that they had moved to the city where everyone believed the biggest collection of relics in Indiana was stored? While the move had been after the foiled attempt, this was still a fact I couldn't ignore. And I'd just sent my father there. Maybe I could keep him busy doing research.

I turned to Kevin. "Do you know where the Goebels live now? I'd like to see if I can interview them."

"I think I have their new address at my house."

"If he doesn't have it, I bet I can get it from someone at church." Janine was gesturing with her hands now, something she did only when she was excited. She definitely wanted to help. Whether it was because of the Schoenings or because she had the chance to be part of an investigation was unknown. "I can check after we finish doing the dishes."

"Mom, I'll do the dishes." Joan patted Janine's hand, which had come to rest on the table. "Nick, what about the Fleischmans? Don't you want to interview them, too?"

I nodded. "If anyone knows how to get hold of them."

Janine spoke up again. "No one in my circle really knew them or liked them all that much. I'd see Gloria, the mother, every once in a while when I went to my hairstylist, Franco. I suppose I could call him and see if he knows where she went."

Kevin had become strangely reticent.

"You said you still see Eddie Fleischman around?" I asked.

He looked at his nearly empty plate instead of me. "Yeah, but he keeps to himself."

"I'd like to talk to him. Maybe you could take me to where you've seen him."

He shrugged.

We were all looking at Kevin. Silence hung over the dining room. A little voice spoke up. "Grandma, can I have a cookie?"

It wasn't that funny, but we laughed anyhow. Everyone but me had finished eating. We had been so focused on how to get information on the two families, we had forgotten the niceties of dinner.

Janine pushed herself away from the table. "Of course, Sweetheart, how could I have forgotten?" She moved her plate into the kitchen and returned with a platter of peanut butter cookies, which we passed around.

Kevin's phone started ringing. He looked at the display. "It's Mom." He got up with three cookies in his hand and went into the living room to answer it. I excused myself from the table and followed him, thinking I should be there for support.

"So, you know how Nick and I left the church after we learned there were dead things in there?" Kevin was saying into the cell. "Well, when Nick got back it had all been cleaned up. That means somebody saw us. So Nick thinks I might be in danger, although I don't really think so."

I could hear the buzz of his mother talking very fast.

"Yeah, he called the police. They came out and took pictures at the church and stuff. But he kept me out of it like he said he would. They don't know I was there."

Brenda buzzed some more.

"No, I don't want anyone to know, not even the police," Kevin said. "Nick said he could get me a bodyguard. I think that's a better idea."

Brenda must not have agreed because Kevin held the phone away from his ear and winced. When the voice had calmed down, Kevin put the phone back to his ear. "Nick's here. Why don't you talk to him?"

Kevin covered the mouthpiece. "No police. Talk her into the bodyguard. If you do, I'll take you to Game Central tonight."

So Kevin was not above bribery.

"How could you do this to my son?" she demanded. "Put him in danger like this?"

"Whoa. I did not put him in danger. He found the church himself. I do agree that, at sixteen, he shouldn't have done it. But he's got good instincts, and I think he'll make a fine reporter someday. The question now is, how do we protect him until this is over?"

Kevin was standing there mouthing the words, "No police," and shaking his head at me.

Brenda asked if I thought the police would put an officer with Kevin all day long.

I turned around so I wouldn't have to watch Kevin. "I'm sure they'd like to do that, but it's a question of manpower. The Jasper police have their available officers tracking Keri Schoening's body, so I don't think they'll be able to help. The sheriff's department has jurisdiction over investigating the cult at the church, but you live in Jasper, which means this is a gray area. Plus, they don't know about Kevin yet since I haven't told them. I don't know how they'll respond. The fact that he's only sixteen might help."

Kevin, who had come around to where I could see him, made a face at me when I said his age again.

"Just for the record, Brenda, I think I can get a bodyguard down here from Indianapolis tonight. If you agree, I'll stay with Kevin until he gets here. My paper is going to stand the cost of this." I trusted I could talk them into it. "Kevin's finding is a major story."

There was some commotion on the other end of the line, and I could hear people talking to Brenda. The noise suddenly muted and I guessed she had put her hand over the speaker. Moments later she came back on.

"I don't have much time to make a decision. Please put Kevin on the phone."

After a moment listening to her, Kevin said, "Yes, Mom, I'd rather have the bodyguard. Yes, I'll stay with Nick. I promise." There was another pause. "Yes, I'll be careful. I love you, Mom. Thanks."

Kevin breathed a sigh of relief. "She said okay."

"I'm going to hold you to your promise to take me to Game Central. Tonight."

He chewed on his lip. "We can go about 8:30. My friends ought to be there by then."

"Is that where you've seen Eddie Fleischman?"

Kevin's mouth turned down. He looked like he was losing a battle to me and didn't like it. "Yeah. He comes late, just about the time we leave. Maybe a little before."

Once he'd spilled his guts, Kevin seemed to warm to the topic. I could see a reporter's curiosity in his eyes. "I've watched Eddie when we've been there together. He plays really violent games, the ones you have to be at least seventeen for. Eddie's in my grade, but it's possible he's that old—you know, if he was held back. I asked a friend who works in the school office to check his birthday, and she said he isn't seventeen yet. Lately when Eddie's there, he disappears into a back room."

"What's in the back room?"

"We don't know. We've tried to get in when the manager was distracted. It's locked."

"How is it that Eddie gets in?"

"Money, we think."

"Any rumors about what's back there?"

Kevin shifted uncomfortably from one foot to the other. "We think it might be underground games."

I may not know video games, but anything that has the word "underground" associated with it is usually bad in one of two ways. "Games so violent or sexual the general public shouldn't know about them?"

"Uh-huh."

Ought to be an interesting night.

CHAPTER EIGHTEEN

The Jasper librarian returned my call and said her initial investigation into county history hadn't yielded anything about local prophets or prophecies. She made it sound like she was busy and had spent enough of her time on it already. I guessed asking her to pursue it further wouldn't net me anything else, so I thanked her and hung up. Then Mark Zoringer called to let me know Miguel was available and would be in Jasper by midnight. I gave him directions to the Mueller's house and asked him to have Miguel call me on my cell before he arrived. Miguel needed some kind of introduction. The last thing I wanted was for him to show up at the Mueller's at the same time Kevin's mother came home from work. With his build and his tattoos, he'd scare her half to death.

Of course, this arrangement still left me taking Kevin to Game Central without backup, but it was a public place and I had 911 on my speed dial. Plus, Kevin's friends would be there. He had called them to make sure.

With an hour or so to spare, Kevin and I excused ourselves into the living room where Hugo and Janine have a computer. Kevin was going to get on the Internet so he could acquaint me with some games. Because the Strassheims have a dial-up connection, I figured there'd be no way we could download the games. I booted up my laptop. There's a wireless card in it, and if any of the neighbors had a wireless Internet connection in their house, I might be able to piggyback. Sure enough, someone did. Under the circumstances, I ignored the ethics of this situation.

The first game site we visited was for soccer. I hadn't played a video game since I left college and was amazed at what Kevin showed me. The players looked almost human. He could choose from 300 teams, a bunch of international soccer stadium venues. He could even control players who didn't have the ball. He explained that he and his friends could play each other or form teams to play other teams.

He moved into another site and showed me a football game that had similar features. Again I was impressed with the realism that had been built into the game—when people got hit, they reacted like real football players.

Kevin said war games were a big attraction at Game Central. We sampled one or two of those. What disturbed me most was the amount of blood in them. A kill could be gruesome.

"I can't believe what I'm seeing." I was looking over Kevin's shoulder at the screen. "That guy you killed couldn't possibly have any blood left in his body, the way it spilled all over the ground. Doesn't that bother you?"

"Maybe a little."

"A little? Isn't that his kidney on your sword?"

"It's a video image, Nick. It's not real. But like I said, we don't play these games much. We'd rather play sports."

"What's the rating on this game?"

He spun around in the chair. "Actually, it's only 'T,' for teenagers. It's worse for 'M.' You have to be at least seventeen."

I could quibble about whether the ratings were strict enough, but sadly, I knew that some parents didn't care anyway, as long as the games kept their kids busy. Store owners might have incentive not to care, either, as long as they kept their customers. "Do they enforce those ratings at Game Central? You said earlier Eddie Fleischman had gotten around it."

Kevin squirmed. "Game Central is a great place. We don't want it to shut down. Most of us abide by the rules. When you log onto a game, they check the rating against the profile you created the first time you were there. So if you were honest about your birthday then, it would keep you honest. But as far as I know, no one checked to see if I entered my real birth date. It might be easy to modify your profile, too, even if you started out being honest."

As capable as some kids are with computers, if they wanted to play a game outside their rating, they could find a way.

I agreed to reserve judgment about Game Central until after we'd been there.

About 8:30 Joan and I put Stephanie to bed, hoping it would be a quiet night for her with no more seeing dead teenagers playing with Mr. Jangles. She said her prayers and turned over, settling in easily. We kissed her goodnight and left.

After saying goodbye to Joan and suggesting she not wait up, I got Kevin and drove the van to one of the old storefronts in the original downtown area, on the opposite end of Sixth Street from the police station. The two-story building was gray stone with large display windows on either side of the main door. A drab beige awning hung over the sidewalk. There were no lights anywhere that I could see in the building, and the "open" sign was not lit.

I pulled up in front. "It looks closed."

"This is the computer repair shop he operates during the day. Game Central is in the basement. The entrance is around the back."

Kevin said we could either park where we were and walk through a short alleyway or drive around the back. The alley didn't look like trouble, but I drove to the back parking lot anyway. It was packed with cars.

"How many people come here?" I asked, maneuvering into

195

the only parking spot I could find, in the back row between two pickup trucks, one of them a red Toyota that seemed vaguely familiar.

"In the summer, it's crowded even on weekdays. During the school year, it's only like this on weekends."

I let Kevin get out of the car and then reached across to the glove compartment and pulled out a set of lock picks, just in case I got a shot at the locked door Kevin had mentioned. The picks had been given to me by my Uncle Angelo, the black sheep of the family until he'd gone legit as a locksmith. He'd included some lessons on how to do unauthorized entries. I slipped them into my pocket.

We walked over to the back entrance. From the rear, the building was the same solid gray stone as the front, but there was more of it since there were no windows except for two tiny ones on the second floor. We took one step onto the stoop, where a single porch light hung over the metal door. The sun hadn't quite set yet, so we could still see well, but I wondered how well lit this area would be in another hour.

Kevin smiled cheesily and waved to the small surveillance camera next to the porch light. He turned to me. "I'm never sure if anyone's watching, but I love to do that." He opened the door and I stepped onto a dimly lit landing with stairs leading down into a basement. Something was swirling around at the bottom of the stairs. The rest of the basement, at least what I could see of it, was dark. Kevin closed the door behind us.

I went into protective mode and blocked him from going into the basement. "There's no one here."

Kevin laughed. "It's dark so people can see the screens, Nick."

He elbowed past me. I followed him into the basement.

Halfway down the stairs I realized the swirling mist was some kind of man-made fog. "Dry ice," Kevin said, seeing me swipe at the air. "Cool, huh?"

In a scary, atmospheric way, it was. We reached the last step, and I could see that Kevin was right about people being there. There were ten computer stations lining each of the two long walls of the basement. An eerie glow emanated from their screens, illuminating the faces in front of them. Down the middle of the room were four large desktops, two of them with groups of three stations, the other two empty. In total, there were twenty-six computers.

"Kevin, we saved you a spot," someone called.

My eyes adjusted to the dim light, and I saw an empty chair at one of the stations to the left. Kevin took the seat. I stood behind him.

"This is Nick," Kevin said to the guys on either side of him. "He's a friend. He came to see what we do here."

They both said "hi," but neither moved to shake my hand. Their hands firmly held joysticks, their eyes fixed to the screens in front of them.

"Login," one of them told Kevin. "We're playing a team from Indianapolis."

I watched as Kevin got into the game. The graphics were amazingly real. Kevin and his friends took the positions of different players kicking the ball around the field. I began wandering around the room, seeing what games others were playing and looking for the locked door Kevin had spoken of earlier.

I stopped behind a kid I guessed to be thirteen. He was controlling an ogre on-screen who was busily dismembering a twenty-something human male. The flesh wounds were frighteningly realistic, and blood was everywhere. I couldn't hear anything because the sound went directly into the kid's headphones, but I guessed it was awful. The agony on the man's face was wrenching. I was trying to control my horror when a stringy-looking guy about thirty rushed over and tapped me on the shoulder.

"I'm the manager, David Haag," he said. He put out his hand. "I don't think we've met."

I turned from the bloodletting. "Nick Bertetto, I'm a friend of Kevin Mueller's."

In the glow of the computer screens, his face seemed gray and his lips black.

"This your first time to a LAN gaming center?"

I must have looked as out of place as I felt. "A *land* gaming center?"

"No, L-A-N, local area network."

I squinted at him.

"It means the games are located on my central processor, and I feed them to the individual stations."

He might as well have been speaking Japanese.

He tried again. "It's a powerful processor, so a lot of them can play together at the same time. It's like having a team of players hooked to an Xbox on steroids."

I knew what an Xbox was. Joan's brother's kids were crazy about theirs.

"I'm not familiar with a lot of these games," I said. "They seem . . . very realistic."

He nodded, and I noticed that his hair moved in clumps, like it either had gel in it or needed to be washed. I didn't want to guess which. "The industry's advanced a lot in the last few years," he said. "It's growing, too. Total revenues from video games are expected to surpass the music industry in a year and a half."

"Do you monitor what the kids are playing?"

Other parents must have asked the same question because his response was automatic. "Absolutely. The first time here they have to create a profile, and I make sure their correct age is entered. After that, any game they play gets checked against their age."

I knew all about the profiles from Kevin's comments. "Who determines the content ratings? This kid here couldn't be more than thirteen, and his game is pretty graphic."

Haag walked me over to a bookcase that contained a variety of video game CD cases. He picked one up and showed it to me.

"The Entertainment Software Rating Board rates the games. They also explain the video content, why they gave it the rating they did." His finger pointed to the big "E" in a black box on a CD case for a football game. "The 'E' stands for everyone."

"And the most forbidden ones would be marked . . . ?"

"A, for adults only."

"Do all games get rated?"

"Yes. All of the games you'll see at a retail store are rated by the ESRB."

"Is that the only way to get a game?"

"No, you can download some of them off the Internet."

"Will those be rated?"

"Sure."

"What about underground games?"

He ran his fingers through his hair. "Look, all the decent ones are rated. Kids would have to surf the Internet to find those other kinds of game, and you can see we don't allow surfing here, only playing. It's their parents' responsibility to stop them from doing that on their home computer, if that's what you're getting at."

He knew what I was getting at and had skillfully avoided the question of whether he had personal knowledge of the illicit games. At this point, pursuing it further would risk Kevin's standing, so I dropped it for now.

On the legal gaming side, though, Haag still had economic incentive to look the other way if the kids wanted to play games outside their rating while they were at his store. "How much does it cost for the kids to play here?"

"If they're using my machines, six dollars an hour. If they're using their own machines," he pointed to the middle tables where the non-uniform computers were located, "three dollars an hour."

"Some of them bring their own computers?" These were *not* laptops. "Isn't it cumbersome to carry them around and hook them up every time?"

He walked over to the middle table nearest the stairs. "The guys who are really into gaming build their own computers. It enables them to put in the latest processors and video cards at much less cost than if they had to buy them assembled. A few of them choose to keep one here and have another at home. Adam does that, don't you, Adam?"

A blonde chubby guy, probably early twenties, glanced up from the helicopter he was guiding into a combat zone. "Damn right. It's the only way to get a decent machine. With mine, I can have two different games loaded and running at the same time." He resumed fighting, sending two helicopters into flames whose missiles had just missed him.

His computer tower was wide and squat. Although I couldn't be sure in the dark, the case appeared to be translucent. It looked like parts of the internal machine were glowing.

"How much would a typical computer like this cost?" I asked.

Adam answered without looking up. "Probably over $1,600 if I bought it on the market. I paid maybe $700 for the parts." When he listed the manufacturer of his processor, video card, and motherboard, none of the names meant anything to me.

Having bought a new computer a year ago, I knew that $700 in the retail market would get you a decent machine, but nothing that could operate the way his did.

I looked at the number of kids at the identical machines on the outer rows. They were full. Twenty kids times $6 an hour meant he was grossing, at minimum, $120 an hour, a little more if we included the ones who brought their own computers. "Do you have to pay for rights to have the games on your processor?" I asked Haag.

"No, I don't. The players are the ones who pay to play the game. They subscribe on a monthly basis. That's typically around 15 bucks."

"Really? How many games do they subscribe to?"

"Usually, three or four."

I looked down at Adam, the chubby guy who had built his own computer. He was old enough to have a full-time job. But what about all the kids who were still in school? When you added up their hours at Game Central, plus fees for the games, it was a tidy sum. Where were they getting the money? Their parents? I'd have to ask Kevin about that later.

In the meantime, I needed to try to find that back room. I shook Haag's hand. "Thanks for the information, David. Do you mind if I just wander around, watch people play?"

"I don't mind, but it's a lot more fun to try your hand at the games. Let me know if you want to give it a shot. I can help you get set up."

I thanked him again and moved on. Haag went to a cubicle office in a back corner of the room. It might have been my imagination, but I thought I could feel his eyes on me as I went from station to station. Of course, since I could hardly see three feet away from the glare of a computer screen, let alone across the room, I couldn't check. I sidled over to Kevin and bent down to whisper, but he had headphones on. I lifted them off. "Where's the back room you were talking about?"

Kevin looked around to make sure no one was watching. "Midway on the side across from us. See the break between the two batches of computers? There's a door there. But it's always locked."

I casually turned to look. There was a significant gap between five computers on one side and five on the other. I could almost make out a door frame. "I see it. Not to worry, I'm good with locks. I'll be back."

The only trick was that the door was fairly close to the office cubicle where Haag sat. Not much of a chance he'd give me the time I needed to pick the lock, but I wanted to see the door.

I wandered over to the other wall and started down the row, watching each player for a minute or two. When I got to the last station before the gap, I lingered a little longer. My head faced forward but my eyes were on the door. In the lack of light, it looked to be metal and painted a dark color, maybe brown.

The door was at least as old as the building, with an antique lock that required a skeleton key. I almost laughed out loud. I remember Uncle Angelo saying those locks were easy to pick, but he'd never showed me how to do it since so few of them were in use. His set of picks, secure in my pocket, didn't have anything shaped for this.

I decided to take my chances that it might not be locked. I walked over, twisted the door knob, and pulled. Nothing. Haag was by my side in a flash.

"Can I help you with something?"

"I was looking for the restroom. Isn't this it?"

Before he could answer, the door opened. I was still holding the knob, so I pulled it back wide to let the person out.

A large, husky kid exited. He was an inch taller than me and probably seventy pounds heavier, pounds he carried mostly in his thick midsection. He wore a black, Insane Clown Posse T-shirt untucked. It hugged the fat around his chest and arms, and rode so high around his big belly I could see skin. I don't think he cared. He seemed surprised to find the door held open. He went out and I slipped in.

Haag was right behind me. He put a hand on my shoulder to

stop me. "This isn't the restroom. You're not allowed in here." His voice was sharp.

I looked around. At one time it was probably a large supply closet. Now it was stripped to the walls with a large table in the middle and three computer monitors on it, similar to the setup in the main room for those who brought in their own computers. All three monitors were on, all of them facing away from the door, and I couldn't see what was on them. In the glow of the farthest one, I could see a face. As my eyes tried to focus on him, he ducked down under the table.

"Not the restroom?" I tried to appear befuddled, which was not too difficult right then. "Where is it?"

"Out here," he said, using his hand on my back to steer me back through the door. When he had closed the door behind us, he pointed to a door on one side of the basement stairs. "There." It was clearly labeled RESTROOM.

"I'm sorry. What was that room?"

"It's for preferred customers."

"What do they do in there? On-line gambling?"

"No, they don't. It just offers them more privacy for their gaming. My highest speed processor runs those machines exclusively."

"Sorry again about the mix-up." I started to walk away.

"The restroom?" He pointed to it again.

"Right!" I said. I went in and stayed a couple of minutes, just to make it look good. While I was in there, I heard something akin to two elephants stampeding. I flushed, washed my hands, and came out.

I found Kevin back at his terminal. He looked like he was only half-heartedly playing soccer, and his headphones were off. "Did you see Eddie Fleischman?" he whispered when I got close.

"The big kid who came out of the locked room?"

"Yeah, he and another guy from the room just left. They were in a hurry."

"Any idea why?"

"Not really. But David went in the room after you left, and the three of them came out. They were having some kind of discussion, and then Eddie and the other guy charged up the stairs."

"I thought I heard a thudding when I was in the restroom."

My cell phone started vibrating. I opened it and looked at the number. Miguel. He said he was outside the city limits. I gave him directions to Game Central and told him we would wait inside.

Ten minutes later Miguel came down the stairs two at a time, his weight creaking the boards. The noise had everyone watching in our direction. Miguel put out his thumb like a hitchhiker and said, "Upstairs."

He went ahead of us and gave the parking lot a quick check before he allowed us beyond the doorstep. "There were two guys waiting here. Don't know if they were looking for you or not, but I chased them away. One of them dropped this," he said.

He handed me a short knife with a small handle and a sharp wavy blade. I had never seen one like it before, but I was fairly certain I knew what it was.

An athame. The knife that had been described to me back at the abandoned church, used in Satanic ceremonies.

CHAPTER NINETEEN

I took the red-handled knife from Miguel and turned it over in my hand. "This is a sacrificial knife they use in Satanic ceremonies. It's called an athame."

"The fat kid dropped it." Miguel made a quick, chopping motion with his hand. "After I persuaded him he really didn't want to use it."

Kevin stared at Miguel as if he were an otherworldly creature. In some ways he looked it. Miguel was an inch shorter than Kevin and wearing one of those compression T-shirts that show off hugely developed muscles. I think Kevin was trying to comprehend that Miguel and his muscles were real.

"I'm Miguel," he said, holding out his hand. "You must be Kevin."

Kevin shook his hand. "You're my bodyguard?"

Miguel turned to me. "Catches on fast."

"He's been through a lot recently."

"How much do you weigh?" Kevin asked him.

"Enough," Miguel answered. "For now, we need to get you two out of this unsecured area. I'll take Kevin back to his house with me. My car is over there." He pointed in the general direction of my van.

"I'm over there, too."

"How did you know what kind of knife that was?" Miguel asked.

I brought him up to speed on what had been going on, how

the animal mutilation didn't connect directly to the missing body but seemed like it should. I also told him what Kevin found and why he needed a bodyguard.

"Before we go to Kevin's house," he said, "why don't you lead me around and show me where all these things are taking place? I should know the location of everything that's relevant to this case."

I looked at my watch. It was close to 10:00. Kevin's mom was due home shortly after midnight, so we had plenty of time to hit the highlights and still get home before her. I wanted to make sure Miguel checked the house over before anyone went in.

Kevin and I talked through a quick list of what Miguel should see. Just as I got in the van, the cell phone rang.

"Nicolo, I am at Augustina's house now," Dad exclaimed too loudly. Sometimes I think his hearing loss makes him do that; other times I think he's just excitable. "You said to call you tonight. What is it you want me to look for again? Something about a break-in at the Old Cathedral?"

It took me a few moments to refocus my attention. "It happened about a year ago, Dad. Thieves were trying to get to the relics that used to be stored in the church. I need you to dig up all you can on what happened exactly—when it was, what the investigators found, and the current status of the investigation."

"That is all?" he asked. He sounded downcast.

"I don't know what could be important, so get everything you can. I suppose this sounds really boring to you."

"I was not doing anything at home, so I guess this is better than that."

"Here's something else," I offered. "See if the name Richard O'Brien comes up in connection with the break-in. He's a relics hunter who may have something to do with the disappearance of Keri Schoening's body. Also, the family of Drew Fleischman, one of the West Jasper shooters, moved to Vincennes a few months ago. If you find anything on either O'Brien or the Fleischmans, I'd like to know."

"Okay. Where should I start?"

"Start with a visit to the Vincennes library. They should be able to call up any articles from the *Vincennes Sun* about the break-in. Also check over the last two years for articles that mention Richard O'Brien or any member of the Fleischman family. If you have to pay to make copies, keep the receipts and I'll reimburse you. After that, call the police station and try to get the status of the break-in investigation, or go down to the Cathedral and see if you can talk to one of the priests there. They might know something."

He paused. "You're sure this will help you?"

I wondered if Dad was on to some of my past tricks to keep him busy and out of harm's way. "Dad, if I weren't so tied up here, I'd do it myself."

"Okay. I will report to you tomorrow."

"*Grazie, Papá. Vi devo uno.*" For all that legwork, I really would owe him one.

With that settled, I started the van. Miguel and Kevin followed. We went to the high school where the shootings had taken place, the cemetery from which the body had disappeared, and the abandoned church where the rituals had occurred. At each stop, Miguel got out, paced around, and asked questions. By the time we got back to Kevin's house it was 11:30. No sign of Brenda Mueller yet, but she wasn't expected for another half hour.

Miguel made us wait in the van until he'd checked the premises inside and out. It took him awhile, and I was so tired I'd almost fallen asleep by the time he got back.

We gathered in the living room. Kevin was far from being tired. He asked Miguel questions about how much he could lift, when he started bodybuilding, and how he became a bodyguard. Miguel was good-natured in his answers. Kevin was about to ask yet another question when his face suddenly went pale.

"Where's Buddy? He should be here. Something's wrong! Buddy!"

There was silence in the house.

Kevin called louder. "Buddy!"

He stood up to leave the room. Miguel quickly grabbed him.

Kevin tried to pull away. "Buddy always comes to greet me when I get home." His voice pitched up. "I didn't notice right away because you guys were with me."

"Didn't you let him outside before we left for the Strassheims'?"

"Yeah, but he came back in right after he finished."

I thought a moment. "Maybe he's afraid because we're here." After all, Buddy had found me a little disconcerting earlier in the day. He could be even more scared if he'd seen Miguel.

Kevin pointed into the hall. "If that were it, he'd be just around the corner."

Miguel let Kevin go but followed closely behind.

There was no dog in the hall.

"Buddy?" Kevin called again, his voice now full of fear. He started down the hall.

Miguel got around Kevin and blocked his path. "Stay with Nick," he said. "I'll go look. Buddy's not dangerous, is he?"

Kevin shook his head.

"No," I said, "but he'll be scared. Let Kevin be the one to approach him if you find him."

I put an arm around Kevin and pulled him back into the living room.

Kevin sat next to me on the couch. "He'll find him, won't he? What if something's happened to Buddy?"

"I don't know. Let's try to keep calm until Miguel comes back."

Minutes went by as Miguel searched. For a man of his size, Miguel was light on his feet. I didn't hear him at all until he stuck his head in the living room. "Broken window in the south bedroom. I didn't notice it earlier. It's a small hole. They must've used it to unlatch the window, come in, take the dog, and then leave by the back door. The door locks itself when you close it."

"Anything else missing?" I asked.

"Nothing obvious. Kevin, let's take a look."

The three of us searched the house, upstairs and down. Kevin said he didn't think anything else was gone.

He was trying hard to stay composed when Brenda Mueller arrived home. She entered through a door in the kitchen. Kevin had heard her car in the garage and was waiting for her.

"Mom, they took Buddy!"

Still clutching her purse, she reached for him and he let her hold him. As Miguel and I approached he squirmed out of her arms, though. Brenda glared at me. "Who took Buddy?"

"We don't know. If I had to guess, I'd say it was Eddie Fleischman and someone he had with him. They tried to attack us in the parking lot at Game Central, but Miguel stopped them."

Brenda's gaze moved from me to Miguel. "You're the bodyguard?"

Miguel could have made another smart comment, but thankfully he didn't. "I am. It's nice to meet you."

She nodded. "How did they get in?" She directed this at me.

"Back window. They broke it."

"Oh, God. They were in our house."

Kevin spoke up. "What will they do to Buddy?"

Neither Miguel nor I dared to answer that question right away. Finally Miguel nudged me.

"Probably nothing in the short term. At least, I hope. They took him for a reason. It could be to scare us, could be to punish us for finding Eddie or suspecting him. Could be to buy our silence. My guess is, we'll hear from them soon."

"Shouldn't we call the police?" Brenda asked.

Miguel gave me a questioning look.

"Yes, I think so," I said. "You should report the break-in and the missing dog. It's relevant to the animals case they're investigating. This also may be a good time to fill them in on Kevin's involvement in finding the site of the Satanic rituals. When he tells them he heard about it at Game Central and what happened there tonight, it would give them another reason to suspect Eddie Fleischman."

Kevin immediately began shaking his head. "Won't they be more likely to hurt Buddy if they find out we told the police?"

"Anything is possible. We don't even know for sure it was them."

Brenda dropped her purse on the dining room table and rubbed her forehead.

"Mom, we can't take the risk they'll hurt Buddy."

"And I can't take the risk they'll hurt you," she snapped.

Kevin put his hands on his hips. "I've got Miguel. And Nick." Suddenly I'm the afterthought.

"I'm all for calling the police," I said. "They have to know we'd do that. They didn't leave us any threats telling us not to."

Almost as if they were listening to us, the phone rang. We all looked at each other. There is nothing quite so foreboding as a phone going off in the middle of the night.

Brenda walked a few paces to where a phone hung on the wall. She took a deep breath and picked up the receiver. "Hello."

Even from six feet away I could hear the sudden yelp of pain from a frightened dog on the other end of the line. Then a male voice with an exaggerated deepness came on. "We've got your

210

dog. Don't tell the police; don't tell anyone. We'll call with instructions tomorrow."

The dog yelped again, the sound sending a chill down my spine. Then the phone went dead.

We sat around for another hour or so, explaining to Brenda what had happened that evening and debating our next move. Miguel was kicking himself now for not bringing us straight back to the house, which, he said, probably would have prevented the intruders from taking the dog. That is, if the intruders were really Eddie Fleischman and his accomplice and if they had come after Miguel disrupted them in the Game Central parking lot. I tried to reason with him that there were too many unknowns and that the dog could have been taken while Kevin and I were at Game Central before Miguel arrived. There was no way to know what would have been the right thing to do. But Miguel was a perfectionist. It didn't help either that Kevin, who had been in awe of Miguel, was now so upset over Buddy's disappearance that he'd become sullen and withdrawn. He wanted someone to blame. His quiet disapproval laid that blame on Miguel.

Finally Brenda said that, in deference to Kevin, we weren't going to do anything until we heard from the dognappers again. Then she told us she was going to bed and didn't want to see any of us until morning. I was more than ready to go back to the Strassheims', and Kevin was also letting out big yawns. Miguel seemed wide-awake. That was good, because I knew that he would be keeping watch for what was left of the night. I said my goodbyes, got in the van, and drove the short distance back to the Strassheims'.

No one was up when I came through the door, which was especially good considering I'd been worried about Stephanie sleepwalking again. Though I was tired, I decided it would be best if I typed some notes into my laptop before I forgot anything. I sat at Hugo's desk in the living room, opened a blank document, and had a page or so done when I fell asleep in front of the screen.

I was jolted awake when Joan began massaging my shoulders. "Hey, if you're tired, you should sleep in the bed," she said.

I calmed down when I realized who it was. "I was just trying to make sure I didn't forget anything overnight."

She put her arms around me. "Did you get it done?"

"No." I read what I had written, Joan doing the same over my shoulder. In one of my recap paragraphs, I mentioned the two shooters in the massacre, Ben Goebel and Drew Fleischman, which brought a question to mind. "Do you know how Ben Goebel met Drew Fleischman?" I asked Joan.

"No idea. You might talk to Father Dan. Apparently he knew Ben from the church youth group."

I looked at my watch. It was almost two A.M. I'd been asleep for about a half hour. "I guess we'd better get to bed."

Joan slid her hands down my chest and onto my abdomen, then began massaging me with circular movements as her hands came back up. She put her mouth close to my ear. "I've got something else in mind. Interested?"

Suddenly I wasn't tired anymore. "Like you wouldn't believe."

She turned the seat around so that I faced her, then sat on my lap, straddling me. She kissed me hard on the lips. "Good," she said.

"Won't your parents hear the awful squeaking that bed makes?"

"That's why we're going to do it in the shower. Up against the wall."

"Let's get clean," I said.

Afterward, we toweled each other off and lay together in bed.

There was a nice breeze that night, so before Joan snuggled next to me she opened the window a crack. We could hear the leaves rustling in the big oak outside, and it lulled us into an easy sleep.

I dozed until sometime around 3:30, when I heard the faint sounds of bells playing. *St. Barnabas's carillon,* I thought sleepily. *I wonder why it's going off now instead of midnight?* I listened to the melody and vaguely recognized it. Maybe "For All the Saints"? Maybe something else. Music was not my strong suit. As I let the melody take me deeper into sleep, I wondered if I could hum it in the morning for Joan. She'd probably know what it was.

Perhaps it'll be a normal morning, I thought hopefully, even though Buddy had been dognapped, there was a Satanic cult operating in Jasper, and I was on the trail of a missing "saint" who had been dug up from her grave. How would I even know what a normal morning was?

CHAPTER TWENTY

My cell phone rang at 8:30 A.M. I knew it was mine, but I couldn't figure out where the ringing was coming from. Joan jumped out of bed first and fished it out of the clothes heaped on the floor, right where we had torn them off each other. She was naked as she handed the cell to me. Seeing her that way, I gave an appreciative moan as Father Vince immediately started talking in my ear.

"Sorry to call you so early, but I've got a busy schedule today. I have to tell you what I saw last night. It was such a coincidence after our discussion yesterday that I almost wonder if God is monitoring my television habits. Did you know that some people believe multiple personalities are the mark of someone who has had an encounter with Satanists?"

"What?"

"True story. I happened to catch it last night on TLC, the cable station. They had this special about Satanism. Since we talked about how there might be a cult in Jasper, I watched it. There are a bunch of churches where the pastors spend most of their time exploring these personalities, exorcising the demons. These pastors resurrect—some would say 'suggest'—memories from fairly normal people about how their families worshipped Satan and blocked their memories of it."

I held the phone away from my ear and shook my head, making sure I was awake. "This was on TLC? Where did they find these people?"

"The churches they featured were in Texas, but they inferred there were churches like them all over. To me, the preachers seemed kind of radical, so that might say something about the idea. But the people they interviewed, the ones that were having the supposedly repressed memories, were from all over the country."

"Did they have an explanation as to why these things would be happening all over the country, but no one knows about them?"

"That was the really interesting part. They said it's a conspiracy. These preachers believe that Satanists are building a national and international network to be ready when Satan returns to earth so they can quickly take over. Supposedly, Satanists—or people with a repressed Satanic personality—have been planted in every powerful organization in the world, including the Vatican."

"Vince, you can't seriously believe in this theory."

"I didn't say I did. I just said it was interesting, especially in light of there being a cult in Jasper. And here's the kicker. Every single person interviewed had some memory of animal mutilation. Every one. Maybe this cult in Jasper is a part of the conspiracy. Or at least believes one exists and wants to be part of it."

As usual, I found myself rummaging around the bedroom for a notebook and pen. Joan found one on the floor as she was picking up clothes and gave it to me.

"Has there been anything in the news about an abandoned church in New Vienna? Police found remnants there of Satanic rituals."

"Page one story in the *Indianapolis Standard*. You haven't seen it yet? It has your byline."

"I just got up."

"Oh. Did I wake you?"

"Yeah, but I needed to get up. Would you do me a favor, Vince? Do you remember that verse that was on the library wall at the site of the West Jasper High School massacre, the one about Satan having his finest hour?"

"Your article says it was on the wall of the church in New Vienna, too."

"Yes, it was. Wish I'd been able to get a photo of the wall. That would have been a great visual. Anyway, the fact that same verse appeared in both places provides a possible link between the massacre and the cult. I Googled the verse, but the only hits I got—about a million of them—were all related to the West Jasper massacre. I'd like to know more about the saying."

"Why would I know anything about it?"

Joan, who had pulled on a nightgown and robe, indicated she was going downstairs. I nodded and turned back to Father Vince on the phone. "You said you knew something about Satanism from a course you took. Could you go back to those sources and see if you can find anything, no matter how obscure, that relates to the verse?"

"I can, but I can't promise when I'll get to it. I have a pretty full schedule today."

"It would really help my story if you could do it today. I could cite you as a source . . ."

"Not sure I want that kind of exposure. But I'll see what I can do. Take care, Nick." He hung up.

A worldwide Satanic conspiracy? I put that in big, bold letters at the top of the page in my notebook and underlined it. Then I got dressed and followed Joan down to breakfast.

Breakfast was a quiet affair. Joan and I were tired and didn't do much talking. Janine asked a few questions about what we had found at Game Central. I wanted to share the details, but deferred much of the discussion by nodding my head in Stephanie's direction. She was eating Froot Loops out of a bowl, no milk, picking them up by hand.

In the midst of this, Kevin Mueller arrived at the front door with the morning papers, both the *Jasper Times* and the *Indianapolis Standard*. Janine showed him into the kitchen. His mood was so dark he practically absorbed light. He plopped into the chair next to me, a frown etched in his forehead.

"Any word on Buddy?" I asked under my breath.

"No." He paused. "Miguel sent me down here."

That alarmed me. "He didn't come with you?"

"He walked me over, but he didn't stay. He said I was safe as long as I was with you."

Great. What was I going to do with him? I'd have to have a talk with Miguel.

"What's Miguel doing?" I asked.

"He said he had to make a few phone calls, and he wanted to have a private discussion with my mom. Personally, I think he just wants to sleep."

"Well, he was up all night." But it didn't give him a reason to dump Kevin on me. I had work to do.

Kevin pulled out the *Standard*. "Did you see this?" His mood brightened ever so slightly. "Your article is on the front page. But I'm still bothered that the carcasses and the blood were cleaned up."

Joan, who was sitting on the other side of me, said, "Kevin! We're eating here!" She gestured at her plate of scrambled eggs and sausages.

"Oh, sorry," he mumbled.

Joan noticed he was sitting at the table with nothing in front of him. "Can I get you something? We have plenty."

"I'm not real hungry, but I might be able to eat something. Thanks."

Joan began to assemble a plate for Kevin. Janine and Hugo

left for their room.

"We really scooped the *Times,* didn't we?" Kevin said. "They don't have anything on the abandoned church."

"No, they don't. On the other hand, they have exclusive interviews with the Goebels and the Fleischmans and inside information that the two families are considering a lawsuit against the police. They say the police have been trying to link them to the missing body, although there's no evidence."

Kevin reached for the box of Froot Loops in front of Stephanie and poured himself a handful, popping a few in his mouth.

"So we're not ahead of them?"

"No, but the *Standard*'s not behind either." Kevin's use of the term "we" made me think I'd better emphasize that he was now out of the investigation. "Kevin, you know I can't get you involved any more than you already are. I'm sorry to have to keep you out of it, but I can't put your life in more danger than it is already."

"But we've got Miguel. We can just take him with us."

Joan came in with a plate of eggs, sausage, and buttered toast for Kevin.

"Thanks," he said. For a kid who wasn't "real hungry," he attacked the eggs with gusto.

I said, "I know Miguel is a big guy, but there's only one of him. There are things he can't protect you from."

Joan said, "He's right, Kevin. Think how it would hurt your mom if something happened to you. If I had my way, Nick wouldn't be involved either. But I know there are things he has to do. When you're an adult, you'll decide those things for yourself."

Kevin pouted and started on the sausage links. "Could I have a glass of milk, please?"

"Sure." Joan picked up my plate and hers and took them over to the sink.

"I still want your advice and your knowledge, though," I said. "For instance, last night we didn't talk too much about the Goebel girl. What do you know about her?"

Kevin chewed a bite and swallowed.

"Her name is Jaime. She's very pretty. We were both on the school paper and had German class together. I always thought she came out of the massacre okay. I mean, even though her brother was involved, I thought she was still kind of popular. But she switched high schools, so maybe I was wrong. We're friends on Facebook and leave messages on each others' wall. But it's just, 'hi, how u doin',' that kind of thing."

Joan put the milk in front of Kevin.

I nodded. It didn't surprise me to learn they kept in touch using Facebook, even though they were casual friends. A lot of kids do that these days. My game-playing nephews have over five hundred friends on Facebook. Their wall conversations are never much of anything, but I guess it lets the other kids know they're thinking of them.

Kevin downed the milk, finished everything on his plate, and munched a few more handfuls of Froot Loops. Teenage metabolism.

Stephanie stared at Kevin. "You eat a lot."

Everyone laughed. I got a second cup of coffee for myself and one for Joan.

"Listen, Kevin, I hate to make you feel like you're being shuttled between Miguel and me, but I've got to do more interviews today, and you need to be at your house in case you hear anything about Buddy. I'm going upstairs to get dressed, and then I need to walk you back home."

Kevin sighed. "Miguel said after we get Buddy back, he'll take me to a gym and set me up with a program for gaining muscle. Is that okay with you? I mean, you did offer to do it for me."

"It's okay, Kevin. He's probably the better one to help you get set up anyway."

"Miguel thinks I do too much stuff that's aerobic, and that's why I don't gain weight. What do you think?"

"I think he's right. But the aerobic stuff you do, you enjoy. You have to figure out what's most important to you. You shouldn't stop playing soccer or riding your bike to gain muscle unless you want to make that a priority."

"Yeah," he said. "Miguel told me the same thing." He took one more handful of Froot Loops. "I hope we get Buddy back."

"I hope so, too."

"Who are you going to interview?"

The fact that Kevin knew Jaime Goebel meant I didn't want to tell him the Goebels were on my list. He didn't know her parents well enough to get me an interview with them, but I didn't want him on Facebook with Jaime letting them know I was coming.

"A few people. I have to call the Sheriff's Department to see if they have anything new on the Satanic ritual site you found for us yesterday. I need to call the paper to talk about stories I have to write today. That kind of thing."

He seemed satisfied.

After I changed, I walked him back to his house. I wanted to question Miguel about why he dumped Kevin on me, but not with Kevin there. Before I had the chance, Kevin asked if they'd heard anything about Buddy. Miguel only shook his head.

I put my hand on Kevin's shoulder. "I'm sure we'll find him."

At 9:30 I drove to the Goebels' address. I didn't call ahead because I wanted the element of surprise on my side. Of course, there was always the risk they wouldn't be home.

The Goebels lived in a Jasper neighborhood straight out of the fifties. Every house was rectangular and almost identical in size, with detached garages facing the street. In Indianapolis I'd seen many neighborhoods like this. They were the infantry of middle class subdivisions decades ago, leading the charge into former cornfields in the name of affordable housing. In Indianapolis, most of those neighborhoods were run down. Here, I noticed as I drove slowly past looking at house numbers, they were still well-kept.

It didn't take long to find the Goebels' house, white with green shutters, midway down the block. I saw no cars in front and no sign anyone was home, but I had to check it out. I rang the doorbell and waited on the "Welcome Neighbors" doormat.

The white front door opened, revealing a young girl about fifteen years old behind it. Her eyes were the color of pool water, and her blonde hair was pulled back in a ponytail. She was dressed in denim shorts and a fuchsia T-shirt, but I was taken by her broad and infectious smile. This had to be Jaime.

"Is your mom or dad home?" I asked.

"Neither," she said through the screen door. "Can I help you with something?"

I always feel weird in situations like this. As a parent, I would hate it if a reporter attempted to interview my child without asking me and especially without me being there to supervise. But I decided if Jaime was willing to engage in a little conversation, I would attribute the information to "background." No one needed to know where I had gotten it.

"I'm sorry to have missed them. My name is Nick Bertetto. I'm a reporter for the *Indianapolis Standard*. I was hoping to ask them some questions."

Her smile faded. "I'll let them know you were here." She started to close the door.

"Wait. Let me give you a business card," I said, stalling.

She paused. I took out one of my cards, crossed out the office number in Franklin, and wrote my cell phone number on it. "This is how they can get hold of me." I held the card out at the side of the screen door. She opened it slightly and took it from my hand.

"I don't suppose you'd be willing to talk to me, would you?"

"Mom and Dad don't like me talking to reporters. We've had bad experiences with them."

I nodded sympathetically. "I'm sure you have. I can't even imagine what you've been through with the national press. I like to think we local papers have been kinder."

"Mom and Dad only trust the reporter who was here yesterday."

"Sally Kaiser? She's a good reporter, I know. I am, too. Do you know why the police are trying to link your family to the missing body?"

Her eyes flashed with anger. "It has nothing to do with us and everything to do with Eddie Fleischman. I wish Ben had never gotten involved with his brother. Our lives were just fine before that."

"Do you know how they met? It seems strange to me that they were even friends. They were so different."

"Talk to Father Dan about it." She practically spit out his name. "He was the one encouraging people like my brother to go after the 'lost sheep.' Like he could have changed Drew Fleischman. Drew changed him."

Father Dan again. He seemed to hold the answers to a lot of questions all of a sudden. I would have to get out and see him as soon as I could.

"What does Eddie Fleischman have to do with the missing body?" I asked.

"Maybe nothing. Maybe everything. Who knows? He's a creep."

"I imagine you were glad he moved to Vincennes."

"He didn't move to Vincennes. He still lives here in town."

"I thought the Fleischmans moved."

"That's not what the police told Mom and Dad."

"Are you sure you heard that right?"

She glared at me. "Yes, I'm sure. You are just like that Sally Kaiser, you know that? She never listens to anything I say."

"What other things have you told her that she ignored?"

Jaime Goebel just shook her head. "I'll tell my parents you were here. But I wouldn't count on an interview." She closed the door.

I was tempted to ring the doorbell again. I really was. Jaime Goebel knew things. Sally Kaiser wasn't listening to her. I wondered if her mom and dad were. I wondered if the police were.

I was willing to. But with her being underage and having just shut the door on me, this session was over. I would have to think of a way to earn her trust. But how?

CHAPTER TWENTY-ONE

So, had the Fleischmans moved or hadn't they? Jaime said they hadn't, but Janine and Hugo knew that Tim Fleischman had taken a job in Vincennes, and the Fleischmans couldn't still be in their former house or everyone would know about it. Would Eddie Fleischman drive an hour back and forth from home just to play at Game Central? Surely there was a similar gaming center in Vincennes, which was a much bigger city. On the other hand, I suspected there was something not quite legal going on at Game Central. If so, what was it? And what did the police have on Eddie Fleischman, anyway? I suspected he was involved in the Satanic rituals, but did they?

It was time to do the one thing I didn't want to do.

I phoned Joan at her parents' house. "You're not going to like what I'm about to ask, but I need your help. Can you call Johnny Day down at the police station and wheedle some information out of him? I'd like to find out what the police have on Eddie Fleischman and if they know where he is."

She thought a moment. "Do I have to?"

"I'm not any more excited about the prospect of you talking to him than you are, believe me. But it would save me a lot of time."

She hesitated again. "I'm not that good at these kinds of things."

"I'd really appreciate it, dear . . ."

"Okay, I'll give it a try."

"That's my girl."

Next I called Deputy Karen Prechtel, hoping to get some follow-up information on what the sheriff's department had found yesterday in the abandoned church. The receptionist asked who was calling. When I told her, she replied that Deputy Prechtel would have to call me back later. I gave the receptionist my cell phone number, but I had little doubt it would be me trying to get in touch with Prechtel again later, rather than the reverse.

Father Dan was next on my list. His name had come up a lot lately, and while I didn't think he was directly involved in anything, he seemed to be one of the hubs around which events were centered.

I jumped in the van and drove over to St. Barnabas. It was hot for June; I turned on the radio with the hopes of getting a weather forecast. When I found it, I was disappointed but not surprised.

"It's another 90 degree day," blathered the cheery DJ. "That's our third this month, and it's only June. If you're hoping for thunderstorms, you'd get better odds playing roulette at the French Lick Casino. And since tomorrow's the longest day of the year, we're going to get a full day of that steamy, hot Indiana weather. The summer solstice occurs at 1:22 A.M."

As I made my way toward the church, it somehow seemed significant that tomorrow was the longest day, but I couldn't quite figure out why. I put it out of my mind and drove on.

St. Barnabas is one of the smaller Catholic churches in the area. Built in the 1920s, it retained some classic design features found in larger churches, such as a bell tower rising high above the entrance, custom stone carvings and woodworking, and small alcoves on either side of the sanctuary where one could pray to the saints. Because it was built to serve rural Jasper before the town expanded outward, it was located where two county roads meet. I drove around the church to the parking lot in the back.

Father Dan's red truck was parked at the rectory in the back lot. I walked over to the brick building and rang the doorbell but got no answer. Jogging back across the street, I decided to try the church office. I walked around to the side entrance and found the office locked with a note saying the secretary would be back after lunch. I looked at my watch. It was only 10:45. They must have generous lunchtimes, I thought.

I circled around to the main entrance, walked up to the main doors, and grabbed a handle.

Suddenly the church bells began to play. I jumped back, then smiled. Of course, it was the carillon. I listened and recognized the melody I'd heard last night. I tried to remember the words. "For All the Saints," was about as far as I could go. I checked my watch again. Quarter 'til the hour was an odd time to play a full melody. Someone had to have set it off—I hoped it was Father Dan.

Trying the handle again, I found the front doors unlocked. I went through the entryway and the next set of doors into the sanctuary. Hearing someone behind me in the choir loft, I spun around and looked up. "Hello?" I called.

Father Dan came to the front of the loft. He looked down at me with a puzzled frown. "Hello, Nick. What brings you here?"

"A few questions. May I come up?"

"Sure. I was just programming some music."

I climbed the stairs and was soon seated next to him at the carillon's "keyboard." Each bell was controlled by a long handle, nothing like what would be found on a piano or organ. The sheet music confirmed I had been right about the title, "For All the Saints."

I pointed to the music. "I heard that sometime after 3:00 last night," I said, "but I wasn't sure of the title. I'm not very good when it comes to music."

"It was after three o'clock? Are you sure?"

"Fairly sure. I guess you weren't up late playing it?"

He laughed. "No, I was asleep. This has a recordable feature on it. You can record your performances and program the bells to play them back at another time. But I'm surprised it went off so late. I'll have to check for what caused the glitch."

"The bells really carry. The Strassheims' house must be five miles away, and I still heard it. Don't people object to it going off at night?"

He shook his head. "The tradition goes back a long time, actually."

"You must be very talented. I can't think of very many priests who know how to play a carillon."

"My mother was big on music. I took lessons in piano and organ until I graduated from high school. I learned how to play the carillon in college—there aren't many people in the country who can play, and you can make good money doing it. It put me through seminary."

"Really? That's great."

I sat for a moment and watched Father Dan pull the handles and play a snippet of a different song. When he paused, I said, "In all the years I've been staying at the Strassheims', I've never heard the bells late at night before."

The sound of the last peal faded away. "Well, the tradition of the bells tolling on the hour and a hymn playing at noon and midnight had stopped long before I came to St. Barnabas. The automatic mechanism had broken down, and the church organist only knew how to play a few bells for Mass, so that's the only use it got. When I arrived, I wanted to revive the tradition. I think it's been about a year now I've been doing it."

"I'm amazed this has recordable and programmable features. Those seem too modern for an old carillon."

He gazed at me, an odd look on his face. "Is it the reporter in you that causes you to ask a lot of questions?"

I smiled. "I guess."

He thought a moment. "It's a new feature. When the church had the carillon refurbished, we upgraded the technology."

"That must have been expensive."

He searched my eyes as though he were checking my sincerity. "Don't tell anyone this, but I paid for the work that was done. The church thinks it was an anonymous donor."

"I thought priests took vows of poverty."

He chuckled. "Not all orders take that vow. Most of us don't have much money anyway, priestly wages being what they are. My family has made some investments over the years, and I thought this would be a good use for the money."

"What are you working on?"

Father Dan glanced at the music sheets. There was another piece sticking out from under "For All the Saints," but I could only see part of the title. Something that ended in "sus." "Jesus," probably. Father Dan shuffled the music together and set it aside.

"Something different, but you didn't come here to watch me play," he said. "Let's sit over in the choir chairs, and we can talk."

We pulled up a couple of wooden chairs. Father Dan sat in one, and I moved mine so we could face each other.

"What can I help you with?" he asked.

"I understand that you knew Ben Goebel and Drew Fleischman before the massacre."

"A little, yes."

"What can you tell me about them? How did you meet them?"

"Why do you want to know about them? I thought you were investigating Keri Schoening's body being stolen."

"I'm hearing rumors that the two might be related."

He didn't say anything for a moment, as if he were weighing whether that could be true. Finally he shrugged. "I don't think I should be sharing information with the press about current or former parishioners."

"I'm not looking for anything they might have said in a confessional. I'm only interested in your impressions."

"Still, I wouldn't want anyone to see that I was quoted talking about them."

"Very well, then, it's all background."

"I'm not even sure what I know is anything of value."

"Just start with how you came to meet them."

"When I arrived at St. Barnabas, I wanted to get the youth program energized. I began meeting with a variety of young people. Ben Goebel was a good kid and seemed to be receptive to some of my ideas. He brought Drew Fleischman to a couple of events. I tried to get to know Drew. For me, he was one of the lost sheep that Jesus asked us to save. But he didn't make much of an effort back. After he stopped coming, there wasn't much I could do. He wouldn't return my calls. I know Ben tried to talk to him, but he seemed to pull Ben down more than Ben lifted him up."

"When did you realize that Ben was starting to act like Drew?"

"Keep in mind I only saw Drew a few times. I think it became apparent to Drew real fast that while we tried to provide some fun times, we were also about God and salvation. It was not his cup of tea.

"Ben was another story altogether. He came from a strong Catholic home. I was surprised when he stopped making time for our youth program. I made it a point to meet with him after a couple of weeks."

"When was that?" I asked.

He rubbed his forehead. "It must have been in November. I

remember that it was after Halloween."

I wrote that down. "What was Ben's story?"

"As I said, Ben was a good kid, but even good kids rebel, especially when they hit that squirrelly sophomore year. They just have to rebel against something, and religion is often an easy mark." He drummed his fingers on the chair seat. "Kids can't afford to shove the schoolwork aside if they're success-oriented, and parents and police can crack back pretty hard. So the church is a good target. Parents figure it's a phase they're going through or that they're old enough to decide if they want to go to church or not. 'Pick your battles,' as the old adage goes. So Ben rebelled against religion. That's how I saw it when he started hanging out with Drew. How it moved to us-against-the-world is difficult to say."

"Did you meet with Ben more than once?"

Father Dan looked down at his hands and flexed his fingers. "Tried to, but I was at a point where the bishop had assigned me extra duties that took up a lot of time. I didn't spend as much time following up with him as I should have. Hindsight is 20/20."

I thought about Father Vince's comments that Father Dan was the exorcist for the area, as well as an administrator for certain programs. No doubt the priest shortage forced things like this to occur. "I understand that you're highly regarded within the diocese."

He smiled at me. "Probably more than I should be."

"Do you still keep in contact with the Goebels?"

"Not since they moved to St. Patrick's parish."

"It's interesting that both families moved."

"What else could they do? With so much resentment from the community, they had to try something. I'm only surprised they didn't move farther away."

"You mean the Goebels?"

"Actually, I mean both families. Vincennes is only about an hour away."

"I heard that the younger Fleischman boy is still in town."

"Eddie Fleischman? Where did you hear that?"

"Actually I saw him. At a place called Game Central. Eddie has a threatening presence."

"Are you judging a book by its cover, Nick?"

I briefly considered telling him about Miguel chasing Eddie and the other person out of the parking lot but decided against it. "You sound like you know him."

"Everyone knows who he is since he's Drew's brother. I'm just surprised at the idea that he's still here. He probably drove in from Vincennes. If he stayed in town, wouldn't he be keeping a low profile?"

"For all I know, he might be. I've only seen him once, and I've only talked to one person who says he's here. My next step is to locate him."

"Good luck."

We sat there a moment looking at each other. I decided to forge straight ahead with my suspicions about Eddie. "Do you know anything about a Satanic cult here in Jasper? And that Eddie might be involved in it?"

He answered quickly. "Certainly not! Why would I know anything about a Satanic cult? The priesthood is diametrically opposed to such a thing."

"I know that. But I wondered if you'd heard any rumors."

He appraised me again, and I don't think it was a positive assessment. "One hears a lot of things, being a priest. There were rumors after the West Jasper massacre that there might be such a cult, but the police never found anything. I think that says something there."

I wasn't sure it said anything conclusively, but I let it go.

"I'm not sure you're on the right track with this angle," he said. "Why do you think the high school massacre is related to Keri Schoening's body disappearing?"

"If Eddie Fleischman is involved, the link is obvious."

"But it doesn't follow. Why would Eddie Fleischman want Keri Schoening's corpse? What possible motive could he have?"

"I don't have a clue. But if he's got the body, he'll have to answer for it. To the police or somebody."

Father Dan looked at his watch. "I'd like to stay and talk, but I'm afraid I don't have a lot of time. I need to reprogram the carillon before I leave for my next appointment."

"That's okay," I said. "I need to get going. Thanks for the help."

Father Dan said goodbye and moved over to the keyboard. I walked down the stairs while he played a few measures of the new song. I recognized the melody, but as always I couldn't think of the title. Just as I reached the bottom of the stairs, my cell phone rang. I checked the number. It was Joan. The carillon would be too loud outside the church, so I answered it inside.

"No go," she said. "Johnny won't tell me much. I got him to admit there is a connection between Eddie Fleischman and Keri's body being dug up, but he wouldn't say what it was or what evidence they have."

"I don't suppose he gave you an address for the Fleischmans."

"Not hardly. Am I losing my seductiveness?"

"Not to me."

"I guess it's okay, then. Are you coming home for lunch?"

"I should be there in about ten minutes."

Father Dan peered down at me over the choir loft, and I realized he'd stopped playing the carillon. "Did you locate the Fleischman boy?"

"Not yet," I said, "but I'm still working on it."

"Good," he said. He returned to the organ and played the

melody again. I still didn't know it.

I spent some quality time with Stephanie after lunch, knowing Joan and Janine were taking her to the water park later. I'd be busy with articles and deadlines then.

"Do you want to play a game?" I asked her. We were sitting in Janine's living room.

"Can I watch TV instead?"

I shook my head. "But I could read you a book. Or you could read me one."

"How about a jigsaw puzzle?" she asked.

Stephanie's jigsaw puzzles are of the 100–150 piece variety, so I knew we weren't getting involved in a long project. "Okay. You choose."

Naturally she chose the one with a cat that resembled Mr. Jangles. She dumped the pieces on the floor. I lay on the floor on my side, separating out the border pieces. Stephanie helped.

"Did you think about Mr. Jangles last night?" I asked.

"No."

"I just wondered why you chose this puzzle."

"I like it."

"Do you remember having any dreams about Mr. Jangles lately?"

She separated more pieces. "No."

"Well, if you do, I want you to tell me about it."

"Why?"

"Because I know you miss him, and if you have any bad dreams, I want to know."

We worked in silence for awhile. It didn't take us long to string the border pieces together. She'd worked this puzzle a bunch of times, so she knew exactly what to do.

"Daddy, can you come with us to the water park?"

"You know I can't, honey, although I would love to do that."

"Grandma says you work too much."

"She's right, I think. Sometimes I feel like I'm working all the time."

Stephanie began to collect the pieces of the cat's face and snap them together. When that part was finished, she stared at it. The stare lasted too long for my taste. I was about to say something when she got up and walked into the kitchen. She headed for the back door. I'd seen this before.

"Joan!" I called.

She must have heard the alarm in my voice because she found me right away. I was kneeling next to Stephanie, who was staring fixedly out the back door.

"What do you see?" I asked.

"Mr. Jangles."

"What's he doing?"

"He's purring. He's winding around a girl's legs."

"Have you seen the girl before?"

"Yes."

"What's she doing?"

"She's watching us. And she's saying something."

Joan knelt down on the other side of Stephanie. She gave Steph's shoulders a slight shake. "Stephanie, wake up."

"Joan, don't," I said.

She ignored me. She turned Stephanie toward her.

Stephanie's voice suddenly sounded more grown up. "Stop them from taking me," she pleaded. "Don't let the prophecy come true."

"Is the girl Keri?" I asked. "What prophecy is she talking about?"

Joan shook her again.

"Don't do that, Joan." I turned to Stephanie. "Who are you?" I asked, but it was too late. Stephanie's eyes refocused, and she looked confused.

"Baby," Joan said and gripped Stephanie close to her.

"Mommy," Steph replied.

I felt tears sting my eyes. I didn't know whether to be mad at Joan or relieved that Stephanie was back to normal.

Joan was still clutching Stephanie to her chest so tightly I couldn't see my daughter's face. My wife's eyes flashed at me.

"What did you think you were doing, Nick?"

I took a deep breath. "We won't get to the bottom of this until we find out who this girl is that Stephanie sees."

"No! We can't let this happen again!"

"We have no idea why it's happening, so how can we prevent it?"

"I'm taking Stephanie to the water park. Maybe it's best she get out of the house for a while." Joan's voice had an edge. She picked Stephanie up and carried her upstairs without another word to me.

I stood there for a moment feeling drained. It was the second time we'd heard about a prophecy. What prophecy? And what was happening to Stephanie? Did she really think someone was out there, or was this connected to her sorrow at Mr. Jangles's death? If it continued, we'd need to get some kind of help for her. For the moment, though, I knew trying to discuss it rationally with Joan was out of the question. I only hoped she'd be more receptive later.

CHAPTER TWENTY-TWO

Moments after Joan swept Stephanie into her arms and left the kitchen, my cell phone began ringing. I answered it as Janine entered, glaring at me.

"Nick, it's Vince. I just returned a phone call from a friend who works in the Vatican archives. He took the same class I did on Satanism. While I was talking to him, I mentioned the particular verse. He said it sounded like it came from a 16th century text he's heard about. It has to do with the nature of Satan and his eventual return to power on earth."

I knew Janine wanted to say something, but I held up my hand indicating for her to wait a minute. "Who wrote it, and how can we get hold of it?"

"I don't know the answer to the first question. But as for the second, it's been a part of the Vatican Secret Archives for a long time. Of course, the documents in the Archives aren't so secret anymore. You can find them online. Only problem is, to read a specific document, you have to know what you're looking for. He said he'd try to find me the title."

"So we could read it?"

"We could view it. The archives have limits, however. The documents are available online in the original language, exactly as you would see them if you could get into the Archives and look at them. There's no translation, no index. So you have to be fluent in the language of the document you're looking for."

"Can he help?"

"He said he'd try to get to it. He thought the original was written in ancient German, and he does have some ability in that. So we may get lucky."

Today's story deadline was pushing in on me fast. "Please let me know the minute you find out anything."

We hung up. Janine started talking the moment I pressed the stop button to end the call. "What's the matter with Joan and Stephanie? Have you done something?"

"I haven't done anything." I heard the weariness in my own voice. I had thought, hoped, that maybe we'd gotten past my role as the bad guy. Janine had apparently relapsed. "Stephanie had another spell. Neither one of us knows what to do about it. We're scared and frustrated."

She turned abruptly on her heels. "I'd better go talk to her, see if there's anything I can do."

The doorbell rang as she charged out of the kitchen. "I'll get that on my way upstairs."

I sank into a chair and rubbed my forehead. Where did Janine keep the aspirin? Maybe there was some in the kitchen.

Kevin appeared in the doorway. "Mrs. Strassheim said you were in here."

I jumped out of the chair. "What are you doing here? Where's Miguel?"

A hint of anger touched his voice. "He said he had to take care of something, and he needed to do it before Mom went to work at three o'clock. He wouldn't take me with him. He said I'd be safe with you."

I crossed my arms over my chest. Just who had hired whom to be Kevin's bodyguard? I would have to have a talk with Miguel.

"Any word from the people who have Buddy?"

Kevin looked in my direction, but not in my eyes. "Nah."

"Miguel didn't say where he was going?"

"No."

"Where's your mom?"

"She went with him."

"She did?"

He nodded. "The two of them have been working on something all morning."

"You have any idea what it is?"

"When we didn't get a phone call from Eddie by noon, Miguel started twitching, like he had the urge to hit somebody. I could tell he was tired of sitting around. He began doing some weird martial art thing, like he was being attacked."

"In karate, it's called a kata. I don't know what they call it in tae kwon do."

"It was fierce, man! You sure wouldn't want to go up against him."

"I'm sure. What did he do after that?"

"He said we need to find out where Eddie was hanging out and get him to tell us where Buddy was. Or who had him."

"We'd all like to do that, but we don't know where Eddie is."

"I mentioned that I knew Eddie's license plate number, but it wouldn't do us any good since it was probably registered to their old house address or maybe their new one in Vincennes."

"You know Eddie's license plate number!"

"He got his brother's truck after his brother died, and he kept the same number. It's not really a number. It's 'S, G, N, a space, then GOAT.' "

I repeated it back, puzzled. Then I wrote it out so I could look at it. I held it up. "SGN GOAT."

"Sign goat," Kevin said.

"That's what I thought."

"What does it mean?"

"I don't know. The goat is the symbol used to represent the god Pan, who is a devil figure. I learned that yesterday from one of the sheriffs at the abandoned church."

"Then it connects to the Satanic cult?"

"I think so, but it's not conclusive. What did Miguel do when he found out you knew Eddie's license plate number?"

"It was Mom who got excited. She and Miguel went off to another room to talk. Then they came back and decided to drop me off here."

"What's your best guess as to what they're doing?"

"Mom has a friend in the sheriff's department. Not enough, you know, to get me a bodyguard, but enough to get some help. I think they're putting out a call to look for the truck with the license plate number."

I pulled out my cell phone and dialed Miguel. It rang three times and then went to voice mail. I hung up. "Let's try your mom."

Kevin pulled out his cell phone and dialed. "Hey, Mom. Where are you? . . . Is Miguel with you? Nick wants to talk to him." He handed the phone to me.

I covered the receiver. "Did your mom say where they were?"

"In Miguel's truck, driving around."

I uncovered the receiver. "Miguel, what are you doing?"

"Trying to take care of this problem. Mrs. Mueller wants Buddy back, and she wants the threat to Kevin neutralized."

"We all want that, but there are other, bigger issues we have to watch, too."

"That's your position. Mrs. Mueller isn't necessarily interested in achieving your goals, only hers."

"Just who do you think is paying you?"

"You were. But Mrs. Mueller has offered me a higher rate to fix things."

I didn't need this, a renegade bodyguard.

"Miguel, please tell me where you are. I won't try to stop you, but at a minimum I need to question Eddie Fleischman and cover this for the paper."

"Mrs. Mueller believes you are a complicating factor. I like you, Nick, you know that, but this is business." He hung up.

I handed the phone back to Kevin.

"What did Miguel say?"

I went through the conversation with him. I think Kevin was angry at his mom for messing up his chance to be something of a reporter and help me with a major story. "What do we do?" he asked.

"If your hunch is right, they've probably got officers looking for Eddie's truck, to figure out where he's holed up. We need to get there faster."

"I've been thinking about that. I wonder if Jaime Goebel knows. I mean, she doesn't like Eddie much, but if the families are considering a lawsuit, maybe she's seen him. I could call her."

"We can try on the way to her house. If she answers the phone, all the better, but if not, let's not waste a moment. I've talked to her once today, and she might talk again, especially if she sees you on the doorstep."

Jaime didn't answer Kevin's call, but he had no sooner hung up than a call came through on my cell phone. I handed it to him. "Answer it, would you?"

He flipped it open and said hello. I could vaguely hear someone jawing at him.

"Wait a minute. You've got the wrong person. I'm not Nick."

Before he could say any more, the person on the other end spoke again.

"My name is Kevin. Who are you?"

Kevin handed the phone to me. "It's someone who says he's your boss."

Ryan. "You're not my boss," I said into the phone.

"Close enough. Whatcha got for me?"

"Nothing yet, but I'm hoping to have something soon. The police's main suspect is likely the same one responsible for the animal killings and tortures. We're fairly confident he broke into a house last night and took a dog. We also think there's a strong link between the West Jasper massacre and the disappearance of Keri Schoening's body."

"That's a lot of supposition. Any proof?"

"We're on our way to get it."

"You'll need it. Yesterday Sally Kaiser debunked the connection between the massacre and Keri Schoening's missing body."

"Yeah, well, I think she just put up a good story for the two families. The Fleischmans might be considering a lawsuit against the police, but it doesn't mean they're as pure as the driven snow, which is how they came off in her interview."

"Do you know something, or is that conjecture?"

"A little of both. The main suspect is Eddie Fleischman, the younger brother of one of the killers, and he's as bad as his brother was. The police must have some kind of evidence, and I'm trying to find out what it is. In the meantime, I did discover that the boy didn't move to Vincennes with his parents. He's still in the area. I'm trying to locate the address."

"That's a lot of ifs and maybes. We need facts."

I glanced at Kevin and told Ryan, "I have one of the best locals helping me dig for information. If it can be found, he'll find it."

"Do you know what Sally Kaiser is up to?"

"If she's smart, she's working on the Satanic cult story I had yesterday, trying to add to it and get her paper caught up."

"What about you?"

"We think Eddie Fleischman is the key. We think he's a part of the Satanic cult, and we think we can tie it altogether."

"Get busy. I need something solid. I'll call you back in a

couple of hours."

He disconnected.

I handed the phone to Kevin. "Study the phone number that guy just called from. If he calls again, don't answer it."

A few blocks from the Goebel's, Kevin said, "Before we get to Jaime's house, there are a couple of things you should know."

"Such as?"

"When Jaime and I worked together on the school newspaper, we were trying to piece together a story on a Satanic cult in Jasper. She always believed there was one here, that her brother had gotten swept up in it, and the cult forced him to be a part of the massacre. Even after she switched schools, she still wanted to prove it. We were following up on rumors when Buddy got grabbed the first time. We both got scared, thinking maybe they knew about us, and she backed out. I would have stopped altogether if you hadn't shown up."

"I'd say I'm sorry I dragged you back into this, but I think you came willingly."

I looked over in time to see him grin. "I just hope Jaime was still interested enough to get some information out of Eddie or his parents."

When we pulled up in front of the Goebel's house, nothing had changed since my earlier visit. There were still no cars in the driveway or out front on the street. This time Kevin stood front and center on the welcome mat when I rang the doorbell.

We waited for what seemed a long time. I was afraid she'd left and almost said that to Kevin when the door opened. Jaime was all smiles for Kevin but gave me a sideways glance that made me glad she'd seen him first.

"Hi Jaime," Kevin said.

"Hey." She ignored me and focused on him, her blue eyes lighting up and making him look at the ground.

I nudged him, and his brain re-engaged. "Jaime, someone's

taken Buddy. They broke into my house and grabbed him."

"That's awful." Her forehead wrinkled in concern. "Who did it? When?"

"Last night."

"We think they may be part of the Satanic cult you and Kevin were looking for," I added. "They've threatened to kill him if we go to the police."

At first they stared at me like I had appeared out of nowhere. Then Kevin said, "This is Nick," he said. "He's a reporter; he's okay."

"We've met."

I kept quiet and let Kevin continue.

"We think Eddie Fleischman is one of the cultists and we're trying to find out where he's staying. He's been showing up at Game Central regularly, and we don't think he's going home to stay with his family in Vincennes. Do you know where he is?"

She leaned in close to the screen door. Kevin leaned toward her. "He didn't talk much when he was here with his folks. They were the ones who initiated the idea of a lawsuit. My parents know the police have been investigating us, but it doesn't particularly bother them. It really bothers the Fleischmans. I did manage to get Eddie aside and ask how he liked Vincennes. He admitted that he hadn't moved, that he was staying near here at his uncle's property."

"Where is it? What's his uncle's name?"

"I don't know exactly. He just said it was out of town, near New Vienna. The old Kitley place, he called it."

New Vienna. Site of the abandoned church that had become home to Satanic worshipers. It figured.

Kevin shook his head. "Doesn't ring a bell with me."

"But we know where New Vienna is," I said. "How hard can it be to find, once we get there?"

"You never know," Jaime said. "There are some old country

roads out that way with farmhouses that are really spread far apart. Anyone within a couple of miles of the town might say they're in New Vienna."

Kevin nodded. "It could mean a lot of searching."

"We can't just sit here, though. Let's get going. We'll figure out where it is when we get there." I grabbed Kevin by the arm and pulled him towards the car.

"Thanks, Jaime," he said over his shoulder.

"Yes, thanks." I needed to keep Kevin on task before he asked Jaime to join us. I didn't need another person involved, especially another teenager to watch out for. Once we were away from the door and he couldn't see her anymore, I stopped pulling. By that time he'd turned toward the car and was running. He beat me back to the van. I got in, and we buckled our seatbelts and took off.

CHAPTER TWENTY-THREE

We drove back downtown on our way to pick up Highway 56 toward New Vienna. My eyes were on the road but my peripheral vision caught a lot of energy in Kevin's hands. He was drumming some invisible instrument.

"The church," he said, excitement in his voice. "I bet anything it's near the church."

"That would explain a lot of things. We know we were being watched during the time we were there, but we didn't see anyone. Easily accomplished if they were holed up somewhere close."

"Do you think Mom and Miguel might be there now?"

I had been thinking along those lines. "It all depends on how good their contacts in the sheriff's department are. Did the police already know where he was staying? Or are they all out looking for it now since you provided the license plate number? It takes a long time to cover the county."

We weren't really battling Miguel and Brenda to find Eddie Fleischman's location first. We just didn't want to get left behind. Now that Kevin asked the question, it occurred to me that we might be the first ones to arrive. I didn't like that idea. Miguel and his skills would be particularly handy.

My cell phone was in the basket between my seat and Kevin's. He must've dropped it there when we went to see Jaime.

"Kevin, would you pick up my phone and call Miguel?"

"Why?"

"We need to make sure he's there, for obvious reasons. If they haven't figured it out yet, we need to tell them we're headed for the old Kitley place. Your mom might even have heard of it."

"Aren't you mad at my mom?"

"Your mom is only thinking about your safety. She thinks she's doing the right thing. If I'm mad at anyone, it's Miguel. I had hired him to do a job. He shouldn't have allowed another job to supersede it."

Kevin found the number and hit redial. When the ringing ended and the voice mail picked up, Kevin held up the phone so I could hear it.

"Damn him. I know he's there. He's just not answering," I said. "Tell him we think we know where Eddie is, and give him the location. Tell him to call me back as soon as he gets the message."

Kevin did that and hung up. As a backup, I had him call his mom's phone and leave a similar message when she didn't answer either.

Next I asked him to call Joan, then give the phone to me. It was one thing to leave a message for Miguel and Kevin's mom, but I wanted Joan to know what was going on, too. We needed to leave traces of where we were so if anything went wrong, people knew where to look for us. There was no answer. Wasn't anyone answering their cell phones today? She'd probably stuck it in her beach bag and wasn't near it. I told her voice mail what was happening.

When we rolled into New Vienna, it was mid-day. I slowed down and read the name of each cross street as we passed. We stared down each road in hopes we'd see something to give us a clue or maybe see Miguel's truck sitting somewhere. Nothing.

I doubled back and turned at the cross street I'd taken days earlier that led to the abandoned church. We checked the street names but again saw nothing. We circled the church but there was no activity. I was ready to start all over again when Kevin pointed and said, "Let's try over there."

He was pointing at a spot about a block away where the roadside had become thick with trees and overgrown bushes. The street sign was hidden by the foliage.

"Good eye." I drove over. A little drainage ditch had been responsible for the plethora of growth which obscured a road that went off to the right.

Kevin read the name off the street sign. "Kitley Way."

"Way" was certainly more accurate than "street." It was nothing more than a gravel road, but in rural Indiana, gravel roads aren't uncommon.

The road was narrow and ran parallel to the ditch. There was a bend to the left after about two hundred yards. Overgrowth obscured anything beyond the bend.

"The house has to be on this road," Kevin said.

I took my foot off the brake. "Let's hope Miguel is already here."

We crept along the road, trying not to kick up dust behind us, but it was nearly impossible. Gravel crunched under the tires, and I wondered if we were really making that much noise or if the anxiety I was feeling magnified my hearing. We made the bend and looked ahead. The road went into a wooded area and then turned to the right. Once again, we couldn't see beyond it.

I stopped the van.

Kevin clapped my forearm. "Why are we stopping?"

"I'm not sure this is a good idea."

"Why?"

"Have you noticed that we haven't come across a single house yet?"

Kevin thought for a moment. "That's not good, is it?"

"I suppose we could keep going until we see a house. Then we could stop from a distance and make a better decision."

"Let's keep going," he said.

I took my foot off the brake again and entered the woods. It felt like we were heading into a forest with no way out. We crept past the bend. Immediately to our right was a squat, flat roofed house set just off the road. It was shaded by a thick canopy of trees. There was no sign of Miguel's truck, but Eddie's truck was parked at the side of the house. And Eddie and Richard O'Brien were out in front. They looked our way.

"They're right there!" Kevin's voice went shrill.

"Don't panic. If we turn around now they'll know we're looking for them. We'll just drive by. Maybe they won't recognize my van."

"I wish Miguel were here."

"So do I."

I pushed the accelerator and proceeded past the house at a normal pace. "Don't look at them," I said. "The windows in the van are dark. Maybe they won't be able to see you."

It was too late for that. Eddie started pointing excitedly at us.

"He knows!" Kevin nearly shouted at me.

I pushed the pedal to the floor and sprinted down the road, spraying gravel behind us. If there were any doubts that we were looking for them, it surely ended with that one action.

Kevin pointed. "They're running into the woods ahead of us." Their path would take them past a wooden shed, beyond which they might be able to cut us off, if that was their plan. So far as I could see they had no weapons.

I floored it. The road made another bend to the right. Although it would take us toward where they were headed, I thought we might have gotten a jump on them.

"Use redial and get Miguel on the phone," I shouted.

Kevin lurched at the cell and hit a button.

I drove as fast as I dared on loose gravel and rounded the bend to find the road dead-ended a hundred feet beyond. I stomped on the brake. The van's rear end slid forty-five degrees to the right. We skidded to a halt.

"Help!" Kevin shouted into the phone.

I shifted into reverse. My plan was to back into a three-point turn. I'd blow past Eddie and O'Brien on my way out.

But before I could shift into forward, I saw through Kevin's window that the front end of a double-barreled shotgun had been leveled at his head. Next to me, Eddie pointed another sawed-off shotgun. It would make a hell of a mess out of either of us.

Kevin dropped the cell phone. I put my hands in the air.

O'Brien motioned us out of the van. He checked the cell phone he saw Kevin drop. "There's no one on. Either they never answered or they hung up," he told Eddie. O'Brien threw the cell back in the van.

Both of them were well-armed. Not only were they carrying shotguns, but each had some kind of handgun strapped to his waist. Eddie had a hunting knife strapped to his right calf as well.

O'Brien took Eddie's shotgun and told him to pat us down. "Keep your hands up and don't try anything," he said, swinging the gun away from Kevin, toward me, then back again. "I'll kill the boy first if you try anything."

Eddie checked Kevin over. "Do you have my dog?" Kevin asked him. He was doing his best not to appear scared, but his voice had a tremor in it.

Eddie put his hand on Kevin's throat and squeezed a little. Eddie was taller and a lot bulkier than Kevin. Kevin's face went pale. "Dragged him right out of your house, yelping all the way. Maybe you'll get to see us carve him up. This time I won't go easy."

"Let go of him, Eddie," O'Brien said. "Just check him for weapons."

Eddie pulled out Kevin's wallet, thumbed through it and found money, which he stuffed in his own pocket.

"People know where we are, O'Brien," I said. "They'll come after us."

"Fortunately we won't be here for much longer," he said. He sounded considerably calmer than I did. The gun stayed pointed at me.

Eddie patted me down next and found only my wallet. He went through it.

"We were right last night," he said to O'Brien. "Nick Bertetto."

O'Brien nodded. "You've written your last column."

Not if I can do anything about it, I thought.

Eddie pulled out two twenties. "Only forty bucks? That's all you got?"

"Okay, we're heading toward the house," O'Brien said. "Try anything and we will shoot to kill."

The first thing we came to on the way was the shed. The door was open, and I looked inside. Guns. The shed was only about 8' by 8', but wherever I looked, I saw guns. All kinds.

"What are you doing with all the guns, O'Brien?"

"No talking. Keep moving."

They marched us toward the house. It was a brown-brick bungalow with a carport to one side. At one time it might have been well-kept, but now there were cracks in the windows and the screen door had a hole. There wasn't much of a backyard because the creek, which ran beside the road part of the way, diverged and went behind the house. It was sunnier by the creek and the vegetation was noticeably thicker.

Kevin reached the door first, Eddie right behind him with the shotgun in his back. "Open it."

Kevin tried. The screen door was only attached at the top hinge and the bottom part swung toward him, the hinge squawking. Flustered, Kevin managed to maneuver the door back into a regular position and hold it open. Then he opened the front door.

"Nice place you've got here," I said.

Rundown as it was, the house at least had an air conditioner that worked. I was cold instantly. "It's freezing in here," I said.

"Get used it. Eddie sweats like a pig. Keeps him from complaining."

If Eddie'd drop a hundred pounds, he wouldn't sweat so much. Another line I wanted to say, but I kept my mouth shut.

We crossed into a short entryway, then entered a sparse living room. The beige carpet was a decade past needing replacement, with stains throughout. In the center of the room, a sectional sofa formed a right angle, creating a sitting area. An upholstered chair sat across from it. Both looked rescued from a dump.

"Get on the floor and lay flat," Eddie told Kevin.

Kevin glanced at me. I nodded. O'Brien whacked me on the head with something hard, and I crashed onto the floor.

"He doesn't need you to tell him what to do," O'Brien said. "He needs to listen to us."

At least, that's what I thought he said. My head was pounding, and I was having trouble focusing. I wanted jump to my feet and fight back, but the little lights wouldn't stop dancing in my head.

It occurred to me that if I faked being out, I might be able to take them by surprise sometime down the road. How this faked unconsciousness would affect Kevin I didn't know, but at that moment I didn't think his safety depended on anything I might do.

Kevin was as worried about me as I was about him. "Nick! Nick! Are you all right?"

"Shut up. He's fine," O'Brien said.

Someone kicked me a couple of times, not real hard but enough to make me uncomfortable, to see if I'd respond. I lay still. The foot found leverage under my ribcage and nudged me onto my back.

"He's out," Eddie said. "I'll get some rope."

Footsteps moved away from me and came back. I opened my eyes a slit. Eddie stood over Kevin and began tying his hands behind his back, then his feet. When he finished, he stood up.

"Put a gag in his mouth and lock him in the basement with the animals," O'Brien said. "Then we need to tie Bertetto up and convince him to give us some information."

Eddie picked Kevin up in a bear hug from behind and left the room. I heard a door open and dogs begin to bark. As tempted as I was to open my eyes, I kept them closed and continued to fake unconsciousness. I felt a pair of arms snake under my armpits from behind me and begin dragging me awkwardly across the floor. Both of O'Brien's hands were occupied, and Eddie was gone. If I was going to have a chance, this was it.

I counted to three, reached for his head, and scrambled to get my feet under me. O'Brien, startled, tried to jerk his head up. That worked to my advantage. I needed to gain some height, and his movement helped lift me. Grabbing fistfuls of hair in both hands, I let my legs go out from under me and dropped backward on my butt, dragging him along. I felt his jaw smash into the top of my head and I heard a satisfying grunt. I'd seen that move in professional wrestling matches; I never thought I'd have the opportunity to try it myself.

Unfortunately, I hadn't thought about my own head. I saw stars again.

O'Brien was on the floor, clutching his throat and making gasping noises. I rolled over to face him, then got up on all fours. I grabbed at his handgun. O'Brien twisted his body away from me, hitting me with an elbow as he did. I saw the shotgun several feet away and lunged for it.

Something soared across the room and landed on top of me, crushing me to the floor. Now I knew what it felt like to be tackled by a piano. It was my turn to grunt.

Eddie's thick hand drove my head into the gritty, smelly carpet and pinned it there. "Don't move or I'll tear your ear off." He pinned my hands behind my back and wrapped the rope around them. Then he did my feet.

O'Brien had retrieved the shotgun. He was still gulping and trying to clear his throat. I wondered if I'd damaged his Adam's apple. I could only hope.

Eddie got off me. O'Brien followed up with a kick to the abdomen. "Bastard." His voice was raspy. He kicked me again, this time in the thigh. I rolled away, longing for two free hands and a crowbar.

"My turn next," Eddie said.

O'Brien muttered something under his breath. "Nah. we've got stuff to finish before the master gets here."

Master? So someone else was the mastermind behind this. But who? And why? What was the purpose behind abusing animals and stealing Keri Schoening's body? Maybe relics was partly an answer, but it didn't satisfy me. Satanism still played into the whole thing, but the concept was so foreign to me that I couldn't get my head around it. And what were they doing with all the guns in the shed? They were risking a lot, especially with the police actively looking for them.

The bungalow had a sliding glass door in the back that looked onto the creek. I caught a glimpse of Miguel off to the side. We made eye contact, and he put a finger to his lips.

Hope surged through me.

CHAPTER TWENTY-FOUR

Maybe we really could get through this alive. In the basement, Kevin was probably safe. At least he didn't have a gun pointed at him. For Miguel to get the best of Eddie and O'Brien, I needed to be out of harm's way, too. As long as either of us was at gunpoint, Miguel was stalemated. I wondered what it would take to get thrown into the basement.

"Is Kevin okay? I swear if you've done anything to him, I'll do the same to you."

"You're in no position to give ultimatums," O'Brien said. "Who knows you're here?"

"Everyone."

Eddie elbowed O'Brien aside, grabbed me by the shirt, and yanked me to my feet. He shoved me against the wall, driving his other fist into my gut. I saw it coming and tightened my stomach muscles. The blow hurt, but it didn't do as much damage as it could have. Thank you, Mark Zoringer, for your ab workouts.

Eddie repeated O'Brien's questions. "Who knows you're here?"

"My family. Kevin's family." I gasped for a breath. "The police will be here any minute."

"I don't believe him," O'Brien said. "He's wasting our time."

Eddie glanced back at the older man. "What if he's not lying?"

O'Brien was unflustered. "We get reporters from out of town, and they do stuff like this."

The way he emphasized "out of town" stopped me. For just a second I thought maybe they were implying that they controlled the reporter "in town," Sally Kaiser. But then I dismissed it. They were just demeaning her abilities.

"We weren't supposed to get any outside attention," Eddie said. "No one was supposed to even find out the body had been dug up."

"You idiot, you just admitted in front of him we dug up the body!"

"No I didn't. I just said that no one was supposed to know it had been dug up. I didn't say who did it. But thanks for telling him, Einstein. Brilliant move."

"Shut up," O'Brien said.

Eddie still had me pinned against the wall with his fist, and he put his face next to mine. His breath was a soured mixture of pizza and Coke. "How did you find us?"

"Rumors. We heard you were holed up in the old Kitley Place, that it belonged to your uncle. I guess that would be your partner there. Problem was, neither of us knew where the house was. That was why we made the mistake of driving by on a dead-end road."

"What were you doing at Game Central last night?"

"Looking for you. Trying to track down who was behind the Satanic rituals, who skinned my mother-in-law's cat. You will pay for that, I promise."

I braced for a hit, but nothing came.

Instead, Eddie smiled. "I did the cat. With my hunting knife. It howled."

If my hands were free I would have wrapped them around Eddie's neck and held on until he stopped breathing. But still shoved against the wall with my hands tied behind my back, all I could do was try to get information. "Why'd you do it?"

"Terror. Make people afraid. Satan loves chaos as much as sacrifice."

"Shut up, Eddie. He's fishing for information, and you're handing it to him on a plate."

Eddie tried to backhand me. I saw it coming and twisted my head so I only caught a glancing blow.

"So, Bertetto, who was the guy in the parking lot?" O'Brien asked.

"What guy?"

"Do I have to have Eddie hit you again? The big karate guy in the parking lot at Game Central."

"He's a bodyguard I hired to protect Kevin."

"Where is he now?"

I went mum. Eddie hit me in the gut. This time I was a little behind in tightening my stomach. It hurt.

"He and Kevin's mom went to the police while we went searching for Eddie's truck. Kevin knew the license plate number. As I said, the police will be here soon."

Eddie relaxed his grip on my shirt for a moment. "They can't trace me to him. He never married my aunt."

"Good," O'Brien said. "That means we've got time for the master to get here. He'll know what to do. In the meantime, we've got to put Bertetto somewhere."

"The basement?"

"I hate to put him down there with the kid, but the rooms up here have windows and Bertetto might come up with a way to get out. It'll have to do. At least the windows in the basement are too small for anyone to get through."

O'Brien got a towel from the kitchen and gagged me. Eddie grabbed me around the waist. He hauled me off like he was carrying a bag of sand. There was a door just off the living room, and when Eddie got to it, he stopped and unlocked it. A set of stairs led down into the basement. The minute the door opened,

256

dogs started barking. I hoped that one of them was Buddy, that he was still alive.

At the bottom of the staircase he tossed me onto a rug. I had no hands to brace my fall and thudded onto my shoulder. The impact jarred my neck. Pain reverberated through my head. Now I knew what a bobble-head doll felt like. Eddie clomped back up the stairs and locked the door as he left.

I looked around. It was a bare basement, more like a cellar. However, it did have the windows O'Brien mentioned. They were small, and about all they did was let daylight in. I could see stacks of cages off to the left of the stairs. Only a few of them were occupied. At least two of them contained barking dogs. All the cages had locks.

I lay on my side, trying to will the pain away. Kevin sat in a shadowed corner. His hands were tied in front. I thought his had been tied in back, like mine. I sat up so I could see better. My abs screamed in pain, but the gasp I made never got past the gag.

Kevin glanced at me but was more concerned with the stairs. He watched them for what felt like a long time. When he was satisfied no one would be coming down, he moved his hands and the rope came apart. He did the same with his feet. Then he crawled over to me and untied the gag, cautioning me to be quiet. He got behind me and began working on the knots.

"They're not Boy Scouts," he whispered. "Not good with knots. I retied mine, but they're really fake." He moved around so I could see how he'd done them. The rope was really only attached to one arm. Clever.

"Won't they remember that they tied them in back?"

Kevin shrugged. "I hope not." He resumed work on my rope.

"Is Buddy down here?"

"First thing I checked once I was free. He's scared but he's okay. There's another dog and several cats. Nick, we have to get them out of here."

"We have to get ourselves out of here, too. I saw Miguel through one of the windows upstairs. He's outside."

"Really? Miguel's here?"

I could hear the excitement in his voice. I could tell the kid had visions of Miguel busting into the place, beating up Eddie and O'Brien and saving us. Problem was, this wasn't a comic book, and it would only take one well-placed bullet to neutralize Miguel, no matter how strong the guy was.

"Actually, I'm hoping he and your mom called the police. This is too big for one person."

Kevin tugged on the rope, but it still didn't loosen. "They tied this one better than mine. I'll get it, though."

I took a moment to examine the windows more closely. There were four of them, spaced evenly across the top of one wall. They were short and narrow, about two feet long and only about six inches high. There was no way we could get through them.

"Doesn't look like we can do anything with those windows," I said.

"I dragged a couple of cages over and got up there, but the handles won't budge," he said.

I felt a loosening of the rope around my wrist. "I've almost got it," Kevin said. Ten seconds later my hands were free. My feet were still tied, but Kevin had a lesser problem with them.

My abs still felt pain, but not as bad. I walked gingerly toward the windows. "I suppose we could break the windows to try to get Miguel's attention, but the noise would have them down here in seconds."

Kevin sat on the floor next to Buddy's cage. He reached a couple of fingers in and petted him, telling him quietly what a good dog he was. Then he wrapped his arms around his knees. He looked pensive. The rope tied to his wrist dangled. "Nick, why do they want Keri's body? Relics seem to be the answer, but I don't think it fits."

"I agree. It doesn't add up. There's something deeper here. Maybe we'll know when their 'master' gets here."

"Do you have any idea who he is?"

I shook my head. "They've mentioned him a couple of times, but no hints as to what his name is. Did you see the shack full of guns? I can't figure that part out, either."

"This'll sound crazy, but it's the only thing I can think of. What's the one thing all those violent video games have in common?"

I saw where he was going. "They all use weapons."

"Exactly. And the ones I've seen people get most excited about at Game Central are the ones that use guns. Now, you don't know these guys, but I do, sort of. I don't think it's much of a stretch to say that if they had the chance to try out real guns, they would."

I turned my full attention to him. "And they probably wouldn't want to go through the paper trail of getting permits."

"I'm thinking that David Haag might have found a way to get illegal guns here, and that maybe he sells them."

"Kevin, the police never did find out who supplied the guns to the West Jasper killers. They were untraceable."

"It could have something to do with that locked room at Game Central."

"Don't ever let anyone tell you you don't have the instincts to be a reporter. This could be the link with the Satanic cult, too. Disaffected youth who feel out of the mainstream are attracted to cults because it gives them a sense of belonging."

"It could mean that David Haag is the master. He meets kids through Game Central, sees where they're at with the games, and then sucks them in."

"Now if we can only get out of here to prove all of this." I looked out the window again. No Miguel. "I've got an idea, but we need to fool them into thinking we're tied up. We'll do each other's gag first, but we won't tie it securely. We'll do the same with our feet. The tricky part will be getting our hands faked-tied behind our backs. You could do mine, but how could you do your own?"

"Let me think about it."

Kevin went ahead and did my legs and my gag. I did his gag before he did my hands.

"Just be careful not to let your hands come apart until you're ready," he mumbled through the fabric of his gag, after he'd finished them. "Once they start to pull apart it'll be obvious they're not tied."

Kevin tied the rope securely to one of his wrists, then put his hands behind his back and tried to loop the end of the rope around his free wrist. "I can't do this, Nick. Can you help?"

With my hands behind my back and Kevin's warning not to let them come apart, it was a struggle. I managed to loop it around and then handed the end to Kevin. "I think you're just going to have to hold the end in your hand and hope they don't notice," I said while trying not to gag.

At that moment, someone fumbled at the lock to the basement door, the door flew open, and both O'Brien and Eddie Fleischman thudded down the stairs.

Kevin grabbed the rope in his fist and turned to face our captors, hiding his hands from them. His eyes looked like they might pop out of his head in fear.

O'Brien seized Kevin by the shoulder and spun him around to face the stairs. "Let's get them upstairs. Carry Bertetto if you have to."

I wondered what caused this panic.

Kevin turned toward me. I shook my head. It was too risky. They both still had their handguns, and Eddie had the hunting knife as well. Even if Kevin were able to overpower O'Brien—

and that was a big "if"—I wasn't sure I could get the better of Eddie. Better for now that we wait and not let them know our hands and feet were actually free, especially since something had them worried.

Eddie picked me up by the waist again and moved me to the stairs. He got me in a bear hug and lifted me up one stair at a time. We were behind O'Brien, who was similarly managing to get Kevin up the stairs. Fortunately, O'Brien seemed to be pre-occupied and hadn't noticed the ropes around Kevin's hands. At the top of the stairs, Kevin hopped with his feet "tied" together until we reached the living room. Eddie just picked me up and hauled me there.

I was dumped on the floor; Kevin got to sit in the scruffy brown leather chair where his hands could be hidden. We were both facing the kitchen. A voice behind us said, "I'm here to negotiate for the release of the hostages."

Eddie and O'Brien turned. They both drew their handguns. I rolled over to face the voice.

Father Dan stood there. He did some kind of fast motion with his left hand. It looked like the signal the Texas Longhorns use, with the index finger and the pinkie raised but the others closed in a fist, except that his thumb wasn't closed. It stuck out. But then he raised his hands, and it was gone, almost as though it were a smooth prelude to having his hands up to show he had no weapons.

Then I noticed that red and blue lights from police cars were flashing through the windows and circled the room. O'Brien aimed his gun at Kevin.

"If you try anything," he said, "we'll kill him."

CHAPTER TWENTY-FIVE

I wasn't sure who was more surprised to see Father Dan—Eddie and O'Brien, or Kevin and me.

He moved into the living room, hands raised. He was wearing a short sleeve black shirt with a clergyman's collar, jeans, and cowboy boots, as if he had been called away suddenly from personal pursuits and hadn't had time to change clothes.

O'Brien seemed unfocused and unsure of what to do. For a second he pointed the gun away from Kevin and halfway toward Father Dan. Then he moved it back to Kevin. As the tense silence held, he did it again. It was so sloppy on his part. I tried to figure out how to take advantage of it. Unfortunately, I would need Kevin's help, and the way he was seated, he couldn't see what O'Brien was doing. Perhaps it wasn't necessary. Perhaps we were in the best shape we could be, with the police having arrived and a hostage negotiator on the scene. He would no doubt get Kevin out first, since Kevin was a minor. Then me.

As if he could read my mind, O'Brien bent over the bulky chair and fixed his arm around Kevin's neck, pulling him back until the teenager was in a chokehold. He placed the gun muzzle on Kevin's head.

The move put O'Brien in an awkward stance. He was half bent over, with Father Dan behind him and Kevin in the chair in front of him. O'Brien tried to scoot the chair, but he couldn't, forcing him to twist into a position where he could watch one while holding the other. When O'Brien touched the metal to

Kevin's head, the boy grunted. I shuffled slightly so I could make eye contact with him, to be sure he was okay. When he saw me, he shifted his eyes toward the kitchen. Without being too obvious, I slowly turned my head in that direction and saw what everyone else, who was facing the opposite direction, had missed.

Miguel was in the kitchen.

He peeked out from above the swinging doors that separated the rooms. I tried to catch his eye, but he was more intent on watching O'Brien, the gun, and Kevin. Our wild card was now in the deck, but I wasn't sure I wanted it played, not while things looked good for a peaceful solution.

"I want some water," Kevin choked out. I had tied the gag loosely, so everyone could make out what he said, even though it was muffled.

"That's a good idea," Father Dan said. "Why don't we all settle down here? Perhaps you could untie the gags on both of them so they can breathe and talk a little easier."

There was a pause, but Eddie moved to comply. He holstered the handgun. "Okay. We can do that." He untied Kevin's first, and then mine.

I gulped a few times. Despite being loose, having the gag in my mouth had made it difficult to swallow.

Kevin took deep breaths. "I really could use a glass of water." He was trying hard to keep his voice even.

I knew what he was doing. I wasn't sure I agreed with it, but I figured the best thing I could do was to keep quiet and play along.

"Shut up about the water," Eddie snarled.

"I think we're all just a little edgy," said Father Dan. "Let's calm down and think things through. Getting Kevin some water won't hurt anything. And when was the last time anyone ate?

263

I'll bet the police would get us some food. And something to drink."

Hostage Negotiations 101. I relaxed just a little. If I was right, pretty soon Father Dan would try to exchange Kevin for the food, leaving just one hostage, me. As least as far as the police knew. They didn't know about Miguel.

O'Brien was frowning as though puzzling over everyone's sudden obsession with food and drink. "I'm not hungry," he said. He glared at Father Dan, then checked to make sure Kevin was in position and the gun was pointed at his head.

"I could eat," Eddie said fervently.

"It's four o'clock in the afternoon," O'Brien growled. "How can you be hungry?"

Eddie looked at Father Dan. "What kind of food can they get us?"

"I'm sure anything you want."

"I could use a hamburger or something."

"Why don't I give the police a call and see what I can have them send out for?" Father Dan asked. "McDonald's okay?"

"I'd rather have Hardee's," Eddie said.

"Hardee's is fine," Father Dan said. "I'm going to pull my cell phone out of my pocket now. I'll do it slowly."

Neither Eddie nor O'Brien prevented him. He dialed a number and waited. "This is Father Dan Klein. I'm the chaplain for the Jasper Police, and I need to speak to the officer in charge of the hostage scene."

After a few moments, he was connected to someone else. He repeated his name and relationship to the Jasper Police, although I was sure it would be the Dubois County Sheriff's department that would be handling this. Still, it established his legitimacy. I was willing to bet most everyone knew him anyway.

"I'm inside the house, sir, and it's a volatile situation. I don't think I should leave, but I do think I can negotiate for the hostages' release." He paused. "Yes, I know I'm not a hostage negotiator, but I am familiar with everyone here." Another pause. "Nick Bertetto and Kevin Mueller are being held. I also know the gunmen. How I got here is a long story. Look, at my request they've untied the gags, and everyone's hungry. Getting us food might go a long way to resolving this peacefully. Can you get us some food from Hardee's? That's what they've requested."

Father Dan listened a bit more, and then disconnected. "They're going to get the food."

Kevin rolled his head back and forth trying to loosen O'Brien's chokehold. O'Brien backed off a bit, letting his hostage breathe a little easier. The teenager cleared his throat. "I'm not sure I can wait that long. My throat hurts from being gagged."

O'Brien sighed. "Eddie, get the kid some water."

Eddie made a move in the opposite direction of the kitchen, toward the bathroom.

Kevin's eyebrows shot up. "Can I have it cold, please? With some ice in it?"

Eddie snarled.

"That's not unreasonable," Father Dan said. "Why don't you do that, Eddie? Nothing's going to happen soon. It won't take long to call in the order, but the police'll have to have it driven out here."

Eddie hesitated a moment, then said, "All right."

Father Dan went to the window and looked out. Eddie started toward the kitchen. For agonizing seconds, different scenarios raced through my head. What if Eddie got the best of Miguel? Miguel was in shape, had combat experience, and the element of surprise, but Eddie seemed like a streetfighter, and he was taller and heavier. Miguel would no doubt see the gun and try to take it away first, but what about Eddie's other weapon, the hunting knife? Would Miguel see it? If something happened to Miguel, how should I respond? Even if Miguel overpowered Eddie, we still weren't out of the woods—O'Brien had his gun trained on Kevin. What if Kevin did something stupid and O'Brien shot him? Or, what if Kevin tried to move on O'Brien and failed, but gave away the fact that his hands and feet were untied? Were we any better off? And should I move to help, giving away the fact that I was free, too?

The slightest of noises came from the kitchen. Knowing Miguel was in there, I guessed he'd probably bumped into something—barely a touch, but enough to make a sound that in the tense quiet of this company was noticeable. Eddie stopped short of the kitchen, his head up and suddenly alert. His eyes darted back to me. With a smirk, he pulled out the handgun and rushed the kitchen before I could warn Miguel.

Whatever advantage of surprise Miguel had was gone.

I yelled anyway, "Miguel!"

I heard a couple of quick pops, like fists connecting with flesh and bone. Something heavy hit the floor, followed by a second thud. Metal clattered against tile.

"He's got a knife, Miguel!"

O'Brien's head had jerked up. His eyes had the wide-eyed focus of a startled deer. His grip loosened just a little around Kevin's neck. "Eddie, are you all right?" He pointed the gun toward the kitchen.

Kevin's hands snaked up. O'Brien, eyes on the kitchen, didn't see. There was no hesitation on Kevin's part. He grabbed O'Brien's gun hand and yanked it toward the floor. O'Brien was dragged half over the chair. Kevin rammed his shoulder into O'Brien's armpit, dragging him the rest of the way. The two of them rolled onto the floor. O'Brien kept his grip on the gun.

My ropes wouldn't give. I tried to yank my way out of them,

but they were tangled. Eddie must've twisted them when he hauled me upstairs. I struggled to get them off.

Kevin scrambled to get up, shaking loose his ropes. O'Brien, off balance, kept the gun in the air, his finger on the trigger. I was afraid he would shoot the first person he could aim at.

From the kitchen, Eddie roared, "You son of a bitch," but he was clearly in pain. I heard the sounds of the two men grappling. Then I heard Miguel grunt.

The ropes on my arms finally gave way. I pushed myself off the floor. O'Brien was a few feet away, and I launched myself toward him. As I did, the ropes around my feet let go, tripping me up. O'Brien's gun swiveled in my direction.

Kevin kicked O'Brien's arm away, then dove square onto his body.

His momentum forced O'Brien flat. Kevin grabbed for the gun hand, but O'Brien recovered and wrapped his legs around Kevin's waist. He squeezed. Kevin gasped and abandoned his reach for O'Brien's arm. He was now positioned between O'Brien and me. I stopped, half-risen from a crouch.

O'Brien gripped Kevin's hair and pulled his face upward. He shoved the gun in between his eyes. "If *anyone* tries *anything* else, I will shoot the boy," he yelled.

An ominous lack of noise settled in the kitchen. I thought I could hear the heavy breathing that comes after exertion, but nothing else.

Then Miguel swore quietly in Spanish. Eddie laughed, a bit too much bravado in it. "Now we'll see if you can take me."

"Miguel, please give up," I called.

No response.

"Bertetto, stand up, hands in the air," O'Brien ordered.

I did. I prayed Miguel would cooperate, too.

"Now turn and face the other way."

As I turned, I noticed Father Dan. He hadn't moved, just

stood there, watching us. Anger welled up in me. I didn't know that it would have changed anything, but we could have used his help.

Father Dan closed his eyes. I wondered if he was praying. As a negotiator, maybe he wasn't supposed to help. If he had tried and failed, he might have sacrificed his position as a third party. Maybe he had done the right thing.

Facing away, I couldn't tell what O'Brien was doing to Kevin. I held my breath, trying to hear something.

"Eddie, bring that other guy in from the kitchen. What's his name, Bertetto?"

"Miguel."

"Miguel," he called, "if you don't cooperate, I will hurt the boy."

There was silence in the room. It took ten minutes for the next few seconds to go by.

"Let's go, muscleman," I heard Eddie say.

Miguel came through the doorway, his hands on his head. Eddie followed, his handgun gone, but he was brandishing the hunting knife. The blade looked to be a good seven inches long. Blood trickled out of Eddie's mouth. His lips were swelling on the right side. Miguel had gotten the best of him. If Kevin hadn't been a hostage, who knew what would have happened?

Then Eddie reached up with the knife and sliced across Miguel's forearm.

Miguel turned quickly, swearing again in Spanish. He put his fist into Eddie's stomach, and I thought it was going to come out Eddie's spine. Eddie went down, gasping for air. He threw up a couple of times. Miguel kicked the knife away, then turned toward O'Brien. O'Brien's eyes widened.

He tightened his grip on Kevin. "Take one step toward me and he's dead! I swear I'll do it!"

Miguel gritted his teeth. The cut wasn't deep, but his forearm was bleeding freely. It had to hurt.

Eddie managed to roll over and get to his knees. He tried to shake off the pain, but didn't get up right away. Miguel was strong.

Father Dan finally moved. "Don't do anything to the boy. I'm going to get Miguel a towel and try to stop the bleeding. We can't have anyone dying here."

O'Brien didn't do anything while Father Dan went into the kitchen and grabbed a dishtowel. He helped Miguel wrap the wound. Blood seeped into the towel.

"Miguel needs medical attention," I told Father Dan. "He could bleed to death." Plus, now they had one more hostage. I was more anxious than ever to get everyone out of there.

O'Brien ignored me. Eddie had staggered to his feet, and the knife was back in his hand. I thought for one moment he was going to be stupid and attack Miguel again. Instead, he circled around Miguel warily and disappeared into a back room. He came back holding a rifle, walked straight up to Miguel and placed the barrel against the other man's temple. "I'm going to blow your brains out, muscleman."

Father Dan spoke up. "No, you won't. It'll only make things worse. You don't want to mistreat a hostage. It could affect how this plays out."

"Get away from him, Eddie," O'Brien said. He nodded at Miguel. "Sit on the couch."

Miguel complied, his jaw clenching and unclenching. I made a move to help him, but O'Brien snapped, "Stay where you are, Bertetto."

Father Dan took a deep breath. "Now that we're calm again, let's just hold on until we get our food, okay?"

O'Brien eased his leg scissors on Kevin. "Don't try anything, boy. Remember I've still got the gun in my hand. I want you to get back in the chair and this time, sit on your hands."

Kevin did as O'Brien directed. The older man followed him, and once Kevin was settled, O'Brien once again placed the muzzle against the back of his head. "Eddie, get the rope. I want you to tie these three back up."

"Okay, but you're gonna have to tie up the muscleman. I'm not getting close to him, not unless I've got this rifle in my hand and you're gonna let me shoot him."

"Just get the rope."

While Eddie went in the other room, I moved to the front window and peered out from behind the drapes. There was a police barricade far from the house, way down the road. I saw the command trailer down by the wooded section Kevin and I had marched through earlier. I was sure the county's SWAT team was set up somewhere, but I couldn't see much except the hypnotic flashing of the red and blue cruiser lights. Television stations had their big vans there, way off in the distance, back behind the barricade. Probably from Evansville. The ones from Indy had a three-hour drive.

I hoped I wasn't still a hostage when they arrived.

Eddie came up behind me. He had the rope in his hands. I tensed for him to tie me up, but instead he pushed me out of the way.

"Hey, that's Sally Kaiser out there!" he said, peering out the window.

I moved behind him and squinted toward the police barricade. Sure enough, Sally was making her way toward the command trailer, snapping photos. How she had gotten past the barricade, I had no idea. Suddenly an officer noticed her and moved to intercept her. He half-dragged her back to the barricade and sent her behind it.

It was no secret how Eddie would know Sally—she'd written the article saying the police had harassed the Goebels and the Fleischmans. Obviously it had been well-deserved in the

Fleischmans' case.

"That's her," I said, secretly delighted she had been removed from the scene. Or maybe I wasn't so secret in the way I'd said it. Eddie gave me a poisonous look and walked toward O'Brien, tying me up apparently forgotten for the moment. I kept watching.

"How're we gonna get out of here?" Eddie half-whispered to O'Brien.

"I don't know. The master will think of something. Give him time."

Where was this "master"?

"The police have the area surrounded," I said, trying to sound calm, not belligerent. "Really, it would be best to surrender now, before anyone else gets hurt."

O'Brien thumped Kevin on the top of the head with the gun, making him yelp. "We don't want to hear your opinion." O'Brien smiled at me.

I let go of the drapes and turned toward Kevin. His eyes were a little glassy from the blow. He moved his hands out from where he'd been sitting on them and held his head. I had to get him out of here.

Eddie remembered what he was supposed to do with the rope, yanked Kevin's hands away, and began to tie them.

Father Dan moved toward O'Brien, but O'Brien shifted the gun toward him, indicating he should stand back. "Just everyone calm down," Father Dan said, his hands half-raised. "I'm sure the food will be here soon."

"My stomach still hurts from where the shithead muscleman hit me. I don't think I can eat." Eddie said. "But I could use a Dew."

Father Dan nodded. "They'll bring lots of food. I'm sure there'll be soft drinks," he said. "Now, I'm sure they're going to want a show of good faith that you want to resolve the situation peacefully. They're probably going to ask that you release one of the hostages when they bring in the food."

"Do we have to?" O'Brien asked.

Father Dan shrugged. I kept my mouth shut for a change.

Eddie finished tying Kevin's hands and moved warily toward me. Everyone else held their position. Miguel, sitting on the couch, pulled the towel tight around his arm. It was nearly soaked with blood now. Kevin sat immobile, O'Brien's gun at his head.

I ignored Eddie and turned back to the window. A police car drove up, lights flashing but no siren. "I think the food is here," I said.

As I spoke, I turned away from the window and saw Father Dan calmly approach O'Brien. He leaned over and whispered something in his ear.

Father Dan's cell phone rang. He answered it. Then there was a knock on the door. "The sheriff's department says the food is outside the door."

Eddie, still a couple of feet from where he could tie me up, yelled at the door, "You aren't getting the hostages."

O'Brien followed Eddie's lead. "Open the door nice and slowly, and come in with your hands up," he said. "I better not see a gun on your person, either."

"They're not coming in," said Father Dan. "They've left it by the door."

O'Brien thought a moment. "Bertetto, bring the food in."

I moved toward the door.

"Just a minute," he said.

I stopped.

"Do I have to tell you not to try anything?"

I shook my head.

Outside I found four bags of food with the smiling Hardee's star on them and a tray of drinks. An older man in a sheriff's uniform nodded to me from the side of the house. I brought the food inside. The sacks were warm and smelled of meat cooked on a grill. There was also the unmistakable aroma of French fries. My mouth watered, despite the fact that I was scared and it hadn't been all that long since lunch. Eddie took a large plastic supersized drink and began rustling through the bags.

Father Dan was still on his cell phone. He listened for a moment and then said, "They want you show some good faith here and let one of the hostages go."

"No," Eddie hollered.

There was a pause in the room. Father Dan said to O'Brien, "It must be done."

O'Brien hesitated. He made eye contact with Eddie. Finally he said, "Eddie, get Bertetto out of here."

Eddie's mouth opened. "Let's get rid of the muscleman," he sputtered. "Either that, or let me shoot him."

"Eddie's right," I said. "Miguel's injured. Send him out. Or Kevin. Not me."

O'Brien glanced at Father Dan. I wasn't watching carefully, but it looked like the priest might have given a slight shake of his head.

But then, I could have been wrong. I kept watching the priest and saw no other movement.

O'Brien said, "Nah, it needs to be the reporter," and Eddie, as though the words triggered him, suddenly shoved me out the door before I could protest. The door slammed behind me.

I blinked and looked around at the police cars at the barricade. I was free, but my friends were still inside.

And at the moment there was nothing I could do about it.

CHAPTER TWENTY-SIX

The deputy by the door grabbed me by the arm and practically yanked me aside. He studied my face. I must've had a bruise from where O'Brien backhanded me. He put his arm around my shoulder, and we made a run for the police blockade.

"Are you okay?" he asked as we ran.

"Banged up a little, but I'm fine. I shouldn't have been the one they released. Kevin is a minor. And we've got an injured guy in there."

"How bad?"

"He's cut on the arm and bleeding. Probably not life-threatening, but he needs medical attention."

"We'll get them out."

The two of us pulled up behind the blockade. I hunkered down with three policemen—the SWAT commander, the guy who brought me back from the house, and the sheriff. I assumed he was the officer in charge. The SWAT commander thrust a piece of paper at me. "We need to know where everyone is in the house. Can you draw it for us?"

I'm no artist, but I drew a top-down view of the house as best I could. "Everyone is in this main room." I said, outlining that part darker. Then I drew in the chair and the couch, and added an 'x' as I explained everyone's position. "Kevin is here, on this chair. O'Brien is here, behind him. He has a gun on Kevin. Father Dan is standing over here. Miguel is seated on this couch, and Eddie Fleischman is located over here. He has a rifle. Most of the time it's pointed at Miguel."

"Who's Miguel?" the sheriff asked.

"He's a friend and professional bodyguard. He's probably the one who called this in."

"No, Brenda Mueller called it in, the mother of the boy. She's in one of the police cars. I don't think she mentioned a bodyguard."

"He might have told her not to. I think he was hoping to have this resolved before you got here. He's a bodybuilder, has lots of tattoos, looks scary. But he's a good guy. And he's hurt. Got knifed in the forearm."

The deputy who'd brought me out added, "He said it's not lethal, but serious. We need to get a medic in there."

"What do they want?" the SWAT commander asked. "Do you know? We want to resolve this without anyone dying."

I shook my head. "This all came on so fast. Kevin and I thought Eddie was involved in the animal torture that's been going on around here, and we heard a rumor he was here. We didn't know it was a dead end street and they caught us, tied us up, and threw us in the basement." I pointed to the door where the basement was. "There are some caged animals down there. When you showed up, they brought us into the main room in case they needed hostages." I explained about the ropes and how Kevin had rigged them, the fight between Miguel and Eddie, and the scrape Kevin and I had trying to wrestle away O'Brien's gun. "I don't think they've thought too far ahead on this thing. They're on their own right now, but they're expecting someone else, their head guy."

"He probably saw the blockade and turned around."

Another deputy came running up. "Something's happening. Father Dan came to the door and said he's bringing out the hostages."

We all stood up to look out over the police cars. The door to

275

the house opened and Kevin and Miguel came out, with Father Dan behind them, his arms on their shoulders as though protecting them. They moved slowly at first, then picked up speed as they approached the safety of the police blockade.

The SWAT team was grouped to one side, waiting on their commander's orders. None of them moved, their eyes fixed on the house. With the hostages out, the rest of us were ready to breathe a sigh of relief, but not them. I looked to the SWAT commander to see what he would do. For a long moment he didn't move, apparently thinking the situation through.

Then we heard a shot. I dove behind the car, and so did everybody around me. After a moment there was a second and third shot. The sheriff shouted something, and the SWAT team went into action.

"The shots were inside," I said to no one in particular.

Kevin, Miguel, and Father Dan, almost to safety, had hit the ground at the sound of gunfire. "Stay down," the sheriff yelled to them.

The SWAT team moved like the rehearsed unit they were, single file until they reached the house, then through the door in button-hook fashion. Shouts could be heard from inside as the team cleared the house. Moments later, one of their men appeared at the door. "Clear! Suspects down, we need paramedics!" he shouted.

And the place came to life.

Officers and medical personnel rushed the house. Kevin, Miguel, and Father Dan were scooped from the ground by the police and separated—Kevin and Miguel to ambulances and Father Dan to a private area where he was met by the sheriff, who looked none too happy, though we were all safe. I mean, the hostages were safe. It didn't sound good for Eddie and O'Brien. Brenda Mueller got out of a police car and ran to follow Kevin to an ambulance.

I tried to go back into the house to see what was going on, but a policeman stopped me and told me I couldn't cross a crime scene. He recognized me as one of the hostages. Nabbing a paramedic, he put us together and shoved us away from the house toward the ambulances. I told the paramedic I was okay and that I had a story to cover, but he was having none of it.

"You have to come with me," he said. "Procedure."

I went along but didn't give up questioning. "Are they dead?" I nodded toward the house.

He wouldn't answer.

The ambulances were hidden by trees on the far side of the properties. There were two of them. As we got closer, I saw Kevin in one and Miguel in the other. I edged toward Miguel. He was lying on a cot as a paramedic attended him, wrapping his forearm in white gauze. A policeman was in there as well, questioning Miguel. Every few seconds Miguel would lift his head off the pillow and look out to see what was going on. He spotted me.

"Nick, what's happening? What were the shots?"

"Can I get in to talk to him?" I asked the paramedic who was with me.

The policeman who was with Miguel answered. "No. You're not allowed to talk to the other witnesses until you've been questioned separately."

"Can I at least ask how my friend is doing?" I said.

"He's going to be fine," Miguel's paramedic said, "but we need to get him to the hospital to suture his wound."

Miguel scoffed. "I've had paper cuts bigger than this. I don't need to go to the hospital."

"Eddie cut across that tattoo of yours," I reminded him. "I'd hate to think what it will look like if a doctor doesn't suture it properly."

While Miguel was thinking about that, the paramedic closed

the ambulance doors and it left. The second ambulance, which contained Kevin and Brenda Mueller, fell in line behind it. A third pulled up, and the paramedic who was with me opened the back and helped me inside.

After examining my face where O'Brien had struck me, he handed me a cold pack and had me hold it to the bruise. Then he ordered me to lie down on a cot, and he checked me over. I kept insisting I was fine, even when he poked me in the abdomen where I'd been kicked and I flinched. Eventually he agreed that I could avoid the hospital, so I escaped with only the cold pack. I dumped it as soon as I got outside.

As one of the hostages, I knew I was due to be questioned. But the reporter in me wanted that to occur on my terms. I moved quickly away from the ambulance. Fortunately, the area around the house was wooded, so I headed in that direction and was able to keep out of sight.

The Jasper police were now on the grounds. I hadn't seen them arrive, but they must have been called to help the sheriff's department. I spotted Officer Johnny Day, hardly a good buddy of mine, but as Joan's not-very-smart ex-boyfriend, I thought I could at least extract some information from him. I stepped out of the trees when he looked in my direction, and I motioned to him. He hustled over.

"Everyone's looking for you," he said, wiping a bead of sweat from his forehead.

"What happened to the two hostage-takers?" I asked before he could get in any questions or call the sheriff over.

"Dead," he replied.

"I was afraid of that. Can you tell me what happened?"

"No. You're a reporter. Besides, the only reason I'm helping you is that I promised Joan I'd try to let her see you."

"Joan's here?"

"Said she drove out as soon as she got the message where

you'd gone. She's back behind the barricade."

"Can you take me back there? I mean, before I get questioned?"

His lips pursed. "Only for a minute or two. You know a lot about what's going on, and they're going to want to take you downtown."

"Thanks, Johnny."

He took my by the arm and escorted me to where Joan was. Since I was being ushered by a uniformed officer we moved quickly through the hubbub, and no one seemed to take notice that I had been one of the hostages. When I saw Joan, I ran over and we embraced. She held me tight, making me wince. "Are you hurt?" she asked, loosening her hold.

"I was kicked a few times, so I'm a little sore."

She kissed me on the cheek. While she was next to my ear, she whispered, "Why do you have to do this kind of stuff?" But it was a rhetorical question. There was no anger in her voice, only relief.

"How did you get here?" I asked.

"I got your cell phone message, and then we heard about what was happening in New Vienna. I rushed over. Johnny was gracious enough to agree to try and find you. I was so worried."

Sally Kaiser elbowed her way next to Joan. She had a small tape recorder in her hand. "What happened in there?" she demanded.

I lapsed into stone-faced silence.

Kaiser frowned. "You might as well talk to me. You're going to be tied up here for hours, and you won't get to file a story."

"Your last article was misleading," I said. "You implied the Fleischmans and the Goebels were innocent and that what the police were doing amounted to harassment. That might have been true of the Goebels, but not the Fleischmans. Did you even notice they weren't all living together? Eddie was here in

Jasper the whole time. Did you think to ask where he was and what he was doing? Or did you conveniently forget because you went into the interview with your own agenda?"

"Sometimes a reporter can be wrong. Even the likes of Nick Bertetto," she said. "Get over it. Now, what happened in there?"

Once again I ignored her.

"Well, be that way. I've already talked to Father Dan and filed three stories today. How many have you filed?" She walked away.

Johnny insisted it was time for him to take me back. I kissed Joan. "Johnny says they're probably going to take me downtown. Will you meet me there?"

It took a moment, but she smiled, shaking her head slightly. "You're going into reporter mode. When they finally get done with you, you'll have people to question and stories to write. I know you're safe. That's what I came here for. I'll be back at Mom and Dad's. I love you," she whispered, and we hugged.

"I love you, too, Joanie." I held her for the best few seconds of the day, then turned and followed Johnny toward the police command trailer.

It was there I got my first break. Five officers had converged on the trailer and talked animatedly among themselves. Two wore the blue Jasper Police uniforms; three were in brown sheriff attire. As soon as they saw Johnny, they absorbed him into their group. I was left on the outside, where I couldn't see their faces, but was able to hear what they were saying.

"Has anyone seen our chaplain?" one of them asked.

"Father Dan?" Johnny asked.

"Yeah, he's disappeared. One minute he was there, the next he wasn't, and the chief wants to talk to him. He's none too happy."

That stopped me. Sally said she had interviewed Father Dan already. How had she managed that, and why was he missing?

"What'd he do?" It was Johnny's voice again.

"What didn't he do? He got here ahead of us and went in the house. He set himself up as a negotiator. If ours hadn't had the day off and been down in Evansville, she would have handled the whole thing and done a lot better job. I mean, the guy could have been taken hostage himself. And when he did get the hostages out, he left without negotiating for the surrender of the gunmen. We've got to find him. He's got to be on the property somewhere."

"Where have you looked?" asked a huskier voice than Day's.

The discussion broke down at that point. Johnny told someone that a reporter said she'd interviewed Father Dan already. Johnny put me back in the trailer for questioning and left to help. I thanked him again for letting me talk to Joan. He waved me off, his mind clearly on the missing priest.

He left, and I got a second break. They were willing to talk to me in the trailer instead of hauling me downtown. Three officers were in on the questioning, including the sheriff, and everything I said was recorded. When I started to speculate about the guns in the shed, I could tell they were surprised. I must've been way ahead of them on that one.

"If I'm right, those guns'll be unidentifiable," I said. "This is kind of a leap, but take a look at Game Central. Something odd is going on there in a locked room few people can enter. Kevin Mueller and I don't have proof, but we think it's possible the guns came through David Haag, the owner of the place. Eddie spent a lot of time there."

I asked my own questions when I could, but they gave very few answers. I had to push hard and remind them of the valuable information I was voluntarily providing them. Finally they decided to tell me a few things. Of course, they made me promise to keep them off the record. I said I would, but I planned to hound them mercilessly every day until they let me use the information.

What I learned was that they had physical evidence—though they declined to give me specifics—to make a case that O'Brien and Eddie were at the cemetery and likely were responsible for digging up the body. O'Brien's alibi hadn't held up under scrutiny. I wasn't surprised. I'd already heard them admit to digging up the body, though in a roundabout way. With both of them dead, the truth might never be known.

"I heard three shots. What happened?"

"At this point we don't know. We know both weapons were fired. The autopsies should tell us something."

"What about the animals in the basement?" I asked.

"We're going to turn them over to the humane society to get them back to their owners."

"Did you find Keri Schoening's body?"

There was silence, and I had to remind them again how much I had helped them and how I had already promised it was off the record.

"Not there," said the sheriff.

"Where could it be?"

He shook his head. "Unfortunately there were no file folders labeled, 'Directions to body.' "

I laughed. "You probably don't get much of that."

In the end, they let me go. The whole thing took over an hour.

By the time I got out, there was less bustling going on at the crime scene, but behind the barricade it was a madhouse. Television stations from all over the state, plus Kentucky and Illinois, were jockeying for position. Well-coiffed journalists were running around with microphones trying to interview anyone they could stop.

I needed to do some work myself.

I patted my pockets for my cell phone and remembered it

was back in the van. Fortunately the van was on the correct side of the barricade, and I was able to get to it without passing by the other journalists.

The phone showed I'd received seven voicemails. The first two were from Joan, earlier in the situation. Four were from Ryan. The other one was from my dad. I called Dad first since I wanted him to know I was okay. Fortunately, Aunt Augustina's number was on my cell phone.

"Nicolo, Nicolo, I have been so afraid for you," Dad said.

"I know, Dad. I was afraid, too, while I was in it. But I'm okay now."

"We have been watching the situation on TV. Your cousin Helena from Clinton called to tell us what was going on. Otherwise Augustina and I wouldn't have known. We have been down at the Old Cathedral all day."

I'd almost forgotten. "Did you find out anything?"

"Not much. The attempted robbery came about a week after All Saints' Day, when the relics were on display at the altar. The police had asked them to make up a list of the people who they knew had been there. The priest and some parishioners made up a list of everyone they remembered, and then they went through the guest book for that day. I have seen the list. The police checked out the names, and none of them had a record."

I thought about that. "So we're either dealing with someone who tried to commit a crime but doesn't have a record already, or a person who wasn't there to see them earlier."

"Not necessarily," Dad said. "They may not have signed the guest book. You do not have to. The parish keeps it at the entrance to the church, but whoever planned to steal the relics could have deliberately ignored it."

I had a sudden thought. "Dad, do you know how often they display the relics?"

"Father says only once a year, on All Saints' Day."

"Do they have records that go back a few more years? Try taking the names from that day every year and see if anything shows up. See if the same people show up every year. If they do, maybe we can contact them to see if they remember seeing anyone suspicious. Or we could take the names of the one-time visitors the year previous and Google them—see if there's anything that comes up."

"Okay. We will do that now. Father is busy most of tomorrow and can't help us, but he did say he would work with us tonight if we wanted. He would love to find out who tried to break in, if possible."

"Dad, thanks so much. Now I owe you twice."

"You bet you do. I'm retired. I do not work nights anymore."

"Ciao, Papá."

I turned to Ryan's voicemail and picked up the most recent call.

"Well, now I know where you are," he said, using his sarcastic radio voice. "I can see you through the lens of Channel 8's camera, which is there on the scene live. You seem to be in the middle of this mess. So I guess you can't be a reporter right now, which, of course, is your job. I'm guessing we're going to miss out on being there first with the news, but I trust we'll get an exclusive from you later. Call me."

There was a pause, but no hang-up, so I waited. "Channel 8 says you were one of the three hostages. I'm glad you're okay, Sherlock. Call me."

I looked around for a place where I could sit down. Not too far from the van was a place by the creek down a slight embankment where I could sit without being seen. I leaned against a weeping willow and tried to relax. I took a breath of air. It smelled of fish and diesel exhaust, and it made me a little nauseous. I focused on the task at hand. Opening up the cell phone, I called Ryan.

He answered quickly on the first ring. "Nick?"

"I'm okay, Ryan."

Ryan paused, cleared his throat. "Well, it's about time you called. Once we knew you were a part of the situation, we rushed Leah Summerlin down there. She's been handling the reporting duties. You need to get in touch with her." He gave me her cell phone number.

"Has anyone reported what happened to the other two hostages, Kevin and Miguel?" I asked.

"Kevin's been released, but his mother won't let him talk to any of the reporters. Miguel—he's a character—he was just released minutes ago and is giving an impromptu news conference outside the hospital. Very colorful."

"Some people love being a celebrity."

"I was worried about you, Nick."

"Thanks, man."

One more phone call to make before I talked to Leah Summerlin. I needed to call Miguel. He might have been interviewed on television, but I hadn't seen it and I needed to know what happened after I left. I punched in his number.

At first, the cell rang a number of times and I thought it would go to a recording, but then he picked up.

"I'm glad it's you, Nick," he said. "I've been interviewed by just about everyone else. You should have been first."

"You could have waited."

"The world should have to wait for Miguel."

I laughed, and he did too.

"I'm glad you're enjoying this. I want to know what happened after I left. It shouldn't have been me they let go. It should have been you or Kevin."

"It was really weird, man. Once you left, Father Dan started being really demanding. He told O'Brien he was taking me and Kevin out."

"That doesn't sound like a hostage negotiator. Do you remember exactly what he said?"

"Yeah. He went over to Eddie—Eddie's a good five inches taller than he is—and he indicates that Eddie should come down to his level. Eddie leans over and Father Dan says, 'It's over now. I'm taking these two out of here. You can't get out, you know.' And Eddie just hangs there, staring. Father Dan motions to me and Kevin. At first Kevin was nervous, but O'Brien drops the gun away from his head. So the three of us go to the door. Father Dan yells that we're coming out, and we did. And then the next thing I heard was a gun going off and we dove for the ground."

"Father Dan did all that?"

"Yeah."

I asked a few more questions and then Miguel had to go. Something about talking to a CBS affiliate.

I shook my head. Father Dan's name kept coming up and coming up, and not in the best ways. Earlier I'd noticed that the priest seemed to be connected to just about everything I was investigating, but I'd never looked on him as a suspect. His status with the church made me think any involvement was just a result of his trying to help. Now he was the number one person I wanted to question. I couldn't put it all together, but something wasn't right about him.

I called Leah Summerlin and fed her everything I knew. When I finished, it was close to 9:30 at night, but it was still somewhat light. I reminded myself we were on daylight savings time, and this was the longest day of the year. I'd have to drive fast when I went past the television vans. I didn't want them to recognize me and try to stop my vehicle.

As I walked back to the van, another Father Dan question came to mind. How had he gotten here so quickly? I tried to think about who knew Kevin and I were headed for the Kitley place.

Janine. I called her home.

"It's Nick," I said after she'd answered. She asked if I needed Joan, and I told her no, that I had a question for her. "Did you tell anyone where I was, after I'd called and left the message about Kevin and me going for his dog?"

"I called Father Dan to ask him to pray for you, that you were going into a dangerous situation. But I told no one else."

"Did he ask for details?"

"Yes. I told him where you'd gone. Did I do something wrong? I've been watching the reports, and it looks like he was a big help."

No point in telling Janine the police felt otherwise. "I just wanted to know how he got here."

"Imagine! He placed himself in the middle of a dangerous situation like that to save people. He is such a good priest."

Maybe. Perhaps I was being overly suspicious. But I didn't think so. "I'm sure he is," I said anyway. We hung up.

Just then another call came through. I checked the number. It was my dad.

"We found something interesting," Dad said. "Now that I know how to 'Google,' I Googled everyone who had attended the All Saints' Day showing multiple years. It was easy because Father already had the lists. Most of my searches came back with no matches. But we did find the obituary for one of them."

"He had recently died?"

"It was a she, and not only was she dead, she had been dead at the time she attended the showing."

It was an hour to Vincennes, but I had the feeling the answer to what happened to Keri Schoening's body lay in Vincennes, that the two relics stories were related.

"Ask the priest if he'll be kind enough to hang around for another hour or so. I'm leaving right now."

CHAPTER TWENTY-SEVEN

During the drive to Vincennes, I made a few calls. Since it was late and there was virtually no traffic, I gave myself a pass on the "no driving while on the phone" rule.

My first was to let Joan know where I was going. I told her to call if she needed me for any reason. Although I didn't say it, I was thinking specifically about Stephanie.

The second call was to Kevin. His mother might not be letting people call on their home phone, but I had his cell number. He answered right away.

"Can you talk?" I asked.

"Yeah. I'm in my room. Mom's guarding the front door and the home phone, but she hasn't said I couldn't use the cell. I was glad to see it's you."

"How are you doing? That was a pretty intense situation we were in."

"I'm okay," he said, trying to sound like it hadn't fazed him at all. But I could hear some false bravado in that.

"If it makes any difference, I was afraid," I said. "You showed a lot of guts, trying to take the gun away from O'Brien."

"I screamed," he said.

"It gave you power. It released your inhibitions."

"I didn't get the gun though."

"But it changed the dynamics of the situation. Who knows what would have happened if you hadn't tried?"

"Maybe you're right." He sounded a little more spirited.

"Anyway, they want me to talk to a therapist."

I thought of Joan and our situation with post-traumatic stress syndrome. "Talking to someone would be a good thing."

"Maybe."

"How's Buddy?"

"Glad to be home. He hasn't left my room since I got back."

"Kevin, Miguel told me that right before Father Dan took you out of the house, he said something to Eddie. Did you see that happen?"

"Oh, yeah. Father Dan was actually scary. His voice got really deep."

"He didn't sound like himself?"

"Not even close. I figured it was something they teach hostage negotiators. I would have been afraid not to let him do what he wanted."

Kevin didn't know that Father Dan wasn't really a hostage negotiator. In any event the odd voice wasn't a strategy I'd ever heard of. "Do you remember what he said?"

"Not the words, just the tone. It was almost like he was willing them to do what he wanted."

I almost told Kevin about my suspicions, but before I could he spoke again. "So, are you still in New Vienna?"

"I'm on my way to Vincennes." I explained why.

"You don't think they're going to find the body at the old Kitley place?" he asked.

"Why would they steal it just to bury it again? No, if they had it, they've put it somewhere. There's a reason why they wanted her saintly remains, beyond the specter of selling it for relics. We have to figure out why."

"Good luck."

We hung up and I slid the phone into the front pocket of my jeans. It took a full hour to get to Vincennes. By the time I pulled into the city limits, the sky had gone from the deep purple of dusk to the black of night. I drove straight downtown on Highway 50 to the riverfront, where the Old Cathedral was located on Church Street. The rectory, a Greek Revival building, was next to the cathedral. It had a small parking lot, and I pulled in next to Dad's car. When I rang the rectory doorbell, Dad and a priest, who introduced himself as Father Philip, answered. Dad gripped me in a bear hug the minute he saw me.

"Nicolo, I am so glad to see you! Let me look at you. Your face is bruised. Are you sure you're okay? Being a hostage must have been horrible."

I smiled and kissed him on the cheek. "It was bad, but I'm fine, Papá. Where's Aunt Augustina?"

"She had to leave," he said. "She said she was tired, but I think she just wanted to get home in time to see Letterman."

Aunt Augustina had eclectic viewing habits. "Where's the list of people you told me about?"

"Right here," Father Philip said, handing me a printed list of names. "These are all the people who attended the most recent All Saints' Day showing of the relics." He looked like he'd had a long day, too, with beard stubble making his face appear rough. I judged him to be in his fifties, about the same age as Father Dan.

Dad pointed to the name that was circled. "This is the one that was dead, at the time she was supposed to be here."

"April Kensington." I tapped the name with a finger. "That name rings a bell." I turned to Dad and Father Philip. "Does it with you?"

"We have had an hour or so to think about it," Dad said. "Father Philip called a few parishioners he thought might still be awake, but no one could come up with anything. They don't know who she was."

"Was she on the list in other years?"

"Yes." Father Philip handed me some additional sheets.

"She'd been here the previous five All Saints' Days."

I looked at what he'd given me. Four of the papers were copies of the church's guest book, the names handwritten, not typed. The most recent list had been typed.

"Why is this one typed, not copied?"

"I had it typed when the police requested it. The book is still in use, in the church."

"Could we look at it?" I had no idea what I was looking for, but the original might give us some kind of clue.

"Let me get my keys. We lock the church after four o'clock."

"Do you remember coming to the Old Cathedral?" Dad asked as Father Philip left.

"As a kid? Not really. Did you bring us here on a visit to Aunt Augustina's?"

Dad nodded. "We took you to the George Rogers Clark Memorial. Coming here was kind of an afterthought. Father Philip took Augustina and me on a tour earlier. It is fascinating, really. They have a crypt in the basement. Four of the early bishops of Vincennes are buried down there. And you should see the murals."

Father Philip returned, and we walked over to the church. He must have heard part of our conversation because he told us a little history. "The church was built in 1826," he said, unlocking the door. "Although we aren't as old as most of the cathedrals you'll find in Europe, we are quite old compared to many in America. In 1970 Pope Paul VI declared us a Minor Basilica, which is an honor reserved for only the most historic churches."

He opened the door and turned on the lights. We went in the main entrance. I saw the stand holding the guest book, and I stopped there, next to a statue of Mary holding Jesus' body after it was taken down from the cross. Father Philip went farther into the church, my dad trailing him, and turned on ad-

ditional lights. I heard the echo of their footsteps in the cavern-
ous cathedral.

"I'm going to look through the guest book," I called inside.

"Of course," Father Philip replied.

I flipped through about a quarter of the pages when I found
the entry for November 1. There were a fair number of visitors
that day. April Kensington's entry was near the top, though. I
compared the backward-slanting handwriting to her signature
on the copies Father Philip had made from the previous guest
books.

"This entry was definitely made by someone else," I said to
Father Philip, who'd returned while I was working.

"It's not the same?" He peered over my shoulder.

I shook my head. The style seemed familiar, however, as
though I'd seen someone else write that way recently.

"Why would someone sign the name of a dead person in the
register?" Father Philip asked. "If she didn't want anyone to
know who she was, she could have easily not signed it."

My dad had returned and was listening to our conversation.

"Augustina and I signed the book this morning simply
because everyone else did," he said. "There's an unspoken pressure to do it, like you would stand out if you didn't."

I thought about that. "It didn't even have to be a 'she.' A
person is here, anxious to get in and see the relics, and for
whatever reason, there's a holdup at the door. Not wanting to
attract attention to himself or herself, our would-be robber
waits in line with everyone else and signs the guest book. Who
looks at the name ahead of their own?"

"He is right," my dad said. "It could have been anyone."

"Father Philip, what would have happened after they signed
the book?"

"They probably went inside and up to the altar rail."

Dad and I followed the priest inside, down the long center
row between the pews until we came to the front of the church,

where we were blocked by the rail. "The reliquaries were set up there on the high altar." He straddled the altar rail and scooted around the near altar, then up several steps to a fancier altar above and behind the more common one. The second altar was tall and wide, with ornate carvings. It looked like the type of altar that was used before Vatican II. After that, priests were instructed to use a low altar and face the congregation during Mass.

It would have been easy for anyone to jump the rail, get to the high altar, and nab the relics, had he or she been left alone in the church.

I asked, "Was this as close as people could have gotten?"

Father Philip stepped down from the high altar. "Generally, they prayed either at the rail or in the pews. We had volunteer parishioners here at all times to make sure everything was orderly. They were asked to keep everyone behind the rail."

"After the visitors prayed, what did they do?"

He shrugged. "They could have done any number of things. Left. Looked around the church. Gone down to see the crypt."

"Can we see that?"

To the right of the sanctuary were narrow steps leading down to the crypt. The priest turned the lights on as we headed down the stairs. In contrast to the warmth outside, the crypt was cool. Father Philip led us into a room, probably twenty-four feet wide, with pews and a small altar on one end. The rounded crypt was at the other.

He beckoned us toward it. "This is where the bishops are buried." The entrance to the burial area was flanked by two large pillars. Past the pillars, evenly spaced around the semicircular wall, were four engraved, inlaid stones, each one commemorating a bishop. In the center of the room, a rectangular stone box like a casket rose out of the floor. A second stone casket was closer to the wall.

"In here?" I placed my hands on the center casket and could feel the cold through my fingers.

"Two of them. The other two are in that one."

Dad came up and stood next to me. He likewise ran his hands over the stone lid. "This reminds me of a book I read once. Not the kind of book I usually read. The casket lid was a barrier between the living and the dead, but if a living person touched it, the warmth of their hand pierced the barrier and the evil spirit could break through. The main character became possessed by an evil spirit."

I jerked my hand off the casket.

Dad and Father Philip laughed, but somewhere in my brain a memory unlocked. "Possessed," I said.

"I hardly think the bishop would want to leave Heaven to possess you," Father Philip said.

But I was thinking along a different line. "Wait right here," I said to my dad and the priest.

I hurried upstairs and back through the church, hit the stickiness of the outside air and ran to the van. April Kensington was the woman Father Dan had performed the exorcism on. I was positive. Somewhere there was a note Father Dan had scribbled to me, and I wanted to check the handwriting. I tore through the notebooks I'd been keeping since I started working on the story until I found it. There it was, the same backward slanted handwriting.

I hustled back into the church. Dad and Father Philip had made their way back to the entrance looking for me. I slid the note next to the "April Kensington" entry.

Father Philip leaned over my shoulder again. "It's an exact match."

"Who wrote that note?" Dad asked.

"It's a long story, and that person has a lot of questions to answer." I gave Dad a hug and shook Father Philip's hand. "I've got to leave. Thanks. You've both been a big help."

"I know that look in your eye, *figlio mio*," Dad said. "I am coming with you."

"You can't, Dad."

"Then I will throw myself in front of your van."

"What about Aunt Augustina? She'll be expecting you."

"She is probably watching Jimmy Fallon, now that Letterman is over. Let me have your cell phone. I can call while you drive."

It would take too long to argue. Dad was very much the stubborn Italian. It runs in our family.

We made a hasty departure from Vincennes. I handed Dad my cell phone, and he called Augustina. Then I asked him go back through the calls I'd made until he found the number for Father Vince at St. Aelred's.

"Surely he would not be there at this hour," Dad said.

"Probably not, but with any luck there'll be a message telling callers how to reach him or someone who can get him."

Dad pressed the dial button and handed the phone to me. It rang several times, and then Father Vince's voice came on with a brief message saying he wasn't at his desk and gave another number to try, "in an emergency." I recited the number to Dad, who wrote it down and dialed it for me. The priest answered on the seventh ring.

"Hello?" The voice was fuzzy.

"Father Vince?"

"Who's calling?"

"It's Nick Bertetto, Father. This is kind of an emergency. I need you to answer a couple of questions for me. I know I'm not supposed to know who Father Dan performed the exorcism on, but I can read upside down and when you had your file open, I thought the name was April Kensington. Can you confirm that for me?"

"Why, Nick?"

"Please humor me for just a moment. Is it possible for a

priest to be possessed by the same demon he's trying to get rid of?"

I heard my father gasp. I glanced over to see him cross himself.

Father Vince stuttered. "W-what?"

"I know it's farfetched. I'm not sure I even believe in possession, as we discussed. But if someone were to believe they were possessed, they would act like it, right?"

"Are you saying Father Dan may be possessed?"

"Or thinks he is." I went back over the strange coincidences I'd seen in the past few days, ending with the discovery of the handwriting sample at the Old Cathedral.

"I'm violating all kinds of rules of confidence in telling you this, but it seems important, so yes, her name was April Kensington. I can't believe what I'm hearing, though."

"Why would someone who is possessed want the remains of a saint?"

Father Vince hesitated before he spoke, almost as if he were afraid to continue with his thought. "In the Satanism course, we learned a little bit about their rituals. Supposedly there's one called 'the desecration of the saints.' It's nearly impossible to do because saints are so holy. But if an evil person can generate enough power to destroy the holiness of a saint, then he or she advances to one of the highest levels of Satanism."

I felt my pulse start to race. "I don't like the conclusion we're reaching."

"Think of what you're saying, Nick. If Father Dan is behind this, then when he failed to get the relics from the Old Cathedral, he set out to create his own saint."

My heart hurt when I grasped what he was getting at. "The West Jasper massacre was staged. Six people were killed to cover the death of Keri Schoening." I paused, thinking. "It's why she was asked if she believed in Jesus before she died. Because

Father Dan knew how she would answer, and in her death, she would become a saint. The police kept looking at her as the exception, but she wasn't. She was the only reason it happened."

"Nick, that simply isn't possible. It can't be." The distress in his voice was palpable.

"No, it *is* possible," I insisted. "Father Dan had connections to the two boys who committed the massacre. And today, he saw to it O'Brien and Eddie Fleischman died so the truth couldn't come out. So many deaths."

The Miraculous Medal weighed heavily against my chest. Everything seemed clear now. The torture and the death of Mr. Jangles was related, too, part of the Satanic rituals conducted under Father Dan's influence. I wanted to cry at the horror of what I'd just discovered.

"Nick, you have to be wrong. I'm going to see Father Dan."

"Don't. Not yet. Wait for me. I hope I'm wrong, too. But I want to be there."

We agreed to meet at the St. Barnabas rectory. It would take him about as much time to get there as it would for Dad and me. We each promised to wait for the other before going in.

"One more thing," I said. "Have you recontacted your friend in the Vatican Secret Archives about that verse?"

"No."

"There's what, a five-hour time difference? So he's probably not up yet, is he?"

"He spent many years as a monk. He may well be up now, but in prayer. I'll try to get hold of him."

I hung up and handed the phone back to Dad. Neither of us spoke as we drove on into the night, speeding toward Jasper.

CHAPTER TWENTY-EIGHT

I filled Dad in on what I thought was going on.

"How is it that you get involved in these things?" he asked.

"I wish I knew."

Both of us grew quiet. I figured Dad was trying to make sense of it all. I know I was.

It might have been the quiet or it might have been the night-time driving, but I found myself yawning and shaking, trying to fight off sleepiness. The day had certainly been a long one. I wished I had a shot of pure caffeine to wake me up.

Minutes later I got a shot of adrenaline instead. It hit me that I kept thinking of this in terms of seeking the truth. This was more than just a search. It was a potential blockbuster story, depending on what Father Vince and I discovered when we confronted Father Dan. I was the reporter who was supposed to be writing it. I needed to think in reporter mode. What would help this story get bold type on page one? Photos. I would need photos. I tried to think where my camera was. The best I could recall was that it was back at Hugo and Janine's house. If it was, I didn't want to stop to get it. One more delay. Then I thought about the rectory at St. Barnabas. There were few outside lights, and at two A.M. there would be absolutely no natural light. Photos wouldn't turn out anyway.

The cell phone rang again. Dad answered and handed it to me.

"You're not back yet, are you?" Kevin asked.

"About fifteen minutes away. What are you still doing up?"

"I can't sleep. All the excitement, I guess."

"Are you okay?"

"Yeah. I wanted to tell you, two cars showed up at the Strassheims' house, one about a half hour ago, the other ten minutes ago, and they're still there. All the lights are on. I think maybe you should be concerned."

"Why? Who was in the cars? Did they look dangerous?"

"Not dangerous in the way you're thinking. I couldn't see for sure who was in the first car, but I had the feeling it was Keri Schoening's mom and dad. I got a real good look at the second car. It was Sally Kaiser."

Hmmm. My good friend and competitor. What was she doing at my in-laws' house, especially in tandem with the Schoenings? Then I had a sudden thought. Sally's grandmother had the night vision camera equipment that took pictures in the dark. I bet Sally could get it.

Perhaps it was time we buried the hatchet.

"I think maybe I need to call over there and find out what's going on. Kevin, you've got good instincts. Thanks for watching my back."

"It's okay," he said. I could hear the satisfaction in his voice. "You've been taking care of me. I'm glad to return the favor."

"Try and get some sleep."

"I will. Bye, Nick."

Dad dialed Hugo and Janine's number. Hugo picked it up. I asked to talk to Joan. He went to get her.

"Joan, is everything okay over there?"

"It's okay. The Schoenings are here. They called ahead and then came over. They're waiting for you. They want to know what happened in New Vienna and if it had anything to do with Keri. The police are tight-lipped about it. How did you know we were up this late?"

"Kevin told me. He's been watching the house. Is it true Sally Kaiser is there?"

"Uh-huh. She's waiting for you, too. She's been trying to pry information out of everyone. We keep telling her we don't know anything, but she's convinced we're lying."

"Let me talk to her."

Joan put Sally on the line.

"Everyone else claims they don't know anything," Sally said, practically braying at me. "I know you know something. Spill it."

"I'll go one better, Sally. You've been a pain in my ass since I got here, and I like to think I've been the same to you. But now I'm willing to share a story—if, and only if—we work together on it."

She was quiet for a moment. I could hear the suspicion in her voice when she finally said, "Give me the details."

"The details are this: can you get the night vision video camera your grandmother has?"

"Take me about ten minutes."

"Okay, here's the deal. For reasons I won't go into right now, I suspect Father Dan is involved with Keri Schoening's missing body. I plan to confront him, but I want photos. Normal photography won't work with what I have in mind because it will be too dark. If I share the story, will you share the photos?"

"Is this a trick? Because this has 'send Sally on a wild goose chase' written all over it. What evidence do you have against Father Dan?"

"Not much, but a lot of coincidence. That's why we're confronting him together. Will you do it?"

"I've known him a long time. This better be good."

"It will be. Deal?"

"Deal. Where do I meet you?"

"At the St. Barnabas rectory."

"I'll be there as soon as I can."

"With the camera?"

"Yes, with the camera."

"Put Joan back on."

When I heard her voice, I said, "Dad and I are headed over to see Father Dan. Don't say anything to anyone. We think he may be involved. Call me if you need me."

We said our goodbyes and I handed the phone back to Dad, nudging the accelerator. Dad looked at me with eyebrows raised. "We need to get there before Sally does," I said. "I trust her, sort of, but I need to be the one in control."

We cruised into Jasper at a good clip. I slowed down after that. I suspected there weren't a lot of cops on the night shift, but I didn't want to find out. Driving through the center of town, we headed west. Five minutes later, we reached St. Barnabas. Both the church and the rectory were dark. Maybe Father Dan was asleep. It had to have been as long a day for him as it had been for me. But I didn't see his truck. I parked in the lot facing the rectory.

Dad turned to me. "Now what do we do?" he whispered.

"We wait for the other players."

Father Vince pulled up a minute later. He got out of his car carrying a large black felt bag. I motioned him into my van and introduced my father. Though it was unlikely anyone would hear us, we all kept our voices low.

"It doesn't look like anyone's there," Father Vince said.

"Could be asleep."

"Well, let's go wake him up and see what he has to say for himself."

I shook my head. "We need to wait for Sally Kaiser. She's going to take pictures for us. There's not enough light, and she's bringing a night vision video camera."

"You didn't say anyone else would be involved."

"I'm sorry, but I'm a reporter. I've got a story to do, and photos are a part of it. I need Sally's expertise here."

He looked at me uncertainly but seemed to let it go as he said, "Nick, I did get hold of my friend. There's something you need to know about the verse that was written on the wall."

Vince was interrupted by the ring of my cell phone. I flipped it open and looked at the number.

"Hang on a minute," I told him. "What is it, Joan?"

"It's Stephanie." Joan's voice was shrill and panicky. "She's sleepwalking again. We've tried snapping her out of it, but it's not working. She's saying over and over that it's the summer solstice. Nick, she doesn't even know what the word means! And now she's pleading with Aaron and Susan 'not to let the prophecy come true'."

I saw headlights coming down the road.

Just then the bells of the church started to play. We were so close to it and the night had been so quiet that the music was nearly earsplitting. I put the cell phone to my shirt to muffle the music. It was the same song I'd heard Father Dan programming earlier.

I turned to Father Vince. "What's that song?"

He listened for a moment. "Victory in Jesus."

I held the cell phone up to my mouth. "Hang on until the music ends," I yelled over the carillon.

Victory. The summer solstice. " 'When night is at its lowest ebb/And Vict'ry's sung from heavenly tower'," I said to Father Vince. "That verse was never about what happened in West Jasper High School, it was a prophecy we were supposed to understand. 'Then evil casts its strongest web/And Satan has his finest hour.' It's happening now."

In a flash I knew what was going on with Stephanie. "Joan, are you still there?" I said urgently. The bells continued to chime loudly.

The voice was barely audible over the music, but I heard a "yes."

"Joan, I think Stephanie is somehow channeling Keri Schoening. Don't try to snap her out of it," I said, my mouth dry. "Ask her where her body is—where the prophecy is going to take place."

Joan's voice broke. "This can't be happening."

I took a deep breath to calm myself. "I know it doesn't seem possible, but . . . please let me talk to her."

Joan put the cell phone down with a clunk.

The headlights came closer and closer to the rectory. There was a second set of headlights tailing the first.

Joan was back on the phone. "Nick, I'm scared for Stephanie." Her voice was strained.

"Keri would not take over Stephanie, Joan, or hurt her. I'm sure of it. Keri just needs our help. Stephanie might even be letting her do it. Stephanie knew Keri when she was alive. Let me talk to her, please."

I heard a soft breath on the other end of the phone.

"Keri," I said. There was no answer. I plunged ahead anyway. "I'm coming for you, but I need to know where you are. Where are you and Father Dan?"

"It used to be a church," the voice was shaky and sounded not like Stephanie, but rather Stephanie trying to imitate Keri. "But not now. It's abandoned."

My breath caught. We were in the wrong place! "Keri, please let Stephanie go. You've accomplished your goal. We know where to find you. We'll get there."

Joan must've been listening in because she took the phone back. "Nick, is she really Keri?"

"Not for much longer. I don't think so. But I've got to get Keri's body away from Father Dan. Look out for Stephanie. If she says anything else I need to know, call me. I love you."

The first set of headlights pulled in and parked between the van and Father Vince's car. The second set of headlights continued down the road, disappearing behind the church.

Sally Kaiser got out of the car. Vince, Dad, and I started to get out, but Vince pulled at my shoulder. Dad went ahead and got out.

"Nick, my friend at the Vatican says that verse was created in the eleventh century by someone claiming to be a prophet for Satan. 'Satan's finest hour' supposedly refers to the successful completion of the desecration of the saints ritual. According to that prophet, when that verse is made to come true, the person who performs the ritual will father the baby that will become Satan in human form."

"That's just too bizarre to be true, Vince."

"Even better, Father Dan took a trip to the Vatican Secret Archives last year, after the exorcism attempt on April Kensington. My friend confirmed it. And remember, Dan is fluent in German."

Dad apparently had introduced himself to Sally and was explaining the situation to her. He had just told her about the desecration of the saints when I interrupted. "Keri's body isn't here, it's back at the abandoned church in New Vienna where the Satanic stuff was found. That's where Father Dan is going to perform the ritual."

Sally turned to me. "I don't believe any of this. You're all crazy!"

"Follow us and you'll see. Or better yet, get in the van and come with us."

The carillon sounded like it was winding down, but then it started the song over, forcing us to continue yelling at each other.

"How do you know where the body is?" Sally asked.

"Too complicated, Sally. You have the camera?"

"It's in the car. I think you're wrong about where the body is, if this is even happening. The church would be too dangerous. The sheriff's department has it blocked off and under surveillance."

This was taking way too much time. "They can't patrol out there all the time," I said. "And crime scene tape only deters the innocent."

Sally shook her head.

"Where do you think it is?" Father Vince asked Sally.

"I'm guessing the body is at the church's retreat house, near the cemetery. Doesn't it make sense? The body is taken out of the grave, and they need to put it somewhere fast. If Father Dan is involved, like you say, then it's a piece of cake to put it in the retreat house. Church volunteers clean the place, but only once a month. If it's well-hidden, the body would be safe there, with no need to transport it."

Father Vince looked confused. "How do you know that, Sally?"

"I . . . I don't," she said. "I've just been thinking about it. It's a more logical place."

"My son knows more about this than she does," Dad said. "I say we go where he tells us to."

Father Vince fingered his clerical collar. He turned to me. "We only get one chance."

"Sally, get the camera and get in the van," I snapped. "All of you get in the van. We're going to do this my way."

Sally stood there obstinately. I started toward her. Before I got too close she pulled a small handgun out of her jacket and pointed it at me. With the other hand, she made the same gesture I'd seen Father Dan use in O'Brien's house. It looked like a Texas Longhorn hand sign except the middle two fingers curled into the base of the thumb, letting the rest of thumb hang down. "You'll do no such thing, Nick. Nor will any of the rest of you."

Time seemed to stop. "What are you doing, Sally?" I asked. "Don't tell me you're involved in all this?"

"We were warned you'd be trouble the minute you arrived, but the problem was the timing. We couldn't wait another week for you to leave because of the solstice."

"Who warned you I'd be trouble?"

She laughed. "You still don't believe, do you, Nick? Father Dan is the head of our cult, and soon he'll be the most powerful demon on earth. And I will be the mother of Satan."

Behind Sally, a figure emerged from the shadows of the church. The bells covered the sound of his footsteps as he approached her from behind. It took everything I had not to give him away. Kevin Mueller.

I kept my eyes focused on Sally, trying to absorb her attention. I hoped the others were doing likewise, but just in case, I moved a little to the right. It forced her to follow me with the gun, keeping her back to Kevin as he inched toward her.

"What was that symbol you made with your hand? I saw Father Dan do the same thing."

"A blessing. It's the Sign of the Goat."

"Like the Sign of the Cross?"

"In opposition to it."

"I can't believe you're a Satanist. Why would you want to be a part of this? What about your career? I thought you wanted to go to a bigger market. You could do that. I could help you."

"My influence will be substantially greater than you could ever imagine when my son is born. *Whatever* I want will be mine."

I sucked in a breath. Everything was coming into focus. "I was confused when I read the interview you did with the Goebels and the Fleischmans, but I didn't think you were actually involved," I said. "Now I see it. You used the innocence of the Goebels to help deflect attention from Eddie Fleischman."

"We needed just a little more time, and we thought that would help buy it. Make the police a little more wary."

"But Kevin Mueller knew," I said. Kevin had slowed his movements as he closed in on Sally. I think he was worried if he was too quick, it might attract her attention, even though the bell ringing was covering the noise.

"Apparently he did. But even then, Father Dan could have managed it if you hadn't hauled in the police. Just one more night and it would work."

Kevin was so close. I had to keep talking. "And this was that night. The summer solstice, the shortest night of the year."

"And now I'm taking care of you three, the last loose ends. No one is going to stop us."

Kevin jumped her from behind. "I am!" he yelled. He forced her to the ground.

Father Vince, Dad, and I rushed to help. I snatched the gun from her hand.

"Thank you," I said to Kevin as he stood and brushed himself off.

"I knew something was going on from the way Sally ran out of the Strassheims' house. I crawled out the window, jumped off the roof, and followed her here in my car."

Dad and Father Vince pulled Sally to her feet. She twisted and turned with every ounce of strength she had, almost serpent-like. The two of them held on tight, though I could see it was a struggle. But the last thing I wanted to do was use the gun.

She spat at me. I dodged the spray.

"Anyone got rope?" I asked.

"I do," Kevin said. "It's in my car."

"Get it."

While he ran to get it, I turned to Dad and Vince. "We'll tie her up. Kevin's good with knots. That should hold her until the police come."

Kevin returned and tied up Sally. I made sure he tied so many knots it would take Houdini all night to get out of it. By the time we laid her in the back of her car, she was spitting and cursing like she was possessed. We breathed a sigh of relief when we shut the car door on her.

I went around to the front seat and pulled out the night vision video camera. It looked like a regular video camera that had a long appendage attached to it. I still needed someone to take pictures.

There was really only one solution. Kevin. I hated to involve him in more danger, but on the other hand, I also knew he wouldn't stay behind, whether we told him to or not. He had a car; there was no way we were going to keep him away from New Vienna. "Kevin, you said you're taking photography this semester. You know how to work this?"

"I think it works just like a regular video camera. I'll figure it out on the way."

I turned to my father. "Dad, I need you to stay here and watch Sally." I handed him my cell phone. "Have some police come here and others to the abandoned church in New Vienna. Have them send EMS there, too. They'll know the church you're talking about."

Dad didn't argue. "Go," he said. *"Stai attento."*

Kevin, Father Vince, and I piled in the van. As we left, the carillon finally stopped playing. The sudden silence was eerie.

"I hope we're not too late," Father Vince said.

CHAPTER TWENTY-NINE

We stormed the roads toward New Vienna. If a policeman wanted to chase us, that would be just fine with me at the moment. But I had the feeling that unless a sheriff's deputy happened to be near the place, we would get there before they did. Whether that was good or not remained to be seen.

The night was moonless. Stars winked at us from in and out of clouds that blew across the sky. We pulled up to the front of the church. There were no police cars and no sirens to be heard. All three of us got out, Father Vince carrying his large black bag.

"I hope we're wrong about this," Father Vince said.

"There's only one way to find out." I held up the police tape so he could duck under it.

He hesitated. "Maybe we should wait for the police."

I smelled smoke coming from somewhere nearby. "We may not have the time."

The three of us went under and headed to the front door. The padlock had been broken.

"Remember, you hang back and take pictures," I told Kevin. Father Vince swung the door out and we went in, Vince and me side by side, Kevin following.

Inside, candlelight flickered eerily. Father Dan, in a hooded black robe, stood over a body lying on an altar draped in black. I recognized the body the moment I saw it. Keri Schoening. The memory of her in the casket, a lovely young girl with blonde hair flowing over her shoulders onto a white prom dress, was etched in my memory. Father Dan stretched out his hands over her and muttered something that sounded like an incantation. Five black candles flickered at the body's head, feet, and arms. Completely surrounding Father Dan were candle stands about five feet high with black candles mounted on them. The flickering lights revealed a pentagram on the floor.

"I'll go for Father Dan," Father Vince told me. "You focus on getting Keri's body to safety."

"You're sure about this? It may take both of us to take out Father Dan."

"I know what I'm doing, Nick. You'll have to trust me."

The Miraculous Medal grew white hot at my chest, a burning sensation like I'd never felt before. It made me want to take it . . .

I yanked at the chain and it gave. I pulled the Medal from around my neck, pressing it into Father Vince's hand. "Take this," I told him. "You know what it is and what it stands for. I think you'll need the gift more than I will."

He slipped it into his pants pocket.

Father Dan pulled his hood back. The candlelight threw odd shadow lines into his face. The effect wrinkled his mouth and exaggerated his eyes, which took on a red glow. "Welcome," he boomed. His voice sounded octaves deeper than it had been. "You are just in time to witness a great triumph for evil, and a personal advancement for me. After which, I'll give your souls to Satan as a gift. It will be easy enough to do. He'll be my son."

"It won't happen, Dan," Vince said, his voice resonating in the building, almost as if it had a life outside of his. "We have Sally Kaiser in custody. You can't father the child without her."

He laughed at Vince. "She's not the important one. I am. There are other women who can bear this son."

311

Father Vince stepped forward, his arms open in appeal, his clerical collar virtually glowing in the light. "I can help you fight this possession. Dan, listen to me. God is calling you back. Stop. Think what you're doing."

"You're not the exorcist, Vince, I am. Or was. Now I'm something else entirely. This power feeds me like nothing else. It's so rich, so amazing! This is the way we're *supposed* to feel. Not humble, not subservient. A *master.*"

Vince edged toward the altar. As he walked he pulled a foot-tall crucifix out of his large black bag and held it upright in his right hand.

"That feeling is temporary, Dan. It's not eternal. I can help you. All priests have the power to perform exorcisms. You know that. Yours was just a special appointment. I've done several exorcisms. If you're a real demon, you should fear me."

I fell in behind Vince as he steadily moved toward the altar. I heard shuffling behind me, and guessed Kevin was working the videocamera. Surely the recording would come out.

Father Vince reached back inside the bag. He pulled out a vial and uncorked it with his teeth. Then, with a sudden movement, he lobbed it at Father Dan.

Father Dan casually flicked his wrist. The vial shattered in midair before it reached him, but water splashed onto the body and the cloth beneath it. "Holy water, Vince? It will take much more than a vial of that to harm me."

"That wasn't for you, Dan. It was for Keri Schoening."

The altar began to shake. Father Dan smiled at Father Vince. "It's too late to stop the fires of Hell," he said. "They'll take her and they'll take you, too."

With that, he turned and swept his hands over Keri. The candle flames surrounding the altar burned brighter. Then the candles on the altar fell to the floor, igniting something there. A ring of fire, burning close to the ground, began to surround the altar and Father Dan.

Father Vince rushed toward the altar, dodging between the candle holders. "I can save you, Dan. Come to me. Take hold of the crucifix. It's not too late."

"Saved? Saved from power like this?" He began to laugh. The laugh was loud, deep, and harsh. It sent shivers down my spine.

Father Vince thrust the crucifix toward Father Dan. Dan backed up and fell, knocking over the candle stands behind him. Fire sprang up.

Father Vince maneuvered around the altar. Dan scrambled to his feet and turned away. Vince tackled him and held the crucifix to Dan's face. Dan began to scream. Father Vince began a ritual of his own. Pinning Dan to the floor with the crucifix, he pulled out another vial.

The fire was now crackling and smoke was forming. The smell of burning fuel was in the air. I wondered where it was coming from. Had Dan sprinkled gasoline around the church?

I saw flames crawl to the black cloth around the altar and begin to climb it. As the fire spread toward the top, it halted momentarily at the side the holy water had touched. I spotted a path through the flames to the altar. Without stopping to think, I rushed for Keri's body.

The heat was intense, the pain prickling over my skin and in my lungs. I reached the altar and scooped up Keri's body. She was stiff, but felt extraordinarily light. I turned to go back out the way I had come, but the flames had closed in behind me.

Kevin stood inside the doorway videotaping. I saw the fire race backward toward him.

"Get out, Kevin. Now!" I screamed over the roar that had built with the fire. I couldn't get through the flames in his direction, so I turned back to the altar to seek a way to the side exit. I could vaguely see Vince, still on top of Dan, through the smoke. His hands held the chain, the Miraculous Medal dangling from it.

And then I couldn't see anything else. Smoke burned my eyes and lungs. I slung Keri's body over my shoulder, freeing up one hand. I grasped the altar cloth where the holy water had held off the fire and flung it toward the side door that led out to the garden. The cloth hit the floor, producing more smoke, but it made a temporary path through the fire.

I danced across the black draping, smoke engulfing me. My throat burned and I put Keri's body down. Gasping, I sank to my knees beside her, trying to find decent air. The flames, thick on either side of me, moved toward the body. I saw the exit again, now about twenty feet ahead. It had a metal door.

I gave Keri's body a shove toward it. The body slid on the concrete floor, pushing flames out of its way. I crawled along behind and reached for the door handle. Too hot to grasp. I flipped over on my back and stretched out next to Keri's body. I kicked upward, banging the hot handle with my shoes. It didn't budge. I tried again. Same result.

Frantic, I stood. I leaped into the air, slamming my foot against the handle with all the weight I could muster. The awkward kick knocked me to the ground, but the door flew open. I jumped to my feet, scooped up the body one more time and charged into the garden. I took in a deep breath and had a coughing fit. Then I noticed the red and blue lights flashing against the burning church.

A pumper truck had set up out front. Firemen sprayed water against the building.

Kevin was there with the camera still taking video. "Where're Father Dan and Father Vince?" he yelled over the roar of the flames and the sirens.

Policemen rushed toward me.

"Don't know," I said. "Haven't you seen them?"

At that moment there was a large crash. We all turned toward the building. A stained glass window, high up in the church building, shattered. A single flame leaped out of the window toward the sky, and then was gone.

The building collapsed on itself. I felt weak at the knees. One of the policemen took Keri Schoening's body from me, and I fell to the ground. Paramedics rushed toward me. The next thing I knew I was being placed on a stretcher and taken to the ambulance. I could hear the sirens blaring. Someone fitted an oxygen mask over my face, and I was carted into Jasper.

EPILOGUE

I was released a few hours later from Memorial Hospital in Jasper. Joan had come as soon as she'd heard I'd been admitted, and Dad was there also. They caught me up on what had happened.

Thanks to Kevin's Boy Scout knowledge of knots, Dad had been able to keep Sally Kaiser on the sidelines and summon the police to both his location and mine. Sally was being held as an accomplice to the murders of the students at West Jasper High School and also in the deaths of Eddie Fleischman and Richard O'Brien. I wasn't sure how well any of that would hold up in court, but we also had her on the lesser charges of holding Dad, Vince, and me at gunpoint. I was glad the police had believed Dad. It had been a touchy situation for them when they arrived at the scene and found an unknown man holding a gun on a car that held a respected member of the community tied up in ropes. It helped that Sally wouldn't talk to anyone and spat at the police. In jail, she went into some kind of trance state. No one knew what to make of it.

The police checked into Game Central and discovered David Haag was using the store as a front to buy and sell guns illegally. They hadn't found evidence that he was part of the cult, but the coincidences were strong. Kevin and his friends were unhappy that the place was going to be shut down, but I told him the economic incentive was there for someone else to open a similar store, this time a legitimate one.

Kevin's mother was angry at me for a long time. I probably deserved it, allowing a sixteen-year-old to get involved in a dangerous investigation like that. In my defense, however, it was Kevin's determination that had kept him involved. Besides, he'd defied me every time I'd tried to stop him.

I made sure Kevin got credit for the video and the photos taken from it and for his role in uncovering Eddie Fleischman's involvement, which gave him a big boost of confidence. He told me he wants to go to a good journalism school when he graduates from West Jasper. I have Franklin College in mind for him, only about ten minutes from our home. His mother may not appreciate it at first, but I would be able to keep an eye on him if he enrolled there.

Stephanie had no more sleepwalking incidents after that night. Days later it seemed like it hadn't happened, almost as if we'd imagined it. Joan and I agreed that her familiarity with Keri and her youthful innocence were two of the reasons she'd been a conduit, if that's what had happened. It sounds unbelievable now.

Father Vince and Father Dan died in the fire. Police found less than they'd expected, just bits of the two men's bones and some teeth. The Fire Department attributed it to the fire's intense heat, which they'd measured at a temperature much greater than it should have been.

How hot were the fires of Hell? I wondered.

The fire had done one other thing. Kevin's photo-taking was wonderful while it was dark, but once the fire got going, the enormous heat enveloped them and the light overwhelmed everything else. The photos of the fight between Father Dan and Father Vince were night vision scrap shots.

There was a significant lump of melted silver that I guessed was the crucifix. I didn't ask, but there was no mention of the Miraculous Medal I'd given Father Vince. I missed it, of course.

317

Joan and Stephanie both noticed that I wasn't wearing it anymore. But I kept reminding myself of the heavenly help which had been promised me, if it was real—and the skeptic in me had never been one hundred percent convinced that I had received a favor—was not dependent on my having the Medal.

More than anything, I wanted to be reassured that Father Vince had prevailed, that right had conquered evil. I got the answer in a roundabout way two days later, when Kevin showed up at the Strassheims' house with additional photos he'd taken at the burned-out property. We were packing to leave for home.

"I'm glad you came by," I told him, holding out an envelope I'd prepared earlier. It was stuffed with some printouts created especially for him. "This is for you."

He took the envelope from my hand. "What is it?"

"Something you asked me for a few days ago."

He opened the envelope and pulled out two charts. One was a three-day-a-week exercise program to help him gain some muscle. The other was a daily meal plan that upped his calorie intake to account for the amount he naturally burned.

A smile lit up his face. "Thanks."

"I called Miguel back in Franklin, and he said that in all the excitement he had forgotten to design a program for you. The two of us collaborated on it. It's our gift."

Kevin handed me the photographs. "Here's a gift for you. I went back to the church grounds last night to take some final video for my scrapbook. These are from the sequence I shot in the garden with Sally's camera. I'll return it to her grandmother tonight. Anyway, I know you want to make sense out of what happened to Father Vince and Father Dan. You're lucky you didn't run into the statues on your way out of the burning building."

I remembered my first encounter with the overgrown garden, how I felt it should contain statues. But it didn't. "There were no statues in the garden," I said.

Kevin gave me an enigmatic smile. He pushed the photos toward me.

"I can't explain it. But they're there."

I glanced through the thick stack. When I saw the images that had been captured on that film, shivers went down my spine. "I've got to go out there," I said.

"I thought you might." Kevin looked at the ground. "Good-bye, Nick. I'll . . ." he started to say something, then coughed. He cleared his throat. "I'll miss you. Friend me on Facebook." He turned and began to walk away.

I caught him and gave him a bear hug. "Thanks for everything you did, Kevin. You're a good reporter now, and you'll only get better. Franklin College has a good journalism program, and it's just down the road from me. Think about it."

He got in his car and left. I told Joan I needed to run out to New Vienna one last time, and she asked me not to stay too long.

Kevin's pictures were on the seat beside me. Every once in a while I would glance at them. I kept thinking that although the garden was overgrown and a mess, I certainly would have seen any statues.

Soon I stood by the ruins of the church. I picked my way through to the spot where the side door had been, the one I had pushed through to save my life. There were no statues there.

I looked at the pictures Kevin had taken. There, in the very ___ I was now standing, was a figure. Although it had an ___ against the dark of the night that obliterated ___ something familiar about the youn___ ___ as though trying to make eye conta___ ___ uch like one I had carried out of ___ in her hands. Both of them seem___

I picked through the rest of the photos, one by one. The last had been taken in a heavily overgrown area. I located the spot, about five yards away. No statue. But in the photo were two chiseled figures. They had arms over each other's shoulders, and they appeared to be happy. One of them had glasses and was just about the height of Father Vince. The second was of a man around fifty years old, wearing cowboy boots and a clerical collar, pointing at something on the ground.

I mimicked his position to see where he was pointing. As I checked the long grass, I caught a flash of metal.

"It can't be," I said.

I pawed the ground in excitement, grabbing for it. When I had it in my hand, I stared in disbelief. It was the Miraculous Medal I'd given Father Vince. It had come home from Heaven.

I knelt on the ground and stayed there for a long time.

ABOUT THE AUTHOR

Tony Perona is a former General Motors advertising/public relations manager who became the first man at GM to take the corporation's two-year leave-of-absence to care for his children. While at home, he kept up his writing skills by becoming a newspaper correspondent and columnist. When the company could not reinstate him, he opened his own business, Tony Perona Writing, to service the writing, marketing, and public relations needs of other companies. Perona's first novel, *Second Advent*, was labeled a "distinctive first novel" by *Publishers Weekly* and termed a "winning first novel" by *Mystery Scene* magazine. The follow-up, *Angels Whisper*, was cited as "the second in a series to watch" by *Booklist*. *Saintly Remains* is the third in the series about stay-at-home dad/freelance reporter Nick Bertetto.